# MISSING FROM ME

## SIXTH STREET BANDS #3

## JAYNE FROST

6TH STREET PRESS
CONTEMPORARY ROMANCE

Edited by: Patricia D. Eddy — The Novel Fixer
Proofreading: Proofing With Style
Cover Design: Pink Ink Designs
Cover Photo: Period Images

*For Patricia—Thank you for all your encouragement. You'll never know what it meant to me. Love you.*

# CHAPTER ONE

4 Years Ago

**Sean**

The front door slammed, shaking the walls in our small apartment. I snuggled closer to Anna's side and buried my face in her hair.

Logan's agitated voice cut through the fog of near sleep.

"Dude, wake up!"

Whatever mess my best friend had gotten himself into, he'd have to solve it on his own. This was one of Anna's rare mornings off, and since we'd had the apartment to ourselves, we'd stayed up late, listening to the rain and having lazy sex until we'd passed out.

Smiling at the thought of a repeat, I grumbled in Logan's general direction, "Go away. I don't have any condoms. Carry your ass to the store like a normal person and leave us alone."

His footsteps echoed in the tiny room, and then he was beside me, his long fingers digging into my shoulder as he gave me a hard shake. "I'm serious. Get up."

*Not happening.*

A frustrated groan escaped my lips when Anna twisted in my arms. She propped herself up on one elbow, wiping the sleep from her eyes. "What do you need, Lo?"

*A swift kick in the ass.*

Rolling onto my back, I smothered my face with the pillow, hoping he'd get the hint. Of course, he didn't.

Cursing under his breath, Logan rooted around under the comforter.

"Hey!" I snarled, tossing the pillow at him. "Whatever you're looking for, I don't have it."

Running an agitated hand through his blond hair, Logan glared at me.

"Where's your remote?" Anxiety laced his tone when I didn't answer right away. "For the TV, douchebag—where's the remote?"

Anna fumbled around on the nightstand and then handed him the clunky device. "What's wrong with the TV in your room?"

Logan walked to the end of the bed and took a seat.

Anna sat up, scowling. "Make it quick." She slumped against the headboard, glaring at the back of Logan's head. "Seriously, Lo, hurry up. I have to pee."

Logan ignored her, all his attention focused on the screen as he flipped through the channels. His shoulders sagged when he reached CNN.

Cable News? Now he had my attention. The only things Logan ever watched were MTV, VH1, or the Cartoon Network.

I popped up to see what was so important, but something told me I didn't want to know. "What's going on?"

"Quiet," Logan whispered.

Buttoning my lip, I reluctantly focused on the screen where a stone-faced commentator stood in a field, fat droplets of rain pelting her microphone.

*". . . live footage from the scene of the tragic accident outside of Fredericksburg, Texas this morning where two members of the super-group Damaged lost their lives in a fiery crash. At this point, we're unable to*

*confirm the identities of the deceased. Damaged, arguably the hottest band in the country, just completed a series of shows in the Southwest and . . ."*

The camera panned out for a wide-angle shot. Wisps of smoke rose from the wreckage, dissolving into the gray morning sky.

A gasp from Anna. "Oh my God."

She crumbled against me, her small hand curving around my waist as she buried her face in my chest. Unable to make sense of what I was seeing, I stroked her hair with numb fingers.

After a few moments of stunned silence, Logan jumped to his feet. "What the fuck is she smiling about?"

Confused, I blinked at him. "Who?"

"The fucking reporter." He pointed at the TV with a shaky hand. "What the hell is she grinning for?"

I shifted my gaze back to the screen, and sure as shit, the reporter was smiling. Just a slight upturn of her glossy lips.

I tightened my grip on my girl. "It's her job, man. She doesn't . . ." Emotion clogged my throat, and I struggled for breath. For words. "She doesn't know them."

But then, neither did we. Not really. Damaged hailed from Austin, our hometown. And over the last five years, as their star ascended, our paths had crossed on occasion.

Our band, Caged, was one of the many groups on Sixth Street that loosely followed the Damaged blueprint. Since high school, we'd been playing the same bars where Damaged got their start, hoping a little of their magic would rub off.

The news report abruptly cut to KVUE, the local ABC affiliate. Terri Gruca, the nighttime anchor, sat stoically behind the half-lit desk, her co-anchor nowhere in sight.

"Thank you, Sandy." Terri blinked into the camera. "We've just got word at the studio that Rhenn Grayson, lead singer for the Grammy winning band Damaged, and Paige Dawson, lead guitarist, were pronounced dead at the scene of the accident on Highway 290 this morning." She looked down at the copy wobbling in her shaking hand. "Rhenn's wife, singer Tori Grayson, and drummer, Miles Cooper, were airlifted to Brackenridge Hospital via

Care Flight. According to band manager, Taryn Ayers, Mrs. Grayson and Mr. Cooper are both in critical condition. The bus driver was also pronounced dead at the crash site." Still photos of Rhenn and Paige appeared on a split screen in the background behind Terri's head. "Our prayers go out to the families. After a brief commercial break, we'll cut to the CNN studio for further updates on this tragedy and a look back at the lives of these two gifted musicians."

My head pounded as a commercial for toaster strudel flickered across the screen. Smiling faces and cheery voices, touting the virtue of strawberry jam tucked inside a fluffy pastry shell. Somewhere, people were probably eating that shit.

But not Rhenn or Paige.

"They were twenty-four years old," Logan murmured.

As he turned to face me, questions clouded his arctic blue eyes. The same questions I'd seen every day since the first time we met. About death, and why it visited some while leaving others alone. Death was what brought Logan and me together, after all. Our shared bond. Two kids whose mothers would never sit at the long table in Mrs. Varner's classroom handing out cookies. Because our mothers had "passed."

That's the polite term people used when someone died. The same folks made sure to tell you they were "sorry for your loss."

Which I always found funny, since my mother wasn't lost. She was dead.

Rhenn's voice boomed from the speaker on the worn-out TV. Smiling his most iconic smile, he stood back to back with Paige as he crooned the band's latest hit.

I leaned forward to drink it all in. Because that's all that was left now, bits of light and shadow caught on tape.

Slithering from my loose hold, Anna stumbled to her feet. "I've got to pee."

Before she got away, I swung my legs over the side of the bed and then slipped my arms around her waist to pull her between my knees.

Resting my forehead against her chest, I breathed deeply, her peach scent soothing me like a balm. "I love you, Anna-baby."

She sifted her fingers through my hair until I stopped shaking, and then kissed the top of my head. "Love you too."

Reluctantly, I let her go, and she retreated into the tiny bathroom. Through the paper-thin walls, I heard her crying softly.

When she returned, her face splotchy and her eyes glistening with leftover tears, I gave her a soft smile and lifted the covers so she could crawl in beside me.

An hour later and we still hadn't moved, like if we stayed here, it wouldn't be real.

But it was.

When they showed the Care Flight helicopter on the roof of Brackenridge Hospital for the second time, I snapped. "Change that, will you?"

Logan flipped the channel to MTV while I reached for the pad of paper I kept beside the bed to jot down lyrics.

Like everyone else, the music channel was covering the Damaged story. But instead of reporting what everyone already knew, they were running a special broadcast about the three lesser-known bands that had followed Damaged up the ladder.

A solemn voice spoke over a montage of snippets flickering on the screen.

*"While it stands to reason that Leveraged, Revenge Theory, or Drafthouse will fill the gaping hole left by today's tragic event, a few lesser-known groups from Austin have amassed quite a following."*

Jolted by the familiar beat, my gaze snapped to the television where footage of Caged performing at the Parish flashed on the set.

*"One such group, Caged, is currently playing the same venue where Damaged got their start some five years ago."*

The camera panned to the front of my drum kit where the band's logo, a lion inside a gilded cage, shimmered under the lights.

*"Like many of the smaller Sixth Street bands, Caged is still fighting for notoriety outside this small, but illustrious, stretch of road."*

"Oh my God," Anna whispered, squeezing my hand. "That's you."

Guilt flooded my insides, sweeping away the momentary jubilation.

*They're dead*, I reminded myself, turning my attention back to my lyrics.

*Voices dying on the breeze, eyes now see what no one sees.*

*Will you be among the masses, forever frozen as time passes?*

As I pondered the morbid compilation, the incessant ringing roused me from my next thought.

"Answer that call, dude," I grumbled to Logan's back.

He glanced down at his hand as if he just realized he was holding the phone. Swiping a finger over the screen, he took a deep breath before lifting the device to his ear.

"Hey, Chase." Logan pushed to his feet and began to pace in a tight circle, glancing at the television every few seconds. "Of course I heard." Stopping in his tracks, he listened intently. "Tonight?" He glanced at me, brows drawn together over troubled blue eyes. "I don't know. Let me talk to Sean first."

Tossing the phone on the bed, Logan dropped his head back and stared at the ceiling. "That was Chase. He wants us to do a set tonight."

My stomach twisted as the shock rolled through me. "Why tonight?"

Logan's eyes met mine, conflicted. "There's going to be some kind of candlelight vigil." He cleared his throat. "They're expecting music, so someone's got to take the stage."

*Might as well be us.*

I could almost hear his unspoken thought.

"What do you think?" he asked, chewing the hell out of his thumbnail.

Looking past him at the screen, I watched as people gathered on Sixth Street. Some wandered aimlessly, tears streaming down their faces, while others stood reverently in front of the poster of Damaged that hung next to the entrance to the Parish. All of them needed one thing—closure.

Pushing aside my reservations, I shrugged. "Whatever. That's fine."

Logan nodded and then gazed at the screen one last time before wandering from the room.

When Anna followed, I assumed she was going to get something from the kitchen.

Burrowing into the pillow, I threw my arm over my eyes.

"Sean?"

Anna's whisper jerked me from my thoughts.

"Yeah?"

She gave me a watery smile as she stood by the door, twisting the hem of her nightshirt.

I offered her my hand. "Come here, baby."

She sank onto her heels at my side. Slashes of sunlight peeked through the slats in the worn mini blinds, turning her red hair into a fiery halo. She looked shocked to the core.

"I don't know what's wrong with me." A tear spilled onto her cheek. "It's not like I knew them or anything."

I wicked the moisture away with the pad of my thumb. "You didn't have to know them, baby. They meant something to you, and you're sad."

"I know." She sniffed, fiddling with her emerald ring. "But it's not like, you know, family." Our eyes met, and I could almost see the thought forming on her lips. "Not like your mom, or . . ."

I watched the column of her throat as she swallowed. The rise and fall of her chest. Anything to avoid the pity in her eyes.

Sliding a hand into her hair, I pulled her close. "That was a long time ago."

When her lips fell open to reply, I silenced her with a kiss. Cradling the back of her head, I reversed our positions. She moaned softly as I pulled her leg to my waist.

"Maybe we shouldn't."

Her breathy pant held no conviction, so I kept going, my fingers gliding to the apex of her thighs. Pushing aside her panties, I parted her slick folds.

"Why not?" I brushed my thumb over her clit, smiling. "You got something better to do?"

Her brows drew inward as she searched my face. "No. I just . . . I want . . ."

Anna wanted what I wanted.

*To feel.*

I slid my boxers over my hips as I continued to stroke her. A whimper escaped when I pulled away.

"Shh." Gripping the base of my shaft, I guided my tip to her entrance. "Is this what you want?"

Past the point of embarrassment, grief, or anything but need, Anna nodded. "Now . . . Sean . . . please."

Burying myself in her warmth, I stilled long enough to push her T-shirt up to reveal her perfect, pink nipples. Scoring my teeth over one stiff peak, I slammed into her again, deeper this time.

We were primal, unrestrained, and when her nails dug into my skin, a jolt of pure pleasure raced up my spine.

*So fucking close.*

But I didn't want this to end, didn't want to face the reality that waited outside this moment, so I rose to my knees and wrapped her legs around my waist. My fingers skimmed her breasts, her quivering belly, and finally the small strip of auburn hair between her legs.

"Let go for me, baby," I grunted, circling her tiny bud with my thumb. "I need you to come."

*I* needed to come. To spill all the pain and the loss and the emptiness coating my insides.

Anna's eyes rolled back and she gripped my arm.

"Sean!"

Her walls closed tight around me as she tipped over the edge, chanting my name like a mantra. Falling onto my elbows, I chased her to the bottom, meeting the end of her with one final thrust.

Anna cupped my cheek as the spasms rolled through me, and leaning into her touch, I pressed my lips to her palm.

"I love you, Anna-baby."

She twined her fingers into my hair, and guiding me to the crook of her neck, she whispered, "I love you too. Always."

# CHAPTER TWO

**Sean**

*I* tossed a handful of clothes into my open duffel. The faint smell of peaches wafted up, warm like pie. Grinding my teeth, I fished around until I found one of Anna's tank tops hidden beneath the folds of a wrinkled T-shirt.

*More liquor.*

As I fumbled to open the half empty pint of Jack I'd pulled from my back pocket, I felt Anna's eyes on me. The drunken half of my brain instructed me to ignore her, but the sober half disregarded the command. Sliding my attention to the head of the bed where she was studying, our gazes collided over the top of her textbook.

Pausing with the bottle halfway to my mouth, I smiled bitterly. "Want some?"

Her lips parted, but then she looked away. Like the sight of me was more than she could bear.

And maybe that was true.

In the month since Caged had been "discovered" and offered our golden ticket—a record deal and a year-long tour to back it up—

Anna and I had exhausted every tactic waging our war of wills against each other. Screaming matches. The cold shoulder. Angry sex that lasted all night. But recently, this was Anna's weapon of choice—silent resignation.

I chuckled dryly. "I guess that's a no, huh?"

Anna frowned as I took a long gulp. Satisfied that she was as pissed as I was, I trekked to the dresser to get more clothes.

Her quiet voice rose from behind me. "Is this really how you want to spend the last night in our apartment?"

Anger flooded my veins as I spun to face her. "It wouldn't be our last night if you'd agreed to come with me."

She chewed the inside of her lip. "You know I have school."

My unfocused eyes shifted to the criminal law text in her lap, the glossy, red cover mocking me. I stalked to the nightstand, snatching the copy of the band's contract with Metro Music.

"Law school will still be here in a year." The papers crumpled in my fist as I shook them at her. "This offer won't be. It's a one-time deal."

Anna pushed to her feet and glared up at me. "I never told you not to take the offer. We'll work it out."

*Work it out?*

All of our conversations tumbled around in my head, a cacophony of compromises and bargains, culminating into one bitter refrain: Anna wasn't coming.

The evidence was all around me. Anna's neatly packed boxes. The two suitcases with all her clothes, ready to be transported to Peyton's dorm. But I'd refused to see it until right now.

Blinded by rage, I swayed in my spot, pointing the neck of the bottle at her. "I think *you've* got a plan. I don't seem to recall having much input."

A red flush stained Anna's cheeks as she folded her arms over her chest. "I do have a plan." Her stone-cold gaze flicked to the whiskey. "And if you weren't drunk off your ass, you'd remember what it was."

Grabbing a hair tie from the nightstand, she stormed away. I knew

I should've let her go. But I didn't. Chock full of righteous indignation and liquid courage, I followed her to the bathroom.

"Don't walk away from me, Annabelle. I'm not done."

*We're not done.*

Sighing, she pulled a hairbrush from the drawer. "Just drop it, Sean. I'll meet you in Phoenix in three weeks." Her gaze met mine in the mirror, pleading. "Can we please stop arguing about this?"

Leaning against the doorframe to keep from falling over, I slurred, "You don't seem too broken up about it, Anna-baby."

Maybe it was the use of the pet name. Or maybe she was just tired of holding all the anger inside. Either way, Anna rounded on me, and the hairbrush went sailing, nearly nailing me in the ear when it hit the wall.

"You don't know what you're talking about."

A tear slid down Anna's cheek, and I was grateful. I could work with that.

Closing the distance between us, I caged her in.

My hand slipped into her hair, and I tilted her chin with my thumb. "Then come with me."

Anguish contorted her features, and for a moment we were on the same side. Then her wall slid back into place.

"I can't. Not yet. We'll make the best of it and..."

The rest of Anna's thought was drowned out by squealing tires and crunching metal as we met the end of the road. Our road. I backed away, stumbling over the rubble.

"How 'bout *I* make the best of it." I cocked my head, my bitter smile firmly in place. "And you get a refund on that ticket to Phoenix?"

Anna blinked, confusion clouding her eyes. "I-I don't understand. What do you mean?"

"You're the smart one. You figure it out."

When I made an ungainly move to escape, Anna lurched forward, fisting my shirt. "No, you tell me what you mean."

*I love you. I want you. I need you.*

I said none of those things. Instead, I pried her fingers from my shirt, the corner of her emerald ring digging into my flesh from the effort.

"It means I'm done." I dropped her hand. "With you and this town."

Anna called after me, but pride and whiskey propelled me out the door and into the humid summer night. Away from the only woman I'd ever loved, and whatever was left of the home we'd built.

I woke up on Cameron's couch, bits and pieces of the previous hours floating behind my lids.

An unfamiliar perfume clung to my skin, overpowering the smell of whiskey, smoke, and stale beer. As I pushed off the sofa, I noticed the long, chocolate brown strands of hair bound to my T-shirt and jeans. Brown, not auburn. Not Anna's.

Pulling on my boots, I yelled a hasty goodbye to Cameron through his closed bedroom door before trudging the two blocks to my apartment.

Dead silence greeted me when I pushed open the front door. "Anna?"

Logan framed the entry of his bedroom, his blue eyes frigid. "She ain't here."

He slung his duffel over his shoulder, gripped the handle of his rolling suitcase, and then brushed past me without another word.

I made it to the toilet in time to spew the contents of my stomach, and after rinsing the foul taste from my mouth, I took out my phone to tap out a text.

*Anna-baby, I'm so fucking sorry. I need to see you.*

I was about to send the message when I took stock of myself in the mirror. Two purple bruises stood out on my neck. I ran my fingers over my skin, my hand sliding farther south to seek out the source of the sting on my chest. Yanking the collar of my T-shirt with enough force to rip the seams, I blinked at the trail of scratches.

This time I didn't make it to the toilet and I dry heaved into the sink until my stomach muscles screamed for relief.

When none came, I peeled off my clothes and then stepped into the shower.

Strands of Anna's long, auburn hair floated in the water at my feet as I scrubbed my skin, trying to wash off the stain of last night's debauchery.

I stopped cold when I heard my phone vibrating on the sink.

Anna.

Dread filled me at the prospect of her call, but a little relief as well.

I jumped out of the tub and made a grab for my phone, but missed the call. My stomach twisted painfully when I realized it was only Logan. A text popped up a second later.

*Bus is here. We're at the Cracker Barrel next door to the Motel 6. Get your ass down here.*

No way that was going to happen. The band's first show in El Paso wasn't for two days, and even if it cost me every cent in my emergency fund, I'd spend it on a plane ticket so I could stay here an extra night and make things right with Anna.

With a plan taking shape, I raced to the bedroom to get dressed. But one look at my reflection in the mirror behind the shabby dresser and I froze. In addition to the welts on my chest, there were finger sized bruises on my shoulders that I hadn't noticed before.

Backing away, I sank onto the edge of the bed.

There was no making things right with Anna. Not now.

And maybe I knew that when I climbed into the backseat of that girl's car.

*Darcy.*

Not even a friend, more like a fixture who'd been following the band around since she heard about our record deal.

*A groupie.*

I laughed out loud because Caged didn't have groupies. Sure, we had fans, but women didn't throw themselves at our feet.

I looked down at my phone, heavy and lifeless in my hand. And with a hard swallow, I pressed the delete button, and my unsent text to Anna disappeared one letter at a time.

I'd make it right. Just not now.

After a long moment of indecision, I tapped out a reply to Logan.

*Wrapping things up at the apartment. I'll be there as soon as I can.*

Tossing whatever clothes I could fit into the duffel, I left the rest of my stuff on the unmade bed. As I headed for the door, I caught sight of a small carton on top of a stack of Anna's boxes.

*Fragile—pictures.*

Opening the lid, I found a dozen photo albums of various shapes and sizes. Picking through the pile, I chose a thick, leather-bound scrapbook, and after tucking the album inside my bag, I paused and took one last look around.

*I'll make it right*, I vowed again.

But when I closed the front door, my insides filled with lead because I knew I wouldn't. Still, I kept walking, down the concrete stairs and straight to my car. And then I drove away, leaving my old life and the biggest piece of my heart behind.

# CHAPTER THREE

Present Day

**Sean**

*J*olted awake by soft lips traveling south over my heated skin, I pressed my head into the firm pillow. Light from the bathroom spilled into the suite, stopping just short of the king-sized bed.

Peering at the nightstand, I spied a plastic room key, a half empty bottle of Jack, and a strip of condoms. But it was the glowing red numbers on the clock that had me transfixed.

*3:37 a.m.*

Clearing away the alcohol induced cobwebs, I tried to piece together the events of the last few hours.

The organizers of the South by Southwest Arts and Music Festival had hosted an event to formally announce Caged's appearance on the closing weekend of the festival. There was an after-party at Maggie Mae's. And that's where things got hazy. The whole night blurred into a string of celebratory shots, courtesy of the cute little waitress who kept filling my glass.

Twining my fingers into the girl's hair, I propped up on my elbow to get a glimpse of her face.

Before I could form a rational thought, her small hand curved around the base of my thickening cock. She took me in her mouth, and with the alcohol dulling my senses, my mind wandered to places it had no business going. Dangerous places. Before I could stop myself, a name coiled around my tongue.

"Anna-baby . . ." She responded with a soft moan, and teetering on the edge, I gave her silky locks a gentle tug. "Look at me."

My heart stalled when she lifted her gaze, blinking up at me with sable eyes. Her hair turned muddy brown in my fist as the illusion slipped away.

I fell back against the pillows, and with my free hand, I made a clumsy grab for the bottle on the nightstand to wash away my disappointment. The whiskey went down smooth, numbing the empty spaces where only memories resided.

"Finish," I grunted, tightening my grip on her hair.

If the girl was offended, she didn't show it. Hollowing her cheeks, she took me all the way to the back of her throat, where I stayed until the last spasm of my release shuddered through me.

Shafts of morning light poured through the floor to ceiling windows as Kimber stalked around my suite at the Driskill Hotel, plucking her clothes from the floor.

Perched on the edge of the bed, my head in my hands and the wrinkled sheet wrapped loosely around my hips, I welded my back teeth together to keep from engaging.

Kimber must've noticed because the room went mercifully silent.

She stopped in front of me, her bright red toenail polish a blur as she tapped out her agitation on the plush carpet.

"Well?" she demanded.

I made a feeble attempt to sit up straight, and quickly decided it wasn't worth the effort, so I merely lifted my gaze. "Well what, Kimber?"

Her eyes rounded. "Are you fucking kidding me right now?" Tipping forward, she poked my shoulder with a manicured, red talon. "I came all this way for your big party, and now you're acting like . . . like . . ." She trembled with rage. "Like you're not even happy to see me!"

If I wasn't so hung over, I might try to play it off, pretend I cared, but as it stood, I was in no mood for any of Kimber's games.

Heaving a sigh, I roughed a hand through my hair. "What do you want me to say? You weren't invited."

Kimber took my cold demeanor in stride. After all, we both knew why she was here. Caged was big news again. And with our upcoming gig at the festival, there was lots of press around. Plenty of opportunities for her to get her photo in the tabloids.

"You didn't have to ask." Kimber's soft tone did little to mask the calculating gleam in her big brown eyes. "I'm here to support you."

A laugh rumbled low in my chest. "Sure you are," I scoffed. "And I suppose it has nothing to do with the new reality show you just landed?"

Surprise flashed across her features, followed by mock indignation and a quivering chin. Since I knew damn well the girl could cry on command, I wasn't moved. This little stunt was too reminiscent of our first encounter at Coachella over a year ago.

Kimber had shown up at one of the after-parties, setting her sights on me from the beginning. Not that I'd resisted. On the contrary, I'd ushered her straight to the limo and took what she had to offer.

Over the next few months, Kimber popped up at several of our gigs, usually with a swarm of paparazzi in tow. A few strategically placed articles in the more prominent gossip rags and we were the new "it" couple.

After Caged fired our manager and retreated to Austin to lick our wounds, Kimber's interest had waned.

Until last night.

Coincidence? Hardly.

Silence swelled between us as Kimber mulled over my accusation.

"That's not the only reason I came," she finally said, turning her head to wipe away a nonexistent tear. "I missed you, Sean."

"Really?" With my aching head, I couldn't offer more than a bland stare. "I heard you signed with Lindsey. Was it her idea for you to show up here?"

Kimber shifted, and even though I knew our old manager had probably put her up to the impromptu visit, I was still surprised when she didn't deny it.

"She's not that bad," Kimber said quietly—as if she'd forgotten that Lindsey had spent the last year trying to ruin my career.

If I could glare without causing more pain to my eyes, I would've. But she wasn't worth it.

"Whatever, sugar. You do you." I lurched to my feet, my stomach pitching from the sudden movement. "I'm going to grab a shower. Feel free to order some breakfast." Stalking to my backpack where I kept a clean T-shirt and a travel toothbrush, I added, "But I've got a busy day, so you need to clear out as soon as possible."

Blowing the girl off was a dick move, but there was no way Kimber was accompanying me to any press events, and with the SXSW show around the corner, the band had a shit ton of media commitments.

"Are you serious?" Kimber watched me with cold, brown eyes as I snatched my jeans from the floor.

"Yep."

Bits and pieces of last night filtered through my foggy brain, none of them good. So I grabbed my phone to check my social media and find out how bad the damage was.

I was mere feet from escaping into the bathroom when Kimber's voice rose up behind me.

"Who's Anna?"

Her question detonated like a grenade, and I rocked unsteadily from the explosion as I turned to face her. "Who?"

"Anna," Kimber repeated coolly, the barest of smiles curving her lips as she closed the gap between us. "You said her name last night when we were fucking."

An image popped into my head of Kimber's eager mouth on my cock. Not exactly fucking, but I wasn't going to argue the point.

"She's nobody." Icy fingers closed around my heart, protesting the lie, but I schooled my features well enough. "You must've heard me wrong." I gave her a smile, then spun on my heel, the world spinning along with me. Pausing at the bathroom door, I closed my eyes, cursing last night's foolish slip of the tongue. "Maybe breakfast isn't such a good idea. It's getting late, and I've got shit to do, so you should probably leave now."

The marble floors in the bathroom only added to the chill that settled in my bones. Dropping the sheet, I slipped into the shower where I stood under the multiple jets for longer than necessary, hoping Kimber had the good sense to heed my advice and get the hell out. My killer headache, burning stomach, and general sour mood didn't bode well for further conversation.

Feeling somewhat revived after the long soak, I cracked open the door on the pretense of letting out the steam, but really, I wanted to see if Kimber was still around. Hearing nothing, I peeked my head out and scanned the room. There was no sign of Kimber, but I laughed out loud when I got a load of her parting shot. Scrawled on the mirror above the dresser in red lipstick was one word—*Asshole*.

Given her flair for the dramatic, it didn't surprise me a bit that Kimber added a smiley face and even signed her name.

After pulling on my clothes, I grabbed a washcloth, a kernel of guilt working its way to the surface as I cleaned the goopy mess.

Sure, I hadn't invited Kimber to the party. But that hadn't stopped me from asking her to come back to my room or letting her deep throat me like a champ.

The mangled condom wrapper on the floor proved I'd at least tried to return the orgasmic favor, though, I wasn't sure how satisfying the venture had turned out to be. I didn't remember shit. And that bothered me. Most of my hookups came courtesy of some type of alcohol haze, but usually, I could recall the basics.

Escaping to the living room to put some distance between myself and the scene of the crime, I dropped onto the couch to scroll through my phone. Finding nothing too urgent, I rang up room service, ordering a pot of coffee and the greasiest breakfast on the menu.

While I waited, I sorted through the newspapers on the table. Settling on the Austin Statesman, I flipped through without seeing much at all until I reached the back page.

My stomach clattered to the floor when I spotted a familiar picture nestled among the obituaries.

*Annabelle "Belle" Murdock, 71 years old, formerly of Austin . . .*

That's as far as I got before the words blurred together. Skipping the bio about her life, which I could recite by heart, I zeroed in on the names at the bottom.

*Mrs. Murdock was preceded in death by Douglas Murdock, her husband of 42 years. She is survived by her two daughters, Alecia Dresden and Patricia Crenshaw, and three grandchildren, Anastasia Crenshaw, Alexandra Crenshaw Burke, and Annabelle Dresden Kent.*

Running a finger over Anna's married name, a wave of emotions crashed over me. Anger, frustration, and above all, soul-deep regret.

Shifting my gaze back to the picture of Gran, I whispered, "I'm so sorry, Anna-baby."

And I was. So fucking sorry, I could barely stand it. And only a little bit of the apology had to do with Anna's grandmother, though that stung as well.

A sharp knock on the door pulled me out of my haze.

"Room service!" a cheery voice called.

"Just a minute," I responded as I painstakingly tore the tiny tribute from the paper.

I fished my wallet from my pocket, and as I tucked the obituary into the secret fold behind my driver's license, my finger brushed the only photo I carried with me—the last picture I ever took of Anna. Things were already going south between us, evident in the sadness that dulled her sparkling green eyes.

I stuck the photo back in its cubby, my throat thick with emotion and the reminder that my worst moments with Annabelle were still better than my best moments with anyone else.

# CHAPTER FOUR

**Anna**

My mom stood among the mourners, holding my dad's arm like she might fall over. As if she could feel my stare, Mom cast a nervous look to me, huddled in the limo.

Ashamed, I dropped my gaze to the wrinkled program clutched in my hand. "Sorry, Gran," I whispered, smoothing the linen paper against my knee.

Sweat from my palm mingled with the tears that wouldn't stop falling, blurring the delicate font.

*Annabelle "Belle" Murdock - January 14, 1945 - March 12, 2017*

I thought I could do it—stand with everyone and watch them lower her into the ground. But I couldn't. If another person told me they were sorry and that Gran went quickly and without suffering, I was going to scream.

I furiously swiped at the moisture on my cheeks as the heavy door creaked open. Dean's cologne mixed with the scent of rain clinging to his dark suit as he scooted onto the seat.

"Are you okay?"

Nodding, I clenched my teeth to keep from snapping.

He blew out a breath and tentatively took my hand. "I think you're going to regret it if you don't say goodbye."

Turning away, I squeezed my eyes shut. There was no saying goodbye. Gran was already gone, and all that was left was this incredible ache that numbed my fingers and stole my breath.

"I will." I sniffed. "Just not right now."

My parents were taking Willow to my aunt's in Houston as soon as the celebration of life for Gran was over. At first, I'd balked at the idea, but Mom was right, I was in no shape to care for my baby with all this grief hanging over me.

Steeling myself, I turned to Dean and gave him a watery smile. "Thank you for being here."

Dean sighed, shaking his head as he looked down at our joined hands. "Where else would I be, Annabelle?" Offense edged his tone as his eyes met mine. "Just because we're separated, doesn't mean I won't be here if you need me."

Dean had always been there when I needed him, and really, it would be easy to lean on him now. But that wouldn't be fair to him. Or to me. But now wasn't the right time to mention it, so I just nodded and let my tears fall freely.

Dean slid his arm around my shoulder. "Shh."

I turned my face into his chest and wondered for the millionth time why I couldn't love him the way he deserved to be loved.

Jerking away when Peyton popped her head in the door, I swallowed the lump of grief that I feared would never truly dissolve.

My best friend knew better than to ask if I was okay. Instead, she held out her hand and said softly, "Come on. The service is over. Let's go say goodbye."

Shrinking against the seat, I shook my head, panic rising like an ocean swell. "I c-can't. I don't want to watch them . . ."

*Put her in the ground.*

I couldn't even say it. But Peyton didn't have to be told.

"They don't do that right now, sweetie."

Dean confirmed Peyton's statement with a solemn nod. Apparently, I was the only one who'd never been to a funeral. My parents were young. But then, so was Gran. Too young to have a stroke in her kitchen.

Pain lanced through me as I gazed beyond Peyton to the cluster of white chairs under the green awning. Now that the service was over, everyone was standing, and I could clearly see the casket.

My eyes darted away, and I found my father among the family members, staring right at me with no reproach.

Holding his gaze, I took a tremulous breath. "Okay."

Dean slid out first, and I followed. One step and my heels sank into the wet grass, but Dean slipped his arm around my waist before I face-planted.

When we reached the chairs, I took a seat in the back row. "Give me a second," I choked, my gaze fixed on the mahogany coffin. "I can't . . . yet."

Dean stood sentry, bracing a hand on my shoulder and intercepting any well-wishers who wandered over.

"Button?"

My dad's voice cut through the fog, and I turned to him, dazed. "Yes."

He crouched in front of me. "We've got to get to the house. Are you ready?"

Sorrow washed over me as I glanced at the casket. I wasn't ready. I might never be ready.

"No, Daddy . . ." I shook my head. "I can't go yet. Please . . ." I tipped forward, burying my face in the crook of his neck. "Not yet."

He rubbed circles on my back, whispering words I couldn't hear, but that soothed me nonetheless.

And then Peyton said, "It's okay, Brian. I'll drive her over when she's ready."

Dad kissed me on the forehead, and though I wanted to grab him and make him stay, I sat stiff as a statue with my eyes on the grass until I heard the car doors slam and the engines purr to life.

When I ventured a glance a few minutes later, the limos were gone.

Dean squeezed my shoulder. "I have to get back to the office." I met his gaze, nodding. "I could come over tonight if . . ." My eyes darted back to my lap, and he took a step back. "Just call if you need anything, okay?"

I wobbled to my feet as he turned to leave. "Dean?" It came out a strangled plea, so of course, he stopped. I threw my arms around him. "Thank you."

The air left his body in a rush, and he folded me into a tight embrace. "Don't mention it." He rocked me for a long moment and then broke away to wipe my tears with the pads of his thumbs. "Call me if you need anything."

If I had any doubt we were over, the kiss he pressed to my forehead sealed the deal. It felt just like my dad's, comforting. And if I only wanted comfort, Dean was the guy.

Peyton linked our fingers as I watched Dean's retreating back, a fresh torrent of tears blurring my vision.

"What now?" she asked after his car sped off.

I let out a shuddering breath. "Now, I say goodbye."

It took another hour, but I finally made it to the casket. While I said my last goodbyes, Peyton ran to her car to grab a blanket to wrap the large, framed portrait of Gran that I refused to leave at the gravesite.

Clutching the rosary Gran gave me, I knelt on the green faux grass in front of her final resting place, fumbling with the glass beads. "Sorry, Gran, I don't . . ." My throat closed as I tried to breathe through the strongest wave of emotion I'd ever felt. "I don't remember all the prayers you taught me." I placed a palm on the coffin. "I love you."

After pressing my thumb to the crucifix and stumbling through a single choppy prayer, I pushed to my feet. As I wiped my knees, I noticed a huge spray of roses. Not just any roses. Peach roses.

*I know you like the red ones, but the peach remind me of you.*

My gaze shifted to three smaller arrangements with those same roses interspersed with baby's breath, lilies, and white daisies—Gran's favorite.

Swallowing hard, I crouched to search for a card. Finding none, I plucked the sticker with the florist's name and number off the ribbon that simply read, "Gran."

Peyton appeared at my side. "All set?"

"Um . . . can you help me grab some of the ribbons? I want to keep them."

She fished her keys from the pocket of her black blazer. "You don't look good, sweetie." She pressed the fob into my hand. "Wait in the car, okay? I'll get these."

I nodded and turned to leave, but then my heart seized, and I spun around. "Goodbye, Gran."

I snapped a peach rose from the arrangement, kissed the petals, and then laid it atop the spray of daisies on the casket. Smiling through the tears, I took off my shoes and then turned and ran for the car.

I poured another shot of Jack into my can of Dr. Pepper as I settled against the couch cushions in my living room.

"Do you want leftover pasta," Peyton called from the kitchen, "or peanut butter and jelly?"

I took a long drink. And then another. "Peanut butter and jelly."

Glancing over my shoulder, I made sure Peyton was occupied

before retrieving the sticker from my pocket. Biting my lip, I stared at the florist's name, embossed on the gold foil.

The Flower Studio—Sixth Street

*It couldn't be. Could it?*

I had to find out, so I picked up my phone and then punched in the number.

"Flower Studio, can I help you?"

"Yes, um . . . my grandmother's funeral service was today and . . ." My heart raced, and I thought about hanging up, but the woman quickly offered her condolences, so I forged ahead.

"Thank you. Someone had several large sprays of roses delivered to the cemetery. Peach roses. But there was no card, and I'd like to send a thank you note."

After telling me she'd check her records, I heard her speaking with someone in the background.

"Yes, I have the order right here. It was a custom job. Tyler roses." A little gasp tumbled from my lips, but she didn't notice. "I don't have a full name, but the first initial is S and the last name is Hudson. Does that help?"

# CHAPTER FIVE

**Sean**

*A* cheer erupted from the crowd as the first of our four limos rolled through the back gate at the Frank Erwin Event Center.

I shrank against the leather seat, watching the stampede of eager fans descend on the first limo. The decoy.

"It's working," I said to Logan, who lounged in the seat across from me.

Shifting his disgruntled gaze to the window, he scowled. "Score."

I rolled my eyes at his sarcastic tone. After a year of fighting off scurrilous claims from our old manager, arguing with our label over the band's latest contract, and more or less getting our collective heads bashed in every fucking day, we deserved this break.

From the reports we'd been given by the South by Southwest organizers, our show was the highlight of the event.

"Dude, stop dwelling on the negative," I grumbled with a shake of my head. "We've got sixteen thousand people waiting to hear us play. Do you really care if we all rode in the same limo?"

Apparently, he did. And I saw his point. Caged had always presented a united front, us against the world and all that, but things had changed.

Cameron was with Lily now. And though Logan originally chalked up their union to a bout of temporary insanity on the part of our guitarist, he'd warmed up to the cute blonde over the last year.

But then Christian met Melody, and now that they were living together, the pendulum had shifted. Their girls were suddenly "besties," which meant double dates and all kinds of other shit that Logan and I had no interest in since neither of us "dated."

I turned my attention back to the window in time to see Cameron and Christian emerge from the second limo with Lily and Melody glued to their sides.

Ignoring the screaming fangirls vying for their attention, they ducked their heads and marched straight to the stage door.

Logan let out an audible groan, slamming the back of his head against the seat. "Did you see that? They didn't even stop to sign any autographs." His eyes found mine, frozen ponds of pale blue, iridescent in the dim light. "How do you think that's going to go over with the press?"

A part of me shared Logan's concern, but I knew better than to give that worry a voice.

Clearing the pebble in my throat, I shrugged. "You worry too much. Plenty of musicians have girlfriends. Besides, you love Lily and Melody. Don't even front."

He frowned, pinning me with his gaze. "Yeah, they're all right."

But I saw it in his eyes, the unsaid "but they're not Anna" dancing on the tip of his tongue.

In four years, Anna's name had never passed Logan's lips. Not since that last morning in the little apartment we'd all shared.

But I felt his resentment.

No, I didn't make Logan choose. He just did. And now he blamed the hell out of me.

I looked away, indifferent. "Well, you better get used to it, bro." I swatted Logan's leg and then scooted toward the door. "Lily and

Melody aren't going anywhere. Get your head on straight. We're golden," I tipped my chin to the fans chanting our name in earnest now, "unless you clock a reporter at the press junket."

Logan's cocky grin returned, but like his mood, the smile was subdued. "No worries. I'm the picture of self-control."

The door swung open, and we greeted our security team.

I slid out first. At six foot one, I stood eye to eye with most of the rent-a-cops, but Logan bested me by three inches, and since he was the fan favorite, it took all four of the behemoths to keep the crowd at bay. Instead of staying put in the tunnel the team had created for us, Logan splintered off and headed for the rope line before we reached the door.

I followed, more than a little amped by the show of adoration from our fans. I tried to tamp down my expectations, the feeling that this show could yield us a new manager and put the band back where we belonged, rocking audiences all over the world, but somehow, I knew this was the turning point.

And after a year in exile, I was more than ready to get out of here. The family dinners at my Aunt Melissa's, seeing the same old haunts, even Sixth Street—it was wearing on me.

Making my way down the row, I came face-to-face with a strawberry blonde, blinking up at me with big green eyes.

Holding out a concert program with a shaky hand, she stammered, "I-I love your music, S-Sean. Could you sign this for me?"

Scribbling my name, I plastered on a smile and gave her the standard, "thanks, sugar," before moving on.

Redheads were off the menu. Unless I was drunk. And then I gravitated to crimson hair, porcelain skin, and green eyes like an addict to a needle.

Spotting a gorgeous brunette with olive skin and sultry come hither brown eyes, I smiled. Since she didn't have anything in her hand for me to sign, the girl obviously wanted more than an autograph.

Obliging, I headed straight for her. "Hey, sugar. You here for the show?"

She tilted her head, amused. "What else?"

I could think of a few things. But since I didn't have much time, I cut through the bullshit and pulled a lanyard from my back pocket.

"What do you say we meet for a drink after the show?"

She looked down at the VIP Pass, mulling over the offer that included much more than drinks. And then she brought her gaze back to mine.

"Don't you want to know my name first?"

*No.*

Since that answer definitely wouldn't get me where I wanted, in between those impossibly long legs, I smiled. "Of course, sugar."

Her thumb skated over mine as she took the lanyard. I guess I'd passed her test.

"It's Beth."

I lifted my chin to the security guard trying to get my attention before leaning in to whisper in her ear, "I gotta go to work, Beth. See you after the show."

I gave her a wink and then headed for the door, ignoring the strawberry blonde with the pretty green eyes who reminded me of things I had no business thinking of.

Four hours later, I was behind my kit, rolling through a drum solo for our last encore of the night. Adrenaline pushed me past the point of exhaustion. Of pain. Of anything but the beat in my head, the sticks in my hand, and the roar of sixteen thousand fans.

Cameron's incendiary guitar licks poured through my ear piece, and I backed off on the bass drum, passing the baton back to Logan who'd appeared from the shadows like a specter to reclaim the spotlight. Prowling the stage like a cat, he belted out the refrain to our latest hit while the audience chanted along.

And then it was over.

The last note died on Cam's strings, and the stage went black.

A sonic boom of applause erupted from the abyss, quickly followed by shuffling feet as the mad dash for the exits began.

Roadies scampered onto the stage, grabbing instruments and handing out water, while I sat anonymously on my perch, waiting for the feeling to return to my legs.

The kid tasked with tearing down my kit approached cautiously, tools in one hand, a Pale Ale in the other.

"Great show, man," he said, holding out the beer.

The burning in my lungs prevented me from offering more than a tip of my chin and a smile as I took the bottle.

His eyes immediately darted away.

Fucking promoters and their damn riders. Since Caged was currently without management, I'm sure the SXSW organizers threw together a standard list of "dos" and "don'ts," including the super douchey "never look the 'talent' in the eye," and "speak only when spoken to" clause.

But that wasn't me. Or us. Caged was born right here in Austin— Sixth Street bred, and the kid probably played in a band himself.

"What's your name?" I asked after catching my breath.

His hand froze on the nut holding my cymbal in place. "Um . . . Zach."

I smiled because his voice rose at the end like it was a question.

"What do you play, Zach?"

From the expert way the kid was tearing down my kit, I'd say drums. But you never knew. I was proficient on guitar and bass guitar, not to mention the violin. But few people knew that.

"Drums," he confirmed. "Bass now and then."

I nodded into my next drink. "Why the skins?"

Zach's eyes lit up, but he played it off with a shrug. "Dunno."

Now, I flat out laughed. "Own it, son." I pushed to my feet and shook the cramps out of my legs. "Nobody purposely sits back here and abuses the shit out of their body unless they've got a beat in their head." I took out one of my lucky sticks from my back pocket and gave it a twirl. "If you don't have the beat, go back to playing the bass. Or better yet take some voice lessons." Zach's gaze followed mine to Logan standing at the side of the stage, surrounded by his usual flock of female admirers. "Lead singers get the most pussy anyway."

Zach let out a nervous laugh. "I'm not worried about that. I got a girl."

Reflexively, my thumb skated over the A I'd carved into the oak base of the stick a million years ago. The smooth initial that I felt regardless of the wear.

"Really?" I forced a laugh. "How's your girl feel about all the late nights?" Again, my eyes wandered to the group of females waiting in the wings. Once the band took our pick of the girls for the after party, the roadies could usually score a little action with the ones who didn't make the cut. "And, you know, all the other perks?"

Zach barely spared the fangirls a glance as he tried desperately to hide the small smile curving his mouth. "It's all about the music. I'm not here for any of that."

The conviction in his voice struck a familiar chord in my chest. "Good on you." I patted his shoulder. "Keep it that way."

I meant it sincerely, but I wasn't about to share my own experiences, so I shoved my sticks back into my pocket and took off. Pushing aside the curtain, I bypassed Logan, who looked like he had his shit under control, and took my place next to Cameron.

Ever since Lily had entered the picture, Cameron kept a safe distance from the fangirls and groupies. Easy to do at the Parish, where we performed a semi-monthly gig in front of a crowd of about four hundred. But this was an arena show, and the mob mentality had set in. It didn't help that Cam was bare chested, having shed his vintage Damaged T-shirt sometime during the show.

He practically jumped out of his skin when one of the bolder girls placed a hand on his chest.

"No touching," he said, the strain in his voice evident through the smile.

I felt a little sympathy for Cam's predicament, but hell, he'd cultivated this persona for years.

"Keep your shirt on, and this wouldn't happen," I said as I took a concert bill from a petite blonde. "Nobody wants to see your scrawny ass anyway." Winking at blondie, I flexed my bicep. "Ain't that right, sugar?" When she nodded vigorously, I raised a brow at Cameron. "See?"

Just having me here, running interference, loosened up Cameron enough to coax a smile from his lips. "Don't be hating." He pointed to his six-pack abs. "We can't all be built like this."

I rolled my eyes. Cameron and I were about the same height, but I had twenty pounds of muscle on the dude and I was rocking an eight pack.

Logan finally managed to tear himself away from his harem, and I was surprised to see that he hadn't picked out a girl for some limo action. He slipped between Cameron and me, snaking an arm around each of our shoulders.

"Listen," he said, his tone low with a hint of urgency. "We've got to wrap this up. I just got a text. We're heading to the Four Seasons."

"What's at the Four Seasons?" I asked, distracted by a willowy brunette propping up the wall a few feet away.

It wasn't Beth, but she had the same glossy brown hair, olive skin, and a body that wouldn't quit. She gave me a brilliant smile when she caught me staring.

Logan tightened his vise-like grip on my shoulder. "Pay attention," he snapped. "The text was from some guy in Benny Conner's camp."

All the white noise faded as I blinked at my best friend. Benny Conner was the biggest concert promoter in the business. If Conner Productions tapped a band for one of their globe spanning extravaganzas, you could write your own ticket when it was said and done. Benny turned nobodies into stars. Or in our case, stars into megastars.

I peeled my tongue off the roof of my mouth. "What did he want?"

Logan grinned. "Us . . . at the Conner hospitality suite."

I knew there was a catch.

Turning my attention back to the brunette, I muttered. "I'm not really into a dog and pony show tonight."

Cameron jerked a nod, concurring. "Me either."

There was a multitude of parties going on to cap off the SXSW festivities, and Caged scored an invite to every one of them. The same assholes that had been avoiding our calls for months would surely be at Conner's party, maybe even a rep from our label, and I wasn't on board with being anyone's window dressing.

Logan heaved a sigh. "It's not like that. The head of Conner's acquisition team wants to have a chat." He lifted a pale brow. "Plus, they've got a shitload of press over there."

Cameron's back stiffened, his easy grin long gone. "We've got a press junket to do at the Parish. And don't even think about bailing."

It was my turn to concur. Leaving Chase to deal with a mob of angry reporters wasn't an option. We owed him more than that. He'd been propping up the band for the last year, keeping us in the public eye with our gig at the Parish. And that wasn't just because he was Cameron's brother. He was family.

Logan thought for a moment before sliding his gaze to Cameron. "Call Chase and tell him there's been a change of plans. Re-route everyone to the Four Seasons."

Cameron pulled a face. "You sure about that?"

"Why not? Have him book us some suites. If worse comes to worse, we'll hold a few interviews there."

Cameron glanced at me, and I shrugged. If Conner was interested, he'd welcome the extra hype. And if he wasn't, it didn't matter anyway. Our reputation was shit; blowing the dude off wouldn't hurt us any.

"Yeah, okay," Cameron finally said, pulling his phone from his pocket. "I'll shoot y'all a text when I get the details. Someone needs to find Christian."

Logan glanced around as if he'd just noticed our bassist had gone missing. "Where is the little dweeb?"

Cameron snorted as his fingers flew across the screen on his phone. "He took off with Melody as soon as the curtain dropped. I'd say he's balls deep in a broom closet somewhere."

Logan barked out a laugh. "Nerd sex doesn't take that long. I'll go find him."

With his long hair and a full sleeve of tats, Christian could hardly be labeled a nerd. But he did have an IQ that rivaled Einstein, making him the resident brainiac of our group.

Logan gave a quick nod, then took off with a security guard to search for Christian.

Hearing our fans' disgruntled sighs, I decided to sign a few more autographs.

The brunette I'd spied earlier muscled her way to the front of the group. Bold little thing, and down to fuck from the look in her eyes.

"Hey, sugar," I said, giving her my full attention. "Did you enjoy the show?"

Her gaze flicked to Cameron who was now beating a path to the dressing room. "Yeah, I did." When our eyes met, a coy grin curved her lips. "But if you take me to wherever he's going, I'll make it worth your while. And his too." Her fingers trailed up my forearm. "If you know what I mean."

Everyone in the vicinity knew what she meant. But threesomes were never really my thing, and a three-way with one of my bros was a definite no go. That didn't mean I wouldn't take her for a solo ride, though, if she were willing.

I dropped my gaze to her tits, sitting somewhere just south of her chin. The chick either had an amazing push-up bra or those babies were fake as hell.

"Don't you read the papers, sugar?" I kept my eyes on hers as I signed a playbill someone shoved in front of me. "Cam's gone and got himself domesticated."

"Well, that sounds boring." Her hand slid farther up my arm. "What about you, Sean," she peered up at me through her lashes, coquettish pout firmly in place, "are you domesticated?"

I leaned in close. "Nope. There's not a domestic bone in my—"

The sentence died when I felt the pull, the jolt that came when I thought of her. My Anna. It was happening more and more lately, likely a result of being here, home, where memories hung as thick and deadly as the ball moss coating the trees by the lake where I lived.

Regrouping, I twined a lock of the brunette's hair around my finger while my free hand slid to the swath of bare skin above the waistband of her low-slung jeans. "There's this after party at the Four Seasons." I smiled against the shell of her ear, and she shivered. "What do you say? You wanna go?"

Over the din, I heard a soft, melodic voice call my name, drifting over me like a warm breeze. And though I was sure I'd imagined it, when I turned to the sound, *she* was there, five feet away, nervously tugging the bottom of her blouse.

A hint of bronzed thigh peeked from the high slit on her black skirt, and I had to look away for a second because I knew what those legs felt like wrapped around my waist. I could practically feel the contours of her body, smell her sweet peach scent, and damned if I didn't get hard.

Regaining my composure, my gaze darted to her face, to those emerald green eyes that sliced through all my defenses. Because I had no defense for Annabelle Dresden.

And despite everything, I smiled at her.

"Annabelle." Her name dripped off my tongue, sweet like honey and just as thick. "What are you doing here?"

# CHAPTER SIX

**Anna**

$\mathcal{I}$'d planned to offer Sean the note it took me all day to write. A small thanks—not from me, but from Gran. I figured with a hundred people around I could find someone to give it to him. But then I'd managed to make my way backstage, and now he was in front of me, mere feet away, enigmatic smile and piercing azure eyes locked on me like a heat-seeking missile.

Whatever he'd just said, I didn't hear. I was too lost in the past, in that place I'd avoided for years.

Sean took a blind step toward me and almost got mowed down by a parade of roadies hauling equipment.

"Anna?" His voice was urgent, demanding. But I heard disbelief as well. Like maybe he wasn't sure it was me.

I should've slipped away. Fallen into step beside the worker bees and headed for the door.

But Sean muscled his way through before I had the chance.

"Hey, Sean." It was all I could manage, and my smile wobbled when the brunette found her way to his side. "I just wanted to...um..."

I swallowed hard when her hand curled around his arm, right below the tattoo of the willow tree on his bicep that matched my own. "I wanted to thank you for the roses. For Gran."

That knocked Sean out of his haze. "Yeah, I'm so sorry about that." His hand went to the back of his neck, and then he smiled. "I just can't believe you're here."

The brunette scowled, expelling a small snort.

I shook my head, more for her benefit than Sean's. "Oh, no, I'm not staying." My attention shifted to the thank you note twisted in my hand, the ink blurred from the sweat on my palm. "Here." I shoved the card at him, my smile thin and tight lipped. "I'll let you get back to your plans. It was a great show, by the way."

Sean took the card, his fingers latching onto mine. And he didn't let go. "You can't stay for a minute?"

The brunette huffed in earnest this time, catching Sean's attention. He gave her a sidelong glance, annoyed, then shrugged off her hand.

"I'm busy here," he said to her, curt and dismissive. "Do you mind?"

She blinked at him, big brown eyes clouded with confusion. "I thought you were taking me to a party at the Four Seasons?"

I took a step back, trying to detach myself from his grip and their conversation, but Sean tightened his hold, long fingers sliding to my wrist.

"Plans change." He cut his gaze to mine for a second, and even though I didn't make any gesture of agreement, he turned back to the brunette. "You should run along now."

The girl appraised me, then turned a coy smile on Sean. "I told you I don't mind sharing."

My stomach hit the floor with a loud thump, and I was surprised no one heard it.

Adrenaline surged, and I freed myself with one tug. "It was nice seeing you, Sean." Painful is what it was, and I only hoped my voice didn't betray me as I spun on my heel. "Thanks again for the flowers."

I shot him a smile over my shoulder before ducking in between a group of fans heading for the red exit sign. My breathing came in labored spurts as I rounded the corner into another hallway.

"Anna!" Hearing Sean's voice behind me like a doorway to the past and all the pain, I picked up speed. "Anna-baby, *stop!*"

Anna-baby . . .

Two words. That's all it took. My steps faltered, time collapsing around me.

Why did I think I could do this?

Determined to try, I turned to face Sean's devastating smile. "Yeah?"

His breathing was as labored as mine, probably the unspent energy from the show. He ripped a hand through his long hair, staring at me.

Shifting under his intense scrutiny as his eyes continued their trek from my face to my body, I wrapped my arms around my middle and went for casual. "Someone's going to scoop Veronica up if you don't get back there."

Sean blinked and then barked out a laugh. "You remember that, huh? Logan still does that you know? All blondes are Betty and all brunettes are Veronica."

My heart squeezed at the mention of Logan. I'd seen him for a split second when he'd come off stage, and it had been nearly as bad as seeing Sean.

I coaxed out a laugh. "Well, I'm sure no one's complaining."

Hell, nobody complained in high school, and Logan wasn't even a star back then.

Glancing Sean over, I wondered what his term of choice was for the groupies and fangirls.

*Sugar.*

Somehow, I knew that was it. He was fond of the phrase but had never once used it on me.

Sean's chuckle died, and his smile lost its luster. "I'm not . . . you know, with that girl. I just met her."

As if he knew that was worse, his gaze dropped to his boots, giving me time to take a step backward.

"I figured," I said. "Anyway, I should go."

He looked up, his face unguarded. "Don't. I mean, unless you have to." After a beat of silence, he asked, "Are you here alone?"

*Lie.*

My brain issued the command, but before I could follow it, I nodded. "Yeah. Flying solo tonight."

Every night.

But Sean didn't need to know that. In fact, I'd gone to great lengths to ensure that he wouldn't. I felt the weight of the gold band on my ring finger, fraudulent since I hadn't worn it in months.

Sean's eyes narrowed as he looked past me, biting his lip. Then, out of nowhere, he took my elbow. "Good. Let's go get a drink somewhere."

Without waiting for an answer, he guided us further into the depths of the arena. It took me a few seconds to pump the breaks. "I don't think that's a good idea."

Running small circles on the inside of my arm with his thumb, Sean gave me a smile that didn't reach his eyes. "Why? You got a curfew or something?"

His gaze slipped to my left hand, gripping the strap of my purse so tight I could feel the leather digging into my palm. After a pointed look at my wedding band, Sean dragged his eyes to mine and waited for an answer.

My shoulders sagged in defeat. "No . . . I don't have a curfew."

Sean's lips turned up at the corners. "Alrighty then. Drinks it is."

"I can't believe you're rewriting history this way," I protested with a snort, sloshing Jack and Dr. Pepper over the rim of my glass and onto the plush leather seat in the limo. "You were the one who stalked me. I didn't show up at any of *your* classes."

Maybe it was the booze. I was three drinks in, not a lot in the old days, but right now my entire body was tingling with awareness. With nostalgia. And a hundred other things I didn't expect and couldn't name. All I knew was that I was having a good time, and none of our baggage followed us when we'd stepped into the limo. It was like we took the best parts of what we were and left the rest on the curb.

Sean smiled into his sip of beer, a chuckle rumbling from his chest. "Maybe, I don't remember."

The downtown lights poured through the moonroof, accentuating his strong nose and angular jaw. But his eyes were mostly shadowed until he lifted his gaze.

I knew Sean's face as well as my own, having traced every inch with my fingers in another life, and right now, I longed to do it again.

Drowning my wild thoughts with another healthy gulp from the crystal glass, I arched a brow. "You really don't remember?"

The silver flecks in Sean's eyes twinkled like tiny sparks in an azure sea. "Of course I do." He smiled, genuine, almost shy. "I was just kidding. I freely admit," he sighed, shaking his head, "I was obsessed with you."

The weight of his words, unabashedly sincere and wholly unexpected, hit me hard. I'd spent years trying to forget *this* Sean existed since he'd largely disappeared in the month before he walked out on me.

Sobered by the thoughts that peeked from the corners of my mind, I shifted my focus to the window and watched the city roll by as the last words Sean had said that night played in a loop.

*I'm done. With you and this town.*

And I had to wonder. How did Sean feel about being back here? Home.

Or maybe he didn't think of Austin as his home any longer.

As if he sensed the change, the uncomfortable turn we'd taken on our trip down memory lane, Sean cleared his throat. "Another?"

I turned to find him motioning to my empty glass. Sean didn't know what I lightweight I was now. And I didn't want to tell him. For one night, I wanted to be the girl I was, so I lifted a shoulder in a casual shrug and then held out the tumbler. "Sure."

Sean's face lost all expression when his fingers closed around mine. Slowly he turned my hand over, spilling the few drops left in my glass onto my knee.

Running his thumb over the emerald ring he'd given me on my seventeenth birthday, his brow creased. "You still wear this?"

The cloudy stone encased in gold filigree was so much a part of me, I didn't think about taking it off before I left the house. And in my defense, I didn't plan on seeing Sean, let alone holding his hand.

"Uh . . . yeah." I licked my dry lips. "Sometimes."

Sean's eyes met mine, guarded. "How does your husband feel about that?"

This time when my brain urged me to lie, I didn't dismiss the order out of hand.

Instead, I misdirected. "He doesn't really have a say so."

Sean stared at me for a long moment, the silver consuming the blue and turning his eyes from azure to turquoise. Without a word, he poured me another drink.

But something shifted as he handed me the fresh cocktail. Sean no longer stole glances but focused all his attention on my face. "So tell me about where you're working now."

My stomach pitched, and I took a long swallow, hoping the alcohol would settle my nerves. "Hollis and Briggs."

Sean's brows crept to his hairline, and I could see the wheels turning in his head. Since I'd promised myself that I'd be as forthright as possible, as feasible, I steeled myself for some type of interrogation.

"You work with Peyton?"

My best friend's father, Mr. Hollis, was the managing partner, but I'd never expressed any desire to hang my shingle at their firm, so I could understand Sean's confusion.

"Yeah."

I was hoping Sean would drop it, because really, why did he care?

But instead, he slid forward and clasped his hands around his beer, eyeing me intently. "How did that happen? Hollis is a corporate firm. You had your heart set on practicing civil rights law."

A spark of humiliation ignited deep inside, engulfing me. My cheeks flamed from the resultant heat. "I'm not a lawyer."

Sean's frosty gaze chilled the air by fifty degrees, his voice dropping to a near growl. "What do you mean you're not a lawyer?

He knew me too well to believe I'd flunked out or that I'd changed my mind. I'd given up everything to pursue my dream until another more important dream came along. A path I'd never expected.

Smiling sadly into my drink, I shrugged. "It didn't work out."

Sean's silence told me more than any words could say, and when I looked up, I could see all the questions dancing above his head in little cartoon bubbles.

But he said nothing, allowing the hurt and disappointment to fill the dead air.

Sean thought he had it all figured out, and I didn't correct him.

I finished my drink, the liquor dulling the sharp edges. "I guess I should be getting back," I said thickly. "Do you think your driver can give me a lift to the Park and Ride?"

Neon lights illuminated the interior as the limo turned onto Sixth Street, but none were as vibrant as the blue in Sean's eyes.

"You can't drive," he said, looking away. "You've had a few."

"I-I wasn't. I'm just going to grab an Uber or a Lyft. There's always one close to the Park and Ride."

After blowing four hundred bucks on the concert ticket on Stubhub, a seventy-five-dollar cab ride to my house in Cedar Park was out of the question. But yeah, there was no way I could drive.

When Sean continued to stare out the window, I took that as a no, and dug my phone out of my purse.

"Where are you headed? I'll just have the Uber pick me up there."

"The Four Seasons."

Sean's hand came down on mine as soon as I swiped my finger

over the screen. His familiar scent invaded me as he leaned into my space, making me think stupid thoughts. But unless I jumped to the other seat, there was nowhere for me to go.

I blinked up at him. "What?"

Despite the lingering anger in his gaze, his thumb swept over mine. "You don't need a ride. I've got a suite. And I'd really like to finish this discussion there."

It was more of a demand than an invitation. And though I'd already revealed more than I intended to, someday when our paths crossed again, I wanted Sean to remember this night. To know that I hadn't run from his questions.

"Okay."

# CHAPTER SEVEN

**Sean**

*W*elding my back teeth together, I did my best to ignore Anna for the three miles it took to get to the Four Seasons. Damned hard to do when every instinct told me to pull her against me and never let her go.

For a million reasons, that wouldn't work. Not only did Anna belong to someone else, but she'd chosen the douchebag over me.

Whatever else happened on that last night before I left, all the sins I carried like stones, it had all started with Anna's rejection.

*I can't go with you. I have school.*

Everything after that—I owned. But those words put an end to us.

The limo coasted to a stop, and I jumped out to scan the area for paparazzi, leaving Anna to fend for herself. Not that I needed to worry. The eagle-eyed valet was Johnny on the fucking spot, helping Anna to her feet, a lascivious grin on his mug.

The band stayed at the hotel often, and the valet was a regular.

He'd seen me bring women here on many occasions, only to have to hail them a cab a few hours later when I was finished with them.

"No bags, ma'am?" The valet's grin turned into a smirk.

Anna glanced at me, her jaw going slack and color rising in her cheeks.

My anger evaporated, for the moment at least, and I pulled Anna flush to my side.

"The airline lost my girlfriend's luggage," I informed the valet. "When it gets here, have it sent to my suite, yeah?"

Nodding, the valet fumbled to grab a ticket from his breast pocket. "Of course." Gulping, he turned his focus to Anna. "Name, ma'am?"

Fuck.

Before I could offer an alias, Anna piped up. "Dresden. Anna Dresden."

Dresden?

If only *that* were true.

Trying not to scowl, I handed the valet a twenty in exchange for the bullshit ticket for the luggage that would never arrive. Then I grabbed Anna's hand, and we marched to the glass door.

As I pulled her inside the lobby, she stumbled, and when I looked down, I found her gazing around in wonder. And for the first time in a long time, I took in my surroundings through the eyes of someone else.

Molding my hand to Anna's back, I followed her to the row of brightly colored glass sculptures. She ran a fingertip over the smooth surface. "Wow." She peered up at me, smiling. "These are beautiful."

*She* was beautiful. And sweet. And so fucking sexy I could barely stand it.

For a moment, I forgot how pissed I was. "Yeah, they are." I pulled my hand away and cleared my throat. "I've got to get the key."

Anna nodded, her attention still on the figurines.

Mandy, the front desk clerk, gave me a smile when I approached. I really spent too much time here if I could recognize all the employees. After a quick greeting, Mandy handed me a little envelope with my key, her focus on Anna.

"Would you like me to set up a car service for your friend, or is the valet hooking you up?"

Mandy continued to smile at me as if I wasn't the biggest douche nozzle on the planet, which, obviously, I was, because I'd sent many a girl packing with her assistance.

"No, sugar," I fingered the edge of the little envelope. "But I will need another key for my girlfriend. Her name is Dresden . . . Annabelle Dresden. If you could add her name to the room?"

Why I was going through all this trouble to make these people believe that Anna wasn't a groupie, I didn't know. But for some reason it was important. Vital, even.

Mandy quickly fixed me up with another plastic card, which I stashed in my pocket. It's not that I wouldn't mind giving it to Anna, along with the key to my house, the pin to my ATM, and any other damn thing she wanted, but I knew she wouldn't take it.

It's a miracle she'd agreed to come to my room, and from the look of dread on her face when she did, it wasn't for anything fun.

I made my way back to Anna, taking her elbow. "All set."

She didn't budge, folding her arms tightly around her middle. "Maybe we should talk in the lounge?"

"Not unless you want to get interrupted every few minutes." I tried for an easy smile. "They're having a shitload of parties here tonight. Closing out the festival and all. They'll probably be photographers as well."

Sucking her lip between her teeth, Anna pondered. I thought for sure the comment about the paparazzi would spook her. Or at least the idea of explaining this shit to her husband if we ended up an item in the paper.

She heaved a sigh. "Okay. Lead the way."

The elevator ride was quiet, and once we exited on the top floor, Anna struggled to keep pace with me. I paused, biting down a smile when she stopped to take off her shoes.

"Surprised it took you so long," I said, glancing at the high heels dangling from her fingertips.

Anna's cheeks flushed. "Sorry. I'm not used to wearing stilettos."

Something about her barefoot was more enticing than her fuck-me heels, and I felt myself hardening behind my zipper.

Anna was right—this wasn't a good idea.

I grunted an incoherent acknowledgment before trekking the last few yards to the suite.

Anna lingered just inside the double doors while I turned on some lights. My backpack and a few personal items were already in the bedroom, and I hoped a bell hop had delivered them and not one of the guys.

If they busted in here and saw us . . .

Dismissing the thought, I made a beeline for the bar. After making us each a drink, I turned and found Anna standing at the wall of windows. Moonlight kissed her skin as she gazed into the distance, palm pressed against the glass and a small frown touching her lip.

I stole behind her, snaking my arm over her shoulder to hand her the cocktail. "You want to tell me what happened to UT?"

"Nothing happened to UT." She tapped the glass, her tone wistful. "It's right over there."

Ready to issue a bitter retort, I noticed two leaves from her willow tree tattoo peeking from the collar of her blouse. And I couldn't help it. Pushing the fabric aside, I ran a finger over the ink.

I'd drawn the tree myself, a replica of the willow that sat by the shores of Anna's parent's cabin at the lake. It was a match to the one on my bicep.

But different.

While Anna's tree was the picture of serenity, long branches and lush leaves brushing the ground, mine was all chaos and fury, with gnarled limbs twisting in the winds of a summer storm.

My name was twined in the bark of the trunk of her tree, camou-flaged, but I saw it clearly.

"Why him?" I asked, meeting her gaze in the glass. "I asked you for one year, and you said no. But you married someone else six months after I left?"

Fire flashed in Anna's eyes when she spun to face me, a little unsteady on her feet. "What does it matter?" The alcohol brought out her southern drawl. "You left, remember?"

After downing the contents of her drink, Anna weaved her way to the bar, and this time she didn't bother with a mixer. She poured three fingers of Jack and then drained the whiskey in one gulp.

I was too damn mad to tell her to slow down. And besides, maybe the liquor would loosen her tongue, and she'd tell me what I wanted to know. The uncensored version.

I joined her as she sloshed more Jack into her glass. "I left after you said you wouldn't come. I wanted you to—"

"To what?" She glared up at me with unfocused eyes. "We had a plan. I asked for th-three weeks," Anna slurred. "Enough time to get my scholarship in order and tell my parents. But no, that wasn't good enough."

She continued to glare at me, swaying on her spot, and the weight of her stare was too much, so I slumped onto a bar stool and stared at my hands. "I thought you were making excuses. That once I left, you'd never come."

*And I guess I was right.* But my pride kept me from saying that out loud.

Anna inched closer, her toes digging into the plush carpet. "Is that why you did it?"

Lifting my gaze, a bitter smile curved my lips. "Did what, Anna? Followed my dreams?" I motioned around the room. "As you can see, I did all right. I never lied to you about what I wanted to do with my life."

She grabbed the edge of the bar for balance. "That's not . . . That's not what I'm talking about."

"What are you talking about then?"

Anna leaned in as if she were about to make a point. Then her eyes widened, and she doubled over, throwing up all over my boots.

I ran a cool, damp washcloth over the back of Anna's neck as she hung her head over the toilet. Her blouse and skirt were long gone, replaced with a large cotton bath towel she'd secured under her arms.

My chin grazed her shoulder as I said into her ear, "Feel better, baby?"

The endearment spilled out unbidden. But in my defense, it was taking all my concentration to keep from molesting her. A nearly naked Anna, puking or not, and my body was on full alert. It didn't hurt that she was situated between my legs, her back pressed against my bare chest. The skin-on-skin contact was driving me crazy.

Groaning, Anna sank back, straight into my lap.

*Fuck.*

Adjusting her body so she wouldn't feel the obvious bulge in my jeans, I eased her into the crook of my arm and gazed down at her. Remarkably, she'd managed to get all but a little of the vomit into the bowl. And even with her eyes squeezed shut and sweat dotting her scrunched up brow, she looked gorgeous.

"Sean . . ." she mumbled without opening her eyes.

I used the corner of the cloth to remove some dribble from her chin. "Yeah?"

"I'm *sick.*"

I bit down a smile. "No, you're drunk."

Which was a little surprising. The Anna I remembered knew her way around a bottle of Jack. Not that she overindulged, but she could hold her own. Whatever she'd been doing these last four years, she hadn't been doing it in a bar.

Anna shook her head vehemently at the affront. "Am not."

"Whatever you say."

She turned her face into my chest, then went limp. I'd nursed the girl through her first drunken episode when we were teenagers and many more since, so I knew the drill—she'd be passed out in minutes.

"Stop," Anna protested with a loud groan when I shook her lightly.

Sighing, I tilted her forward and said, "Grab the bowl."

Thankfully, this was the Four Seasons, and not one of the rat traps the band had stayed in during our first year on the road.

Once Anna's uncoordinated arms were wrapped around the gleaming porcelain, I pushed to my feet, cursing when my leg cramped.

She looked up at me with heavy lids. "Sorry."

"It wasn't you." I rubbed my thigh. "My legs always give me trouble after a long set."

"I remember." Brow furrowed, her gaze lingered on my bare chest. "Why don't you have a shirt on?"

*Because I'm a selfish bastard who wanted to rub against you in your time of distress.*

Keeping that thought to myself, I plucked my T-shirt from the floor. "I didn't want it to get dirty."

Dirtier, I realized as I glanced at the wrinkled cloth. Still, it was better than Anna's puke-covered blouse.

"Let's get this on you." My tone was gruffer than expected, full of unspent lust. "Lift your arms." When Anna's eyes widened, I smiled at her. "I won't peek. Unless you want me to."

Something about taking care of Anna brought a slew of emotions to the surface. Not all of them pure. If fucking her right here on the tile floor was an option, I'd take it.

*Pathetic.*

I didn't have time to ponder my depravity because Anna pushed herself off the bowl and slowly raised her arms. The towel slid off, and thank fuck, her back was to me because I couldn't move. My hungry gaze ate up all her smooth skin, lingering on her willow tree tattoo.

She finally looked over her shoulder at me, a weak smile ghosting her lips. "Is this some weird new fetish? Are we playing cops and robbers?" She snorted a laugh, wiggling her fingers. "I surrender already." Confusion crinkled her brow when she looked down. "Holy shit . . . my nipples are hard as hell," she mused. "What's that about?"

Before I was tempted to do a thorough inspection of the stiff peaks with my tongue, I yanked the T-shirt over her head, "You're just cold."

Anna continued to chuckle as I pushed her loose limbs through the sleeves.

Slipping an arm around her waist, I pulled her upright. "Up you go."

Anna's legs weren't on board with the plan, so I molded myself to her back and walked us to the sink.

She gripped the edge of the granite while I held her in place with my hips so I could sift through the complimentary basket full of toiletries.

Finding two toothbrushes, I peeled off the wrapping and then loaded the bristles with toothpaste.

Prying Anna's hand from the counter, I pressed the toothbrush into her palm. "Brush."

Anna wrinkled her nose as she tried to find her mouth. When her cheeks were sufficiently covered with gel, I took pity on her and guided the instrument to her lips. "Open, baby."

Anna did as I asked, her hand covering mine as I swept the bristles over her teeth.

"Good girl. Now, spit."

Our eyes met in the mirror, and she blinked, foam dribbling on her T-shirt. My T-shirt. And something about her wearing my clothes was hot as fuck.

Cupping the back of her neck gently, I tipped her forward. "Spit, baby."

Once she'd expelled most of the bubbles, I drew her back so I could clean the mess off her face.

Her gaze never left mine as I made quick work of brushing my own teeth.

"Can you walk?" I asked when I was finished.

Anna jerked as if she just realized she'd spent the last five minutes with my hard-on pressed against her back.

I snaked an arm around her waist as she tried to scoot away. "Whoa, hold on."

Her wobbling legs guaranteed an inevitable crash to the unforgiving floor, so I scooped her into my arms.

"Stop squirming," I said as I carried her into the adjoining bedroom.

When she complied, collapsing against me, I gave serious thought to taking a lap around the suite just to hold her for a few extra minutes. But I wasn't that fucking desperate.

Pride notwithstanding, I pressed a feather light kiss to the top of her head before easing her between the sheets on the king-sized bed.

Anna grumbled, then rolled onto her side, burrowing into the pillow.

Sinking into a chair, I watched her for any signs of distress. "Sean?"

Inching forward, I lowered my head to catch her eyes. "Yeah?"

Anna blinked slowly. "Am I dreaming?"

I laughed because it was a distinct possibility. She'd always talked in her sleep, sometimes with her eyes open. We used to have disjointed conversations about flowers and bicycles and birds. Mindless chatter that she couldn't remember and I'd never forget.

"No, baby, you're not dreaming."

She frowned, her eyes drifting shut. "Why aren't you in bed, then?"

Since Anna's subconscious was taking a walk down memory lane, I decided to call the front desk and get my own room before I lost all reason and took her up on the offer.

After securing the black-out drapes so the sun wouldn't blind her in the morning, I crouched next to the bed.

Tracing a finger down her jaw and over her bottom lip, a lump of regret formed in my throat. "It was nice seeing you, Anna-baby."

Her eyes popped open. "Sean . . . ?"

Alarm etched her tone, and before I could say anything, her palm was flat against my cheek.

I leaned into her touch. "Yeah?"

"Do they have good pancakes here?"

"They have good everything here."

Anna hummed, her eyes fluttering closed and her hand falling away. Seconds passed, and when her breathing evened, I got up.

I was headed for the door, to the freedom from all the turmoil twisting me in knots, when I heard her voice, soft as a whisper.

"Can I have some in the morning?"

My every instinct prodded me to keep walking, but when I swung my gaze to the tiny lump huddled on the side of the huge bed, I lost my will to be anywhere but here.

Closing the door, I sealed out the rest of the world for the little while we had left. When morning came, Anna would go, but right now I could pretend. Easing onto the mattress, I stayed on my side of the bed until I felt her roll over.

"Can I?" she asked, groggy. "Have pancakes . . . with you?"

Even though I knew it would end badly, I turned and faced her, sliding down until we were nose-to-nose. Her eyes twinkled faintly, and I found her hand, tangling our digits.

"You can have anything you want." Brushing a kiss to her knuckles, my lips grazed her emerald ring. "Anything."

# CHAPTER EIGHT

**Anna**

My heavy lids felt like someone soldered them shut, and the room was spinning like a carnival ride.

"Oh, God."

My groan echoed in my ears, barely audible over the pounding in my head.

Rolling onto my side, I pressed my face into the soft pillow. The cotton smelled earthy, like the outdoors, with a hint of something else.

*Sean.*

Flashes of memories bubbled to the surface.

The concert. The limo ride. Cocktails and confessions in Sean's suite.

And then . . . nothing.

The mattress dipped, and a damp washcloth grazed the back of my neck.

"Anna, are you okay? Do you need to throw up again?"

Again?

Jolted by his words, I recalled cold marble under my knees and Sean's eyes on mine while he removed my vomit splattered blouse.

Unwilling to face him, I mumbled, "I'm okay."

Another piece of the puzzle clicked into place when I tasted mint on my tongue.

*Sean's rock-hard chest pressed against my back, holding me upright while I brushed my teeth.*

Or did he brush them for me?

Twisting to look up at him, light from the bathroom sliced through the darkness, illuminating his liquid blue eyes.

"Did I use your toothbrush?"

Given my current circumstances, I didn't know why that was relevant.

And apparently, neither did Sean, because he barked out a laugh. "That's what you want to know?" He flopped onto his back at my side. "If you used my toothbrush?"

I was fairly certain we hadn't had sex. There was no telltale throb between my legs. And with Sean, there would have been. But I didn't need to give his over inflated ego a boost by mentioning that.

"I don't know where your mouth has been," I replied flatly, gazing from his bare chest to the dusting of hair below his navel. My eyes lingered on the deep V that disappeared into the waistband of his worn jeans. "And why aren't you wearing a shirt?"

He faced me, his lip twitching as his focus dropped to my chest before slowly returning to my eyes. "Because *you're* wearing it."

Of course I was.

Everything was coming back to me now. The way Sean's fingers twined in my hair as he helped me wrap my long tresses in an off-kilter ponytail. His hands on my waist as he maneuvered me under the covers. The way he scooted as far from me as possible when he slid into bed next to me.

"And you didn't even try anything," I said, cursing the wistfulness that colored my tone.

Sean tucked a strand of hair behind my ear. "Did you want me to?"

*Did I?*

For years, I'd pictured myself showing up on Sean's doorstep and revenge fucking the hell out of him. That was when I was still angry. And like my mama always said: holding onto anger was like drinking poison and hoping the other person would die. And she was right, sort of. If I fucked Sean, I'd surely vanish, the last piece of me dissolving into the ether when he walked away. And he *would* walk away.

"No." My hand followed my gaze to his mouth, and I ran a finger along his bottom lip. "Yes."

Sean nipped the pad of my thumb, then pressed a kiss to my palm. "Which is it, Anna-baby?"

I wanted him. Four years or four hundred years wouldn't change that. But the ravine separating us was larger than ever. Once, I believed Sean loved me with his whole heart. And even that wasn't enough. Now we were strangers. And I had too much to lose.

"It's a no," I said softly before shifting onto my back to look at the ceiling.

"Because you're married?"

*Because I'm not.*

The gold band pinched my finger, foreign and even more fraudulent without the benefit of a few cocktails.

I shook my head, and that's all it took. Sean was above me, his elbows bearing the brunt of his weight as he looked down at me.

"I want to kiss you," he murmured, his lips brushing my cheek.

When I couldn't muster the tiniest protest, his mouth crashed into mine. It wasn't gentle. Teeth clacked and tongues tangled and my hands molded his shoulders, either to hold on or to keep from climbing inside him.

Sean tasted like he smelled. Like sunny days at the lake. And a bowl of fresh oranges.

*And home.*

He slid his hand to the back of my neck, to the place he owned. Diving in again and again, he teased and tasted, his hips grinding against my bare thigh.

And then he stopped.

Conflict creased his brow as his thumb caressed the column of my throat. "I can't," he rasped, his voice a harsh whisper. "Anna...I just..."

My limbs went numb as Sean's rejection sank in.

*I'm done with you. And this town.*

All the women I'd seen him photographed with over the years flashed in my mind, a parade of long legs, toned abs, and perfect smiles.

Balling my fists against his chest, I pushed lightly. "I can't breathe. Please . . . I can't . . ."

Sean's azure gaze locked onto mine as he grasped my chin, holding me in place. His long hair fell around his face, trapping me behind the curtain with him, where there was only his scent, and our breath, and a memory of what used to be.

"Listen to me. It's not because I don't want to." Pressing his forehead to mine, he murmured. "I just don't want you to do anything you'll regret. You're not a cheater, Anna-baby."

Four years' worth of pent up anger lit my insides, boiling my blood and charring what was left of my heart.

"But you are." I flung the insult like a dagger. "Aren't you?"

Sean blinked and then slowly rose to his knees with me still beneath him. "I . . ." He narrowed his gaze. "What?"

"You're a cheater. You cheated on me." Defeat infused my tone. "The day before you left town." His mouth dropped open, genuine surprise coating his features. "Don't deny it. I was there, in the parking lot at the bar. I went to find you."

Sean blanched, his eyes glued to the tears sliding from my eyes. The hot, salty testaments to his betrayal glided over my temples and disappeared into my hair.

"You were there?" His Adam's apple bobbed as if he were fighting to breathe, to keep from drowning, and maybe he was.

Taking advantage of his surprise, I wiggled out from under him, repositioning myself at the head of the bed with my legs drawn to my chest. Protecting my heart, even as I was laying it bare.

"I saw you getting out of that girl's car, buckling your jeans." My vision blurred and now there were two of him. "And then I talked to her, and she confirmed it."

We stared at each other for a long moment, and then Sean flopped onto his back.

"You didn't know?" I asked, sniffling.

He draped his arm over his eyes. "Of course not. How would I know?"

The anguish in Sean's voice told me he wasn't lying.

Scooting to the side of the bed, I swung my legs over the edge, but his hand darted out to catch my wrist before I could escape.

"Tell me, Anna. How would I know?"

My attention shifted to the clock with 3:11 a.m. glowing in red.

I had nowhere to go at this hour so I might as well let it all out.

"I thought Logan would've told you."

Willing the emotion from my voice, I fought the fresh batch of tears stinging my eyes. Sean didn't deserve them. I'd cried an ocean and didn't have any to spare.

Sean's hand slid up my arm. "What does Logan have to do with this?"

"He was there." My voice cracked, brittle shards falling into the space between us. "He found me."

Sean rose on one elbow, color draining from his face. "He was there?" Shaking his head like he couldn't believe it, his jaw hardened. "What did he do?"

Anyone else, and the question would've sounded like an accusation. But Sean knew how close Logan and I were. Like brother and sister, closer than Peyton and I were in many ways.

Sean took that from me too.

I wicked the moisture from my cheeks with my free hand. "Logan took me back to the apartment, and we waited for you to come back. But you didn't."

Even though the burden was Sean's, a weight lifted off my shoulders, and suddenly I was too tired to keep my eyes open. I suspected I wasn't quite as sober as I thought. The fact that I let Sean pull me against him proved the point.

"I did come home," he roughed out, his tone gravel and grit. "But you were gone. And I couldn't . . . I couldn't face you, so I left. It was a mistake." Sean's arms fell around me as he kissed my temple. "The biggest fucking mistake of my life. But I was going to come back for you after the tour. And explain. I swear it."

Sean buried his face in my neck, the rest of his confession muffled by my hair. And though I knew it was wrong, that we were wrong, I let him rock me until I fell asleep.

# CHAPTER NINE

**Sean**

*I* cursed the sliver of gray peeking through the tiny slit in the blackout drapes. I hadn't so much as flinched in three hours, too afraid that if I moved, Anna would come to her senses, get up, and call a fucking cab.

*She knew.*

The notion rolled around in my head as I stroked her back with numb, tingling fingers.

I'd been carrying the guilt of my betrayal around for all this time, telling myself that even if I was the one who started us down the path, Anna had ended us. That she'd moved on.

But it was all me.

Anna stirred in my arms, catapulting me into the present.

She looked up at me with that not-quite-awake stare and said, "Can we open presents?"

Anna was the fucking present, and I'd love to unwrap her, peel back every layer.

Instead, I smoothed the hair from her face and tried to figure out what time or place she was visiting in her dreams.

"Is it your birthday, Anna-baby?" She frowned, confused, so I tried again. "All right then, what do you want for Christmas?"

A small smile curved her lips, and her lids fluttered closed. "Padre Island."

I chuckled. "The whole island?" She shook her head, then nodded, and it took all my effort not to laugh. "All right, pretty girl. I'll get you Padre Island. The whole damn thing."

She rolled away from me, and though it sent a pain straight through my fucking heart, I let her. After pulling the covers to her chin, I scooted off the bed.

Grabbing my phone from the nightstand, I skimmed all the alerts, but it was Anna's soft sigh that drew my attention. I glanced at her auburn hair fanning the pillow.

*More.*

That's all I wanted.

More of Anna. More of this. Just . . . *more.*

Looking down at my phone when it buzzed, I walked into the living room and hit the first link that populated the screen.

*Mega concert promoter Benny Conner wooing Caged for the Euro-Trash Rock Festival tour.*

Fuck me. I hadn't even thought about Benny, the band, or the meeting I'd blown off. Since the moment I'd followed Anna down that hallway at the arena she'd consumed me.

Instead of reading one of the hundred texts, I dropped onto the couch and perused the breakfast menu. Only after I'd called room service and ordered every kind of pancake known to man did I pick up my phone.

Before I could respond to any messages or emails, a loud knock echoed in the suite. I jumped to my feet, rushing to the foyer before the pounding woke Anna.

Yanking the door open, I met Logan's frosty glare over the top of his sunglasses. "What the fuck happened to you last night?" He brushed past me, and when he nearly tripped over Anna's discarded stilettos, he jerked his gaze to mine. "You've got to be fucking kidding me? You ditched a meeting with Benny C for a—"

Before he could finish, the bedroom door creaked open, and then Anna was there, twisting the sash on the oversized robe the hotel provided.

"I didn't know anyone was here," she said, her eyes jumping from Logan to me.

I cemented on a smile. "That's okay. Look what the cat dragged in."

Logan didn't even look at me as he stalked straight to Anna. A brief second passed and then she was off the ground, in his arms. "I can't believe this," he said as he swung her around. "You're really here. How?"

Setting her on her feet, he waited for an answer.

Anna pulled in a slow breath. "Well, I came to the show last night, and . . ."

Her gaze shot to mine.

"And we had a few drinks," I said to Logan as I sank into the wing backed chair. "Since Anna was a little tipsy, she decided to crash here."

Anna turned a deeper shade of red, knowing exactly how this looked. I knew as well, but the difference was, I didn't care. I'd already resolved myself to the fact that I wanted Anna in my life. Any way that she'd have me.

Logan glanced between us, and for a moment, I thought Anna's crimson flush might deter him. But, no.

"Yeah, right," he scoffed. "Go sell crazy somewhere else. We shared an apartment, remember? No way y'all spent a night in the same room without—"

"Dude!" I barked. "Don't."

Anna's snort of laughter broke the tension, and when I saw the small smile curving her lips, I relaxed.

Smirking at me, Logan grabbed Anna's hand and led her to the couch.

Leave it to the jackass to break the ice without falling through it.

Logan pulled Anna down next to him, his questions coming fast and furious. And to my surprise, she answered, providing bits and pieces about her life.

Logan met my gaze, a question furrowing his brow. Since I didn't have a fucking answer, I merely shrugged.

Tuning them out when Logan delved deeper into Anna's personal life, I picked at the hangnail on my thumb. I couldn't bear to hear the details.

I jumped to attention when Logan snapped his fingers.

"Dude, someone's at your door," he said, both brows raised in an exaggerated gesture. "Do you want me to get it, or what?"

There was no mistaking Logan's implication, or his intention to throw himself on the sword if some chick had found her way to my suite. Anna's fidgeting and refusal to meet my eyes proved that Logan wasn't the only one with an over-active imagination.

"That's room service." Hauling to my feet, I smiled at Anna. "Pancakes."

Moments later, two rosy-cheeked attendants followed me into the room, each pushing an overfilled cart. Logan and Anna took a seat at the dining room table while the servers busied themselves unloading platters of pancakes.

Anna pressed her lips together, biting down a grin.

I grinned back, because really, what else could I do? The girl wanted pancakes. Maybe not four dozen, but hey, better safe than sorry.

After helping the servers with the cart and signing the check, I returned to find Anna scowling as Logan loaded her plate.

"Lo," she griped. "That's too much."

He snorted as he set the feast in front of her. "Don't give me that shit. You know how hungry you get after—"

Anna elbowed him in the ribs. "Don't you dare finish that statement."

Rubbing his side, Logan scooted away from her. "A concert! You get hungry after a concert. Geez, girl, put that bony elbow away, and get your mind out of the gutter."

Smiling, I trapped Anna's foot between mine as I poured her a cup of coffee, light with two sugars. She didn't try to move, so I counted it as a win.

"Anna said she'd come out to the Parish for our next show," Logan said in between bites. "Just like the old days."

Anna stared down at her plate, pushing her food around.

Filling my cup, I caught her gaze when she looked up. "You're going to the Parish?"

She lifted a shoulder. "Logan invited me. But it's no big deal. I won't go if you don't want me to."

"Of course you're going." Logan glowered at me. "I would've invited you sooner if I'd thought you'd come. Shit, you won't even meet me for coffee, so I didn't think you'd be down to come to a show."

I froze with the cup halfway to my lips, glancing between the two of them. I hadn't forgotten about Anna's confession or Logan's four-year omission, but I'd deal with that later. Right now, I was more interested in how long they'd been in contact.

Anna didn't notice my frozen expression.

She gave Logan a little nudge with her shoulder. "You don't drink coffee."

"For you, I would." Logan's eyes locked on mine as he pushed to his feet. "I got to take care of that business we were talking about." I nodded, and he planted a kiss on the top of Anna's head. When she looked up, he said to her, "I'll see you next Saturday."

She smiled, then promptly refocused on her plate.

I hopped out of my chair, following my best friend to the door.

"We need to talk," I said, grabbing his arm before he slipped away.

Logan looked down at my hand, then up to my face, smirking. "Name the time."

I gave Logan's bicep a hard squeeze before I released him so that he'd know I was dead serious.

He searched my face for a long moment, then he left.

When I reclaimed my seat across from Anna, I noticed that her pancakes were now a pile of blueberry mush.

"I don't have to go to the Parish if it makes you uncomfortable," she said quietly, without looking up. "Logan's just . . . you know . . . Logan."

"Baby, I want you to go." I took a sip of my coffee, and when the silence got too hard to ignore, I said carefully, "So you and Logan talk, huh?"

Anna looked up, her wall firmly in place. "Yeah, a little bit."

I watched her over the rim of my cup as I took another drink. "How did he know where to find you?"

Anger sparked in her emerald gaze, the gold flecks burning orange. "He didn't have to find me, Sean. I wasn't lost. Unlike you, I have the same email address and the same phone number."

I sank further into my seat, absorbing the blow. All this time, Anna was only lost to me.

"I thought he'd mention it, that's all," I said as I examined the left-over grounds in the bottom of my cup. "How long have y'all been talking?"

Anna's silence drew my attention, and she gave me a look that said I didn't want to know. But then she sighed. "I contacted Logan about two months after you left, just to see if you were okay." Her focus shifted to some spot on the wall, and she continued, "He told me it would be awkward if we, him and me, kept in touch. Then about a year and a half ago, he sent me an email and apologized. I just thought he was having a moment, you know?" Our eyes met, and unable to hide the pain, she whispered, "No, I guess you wouldn't know."

A pitiful apology clawed at my throat, but I swallowed it because anything I said would only serve one purpose: getting her to stop. And knowing Anna, she probably would, just to spare me.

A dull ache settled in my chest. "So he apologized, and . . . ?"

"I figured he'd said what he needed to say, so I was shocked when he kept emailing."

I forced my lips to bend, mostly because I was thinking about all the ways I was going to kick Logan's ass. "What do y'all talk about?"

"Lots of things." Anna laughed. "Girls. The band. Music. Besides you and Peyton, Logan was my best friend. I lost all my closest friends when we split. It was hard." Squinting like she was reliving a physical pain, Anna looked away. "Really hard. But we don't talk about you, though. Logan said you never mention me, so . . ."

Anna's thought trailed, but the implication was there—I didn't care. I'd never cared.

The blow hit me square in the gut, and I offered a truth of my own, selfish as it was. "I don't talk about you, Anna. It hurts too much."

A practiced smile lifted her lips. "Don't feel bad. It was a long time ago. I'm glad you're happy."

Happy? Was I happy?

*Sometimes.*

But the empty space was always there, the Anna-shaped void that I'd tried to fill with music and women and parties.

"So," Anna continued, snapping me out of my inner thoughts, "y'all have been in Austin for quite a while. What's next?"

If I didn't know any better, I'd think the girl was fishing. And since I was more than willing to get caught, I smiled.

"Nothing much."

It was the truth. Nothing seemed as important as keeping Anna in my life. As friends or maybe more. The *more* I was still trying to figure out.

Taking her hand, I looked into her eyes. "What about you? Are you happy?"

Anna tilted her head, pondering. And then she smiled weakly. "At times, yes. Very happy."

I nodded, accepting Anna's hedging, because if she were truly content, she wouldn't be here.

Testing the theory, I moved to the seat Logan had vacated. "So, you and Dean?"

Anna looked down and fiddled with her emerald ring. "I don't want to talk about Dean with you."

I closed my hands around hers, and again, she made no move to pull away. "Fair enough."

I'd never knowingly gone after another man's girl, let alone their wife. But this was Annabelle. She was mine first. And if Dean Kent made her happy, I'd back the fuck off. But first, I needed time to assess.

Skimming my hand up Anna's arm and over her shoulder, I cupped her nape. "You know I built a house out at the lake?" I tilted her chin with my thumb, and she met my gaze, nodding. "How about you give me a ride home, and I'll give you a tour of the place?"

# CHAPTER TEN

**Anna**

*W*hen we arrived at the Park and Ride, a crowd gathered around Sean. He gave me an apologetic smile as he posed for a couple of selfies with some fans. Funny as it sounded, I didn't know how big Caged really was. My cyber stalking was limited to Sean, and nobody who knew me ever mentioned the band.

Smiling back, I motioned to my car before wandering to the aisle where I'd parked my Audi.

As I slid behind the wheel, I noticed the crowd had grown around Sean, and for a moment I seriously considered leaving.

Because this was crazy. Over the course of twelve hours, he'd not only convinced me to have drinks but to go to his hotel suite and take a tour of his house.

I'd texted Peyton after breakfast to let her know where I was so she wouldn't worry, but I wished I hadn't.

My phone buzzed in my pocket with her ongoing diatribe, though I'd stopped responding five messages ago.

I looked down at my hand, to the gold ring cutting into my finger, and screw it; I took the damn thing off. And then I settled into the leather seat to read my texts.

Tucked amid Peyton's warnings was a short video from my mother. I smiled as I watched my dad lead Willow around the corral at my aunt's house.

With tears lining my eyes, I tapped out a reply.

*Miss y'all. Please be careful.*

"Everything cool?"

Startled, I looked over at Sean, who'd somehow managed to open the door without me hearing him.

"Yeah, fine."

While he was busy folding himself into the seat, I waited for Mom's reply. She was terrible about checking her phone, so I finally gave up and tossed the device into the cup holder.

As I pulled out of the parking space, Sean noticed my small suitcase in the back seat.

"Going somewhere?"

The question came out as brittle as his smile.

"To the cabin. You know, to clear my head after all the stuff with Gran."

Sean rested his arm on the console next to mine, and when he linked our pinkies, I had to smile. He made me feel sixteen, which was not only dangerous but foolish as hell.

"I meant to ask," he said as I pulled into traffic. "What happened to Gran?"

My heart stuttered, and I had to wonder if talking about Gran would always be this painful. "Stroke. It was quick."

Cutting my gaze to Sean's, I understood now why people said stuff like that. Even if there was little consolation for me, he seemed relieved. Sean's mother had died a slow, painful death from cancer. And he never got over it.

"Thanks again for the flowers." I forced a tight-lipped smile. "She would've loved them."

Sean frowned before shifting his focus to the side window. "I should've gone. To the funeral, I mean."

When he turned back to me, he was the boy I'd met in high school.

"It's okay."

We drove in silence until we turned down the two-lane highway leading to the lake. Once we were on the back roads, I rolled down the window, and cedar scented air perfumed the cabin.

Sean squeezed my pinky. "Turn left up here."

He motioned to the lane that seemed to lead straight into the preserve. But that couldn't be. The preserve was off limits.

I waited for traffic to clear, then made the turn, my heart racing as we passed under a canopy of trees.

After a stop at the guard shack to collect a visitor's pass, we pulled into the gate.

"Look familiar?" Sean asked when we crested the top of a small incline, and the waters of Lake Travis peeked through the trees.

I slammed on the brakes. "We used to camp right down there."

Sean chuckled, a faraway look in his eyes. "I guess that's one way to describe it. There was a tent and a couple of fishing poles."

He was right. Our weekend jaunts usually consisted of skinny dipping and hot sex under the stars. And all we managed to eat were the s'mores we cooked over the campfire as we discussed all of our plans for the future.

When we had a future.

Sean squeezed my hand. "What is it, baby?"

I shook my head, a little dazed.

Sean did everything he'd set out to do. Built his house and his life and his music. He'd just done it alone.

"Nothing." I lifted my foot off the brake. "Tell me where I'm going."

Following Sean's directions, we ended up at the bottom of a hill in front of a security fence.

Craning my neck, I looked up at the spikes on top of the twelve-foot gate and then over to the keypad next to my window. "Is there a code or something?"

Anger flared when Sean crossed his arms over his chest, shifting in his seat. Was he kidding right now?

"Look, you invited me," I bit out. "If you think I'm going to show up here some time out of the blue and bother you, you're sadly mistaken. So either give me the code or get out of the car and punch it in your damn self."

A smirk twisted Sean's lips but he continued to stare straight ahead. "Zero-five-two-four."

The air left my body in a rush. "What?"

Sean finally looked at me. "Zero. Five. Two. Four."

I blinked. "But . . . that's my birthday."

He eased a strand of hair behind my ear, smiling. "I'm aware."

Flustered, I rolled down the window and then punched in the code, only to have the box squawk in protest. I tried again with similar results, and Sean laughed.

"You only get three tries until they lock you out. Unless you want to climb that fence, you'd better concentrate, Anna-baby."

Steadying my hand, I slowly punched in each number, and a loud beep signaled my success.

I stared at Sean's profile as the gate slid open. "Why?"

He shrugged. "Why not?"

Exhaling a slow breath, I drove up to the mini-mansion. Before the car rolled to a complete stop, Sean was out the door with his backpack and my suitcase in his hand.

"Hey!" I called as he strolled toward the garage.

He shot me a grin over his shoulder. "Sit tight."

Still a little off balance, I sank into the seat and took a look around. My heart jumped into my throat when I saw the little meadow surrounded by a picket fence, and before I could think better of it, I was out of the car.

"Anna!"

Sean's boots thundered behind me, but I kept on running.

I stopped in front of the gate, giving it a hard shake.

"Easy, baby," Sean said, reaching around me to find the hidden latch.

Impatient, I slipped inside, and then came to an abrupt halt in front of the full-grown willow tree. Curling my fingers around a low hanging branch, I swayed in my spot.

"It's a willow tree." My voice cracked as I spun around. "Why do you have a willow tree in your front yard?"

Sean squinted up to the sky, to where the leaves were so dense they nearly blocked the sun. "The same reason I have a willow tree tattooed on my arm. To remind me."

"Remind you of what?"

I stumbled backward as he closed the gap, pressing me up against the tree trunk.

Touching his forehead to mine, he smiled. "Of you."

# CHAPTER ELEVEN

**Sean**

*I* pressed Anna against the tree, my hand in her hair, and my lips so close I could feel her breath.

"Tell me to stop, Anna-baby."

The low growl was somewhere between a challenge and a plea. And then, just to remind Anna of what this was, what we were, my hand found hers, seeking the gold band.

But her finger was bare. Not even a groove on her skin. Like the last four years had left no impression.

"Tell me," I repeated, tightening my grip so she'd know I was serious, that I'd take her right here, claim what wasn't mine. What should've been mine.

Anna held my gaze, fingers treading lightly up my arms, over my shoulders, and into my hair.

And then she pulled me down, and her pillow-soft lips met mine. "Don't stop."

Her tongue slipped into my mouth, twisting and tangling and

blurring all the lines. But I wouldn't cross over only to have her hate me, or herself. So, I let her steer the ship.

When she guided me to her neck, panting in my ear and seeking the button on my jeans, I broke our connection.

Her lids fluttered open, her emerald gaze dark with lust. "What?"

"You ready for that tour?"

Anna studied my outstretched hand. Because she knew what it was. An invitation. A disaster. The point of no return.

And she took it.

This wasn't how I wanted things to go down. Not that I believed that Anna would ever see this house, but when I indulged in the fantasy, I somehow thought she'd be more impressed.

Instead, she'd trailed behind me as we went from room to room, hands clasped in front of her like she was afraid to touch anything.

Maybe Anna was having second thoughts. Or maybe I'd only imagined the whole thing by the fucking tree and all she wanted to do was tell me to go straight to hell and then offer directions.

And really, could I blame her?

Lost in thought, I topped the marble stairs and then headed for my bedroom to stow my backpack and her small suitcase, which I still had in my hand.

Yeah, wishful thinking.

Glancing over my shoulder when I realized Anna wasn't following, I froze when I spotted her in front of the pictures lining the glass table in the alcove.

Retracing my steps, I cringed when she dropped to her knees in front of the photo album on the bottom shelf.

Brushing a hand over the leather cover with the picture of us encased in plastic, Anna looked up at me with questions in her eyes. "*You* had this?"

I closed the distance between us as casually as possible. "Yeah. I found it when I was unpacking."

A faint smile touched Anna's lips, but she didn't call me on the lie. Instead, she pulled the album onto her lap and then carefully cracked open the cover. "I wondered where it went." She looked up at me, smiling. "I'm glad you saved it. I don't have copies of these."

I crouched at her side. "Do you want copies?"

Anna went still, examining one of the photos from our prom. "If you don't mind. I want to save them for—" She caught herself and then cleared her throat. "For old time's sake. You can mail them to me or whatever."

Anna closed the cover, but before she could put the book back on the shelf, I scooped it up. "I haven't seen these in a while. Let me drop this stuff off in my room, and we can take a look, yeah?"

Nodding, she hauled to her feet, smoothing her hands over her wrinkled skirt.

"Your house is gorgeous," she said, peering up at me as we made our way down the long hallway.

"You sound surprised."

Anna laughed, and the sound struck a chord deep inside, a place where there was no music. Just her.

"You used an empty keg for a chair in our old apartment."

"True." I pushed open the door to my bedroom. "But I can't take all the credit for this place. I had a decorator."

I dropped the suitcase and my backpack on the small couch and then placed the photo album on the bed, hoping Anna would take the hint. I wanted *her* on that bed, branding my sheets with her peach scent and leaving strands of auburn hair on my pillowcase.

Adjusting my semi hard dick, which showed no signs of cooperating, I dug around in the fridge behind the bar. "All I've got is Pale Ale up here. I'm sure there's some Dr. Pepper downstairs if you—"

Whatever I was about to say died on my lips when I turned and found Anna on the bed, the album in her lap. She wasn't looking at the pictures, though.

Easing behind her, I brushed the hair off her shoulder. "I saved the best view for last."

"You think the dam is the best view?" she asked quietly.

Banding my arms around her waist, I stared out at the water. "It's my favorite view."

Mansfield Dam towered in the distance, just inside the window frame. Anna's parent's cabin sat on the other side of that dam, tucked away in a small inlet. The best days of my life were spent there, with her. And when I'd proposed to Anna under the willow tree on her seventeenth birthday, I'd promised to build her a house with a view of the dam.

And I did. She just didn't know it.

For over an hour we sat in silence, fingers entwined, my chest pressed against her back, watching the breeze blow across the water. My stomach tightened when the sun dipped below the tree line, the invisible clock in my head ticking louder and louder.

"Stay with me tonight, Anna-baby." I kissed her temple. "One night."

Her back straightened and she looked up at me with a heavy-lidded gaze. "Why?"

*Because I want to live inside you. Wake up with you in my arms. Watch you drink coffee and eat pancakes. And then do it all over again.*

Blowing out a breath, I went for honesty. "Because I miss you."

Anna scooted away from me, and I squeezed my eyes shut, biting back a string of curses when she hauled to her feet. I'd pushed her too far, asking for something she couldn't give.

But then I heard the snick of her zipper.

Eyes locked on mine in the fading light, Anna wiggled out of her skirt. "One night. And then I can't see you again, Sean."

It was a hollow victory. Like eating cake without the frosting. But damned if I wouldn't take it.

I tried for that carefree smile I could usually conjure on

command. But I only succeeded in a small curve of my lips. "Okay, baby."

Anna slid under the covers while I toed off my boots. She was still wearing the baggy T-shirt I'd loaned her this morning at the hotel.

*Was it only this morning?*

It felt like time was moving too slow and too fast. Probably because I was cataloging every second.

Easing on top of her, I pressed a kiss to her lips, drowning in her sweet scent. Her fingers dug into my wrist when my hand slipped under her T-shirt, and I pulled away, sobered by the thick clouds gathering in her emerald eyes.

"What is it?" She snagged her lip between her teeth but said nothing. Resigned, I rested my forehead against hers. "Anna, we don't have to do this."

I wanted her so fucking bad, I could barely say the words without choking on them.

"It's not that," she finally said, her voice quavering. "Four years is a long time. We don't know each other anymore. Not like this."

I blinked, astounded. "You don't know me?" I slid my hand to her knee, fingering the one-inch scar that she got from the fall she took when we were hiking in the hill country at sixteen. "You sure about that?"

Maybe it was true for her. But I'd never moved on. Everything about Anna was fresh in my mind. Her scent. Her smile. The way she looked at me when she tipped over the edge, it was all there.

Anna blinked, her plump lip firmly entrenched between her teeth once again.

Holding her gaze, I rose to my knees and then stripped off her T-shirt. My lips found hers for a quick kiss as I worked the tiny clasp on her bra, nestled in the valley between her perfect breasts.

Peeling away the lace, I said, "Let me see if I can change your mind."

Anna's back bowed when I sucked her nipple into my mouth, and she jerked, gasping, as I scored my teeth across the stiff peak. I'd forgotten more than anyone else would ever know about Anna's body.

Including the fact that she liked a little pain with her pleasure. Not a lot. Just enough to feel.

Groaning, she fisted my hair. Hard. And I smiled then because Anna knew what I liked too.

I just had to remind her.

Abandoning her needy breasts, I worked my way south, lingering at her navel piercing, which, thank fuck was still there. I gently tugged the barbell with my teeth while I slid her panties over her hips.

"You like that, don't you?"

Anna writhed against me while I teased her with my tongue and my teeth, blazing a trail down her belly and past her hips. I settled between her thighs, hiking one leg over my shoulder.

*Home.* I was almost home.

As I moved lower, peppering kisses over her smooth skin, my lips grazed a thick scar above her mound, and I froze.

Anna went stone still as I ran a finger along the jagged ridge.

Resting my forehead on her stomach, I swallowed the lump of regret. Any fantasies I'd entertained about this being anything more than what it was, a final gasp, a goodbye, a period at the end of the sentence that was us, evaporated into the chasm between our past and our present.

Because there was no future. Not now.

"So," I curved my hands around her hips, my thumbs tracing small circles over what wasn't mine. "Did you have a boy or a girl?"

# CHAPTER TWELVE

**Anna**

*A*nd this is why I should've never gone to the hotel with Sean. Never let him buy me a drink. Never spent the night in his bed.

There were too many landmines, things he didn't know, and he'd just tripped over one of them.

Stumbling out of the rubble, I tried to sit up, but Sean's hands were unyielding, and the look in his eyes brooked no argument. It said, "you're going to tell me," and gazing into the blue depths, identical to my daughter's, I realized that I would. I'd answer any question Sean had. And if he asked the right one, everything would come crashing down.

"I have a little girl," I replied, making a vain attempt to keep my voice steady, my features schooled, and my hands from shaking.

*Ask me her name.*

I forced the notion from my mind. Sean had a place reserved in my head, and the bond we'd shared was almost eerie at times. He used to finish my sentences, know what I thought before I thought it.

Not now, though.

Sean's eyes dimmed, the light bleeding from the azure pools as if someone pulled a plug. He loosened his grip, and I wriggled free.

He sat up, swung his legs over the side of the bed, and stared out the window. It was nearly dark outside now, a faint moon rising in the sky.

*Ask me her name.*

But he didn't.

Lips turned downward and brows slashed in an angry line, Sean stared vacantly at the water while I studied his reflection in the glass.

I guess fucking a woman with a kid was a turn-off. And on some level, I knew that.

Why would Sean choose me, with my less than firm tits and faded stretch marks, when there was a bevy of women out there with perfect bodies, just waiting for him?

I'd embraced the changes in my body over the last four years. I was young, and I'd bounced back. But my hips were a little wider, my breasts a little fuller, and no amount of exercise would get rid of the stubborn little bulge above my scar.

I guess that's what happens when a doctor rips you open and takes out a small human.

As I sat pondering my shortcomings, I continued to watch Sean, and when he buried his head in his hands, gripping his hair and looking down at his feet, I knew it was time to leave.

I found my panties in the sheets and then slowly got out of bed. I'd just slipped the lace over my thighs when Sean's fingers circled my wrist.

Startled, I looked up.

"Where are you going?"

His voice was like sandpaper, scraping the inside of my ears.

"I just thought . . ."

I didn't know what I thought. Or what I felt. The only thing I wanted was to spare us both the embarrassment of this conversation.

Sean was looking at me now, his gaze crawling over me from tip to toe. Checking for imperfections, I assumed. He'd always regarded me with lust, a huge boost to my ego, even when I was young and I wasn't sure what that look was all about.

I saw it last night and today, but now his eyes were shuttered. Not cold exactly, but inscrutable.

"You don't have to leave, Anna."

Of course, he would say that.

I tugged free of his hold, smiling through tears I refused to let fall. "I only live a few miles from here. It's no big deal."

When I made to brush past him, he grabbed me and then shoved his hands into my hair. He stared down at me, cradling my face in his palms. "You promised me one night." His lips found mine. Firm. Demanding. "One night."

We tumbled onto the bed, a tangle of limbs, our mouths searching for one another.

Sean's hand dipped into my panties, long fingers parting my folds, slick with arousal, because, yeah, he did that to me. Always.

And then his fingers were inside, and I gasped. "Oh . . . God . . ."

Maybe it was that rhythm Sean was always talking about, but he could play my body like no other. Not that I had a lot of experience. Two men, total. But Sean knew all the secret spots, coaxing the pleasure from inside me until I was a raw bundle of need.

His thumb glided over my swollen nub while he pumped his fingers in just the right way, and I squeezed my eyes shut.

"Look at me, Anna. Stay with me."

I'd heard those words from him a million times when forever was an option. Now it was all about a moment, *this* moment, and nothing else.

"I'm here . . ." I managed to say before Sean sealed his mouth over mine, his tongue exploring, pushing me to the edge.

And when I shattered he swallowed every moan.

I was still somewhere else, floating above, when his teeth grazed my nipple.

"Don't stop." I fisted his hair, still grinding against his hand. "Please . . ."

He worked his way down, found my belly button ring and gave it a single pull. And then his mouth was an inch from my most sensitive spot, his warm breath tickling my clit.

My back arched the second Sean's tongue swirled over my tiny bud. His arm circled my thigh, fingers digging into my flesh with the right amount of pressure.

"Fuck," he murmured. "You taste so good. So fucking sweet."

His words sent me over the edge, riding the wave of another release, and my vision went dark.

I was a shuddering mess, on the verge of tears when Sean finally pulled away. He pressed me into the mattress, his body covering mine as he kissed me, long and slow.

"Believe me now?" he asked, brushing the hair off my sweaty brow.

"Huh?"

"I know you, Anna-baby. All of you."

Burying my face in his neck, the thrum of his pulse against my lips was almost enough to let the truth spill out.

Before I could speak, Sean was on his knees, ripping the condom wrapper with his teeth. Desire darkened his irises, the silver threads burning bright.

With his arms coiled around my thighs, he pushed in slowly.

Arching to meet his thrusts, I pressed my head into the pillow.

"Eyes, Anna," he grunted. "Show me your eyes."

I did as he asked, holding his gaze as he moved with purpose, his jaw torqued tight, a deep crevice between his brows.

"Sean . . . I can't."

He eased on top of me, his forearms braced on either side of my face, our noses less than an inch apart. And then he kissed me.

"Fuck . . . fuck . . . fuck, Anna," he bit out, his mouth sliding from mine. "I'm not . . . I'm not going to last."

He reached between us, then stroked my clit, teasing yet another orgasm out of my limp body. But this time he followed me over the edge, meeting the end of me as he came. When he pushed to his palms and looked down at me, his brows drew together, worry chasing away any residual lust in his gaze.

"What is it, baby?" His thumb skated over my cheek, spreading the moisture I didn't realize was there. "Don't cry. Shit."

He kissed away the tears while I tried to melt into the pillows, embarrassed and overwhelmed. It wasn't him, I told myself. But that was a lie as well. It was always him.

"I'm fine," I croaked.

He rolled off me and then disposed of the condom before joining me under the covers.

"Come here," he said, entwining our fingers so he could pull me close. "Tell me what happened."

*You* happened. *This* happened.

"Nothing. I'm just a little emotional. It's been a hard week."

He nodded, and though I knew I'd probably regret it, I snuggled into his arms and let the steady beat of his heart lull me to another place and another time. When I was happy.

# CHAPTER THIRTEEN

**Sean**

*I* stroked Anna's hair until her breathing slowed.
Even now, I could feel the hot, salty tears on my
thumbs. The evidence of her regret.

The problem was, I couldn't find it in me to feel sorry for what
we'd done.

Alive; that's what I felt.

My phone buzzed, and reaching for it out of habit, I skimmed
Logan's text.

*Party tonight at Maggie Mae's. You in?*

He was either the dumbest fucker on the planet or he was fishing.
But my answer was the same.

*No. I'm good.*

When I stretched to set the phone on the nightstand, Anna rolled
onto her side.

"I love licorice," she mumbled.

Tucking in behind her, I molded my chest to her back, spooning.
How long had it been since I spooned?

Almost four years.

"Me too, baby."

She hummed. "And Willow."

Smiling, I pressed a kiss to her shoulder somewhere on the branches of her tattoo.

As my eyes grew heavy, my subconscious surrendered to the beat in my head, the familiar tune I'd vanquished to the archives the day I'd left Austin.

The song of Anna.

Whether she invaded my dreams or I occupied hers, I wasn't sure. But when I drifted off, Anna was with me, beneath our willow tree, with lips that tasted like candy.

Cursing, I scooped the broken egg from the skillet, my fourth, and then looked around in a panic. The mangled, empty carton lay on the counter amid the debris of mixing bowls, utensils, and other ingredients.

"Lola!"

My housekeeper strolled in, a basket of clean laundry under her arm. She didn't answer, preferring to snicker at my distress.

Swinging my gaze to hers, I glared. "Do we have any more eggs?"

Unfazed by my glower, she set the basket on the table. Plucking a clean T-shirt from the pile, she tossed it to me, staring pointedly at the scratches on my chest. And the bite marks on my neck. My just-fucked hair.

In my defense, I didn't know about the scratches or bite marks until I saw my reflection in the mirror this morning when I came downstairs.

The night was a blur of peaceful sleep, vivid dreams, tangled limbs, and sweet lips that tasted like licorice.

Arching a brow, Lola meandered to the refrigerator. "You got a girl up there, or a lion?"

I pulled the T-shirt over my head while she poked around in the Sub Zero, producing a dozen eggs from a compartment I'd never seen.

"I thought you told me that you didn't bring your floozies back here, Mr. Sean." Lola sighed her discontent, laying the fresh carton of eggs next to the stove. "You're free to live your life any way you see fit, but I'm not going to be cleaning up their messes. I told you when you hired me, I used to work for someone in the movie business. Brought a different gal around every day." Clucking, she shook her head. "Those girls started ordering me around. And, lordy, they were slobs."

Normally, I'd laugh if someone used the word "floozies" but instead my back stiffened in defense.

"Anna's not a floozy," I muttered. "She's my . . ."

Hell, I didn't know what Anna was. And even if I did, I couldn't describe her in a word. It would take a book. And besides, Lola was my housekeeper, not my mother.

"You going to turn that pancake, Mr. Sean?" Lola asked. "Or are you planning on burning the house down?"

I jerked my gaze to the stove where a plume of black smoke hovered over the burners.

"Shit."

I grabbed a pot holder so I could toss the pan into the sink without burning the hell out of my hand. The automatic faucet spluttered to life, dousing the charred remains.

Fucking perfect.

Raking a frustrated hand through my hair, I surveyed my mess through watery eyes. Burnt pancakes, singed bacon, and something that resembled eggs, but not quite.

Blowing out a defeated breath, I ignored my rumbling stomach as I searched the cupboards for clean bowls.

I hadn't eaten a full meal since breakfast yesterday morning at the Four Seasons, though I seemed to recall some dried fruit snacks

Anna pulled out of her bag sometime before dawn. Or maybe it was licorice.

Shit . . . I didn't know. It was good, though.

Lola elbowed my ribs. "Move, Mr. Sean. Whoever you got upstairs is going to starve to death. 'Sides, you're just causing more work for me. It's going to take an hour to clean up this disaster area as it is."

I held my ground until my stomach let out another loud roar, then reluctantly backed away from the stove and my surly housekeeper.

Lola got right to work, expertly dropping an egg into the skillet with one hand while simultaneously peeling bacon from the one-pound package with the other.

Even with all that, Lola still managed to shoot me an admonishing glare. "Make yourself useful and fetch me some orange juice from the fridge." She snorted. "I would tell you to squeeze some fresh, but that juicer of yours takes an advanced degree to operate."

"I have a juicer?" I set the jug of OJ on the island, then opened a cupboard filled with canned goods. "Shit, where are the glasses?"

Lola snapped me with a towel.

"Ouch!" My hand shot to my arm, which stung like a bitch. "What the hell?" Clamping my mouth shut, I jumped out of the way as the tiny tyrant lifted the towel in preparation for another assault.

"No need to cuss. Your glasses are up there." Lola pointed to a cabinet above the dishwasher. "Didn't you buy anything in this house for yourself, Mr. Sean?"

"Just, Sean," I corrected, the way I had done a dozen times. But Lola never took the hint. "And, no, I didn't."

Ladling four scoops of pancake batter onto what I thought was a burner cover, she tutted. "You got a built-in griddle, dummy. Why are you using a fry pan?"

I glared at the beast of a stove. Two ovens, eight burners, and apparently, a griddle. Who knew?

Lola snapped her fingers. "Fetch me a tray from the pantry. A wooden one."

She pointed at the door next to the laundry room, and when I didn't move, she rolled her eyes.

"I know where it is," I grumbled.

"It's a miracle."

Biting my tongue, I stalked away without a reply. The little dictator could easily hold my breakfast hostage, and I was already feeling light headed.

Poking around the large storeroom, I found the trays on a bottom shelf tucked between the juicer and some kind of tiny coffee machine. I didn't know who my decorator thought I'd be entertaining, but at least I figured out how she spent so much money stocking the kitchen.

As I turned to leave, a beat-up box with "Grace's Jars" scrawled on the side in Anna's handwriting caught my eye.

Memories of my mother came rushing back as I pulled off the lid.

Every spring, Mom would gather bluebonnets and display them in Mason jars.

After we'd moved in together, Anna heard about the tradition, and I guess she'd asked my aunt for the jars because I came home one afternoon and found bluebonnets on every table.

Peeling back the newspaper from one of the jars, I read the date in the corner.

Two weeks before I'd left for the tour.

Even with our relationship fucked beyond reason, Anna had lovingly boxed the treasures.

"Mr. Sean, would you like coffee or—"

"Coffee's fine, Lola," I mumbled, dropping off the tray on my way to the back door. With one of my mother's jars in hand, I hopped off the deck and then headed straight for a patch of wildflowers growing by the shore.

Sorting through the brush, I picked a few of the most colorful blooms.

As I retraced my steps, I heard Anna's voice, and when I looked up to the second-floor balcony, I found her propped against the railing with her back to me and the phone pressed to her ear.

It was wrong to eavesdrop on Anna's conversation, but I couldn't help myself, so as quietly as possible, I edged toward the house.

"No . . . it's in the blue bag," Anna said, agitated. "No more than three or she'll get jittery." She paced in a tight circle, nodding absently. Her face lost all expression when she noticed me. "I've got to go," she said, her tone devoid of emotion. "Yeah . . . you too."

*You too . . .*

I'd been on the receiving end of enough of her calls to recognize the familiar response.

Anna forced a smile. "You should've woken me up."

When the phone rang again, her gaze shot to the screen, and without a word, or even a glance my way, she turned on her heel and walked into the house.

*You have no right to be upset*, I reminded myself as I filled the jar with water from the spigot next to the back door.

I took a deep breath and wrestled the jealous beast trying to claw its way out of my skin.

Lola eyed me with concern when I flung the back door open. "You okay, Mr. Sean?"

"Fine," I snapped as I arranged the silverware on the tray. Blowing out a breath, I met Lola's gaze and smiled. "Sorry."

A thud against the marble steps, and then another, prompted Lola to step out from behind the island.

"I got it," I said on my way out of the room.

Meeting Anna halfway up the stairs, my focus shifted to the suitcase in her hand.

"What's going on?"

She blinked at me. "I have to go."

Molding my palm to her hip, I held her in place. "Go where? What's the matter?" Her chest heaved, heart thumping so loudly, I could practically feel every beat. "Anna, tell me. Whatever it is, we—"

"There is no we!" she cried. "I told you one night, and now I have to go."

Seeing the tears well in her eyes, I let my hand fall to my side. "You don't have to do anything. Whatever it is, we can work it out."

Anna looked at me for a long moment, her eyes roaming over my face. "No, we can't. I'm sorry."

I clenched my hand into a fist to keep from hauling her into my arms. And then I smiled. "I'm not."

Whatever that said about me, and my morals, I wouldn't trade the last thirty-six hours for anything. In fact, I wanted more.

Anna glanced to the foyer and then back to me, so I gave it one last shot. Crossing my arms over my chest, I locked our gazes. "You can stay, Anna. For as long as you want."

The indecision faded from Anna's green eyes. "No, I really can't," she said flatly. And then she rushed down the stairs. Turning to me at the bottom, she frowned. "Goodbye, Sean."

I didn't say anything, didn't move. But then the front door clicked shut, and my knees got weak.

Sinking onto the step, the unforgiving marble chilled me straight through my jeans.

"Can I help with anything, Mr. Sean?" asked Lola, hovering near the entrance to the kitchen.

I smiled, fake as hell. "No thanks, I'm heading out to meet the guys. Might be gone a few days." The thought of sleeping here—no, I couldn't do it.

"Hey, Lola?" She paused, then turned back to me, her smile as fraudulent as mine. "Change the sheets, will ya? And get rid of the flowers."

# CHAPTER FOURTEEN

## Anna

$S$itting in the parking lot at the Iron Cactus on Trinity
Boulevard, I tipped my head back and stared out the moonroof of my car. The wispy clouds blended into the evening sky, their
edges burning pink against the violet sunset.

"Jolene," my favorite Ray LaMontagne song, whispered softly
through the speakers. It was an anthem for my life after Sean had left,
and the refrain hit me hard, like a hammer to the chest.

I'd found the CD in a box in the garage, tucked away with the
other relics from my old life. Pictures and poems and other trinkets
that told the story of our shared past.

That was the price of seeing Sean again, I guess. Letting him
inside me, both literally and figuratively. Four years of progress
erased in two days. Followed by four days of utter misery.

If Mom hadn't called me that second day and told me that Willow
was having an asthma attack, prompting me to freak out and demand
that she bring my child straight home, I might still be at Sean's.

Since Willow ended up in the hospital, it was a good thing I'd followed my instincts.

Still, it hurt like a bitch, leaving Sean that way.

I shook my head, dismayed. I really had fallen into old habits, stalking Sean's social media, Google searching anything related to Caged.

And what did I find?

An article on that reality star, Kimber what's-her-face, talking about how good it was to see Sean when she was here.

*Here.* In my hometown. The thought of her in Sean's bed, looking out the same window that faced the dam . . . I couldn't even think about it. The tabloids claimed that Kimber was planning another trip to Austin, so it was a good thing I got out before she showed up on his doorstep.

Knocked out of my trance by a tap on the passenger window, I shifted my gaze to Peyton, arms crossed over her chest, scowling at me with her stormy gray eyes.

Reluctantly, I unlocked the door.

Sliding into the seat, she stared straight ahead. An awkward silence hung between us. Since I was the one in the wrong, I spoke first.

"I'm sorry, Pey."

Ever the dramatic, she turned slowly. "You're sorry. You haven't returned my calls in four days, and you're *sorry*?"

Hands knotted in my lap, I twisted my emerald ring.

"I went to your house last night," Peyton continued, accusation dripping from her tone. "Didn't you hear me banging on the door?"

Guilt bloomed in my chest when our eyes met.

I'd spent the last forty-eight hours lounging with my little girl inside the pillow fort I made on my living room floor, ignoring my phone. The only knock I remembered was from the pizza delivery guy.

"I swear, Pey, I had no idea. Willow was really sick when she got home and we just . . ." Peyton wasn't buying what I was selling, so I gave up, offering a conciliatory smile. "I didn't mean to freak you out. I did text though."

*Once.*

Not cool.

Peyton tossed her designer bag on the floorboard and then twisted in her seat. "You *texted*?" Leaning against the car door, she scrutinized me like a hostile witness she was about to interrogate. "I figured your rendezvous with Sean was at least worth a phone call."

My cheeks flamed, heat crawling up to my hairline. "It wasn't a rendezvous. We had a few drinks and I went back to his suite. And I was kind of buzzed, so I stayed the night."

"Whoa, whoa, hold up." Peyton lifted her hand in the universal don't-you-dare-say-another-word signal. "You spent the night in his suite? I thought you just had drinks. Isn't that what you told me?"

We'd been best friends since we were six. I never lied to her. "Well, yeah, but it was at the Four Seasons."

Her eyes narrowed, growing darker by the second. "So y'all had a tryst in his suite?"

I shook my head. "No tryst in the suite."

It wasn't a lie. Not technically. But still, I had to work hard to keep from melting into the plush leather seat.

Peyton let out a relieved sigh. "Thank fuck. It would be just like the slimy asshole to take advantage of you after everything with . . ." Her eyes darted to mine and she softened considerably. "With Gran."

At the mention of Gran, the familiar lump hardened in my throat. "It wasn't like that. Sean loved Gran." Gazing at the traffic, the lights blurred when tears formed. "He even sent flowers to the cemetery."

"How chivalrous of him."

Her sarcasm drew my heated glare. "Drop it. You don't know how Sean was with me."

The vein on the side of Peyton's head pulsed. "Then tell me!"

My teeth dug into my bottom lip as I weighed the pros and cons of getting into this with my best friend. If anyone deserved an explanation, it was Peyton. She was the one who'd glued me back together after my breakup with Sean.

But, no, it was too soon, and I was still too raw.

Instead, I took her hand. "What does it matter? I was bound to see Sean one day." I gave her a small, knowing smile. "Someday I won't have a choice, and we both know that. Let's save the dramatics for that day. Okay?"

After appraising me for a long moment with her face pinched as tight as her brows, Peyton's mask fell away. "I just don't want him to hurt you again."

My attention shifted to the emerald ring on my finger. Yes, Sean had outgrown me, outgrown us, but I had the evidence of the great love we'd shared, the best part of Sean Hudson, whether he knew it or not. And for that reason alone, my ability to hurt him far outweighed his ability to hurt me.

"You can't talk about him like that, Peyton." I tipped my chin at her, defiant. "He's Willow's father."

Hearing my daughter's name in the same sentence with Sean's sent my stomach tumbling. They didn't exist in the same space in my head. In my mind, the Sean I knew when we made her was gone, his love and light extinguished by the rockstar he'd become.

But I'd glimpsed something in the hotel suite and again at his house. An echo of the past. I'd chalked it up to geography, sharing the same space, breathing the same air. But it had been four days, and the feeling hadn't diminished.

Peyton touched my arm, bringing me back to the here and now. She blinked at me, her face pale in the reflected light from the dashboard. "You didn't tell him about Willow, did you?"

I shook my head. "No."

*He didn't ask.*

I left that part out.

Peyton's shoulders sank as she released an audible sigh. "That's good."

"Willow will find out someday, Pey. You know she will. And then they'll both hate me."

Peyton straightened, setting her jaw. "Dean is on her birth certificate, so Willow doesn't ever have to know."

Frustrated, I shook my head. "Dean doesn't want anything to do with her." Peyton cringed at my harsh tone and harsher words. But it was the truth. Before I could stop myself, I blurted, "Which do you think is worse, a father that doesn't want you, or a father who'll show up on occasion?"

Peyton scrutinized me with a cocked brow. "Remind me again, which one is Sean?"

Anger surged through me on Sean's behalf, indignation he didn't ask for and likely didn't deserve.

"I didn't give him a choice. I didn't—"

"You found Sean with a groupie," Peyton shot back. "Before he even left town. He didn't give *you* a choice."

Peyton's gentle reminder knocked me back. All the way back to the frantic eleventh-hour phone calls I'd made that she knew nothing about.

Admittedly, I was weak back then, and the day before I'd married Dean, I tried to find a way out.

But Sean had changed his number, shed the vestiges of his old life, like a worn-out piece of clothing that no longer fit.

And I was part of that old life, so I let it go.

"It doesn't matter now anyway," Peyton grumbled. "Once Caged signs the offer from Benny Conner you won't have to worry about Sean for at least eighteen months. Probably longer."

My heart slammed against my ribs with such force that my hand crept to my chest to make sure there wasn't a hole. "What offer?"

Peyton's face fell, pity swimming in her stormy eyes. "I thought you knew. Benny Conner retained the firm to draw up some papers to open up negotiations with the band for a tour of Europe and Asia. The Euro-Trash Festival. Memos have been flying around the office for the last couple days."

And if I checked my email, I would've known that. But apparently, I was too busy reliving my past to be bothered with the present.

*Stupid.*

I forced my lips to bend, my cheeks nearly cracking from the effort. "That's great."

The understatement of the year.

Benny Conner was the pot of gold at the end of the rainbow, a sure-fire ticket to superstardom for Caged.

I took a fortifying breath and then grabbed my purse. "I'm happy for them." Walking the tightrope between the truth and a lie, I pinned the smile to my lips. "Let's go eat. I've got to pick Willow up in an hour or so, and I'm starved."

Peyton looked around as if she just realized why we were here. When our eyes met, her lips parted, but I shook my head, signaling an end of the discussion.

My chest constricted under the weight of everything said and unsaid in my life as I climbed out of the car.

Peyton stole concerned glances at me as we crossed the parking lot.

But I held my head high, determined to prove to her that I wasn't the fragile girl Sean had left behind four years ago. I'd survived the storm then and found beauty in the chaos.

*Willow.*

She was my reward.

"Are you okay?" Peyton asked as she pulled the door open to the cantina.

"Yep."

Breezing past the hostess, I headed for the stairs, for the rooftop bar, and all the twinkling stars just beyond my reach.

# CHAPTER FIFTEEN

**Sean**

The sun sank low as I pulled my boat into the slip at the Oasis, the trendy three-story restaurant directly across the shore from my house. My gaze shifted to Mansfield Dam as I wrapped a thick hank of rope around the metal post on the pier, mooring the boat to the dock.

This made the fifth sunset since Anna had walked out. I'd seen them all. The first two days I'd spent in a drunken haze, but I swam up from the bottle every evening like clockwork, just to watch the sky turn.

Sliding my sunglasses on my nose, I ambled down the pier, hoping to blend in with the dinner crowd.

Caged was a solid band with a good-sized following, but it was only here, in Austin, where I got recognized daily. Love us or hate us, people knew who we were. Maybe because we were born and raised here. And there were only so many places to go in this city. I'd visited them all at one time or another, before they were tourist traps.

The Oasis was one of those places. The multi colored umbrellas dotting the patios at the rear of the restaurant provided optimal shade to enjoy the view of the lake, even in the summer.

I spotted Trevor as soon as I slipped through the door, so I bypassed the hostess stand and then climbed the three steps to the premium tables.

"Look at you." I held out my fist for a bump, smiling. "Shunning the commoners up here in the VIP."

Trevor laughed, slinging his arm over the back of his chair. "Dude, I used your name. I'm but a lowly attorney. I can't compete."

I tossed my glasses on the table as I slid into my seat. "Glad my name is good for something."

Unable to keep the edge out of my tone, I scrubbed a hand down my face.

Trevor eyed me as he took a sip of his beer. "Why do I get the feeling this ain't a social call? You in some kind of trouble, Hudson?"

I was in a shitload of trouble. But not the kind Trevor could solve.

Picking through the bevy of appetizers on the table, I popped a shrimp into my mouth.

"If I wanted to talk business, I'd come to your office, and you wouldn't be using the word 'ain't.'" I laughed. "Not for seven hundred and fifty an hour."

Trevor scoffed. "I've never charged you seven fifty in your damn life. You got me cheap."

Trevor's firm handled some of the business for the band. Or, rather, Trevor's daddy's firm. Trevor Sr. charged full price to look over all of our contracts and such, but I'd known Jr. since our dive bar days. His and mine. Considering the amount of alcohol Trevor had imbibed during his years at UT, I wasn't sure how he managed to graduate.

We made small talk over a bucket of beer while we waited for our fajitas. Once the waitress dropped off the sizzling plates of beef and shrimp, I got to the point.

Dipping a tortilla chip in salsa, I asked, "You know anything about Dean Kent?"

Trevor shoved a wedge of lime into his bottle of Corona, chuckling. "So that's what this is about—Anna's husband?" he took a sip. "Or ex-husband, I guess."

He belched loudly, which was a good thing since my stomach hit the floor with a thud that could probably be heard at the next table.

I chugged half a glass of water, forcing the chip down my throat. "Ex . . ." I coughed. "Ex-husband? Since when?"

Trevor lifted his gaze to the ceiling, pondering. "Not sure. They may not even be officially divorced." He shrugged. "They're separated, though. Have been for a while. It's been over a year since I've seen them together at any parties."

I pushed a piece of beef around my plate. "Maybe Anna just doesn't like to go out."

From the way she was heaving her guts out the other night after a few cocktails, I'd say it was a distinct possibility.

Trevor sighed. "Yeah, no. First of all, if you're married, you show up for these parties together. Second," he pointed his fork at me, "people talk. And Anna and Dean's impending divorce has had everyone's tongue wagging for a year."

Digesting the information, I tried to hide my shock. "That's interesting . . . I guess."

Trevor's boisterous laugh filled the room. I swear people turned to stare. "Cut the crap, Hudson. If you're asking about Anna-baby, you've either seen her, or you want to."

The asshat continued to smile, piling more food on his plate while he waited for me to elaborate.

After four sleepless nights, my patience was less than zero, but I played along. "I might have run into her."

He shoveled another bite into his pie hole. "Why don't you ask *her* then?"

"Dude." I wrinkled my nose. "Don't talk with your mouth full."

Trevor took a sip of beer to wash down his food. "I said—why don't you ask Anna?"

I heard the fucker the first time. I only hoped a little misdirection would aid my effort to shift the conversation.

Since it didn't look like it was working, I lifted a shoulder. "We only saw each other once. We didn't really talk."

Trevor clinked his bottle with mine, grinning broadly. "But did you fuck?"

Red painted the corners of my vision and white-hot rage boiled under my skin. "Don't fucking talk about her like that. You got a death wish?"

Genuine confusion furrowed Trevor's brow at my snarled retort. "Damn, Sean, lighten up. I was only kidding. If you didn't even know about the divorce, no chance you two were hitting the sheets. Anna would never fuck around, not even on Dean."

I grabbed another beer, and ice rolled down the bottle, stinging my hand, but I didn't flinch. Hell, the pain barely registered. Because I *did* think Anna was married. No, I'd never asked her outright. But the ring.

Trevor's last comment finally caught up with my whirling thoughts. "What do you mean, 'not even on Dean'?"

Trevor looked me in the eye, clasping his hands in front of him in what I assumed was his courtroom demeanor. "How much do you know about Anna and Dean?"

I shrugged, pulling a face. "Nothing."

At least that was the truth.

Trevor blew out a breath, exasperated. "Okay, so you don't know anything now. What about when they first got together. I mean, you two had to have talked about . . ." His brows shot up as I shook my head. "Are you telling me you haven't spoken to Anna in all this time?"

Disbelief shrouded his features, and I averted my gaze. "We broke up. Do you speak to your exes regularly?"

Trevor slumped in his chair. "Well, no. But, shit, y'all were together since what, first grade?"

I rolled my eyes. "Sophomore year, asshole."

He chuckled as if I'd proved his point. "That's what I'm saying. I still talk to Jilly, and I was only with her a couple of years."

I lifted my beer in a mock toast and smiled bitterly. "Good for you."

Glancing in the mirror behind Trevor's head, I paused with the bottle halfway to my lips as a tall brunette walked up the steps, straight out of my past. Out of a dream. Or a nightmare.

That had to be it. Four nights without sleep and I was conjuring ghosts.

But as she got closer, her high heels clicking a staccato beat against the wood floor, I realized this was really happening. She was here.

"I thought that was you," Darcy said smoothly, resting her hand on my shoulder. "Sean Hudson, in the flesh."

I'd long suspected the events that destroyed my only chance at happiness were inexplicably woven into the fabric of the universe. Like the Big Bang. And now, in exchange for Anna making a guest appearance in my life, karma had brought Darcy along for a cameo.

My focus shifted to the gold name tag on her blouse for confirmation. Our hookup came courtesy of too much booze to be sure it was her. Though I knew it was. "Hey, Darcy. Long time."

She tapped her lips with her finger, smiling. "Yeah, almost four years."

"That long?"

In my periphery, Trevor's gaze volleyed between Darcy and me. She'd yet to look at him, which spoke volumes. Trevor wasn't famous, but the dude's all-American good looks drew women like flies to honey.

Darcy gave me a small pat and made a show of perusing my plate of fajitas. "I saw your name on the reservation list, and I thought I'd say 'hi' and make sure you were enjoying your meal."

If the glint in Darcy's eyes was any indication, the only thing she wanted me to enjoy was E-coli or something equally heinous.

"Well, thanks for that." I forced a smile. "Food's great. It was nice seeing you again."

"Are you dismissing me?" she snapped, her tone shrill. "Because I'm a manager here. So I'm not going anywhere. If you've got a problem with me then *you* can leave." Her eyes narrowed to slits. "You're good at that, aren't you? Last time I don't think you bothered to zip your fly before you ran out on me."

Trevor cleared his throat, but Darcy didn't flinch. Either she knew he was there and didn't give a shit or she was too wrapped up in telling me off to notice.

Either way, I felt bad. None of this was Darcy's fault. It was on me. But she'd pay the price if she lost her shit in the middle of the dining room. I doubted her boss would take kindly to one of his employee's cussing out a VIP, justified or not.

"Darcy," I warned, "keep your voice down."

"Why? It's not like you have a girlfriend anymore. Nobody's going to jump me in the parking lot."

The buzzing in my head rose in pitch, and I half expected my eardrums to shatter.

"I don't know what you're talking about, sugar, but you need to run along."

A smile crept over Darcy's lips. "Oh, I think you know exactly what I'm talking about. The redhead. Annie something or other."

My jaw clenched reflexively, trapping Anna's name behind clenched teeth. "You mean Annabelle?"

"Yeah, her."

Lifting the beer to my lips, I wondered when the man on the pale horse was going to arrive because surely this was the fucking apocalypse. I'd already heard this story once, and it nearly killed me.

"The crazy bitch accosted me in the parking lot after . . ." Darcy got hold of herself at the last second, her attention shifting to Trevor, scowling into his beer. "After you left."

Somehow, I managed to form a thought. Because only one thing mattered more than my pride, and that was preserving Anna's dignity.

So I laughed. "I doubt Anna was that concerned. She kicked me to the curb before you and I hooked up.

The lie slipped out, smooth as a greased pig. But Darcy wasn't buying it, and from the look of reproach on Trevor's face, neither was he.

"Could've fooled me," Darcy singsonged, examining her nails. "She was crazy hysterical. Logan had to pull her off. She crumbled right there in his arms."

Looking me in the eye, whatever Darcy saw was enough to satisfy her need for revenge, because she plucked the check from the table and said, "Your meal's on the house." She gave Trevor a brilliant smile. "Y'all have a good night."

I fished my wallet out of my pocket for a tip while Trevor watched Darcy saunter away.

He met my gaze with thinly veiled disdain, and I couldn't blame him. "You want to tell me what just happened?"

I took a deep breath.

"It's a long story," I said as I grabbed the last beer. "And I don't mind sharing. But first, you need to tell me everything you know about Anna and Dean."

# CHAPTER SIXTEEN

**Sean**

*L*ater that night, I turned into the quiet cul-de-sac in Cedar Park where Anna lived. I didn't plan on going to her house straight away. At least that's what I told Trevor when I'd convinced him to pull up her address on the tax assessor's website.

But here I was, squinting at the house numbers stenciled on the curb. Most of the designations were plain, with a white glow in the dark paint on a black background. But only one had a UT Longhorn logo.

I made a quick pass in front of the house to verify the address before parking across the street.

When Anna mentioned that she lived close, I didn't realize it was *this* close. Seven-point-three miles from her door to mine according to the GPS. I could run it in less than a half hour and drive it in five minutes.

Sipping the coffee I'd picked up at Starbucks on the way here, I looked around the upscale development. All the homes had well-manicured lawns and expensive cars in the driveway. But the charming red brick two story had Anna's fingerprints all over it. An oak tree stood tall in the front yard with limestone bricks stacked neatly around the base of the trunk. Manicured hedges cupped the arched entryway, and brightly colored perennials peeked from the flower beds in front of the windows. And then there was the orange tricycle tucked against the garage, white streamers dangling from the handlebars.

I'd come here with every intention of letting Anna know that I was on to her and that I was totally cool if she wanted to use me. But first she needed to tell me why.

As I finished the Americano, the truth seeped in along with the caffeine. I wanted the girl, my girl, as much as the explanation.

Jumping out of my skin when Logan's ringtone bled through the speakers, I gritted my teeth and ignored the call.

The phone rang again.

Without taking my eyes off the house, I tapped the button on the steering wheel. "What?"

Over the loud music in background, Logan said, "Dude, if you don't start answering your phone, I'm implanting a fucking chip in your arm. Where the hell are you?"

I bit my tongue until I tasted blood to keep from tearing into him. We still hadn't had the talk. The one where my best friend explained why he didn't tell me about seeing Anna at the bar the night before we left town. And oh, by the fucking way, why in the hell have you been emailing her for a year?

Tamping down my anger, I replied, "Out."

"What's up your ass, Sean? I haven't seen you in three days."

"I've been busy."

"With Anna?" When I didn't answer, Logan sighed. "She wasn't at the show last night."

My anger reignited, scalding my tongue as the words flew out. "Why the hell were you looking for her?"

"Because I invited her, dumb fuck."

Before I could reply, Anna's garage door slid open, spilling bright light onto the driveway.

I hunkered down in my seat as she stumbled out, dragging a large trash can behind her. "I gotta go."

"Wait a minute!" Logan barked. "Benny called. He wants us to come to LA next week."

"Fine, whatever."

Distracted, I disconnected the call and watched as Anna walked backward down the steep incline. Under the street lights in her flimsy nightgown, I could see every curve, every slope of her body. And I glanced around to make sure nobody else was watching.

*Mine.*

Unable to sit still any longer, I hopped out of the car. "Anna!"

She whirled around, shock painting her features. "Sean, what are you doing here?"

Her mouth formed a little *o* as I marched toward her.

"I want to talk to you." When she turned, bolting for the safety of the garage, I cursed under my breath and then broke into a sprint. "Anna, stop!

Glancing over her shoulder, her eyes widened as I closed the gap. "Go away!"

She wasn't looking where she was going and she tripped over the tricycle, landing on all fours.

Flipping onto her backside, Anna cursed and then bowed her head, like the weight of the world just descended on her shoulders.

*Me.*

I was the weight.

"Are you all right?" I held out my hand as I approached. "Let me help you."

Daggers shot from Anna's pretty eyes as she looked up, scowling at me. I suppose she thought it was fierce. Cute is what it was, and all my anger fled.

"I'm fine." She swatted me away. "I don't need your help."

I crouched in front of her, my fingers itching to touch her. "What are you running from, baby?" I swept a curl behind her ear. "Huh?

She blinked up at me, defeat written all over her face. "You shouldn't be here."

Easing down beside her, I offered a small smile. "You're probably right. But I am, so what are we going to do about it?"

Anna struggled to her feet. "You're going to get in your car and leave, and I'm going inside."

She tapped her foot impatiently. But I wasn't going anywhere.

I glanced over my shoulder at her car. "Is Dean-o home?"

Her brows dove together, and she took a step back. "No."

"Good." I climbed to my feet, then took her hand. "We'll talk inside."

In Anna's state, half naked and pissed as hell, she wasn't concerned about her neighbors sneaking a peek at her goodies. But I was.

*Mine.*

Anna pulled her hand free and growled, "We will not." Wincing, her gaze shot to a small gash on her palm. "Shit." In seconds, a thin rivulet of blood trailed to her wrist. Dazed, she blinked up at me. "I think I cut myself."

The sight of blood had always turned her to stone.

"You did, but it doesn't look that bad." I guided her to the door. "But we need to clean the dirt out."

As I crossed the threshold, my feet tangled around a pink Big Wheel, giving Anna time to slip around me and rush to kitchen.

I was still staring at the toy like it might sprout wings when Anna called, "Hey, can you get me a Band-Aid?"

She pointed to a door right behind me.

I nodded, and then stepped inside a tiny washroom. Sorting through the medicine cabinet, I finally came across a couple of stray bandages imprinted with Disney princesses. I picked the one with the red hair.

Joining Anna at the kitchen sink, I laid the Band-Aid on the counter. "I think this is Aurora."

Aurora was the only princess I knew by name, and only because my cousin went through a Sleeping Beauty phase. The kid refused to get out of bed for an entire weekend, insisting her prince would come. I finally had to pay the little boy next door two bucks to give her a damn rose.

Anna glanced at the package and rolled her eyes. "That's Ariel." She hissed a breath, her attention back on her wound. "It stings."

Brushing aside her hand, I sloughed off the soap so I could get a better look. "How do you know?"

Anna tore her gaze from the pink water circling the drain. "Know what?"

"How do you know it's not Aurora?"

"Because Aurora's a Betty." She tugged on her hair. "A blonde. And she doesn't have a tail."

I laughed. "Why in the hell would a princess have a fucking tail?"

"Because she's a mermaid."

Anna actually knew this shit. Amazing. And then I thought of her kid, her little girl, and my gaze flicked back to the Big Wheel by the door.

When the bleeding dwindled to a trickle, I turned off the water, smiling. "You don't need stitches. Let's get the Band-Aid on."

Things got awkward, and Anna slipped free of my hold. "I've got it."

Before she could ask me to leave again, I wandered to the living room to take a look around. The house was half the size of mine with none of the custom finishes, but unlike my mini mansion, this place screamed home.

On the coffee table, a half empty can of Dr. Pepper sat next to a John Grisham paperback and a coloring book, and Gran's quilt lay in a messy ball at the foot of the couch.

I fingered a crocheted square. "I wish I could've seen her one last time before she . . ."

*Died.*

For someone intimately familiar with the concept, I couldn't bring myself to say the word. Like if I never actually said it out loud, death would forget where I lived.

But who was I kidding?

Death had come to visit before I was born, stealing my father and my grandmother. And just to make sure he had my full attention, the grim reaper came back to take my mom.

Head bowed and lost in my own morbid thoughts, I didn't realize Anna was in front of me until her hand sifted through my hair.

The girl knew how to chase away all my demons with only a touch. How did I ever forget that?

Resting my forehead on her chest, I breathed her in. When my arm banded around her waist, she stilled, and I lifted my gaze.

"You should go," she said, a weak smile playing on her lips.

Taking Anna's hand, I pressed a kiss to the shiny new Band-Aid. "Why? You got a boyfriend or something?"

My attempt at humor fell flat, and she pulled away. "Of course not, I'm . . ."

Folding my arms over my chest, I waited for her to finish, but Anna was such a shit liar, she didn't even try.

"You're not married, Annabelle," I said flatly.

Her eyes widened, but only fractionally. "Yes, I am. I'm just . . ."

"Separated?" I cocked my head, scrutinizing her with a frown. "Is that the word you're looking for?"

Her lips parted, but then she went still, lifting a finger. "Shhh."

I was about to ask why the hell she was shushing me when a child's voice called, "Ma!"

The little cough that followed sounded like a bark.

Anna stepped back, her eyes as cold and distant as I'd ever seen. "You need to go." Another cough and her steely determination crumbled, along with her composure. "Leave, Sean. *Now*."

And then she was gone, up the stairs without a backward glance.

Obviously, whatever was going on with her kid took precedence. We could finish later.

But as I headed for the door, Anna's panicked voice floated from above.

"Breathe, baby, big breaths," she pleaded. "Please, for Mommy."

My feet moved of their own accord, taking the steps two at a time, and before I knew it, I was standing in the doorway of a cheery pink bedroom.

"Is everything okay?"

Anna rounded on me, eyes large and frantic. "I need your phone!" My attention slid to the clear plastic tube snaking from the headboard and the clunk, clunk, clunk, of a machine. A penguin? "Sean! Your phone!"

I snapped out of my stupor and dug the device from my pocket. "Here. What else can I do?"

Anna pried the phone from my hand while I stood, transfixed by the tiny figure tucked under the lavender sheet. Wisps of copper curls framed the little girl's angelic face, falling over her eyes, scrunched tight in distress. She held onto the mask affixed to her nose as her chest rose and fell with labored breaths.

"What's the matter with her?" I cut my gaze to Anna. "Why can't she breathe?"

"Asthma." Anxiety etched Anna's tone, but she sounded a hell of a lot calmer than I felt. "She's stable right now. I'm calling the doctor."

I blinked at Anna and then back at the baby. Was she a baby? It was hard to tell.

"This is stable?"

Anna nodded, and then spoke into the phone. "Yes, this is Anna Kent."

Stepping away, she continued to relay information, but whatever she said faded to white noise because all my attention was focused on the little girl.

Until that moment, I'd put the notion of Anna's kid to the back of my mind. But now she had a face. Anna's face, apparently, because even with the mask obscuring her features, the resemblance was remarkable. Same alabaster skin. Same delicate fingers. And that hair.

I swept an auburn curl from her brow. "You look just like your mama."

Her eyes flew open and inquisitive blue orbs searched my face. *Blue.*

Not brown like Dean's. Or green like Anna's. Azure, with tiny filaments of silver spreading from the pupils.

My mom used to say we were lucky because we carried lightning in our eyes.

Just like this little angel.

Anna nudged me out of the way. "I have to go. Her doctor's meeting us at Brackenridge."

The electricity flowing between us arced into a circle, engulfing the little girl with the red hair and the blue eyes. And I knew.

Meeting Anna's resigned gaze, I swallowed hard. "I'm driving you."

# CHAPTER SEVENTEEN

*Anna*

$\mathcal{T}$here are moments in life when everything changes. When the earth shifts, and the ground crumbles beneath your feet.

Most of the time, you never see it coming. You certainly don't invite it.

But I had.

The moment I'd decided to go to that concert, I'd summoned the chaos.

That's what I thought about as I climbed into the backseat of Sean's car—how I'd done this to myself and now I was going to pay.

While I attempted to strap the safety belt over Willow's lap, Sean drummed his fingers frenetically against the steering wheel.

I probably should've grabbed Willow's car seat, but she was already looking at me with wide eyes, and with the time I'd wasted throwing on a pair of jeans and grabbing my go bag, we didn't have a moment to spare.

Yes, I had a go bag. When your child has health issues, it only takes one trip to the hospital in the middle of the night to learn your lesson.

Willow wasn't in distress at the moment, her breathing even, but shallow. Normally, I wouldn't have freaked out. But with Sean in my living room and my daughter barking out little coughs, my composure had snapped.

After four years of holding my secret, I knew I was on the verge of being detected, and I'd panicked. Or maybe, on some level, I wanted Sean to know.

"Damn it," I muttered, tears welling in my eyes when I couldn't free the seatbelt from the frame of the car. "I-I think it's broken."

I cringed when the driver's door creaked. And then Sean was there with me, eyes locked on mine, brushing my hands away.

"Easy, baby."

I wasn't sure if the endearment was for Willow or me.

I didn't deserve it, and the fact that Sean felt comfortable enough to bestow it on my daughter was terrifying. And exhilarating. Mostly terrifying.

The traitorous little strap unfurled, and Sean leaned forward, securing the fastener into the slot.

His gaze met mine again when he finished, and time stood still as our entire past played in his eyes, the silver gossamer weaving our story like a web.

When the reel ended, he shifted his attention to Willow. Then he quickly backed out and reclaimed his seat behind the wheel.

"You ready?" he asked in a hollow voice.

*Was I?*

"Yes."

Sean put the car into gear and then backed out of the driveway, while I pressed Willow's hand to the hollow of my throat so she could feel my words.

"What's her name?" Sean asked when our eyes collided in the rearview mirror.

While I'd longed for him to ask that question a few nights ago, now I wasn't sure why.

As I held my daughter closer, I glanced at the tattoo on his arm. "Willow."

I waited for the requisite, *"Is she mine?"* but it never came.

Sean just nodded to himself, tightened his grip on the wheel, and drove.

# CHAPTER EIGHTEEN

**Sean**

*W*illow.

Stunned into silence after hearing my daughter's name, I drove like a bat out of hell. Now and then, I peeled my eyes from the road and looked into the rearview mirror.

Light spilled through the windows, framing the angel molded to her mother's side. It was like the moon was drawn to her, painting her little features with a luminescent brush.

My gaze found Anna's, and I held on tight to those green, green eyes. I was all questions, and she was nothing but answers, but I didn't say a word, too afraid to open my mouth and unleash the fury clawing its way up my throat.

*How could you not tell me?*

As if she'd heard my inner thoughts, Anna smiled, soft and hesitant, and then she looked down at Willow, like maybe that was her answer.

I drew a blank as I tried to recall anything that I'd accomplished in the past four years that I wouldn't sacrifice to know her, that little angel with my eyes and her mother's face.

Pulling my car under the awning next to the emergency room door, I found my voice when Anna jumped out.

"Anna!" I barked, my feet hitting the pavement as she hustled to the automatic doors, cradling Willow in her arms.

Anna froze, hesitated for a long moment, then turned. "Thank you for the ride. You don't have to stay, though. My mom's coming."

Incredulous, I closed the distance between us. "I'm going to park the car." Infusing calm into my voice my eyes dipped to Willow. "Where can I find you?"

Anna's silent scrutiny caused a chemical reaction that set my blood on fire.

If she thought she could dismiss me without an explanation . . .

"Fourth floor. Pediatrics."

Anna's voice was hushed, and I strained to hear her over the hum of traffic from the busy street.

"I'll be right up." With a last look at Willow, I turned on my heel and then stalked back to the SUV.

Once I was behind the wheel, I sucked in a breath and cut my gaze to the door. Anna was nowhere in sight, and that old feeling crept from a long-buried place. The same thing I'd felt when Anna walked out of my house a few days ago. Despair. Only now it was worse.

I found the first available parking spot and then jumped out of the car, the white cross on the side of the building illuminating my path to the door.

I didn't have to look to know it was there. On my mother's final stay, her hospital room sat in the shadow of that cross. Every day I stood at her window, praying that God would spare her, and when he didn't, I vowed never to set foot in a church or Brackenridge hospital again.

Shattering that promise when I marched through the doors, all the sights and sounds came back to me in a rush. I was twelve again, and as I stood there reeling, I couldn't for the life of me remember where Anna had told me to go.

"Excuse me." Addressing the nurse behind the high desk below the sign marked information, I waited for her to look up, and when she did my overstimulated brain shut down.

She lifted a pale brow. "Yes?"

"The baby floor, where is it?"

*The baby floor? Jesus.*

The nurse cocked her head, her gaze traveling the length of my long hair. "You mean, pediatrics?"

"Yeah ... er, yes. Pediatrics."

The nurse clasped her hands in front of her, all business. "Who are you looking for, sir?"

I felt my patience ebb, but one glance at the security guard posted a few feet away, and I got my temper under control so that I wouldn't end up in jail.

"My friend, I gave her a ride. Her baby was having an asthma attack."

The nurse sighed, pushed her frameless glasses up her nose, and then turned to her computer screen. "Name?"

Shaking my head, I bit down my frustration. "Listen, she just got here. I don't think—"

Without looking up, she repeated. "Name?"

"Kent." The wave of bile that accompanied Anna's married name threatened to spill all over the nurse's white uniform. But I swallowed it down, along with my pride. "Willow Kent."

Gnashing my teeth, I looked up at the ceiling while the nurse pecked away on her keyboard. I was about to go thermonuclear when she said, "Yes, Willow Grace Kent. She's been a patient here a number of times." She blinked at me, wrinkles furrowing her brow. "Sir, are you all right?"

"Um ... Willow Grace, you said?"

My mother's name rolled off my tongue like thick molasses.

"Yes." Wary, the nurse glanced at her screen to confirm. "Willow Grace Kent."

"Where . . ." I cleared my throat. "Which floor, ma'am?"

A stiff breeze could've bowled me over, so any threat I posed was long gone.

The nurse softened, expelling a sigh. "I'm sorry, but pediatrics is a locked ward," she explained with a smile. "You'll need a member of the child's immediate family to escort you in. You said you came here with her mother?" I nodded dumbly. "Well then, if you could call her, I'm sure they'll let you in."

Anger, frustration, and helplessness collided and I was about to lose it, security guard or not, but in the nick of time, I heard my name. Turning to the voice like a drowning man in search of a life jacket, I lost my breath when Alecia Dresden flung her arms around me.

"Oh my God," she whispered. "You're really here."

Engulfed by the scent of floral perfume, I squeezed my eyes shut, melting into Anna's mother's embrace. She smelled like home. Like reassurance. All the things I had no right to demand, but couldn't decline.

Pulling away, she asked, "Is Anna upstairs with the baby?"

The baby. Willow.

*My daughter.*

I couldn't speak or think, and Alecia's smile faded before my eyes. "Anna said you were coming." She took a step back, settling her tote over her shoulder. "Were you just giving her a ride?"

"No. I just . . . I can't get in." I licked my dry lips. "It's a locked floor, and I'm not . . ."

*Anything.*

The realization stifled my stammering attempt to explain.

Alecia nodded, then flashed a smile to the woman behind the desk. "I'll get him out of your hair, Shelly."

And with that, Alecia slipped her arm in mine and guided us to the elevators.

As we waited, she let out a weary sigh and then lamented, "Unfortunately, I know this place like the back of my hand. What with Willow's issues and all."

*Issues?*

I lost feeling in my limbs, and unable to form a question, I followed her gaze around the vast space.

When I spotted a kid of about fifteen staring bleakly at the screen on his laptop, his eyes darting to the doors with the big red sign that read TRAUMA every few seconds, my throat constricted.

The kid could've been me when I was twelve, waiting for my mother to emerge from her latest round of chemo. The only difference being, a glimmer of hope still shined in his eyes, and by the time I was twelve, I had none.

Shaking off the memory, I sidestepped the horde of people spilling from the elevator and then joined Alecia in the back. My eyes took permanent residence on the ground, on the faint but visible stains discoloring the tile. Blood and tears and other things that wouldn't wash away.

Alecia tugged my hair and I looked up. Her lips twitched as if she were trying to suppress a smile. "How does Melissa feel about this mane of yours?"

It was odd talking to anyone about my family. Because both my parents were dead, reporters steered clear of those questions, and as a result, my aunt Melissa and her daughter Chelsea had remained mostly hidden from the public eye.

Relaxing for the first time in what seemed like hours, I shrugged. "She says I'm the niece she always wanted." Recalling Anna's hands in my hair, gripping and tugging and pulling me against her, I smiled. "Your daughter likes it, though."

Which, sadly, was the main reason I wore it so long. Pitiful, but Anna's fingers twining in my hair was something I'd missed these last four years. Alecia *tsked*, but I continued to smile because she'd just reminded me of how I felt about her daughter.

Yeah, I was pissed as hell at Anna right now, but I was madder at myself.

My anger took a backseat as the elevator coasted to a stop on the fourth floor. It was one thing to make it through the lobby at Brackenridge and another to enter one of the wards.

To my surprise, when the doors snicked open, the utilitarian concrete floors were no longer plain white tile but covered in stickers shaped like bricks. A sunny yellow path that led to a mural of the emerald city painted on the wall.

*Follow the yellow brick road.*

Falling into step behind Alecia we headed for another desk.

"Hi, Mrs. Dresden." A nurse with a bright smile passed Alecia a green sticker with a smiley face imprinted in the center. "Anna's in Room 437." Frowning, she added, "I'm sorry about Willow. Poor little thing's had a bad week."

"Indeed," Alecia replied, her gaze flicking to mine. "This is Sean Hudson. You can add him to the list of approved visitors."

The nurse turned to me, and her jaw dropped open. "Um . . . sure. Sean Hudson, you said?"

Color sprang to her cheeks as she waited for confirmation of what she already knew.

I nodded, wearing the neutral expression I used in public when I didn't want to be bothered.

The nurse handed me a yellow sticker. "You can go back with Mrs. Dresden, but no longer than fifteen minutes." She smiled apologetically. "Immediate family only after visiting hours."

Taking the sticker, I stared at the imprint, a protest on the tip of my tongue. I was Willow's family. Her father.

Luckily, Alecia came to my rescue. "Sean is family. He's Willow's..." Flustered, she struggled to find a word for me, and when none came, she waved her hand. "Like I said, he's family. Anna will call and straighten it out later."

The nurse's eyes volleyed back and forth between Alecia and me as she fiddled with the spool of green stickers. I'm guessing those bad boys were the keys to the emerald city, and at the moment, I'd trade anything in my possession for just one.

Before I embarrassed myself by resorting to bribery, the nurse peeled off a sticker and turned it over to Alecia. "I'll give this to you," she said, her tone just above a whisper. "I don't want to get into any trouble with Mr. or Mrs. Kent."

Alecia's smile tightened. "Oh, is Dean here?"

The nurse shook her head. "No. I just meant if he comes by . . ." Her thought trailed, her dreamy gaze returning to my face.

I tried not to grimace, both from the look and the mention of the dude who was posing as my child's father.

Alecia offered her thanks to the nurse, and coaxing me from the desk, she whispered out of the corner of her mouth. "You'd think we were trying to sneak into the Pentagon." She sighed as we stepped through the double doors and onto the ward. "But then again, she's only trying to protect your daughter, so I can't fault her."

*My daughter.*

The first time anyone said those words, and it wasn't Anna. Questions piled up like stones, weighing me down as we walked to the end of the busy corridor.

Alecia came to an abrupt halt in front of Room 437.

"Before you go in, we need to talk." As if it were a foregone conclusion, she dropped onto one of the god-awful plastic chairs lining the wall.

Every fiber in my being gravitated to the door and what was behind it, but since Alecia seemed to be my only ally, I took a seat beside her.

"I don't know what happened between you and Anna and I gave up asking a long time ago," Alecia said. I shifted my gaze her way, but her attention was elsewhere. Like she couldn't look at me. "But Willow . . ."

The slight I felt at being labeled a deadbeat dad evaporated with those two words. Any way you sliced it, my choices had reduced Anna to a footnote in my life, and now our baby was a "but."

I sighed heavily at the realization.

"I'm sorry I wasn't around," I roughed out, hanging my head. "I'm still trying to figure everything out, but If I would've known, I would've been here."

My head snapped up when Alecia grabbed my arm. "What do you mean 'if you would've known'?" Her blunt nails dug into my skin. "Are you telling me that you didn't know about Willow?"

She stared at me, eyes narrowed in disbelief.

Resisting the urge to vent, I shook my head. "Not until about an hour ago." Alecia shot to her feet, and reflexively, I caught her by the arm. "Where are you going?"

"To talk to Anna."

"Don't you think I should be the one to do that?"

Alecia pondered for a moment and then dropped back into her seat. "Oh, Sean . . . I just assumed." She shook her head and cursed under her breath. "Anna refused to talk about you, except once, when her father wanted to find you and separate your head from your shoulders. I made Anna tell me why I shouldn't let him."

My gut twisted at the thought of Anna defending me.

"What did she say?"

She looked down at her hands. "That you outgrew her. And Austin. That you wanted a different kind of life. And I thought Anna wanted a different kind of life too. Different from me." Glancing to the room where her granddaughter was secreted away, Alecia's voice fell to a whisper. "That's why I told Anna . . . why I suggested . . ." Frowning, she looked at me and sat straighter in her chair. "She had choices, Sean. And I wanted her to know it."

*Choices?*

If I thought I couldn't feel worse, I was wrong. But what could I say? I'd given up the right to an opinion the minute I walked away from Anna.

Alecia sighed, then continued, "It backfired, though. Anna got it in her head that I didn't want her to have Willow. So she up and married Dean, complicating things even more. She never loved him, you know, not the way a wife should love her husband."

Alecia's face contorted, caving under the weight of whatever she thought she'd done.

Which was nothing.

It all came back to me, to my ultimatum, and the night I wanted to forget but never would.

Looping my arm around Alecia's shoulders, I brought her in for a hug. "It's not your fault."

She smiled, covering my hand with hers as she tipped her chin to the door. "We'll talk later. I need to call Brian and tell him to keep the gun at home if he's coming down here."

I hadn't given Brian a second thought until now.

"I'll talk to him."

Alecia cut me off with a snort. "You absolutely will not. Someday soon I suspect you'll realize there is no reasoning with an angry father. I know my daughter, how willful she is, especially when it comes to you. But Brian?" She sucked air through her teeth. "He's blind for Anna. From the first day they put her in his arms, she could do no wrong. It was hard enough for him to accept that Anna was pregnant since he'd convinced himself she wasn't having sex." She smiled at me. "And we both know that ship sailed on prom night."

I'd had some uncomfortable conversations in my life, but this one took the cake.

My burning cheeks forced me to my feet. "I'm going to go in."

Alecia pulled a book from her tote. "You do that, sweetheart. And another thing?" Her smile wavered. "Try not to be too hard on Anna, okay?"

Pleading underscored her light tone, so I nodded. "I'll try."

It was the most I could promise.

Blowing out a breath, I reached for the knob, but the door swung open, and I had to move out of the way to make room for the nurse to exit. When she stopped to scribble something on the dry erase board on the wall, I lingered, hoping to glean some information about Willow's condition.

The nurse smiled at me and then walked away, leaving me to gape at the two words she'd scrawled in red marker.

*Hearing Impaired.*

I jerked my gaze to Alecia, engrossed in her book.

She looked up. "Anything wrong?"

From the corner of my eyes, the red letters loomed.

*Hearing impaired.*

"No . . . I'm good."

But I wasn't good. The light from good was a pinprick in the distance, so faint I could barely see it.

I stepped inside the room before Alecia could say anything more. This was one explanation that I wanted to come straight from Anna.

As the door whooshed closed behind me, I cringed at the bolt clicking into place. It sounded like a gunshot. In fact, everything sounded louder—the humming of the machines, the annoying J. Lo ringtone one wall away, the nurses' shoes squeaking on the polished floors in the hallway. And Anna's breath.

It left her body in a soft exhale as I took my place at her side, gazing down at the most beautiful thing I'd ever seen.

Willow dozed with no outward signs of distress, thick auburn lashes caressing her cherub cheeks. The bulky mask was gone, replaced by a tube attached to her button nose.

"I'm so fucking pissed at you, Anna," I whispered through gritted teeth.

"I know."

"How could you not tell me?"

I glared at her out of the corners of my eye, but her gaze never left Willow's face.

"You don't have to whisper, Sean." A sad smile curved Anna's lips as she adjusted the thin blue sheet around our daughter. "She can't hear you."

*Hearing impaired.*

"She's completely deaf? I heard you talking to her . . ." I ducked my head, searching for Anna's eyes. I had to see her face. To know everything was all right. "You were talking to her, right?"

Anna eased onto the bed, legs dangling over the side.

She took the longest moment of my life to compose herself and then began in a quiet tone, "She's not completely deaf. But it's hard to say what she can and can't hear. The tests . . . they're hard to perform on a baby. As far as the doctors can tell, Willow hears at about fifty percent with her hearing aids. But she's only had them a few months. There was a long period of time when we didn't know what the problem was." She sighed wearily as if reliving the memory. "And once the doctors confirmed her hearing loss, we had to go slow. So yes, Willow does speak, but not very much."

Maybe I was the one with the hearing problem, because I couldn't process a damn thing Anna'd just told me.

I dropped into the plaid chair with a thud, my focus on Willow. "I don't understand."

Anna squeezed my hand, which I just realized was tangled with hers in a death grip. "Willow's only had the hearing aids for a few months. We're turning the volume up a little at a time, so we don't overload her system. She might hear better than we think. Or worse. She's going in for another hearing test soon."

I rubbed my brow, willing away the headache thudding at my temples. "Does she need anything? Special classes? Education?" I offered helplessly. Stupidly. "Just tell me, baby. Whatever I need to do, I'll do it."

Anna looked down at our joined hands. "Willow's hearing loss— it's most likely temporary. She'll have surgery when she's about five. Right now, she sees a speech therapist. But she's going to pre-school." Anna looked me in the eyes, resolute. "A regular school. She's not deficient in any way. She's very smart."

*Deficient?*

Even under the harsh lights with their aged covers tinting every-thing a sickly yellow, Willow looked perfect.

I scrubbed a hand down my face, hoping the right words would find their way to my thick tongue. "I'm just trying to find my way here, Anna. So cut me some slack, all right?" I pressed a kiss to her palm. "I'm still really fucking mad at you."

Anna cupped my cheek, and just like that, she silenced the riot in my head. Leaning into her touch, I closed my eyes. We drifted like that for a moment, until the monitor above Willow's bed let out a shrill beep. The other machines followed suit.

Every cell in my body jumped to life when Willow rasped, "Ma?"

Cataloging the tone and the pitch, I added it to the symphony of sounds seared into my brain. And I knew without a doubt that in a sea of voices, I'd always hear hers.

Anna was on her feet, fishing something from her pocket, so I stood too. She leaned over the little angel and popped an earbud into Willow's ear.

"There you are." Anna's tone was a few decibels above conversational, but gentle, soothing. "Are you feeling better, Willow-baby?"

*Willow-baby.*

I watched my little girl's lips curve into a sleepy smile. Adoration sparked in her azure gaze as she cupped her mother's cheeks with tiny hands.

Inching so close that my chest fused to Anna's back, I whispered, "Is she okay? Can you tell?"

Willow's eyes found mine, curious.

"She's fine," Anna said. "But you're going to have to speak up. She can't hear what you're saying."

Making space for me directly in front of our daughter, Anna said to Willow, "This is Sean, he came to visit you."

Hearing Anna refer to me by my given name drowned me in so much regret, I had to fight to keep my smile cemented in place. "Hi, Willow."

"Sean's worried about you," Anna continued in her soft but loud tone. "Can you give him a thumbs up and let him know you're okay?"

I'd never had my breath taken away, not by a crowd of ten thousand, but Willow did it just by raising her little thumb.

And when she smiled my whole world flipped upside down.

# CHAPTER NINETEEN

**Anna**

*I* heard my name over the faint whirring of the machines, and in a flash, I was fully awake and hyper aware.

"What?" The word scraped my dry throat as my heavy lids fluttered open.

I blinked down at Willow, pressed to my side with her thumb in her mouth and her eyes fused shut.

Jennifer, the day nurse, touched my arm, and I nearly jumped out of my skin.

"Sorry to disturb you, Mrs. Kent." She smiled a little wide to be apologetic. Beaming was a better description. "The doctor will be in here in about an hour. He'll probably have your discharge papers ready."

Rolling Willow onto her side so I could sit up, I winced at the crick in my neck. My back decided to join the party and sent pain shooting down my leg. Apparently, lying in the same position with a small human draped over me like a shawl wasn't optimal for sleeping.

But I insisted on it when Willow was sick. Chest-to-chest so I could feel any rattles.

I scrubbed a hand over my face. "Yeah, okay."

Why Jennifer felt the need to deliver this news in person, at 7:00 a.m., was a mystery. The pediatrician on duty had already come by a few hours ago, and after checking Willow's vitals, he removed her oxygen tube and told me we could go home after morning rounds.

My confusion cleared up when Jennifer let out a sigh. I quit rubbing my shoulder mid squeeze and turned my attention to the nurse who was now staring dreamily at Sean. He was asleep in the tweed chair that he'd dragged to the window. With his long legs stretched out in front of him and his head lolling to the side, he should've been uncomfortable. But he didn't look it.

"Gah, he's gorgeous." Jennifer's guilty gaze snapped to mine, and her cheeks bloomed with color. "Did I say that out loud?"

"Yeah."

I smiled, letting her off the hook because Sean *was* gorgeous. Even drooling, with all his hair tied up in one of my pink hair bands, the guy was smoking hot.

Jennifer cocked her head, surveying Sean like he was some kind of exhibit in a museum. "You know, I've never liked those man bun things. But . . . wow . . . he wears it well." She tapped a finger against her lip, narrowing her eyes at me. "I've read his bio, and he's an only child. Are y'all cousins or something?"

"Eww . . . *no.*" I shook my head, laughing. "We're not related."

The second the words left my lips, I kicked myself.

Jennifer's gaze shifted pointedly to the green sticker on Sean's chest, the little badge that clearly stated that we were family. Immediate family. Which meant Sean was either related to me or related to Dean.

Since I'd managed to confuse the hell out of the situation without meaning to, I sealed my lips, and Jennifer returned to her ogling.

After a moment, she huffed and then grabbed Willow's chart. "I wanted to meet him. I guess he's a heavy sleeper."

I watched Jennifer sashay out of the room, blowing out a breath when the door slid closed behind her.

"Is she gone?" came a raspy voice.

I jerked, my heart leaping into my throat. "Dammit, Sean." My hand flew to my throat. "Have you been awake this whole time?"

He sat up, wiping his mouth with the back of his hand. Then he gave me a devilish smile. "Not the whole time. But I cracked an eye open and caught Jenny's creepy stalker vibe, so I figured I'd play dead."

Not exactly the most comforting words to say in a hospital. But Sean was always funny about death. He either made jokes, or he didn't speak about it at all.

"Good plan," I agreed, hopping to my feet.

Folding my arms over my chest, I scrutinized Willow's monitors, relieved that all the indicators fell into the normal range.

Sean came up behind me, and I froze. Last night's anger was still there, I could feel traces of it in his touch, but he was doing a damn fine job of hiding it.

Sean slipped his arms around my waist, and when his chin landed on my shoulder, his scruffy beard tickled me through my threadbare T-shirt and my nipples hardened.

I'd resolved not to blur the lines. One of us had to be rational, and since Sean was bound to have feelings for Willow that didn't extend to me, I couldn't take anything he did seriously.

But then he nuzzled closer, his voice a sexy rumble in my ear. "Morning, Anna-baby."

Caffeine. Surely Sean's ability to light up every cell in my body had more to do with lack of coffee than his charm.

I was about to suggest that he make a Starbuck's run when his lips grazed my temple.

"Do you know what all this means?" he asked, indicating the monitors. "Can you tell if she's okay?"

His bright blue eyes clouded with apprehension as he looked down at me, waiting for an answer.

I touched his cheek. "She's fine."

"You're sure?" The worry etching his brow deepened when he looked past me to where Willow slept peacefully. "She hasn't moved."

I bit down a smile because soon he wouldn't have to worry about that.

"They gave her something to sleep around 2:00 a.m." He blinked, biting his lip furiously. "Don't worry. It was just some Benadryl. Anyway, let me explain what all this means." Sean reluctantly tore his gaze from our daughter and then focused on the monitors. "That's her oxygen level. The saturation looks good."

Sean pressed a feather light kiss to my shoulder. "Okay. What else?"

My pulse quickened, and I flushed. So much for my caffeine theory. "Her heart rate is good." Another kiss. "And the um, corticosteroids . . . they worked."

He rocked me gently, and as I relaxed into the sway, my heart falling into step with his, he said softly, "Why didn't you ever tell me?"

Sneaky bastard, lulling me into a false sense of security so he could bring out the big guns. Sighing, I broke free to get a little distance. But when I took a seat on the edge of the bed, he was right there in front of me, his hands molded to my hips.

"I never wanted you this way," I confessed, tracing a finger over the amulet on his neck with the Caged logo.

Sean tipped my chin with his finger, forcing me to look into his eyes. "Which way?"

"Trapped." I smiled nervously as my first bit of truth slipped out. "That's why I didn't tell you before you left."

"You knew before I left?" His anger was back, along with a good bit of shock. "And you still didn't tell me?"

I stiffened at his demanding tone. Sean would never know all the things I'd done to ensure he'd get his chance. "Because I wanted you to have your shot, even if you didn't give a shit about mine." I glared at him. "And besides, we had a plan. Three weeks, remember?" My quivering chin gave me away as I recalled the preparations I'd made to meet him in Phoenix. Tears stung my eyes, and I repeated, "Three weeks."

Sean dropped his head back, grimacing. "I just . . . I made a mistake. And I'm so fucking sorry."

He lowered his gaze, his wounded eyes digging into my soul.

I didn't want Sean to hurt any more than he already was, but he had to know everything, so I took a calming breath and began in a steady voice, "Do you remember the girl Cameron used to date—the one that worked at the Daily Texan?" Sean's blank stare drew a lethargic smile from my lips. "The UT campus newspaper? She's a DJ in Dallas now."

"Oh, yeah." He chuckled. "Wicked Wendy."

I nodded, looking down at my hands. "Well, after y'all left, she wrote a weekly article with pictures from all your shows. Insider stuff that Cameron gave her from the tour bus and the dressing room."

I watched as the realization broke on Sean's face. His smile vanished, his lips parted, but nothing came out, so I kept going.

"By the time you reached Phoenix, you'd dumped the blonde you picked up in El Paso and moved onto the brunette you hooked up with in Tucson." I felt the tears spill onto my cheeks but didn't attempt to wipe them away. "I don't remember her name, and you probably don't either, but after seeing the pictures, I didn't exactly feel welcome."

The color washed from Sean's eyes, and his fingers tightened around me. I gave our sleeping child a sidelong glance, my assurance to Sean that I'd never bolt, and then curving my hands around his, I peeled them away. "I need to use the bathroom."

The tears were flowing freely now. Too many tears. And I had to get away.

Sean's forehead lined with worry. "I'm so sorry." He stroked my hair. "So fucking sorry."

He might as well have been apologizing for having brown hair or blue eyes. This was him, or who he'd become. He fucked women indiscriminately. And damn my stupid heart for feeling things I shouldn't.

"I believe you." I shrugged, forcing a smile. "But I still have to pee."

Sean reluctantly let me go. And while I searched for my portable toothbrush in my tote bag, he dropped into the chair in front of the window. He stared at the big white cross, then down at his hands, and if I didn't know better, I'd think he was praying.

I left him to it and headed for the small bathroom to pull myself together. I'd just finished brushing my teeth when I heard the commotion.

I threw open the door, and two sets of eyes turned my way, one azure blue, and one chocolate brown, both angry as hell.

"You want to tell me what he's doing here?" Dean growled, nostrils flaring.

I moved to position myself between the two, but Sean stepped in front of me. "The name's Sean."

"I know who you are." With a disgusted glance in Sean's direction, Dean added, "Now, why don't you get the fuck out of here and let me talk to my wife."

Casting Dean as the aggressor in this scenario seemed unfathomable. He was a trial attorney, unflappable. But from the look of the vein throbbing on his temple, *that* Dean had left the building.

I shuffled to the side, but Sean was quicker, blocking my path.

"That ain't happening right now, bud," Sean said in a no-nonsense tone. "Not here."

"Fuck you," Dean spat through clenched teeth. "I'm her husband."

The word was like kryptonite, and Sean froze, allowing me time to get around him. Standing in front of Dean, I realized the murder in his eyes wasn't reserved for the man behind me.

"I wasn't expecting you," I said, my voice flat, hollow. "What do you need?"

Dean's fury mounted, and he ripped a hand through his hair. "What do I need? Are you for real? We're married. I don't need a reason to be here."

Emphasizing the word "I," Dean tapped his chest.

"We're separated," I reminded him. "I haven't talked to you since Gran's funeral."

I pleaded with my eyes, but the gesture only added fuel to the tumultuous fire swirling between us.

"I thought you were grieving, so I left you alone." Dean's gaze shifted to Sean. "But I can see that wasn't the case."

I *was* grieving, and for a lot more than Gran it seemed. I mourned the life I once had, the happiness. And Sean was part of that life. Of course, I couldn't tell Dean that, so I bowed my head and let him fume.

"Listen, dude," Sean snarled, hands glued to my waist. "This isn't the time."

Ignoring the threat in Sean's tone, Dean leaned in so we were at eye level. "I asked you for one thing," he waved a finger in my face. "Only one. That you'd never see Sean Hudson again." Hurt shone through the anger, gutting me. "What happened to that promise, huh?"

I inched forward, wanting to provide some comfort, but with Sean's hands on my waist I got nowhere fast. "I kept my promise," I insisted. "I never saw Sean until we were separated. If you don't believe me, we can talk about it later. Please, Dean, Willow is right over there."

His eyes drifted to the bed. "She can't hear us, though, can she?"

I was off the ground for a second, in Sean's hold, before he deposited me at his side and out of the line of fire.

And then he was in Dean's face, nose-to-nose, his composure a distant memory. "You're lucky you're already at the hospital," Sean rumbled. 'Cause I'm about to make you bleed."

Panicked, I curled my fingers around Sean's bulging bicep. "Sean...stop," I pleaded. "You don't understand."

Dean's sardonic laugh filled the room as he glanced down at my hand, still curved around Sean's arm. "Who are you protecting, me or yourself?"

The shudder that rolled through Sean was like thunder.

Before the lightning hit, I said to Dean, "You need to go. We'll talk later."

"I'm Willow's father," Dean roared. "And you will not dismiss me."

With super hero strength, I pushed Sean out of the way and glared up at Dean. If he wanted the truth, I had it. In Spades. "You haven't seen Willow in over a month. You haven't asked about her, even though she was in the hospital four days ago. You have no right to say anything about her to me now."

Dean cocked a dark brow, and I deflated. He had as many rights as I did. And worse yet, he knew it.

"Maybe you were absent the day they taught family law," Dean said. "But a child legally born of our union is mine. And in case you forgot," he flicked a malicious smile at Sean, "we were married at the time of Willow's birth."

"Don't spout the law to me," I choked, tears clogging my throat. "You're not her father."

The words flew out with more venom than I intended. Because as much as I'd like to believe that Dean was standing here out of love for my daughter, it just wasn't true. He wasn't Willow's father, and it had nothing to do with biology. The older my little girl got, the more Dean had distanced himself from her questioning blue gaze.

Dean's cold glare shifted to Sean. "I can assure you, Anna knows less about the law than I do." A bitter smile curved his lips. "You did know she dropped out of law school, right?"

So this was the game. I hurt Dean, and in turn, he taunted Sean.

"She fought the good fight for half a term," Dean continued, shaking his head ruefully. "But she was just too sick. What was it the doctors called it? Preeclampsia?" He gave me a pitying smile. "Pretty rare for a twenty-two-year-old, but I guess it had something to do with seeing you parading around with all her replacements." Dean shrugged. "Doesn't matter. The point is, Anna almost died. You've seen her scar, right?" Another laugh. "Yeah, I guess you have."

Sean let out a curse, and his chest heaved against my back. Another minute and he'd lose his shit.

"Dean, stop," I ordered. "*Not now.*"

Shaking his head at me in disgust, Dean ignored my warning.

"And where was your drummer boy when you were getting all those pretty stitches? I'll tell you where, with that girl from the music video, the *other* redhead. You remember, don't you? You read all about it when you were in the hospital."

"You motherfucker!" Sean growled, and when he made his move, I did the only thing I could do. I rushed forward, my palms landing on Dean's chest.

"Get out," I cried, shoving him toward the door.

Dean stumbled backward, surprised, but I kept advancing until we were in the hallway. "Go!" I pointed at the exit. "Now!"

Too focused on my own little melodrama, I barely registered the ruckus at the end of the hall.

That is, until I heard Logan bellow, "Call the fucking cops if you need to. But you'd better get out of my way, or I'll lay you flat."

Pushing past two orderlies, Logan thundered down the hallway with Christian and Cameron on his heels.

"Lo," I said, holding my hand out in a panic. "Stop."

Sidestepping me like I was standing still, Logan grabbed Dean by his starched white shirt. "I think you overstayed your welcome. So unless you want me to hurt you, you'd better move along." A maniacal smile played on Logan's lips. "Do you want me to hurt you?"

The nurses appeared too enraptured by the four rockstars in their midst to intercede.

Sean nudged me out of the way. "Dude, not here," he said to Logan, bracing a hand on his best friend's shoulder. "They're going to call the cops."

"Not before I beat the shit out of this guy," Logan replied, his gaze never leaving Dean's face.

Easy going as ever, Cameron stepped into the fray, snaking an arm around Logan's chest. "We'll just go back to the waiting room. It's safer that way." Walking backward with Logan in tow, he grinned at Dean. "For you, that is."

Dean adjusted his shirt. "Real nice," he muttered. "I thought you wanted better for Willow. Isn't that why you married me? Because you didn't want all of this?" My lips parted, and I grappled for a response, but then Dean softened. "She deserves better than a father who waves to her from a rope line."

"You don't know Sean like I do," I whispered. "He wouldn't do that to her."

Dean took a deep breath and then brushed a strand of hair from my face. "So it's only you he treats like shit?" I flinched, and his arm fell to his side. "If this is what you want, Annabelle, I can't stop you. But I won't help you either. The house is in my name. And the health insurance. If you want out, I'd suggest you get your shit and leave."

Dean could have the house, it was his. But the health insurance?

"Be reasonable," I implored. "You know I need—"

"We had an agreement," Dean interjected. "And you broke it. You want to fight me in court?" He shrugged. "Property rights are the least of your worries. Fraud is a felony."

"Fraud?" Sean growled. "What the fuck are you talking about?"

Dean turned on his heel. "Ask Anna."

The squeak from his loafers grew fainter as I gazed down at the floor crumbling beneath my feet. We'd never fought like this before, and I could feel a piece of me breaking away. The piece I gave to Dean. Not love, but trust.

"What's he talking about?" Sean asked as he ushered me back into the room and away from the gaggle of nurses.

Squeezing my eyes shut, I pressed the heel of my hand to my forehead. "If Dean claims I tricked him into marrying me, that's fraud."

Dean wouldn't do it. I was relatively certain, but still, the threat was there.

"How can he do that?" Sean asked, taking my hands.

"Because it's against the law to sign a birth certificate you know contains false information. He's an officer of the court."

Sean pulled me into his arms. "But you didn't even know him before I left. Did you?"

I peered up at him, and the look on his face—it was like someone told him an awful joke.

He backed up, and I took the opportunity to walk to the window. "Dean was a TA in one of my classes."

"Tell me what the fuck you're talking about, Annabelle. Because I'm about to—"

"It's not what you think," I said evenly. "I'd never spoken more than a few words to him until that night."

"What night?"

"The night you broke up with me." I closed my eyes, the scene playing behind my lids. "I was in the parking lot at the apartment, trying to start my car so I could go find you. But the battery was dead. Dean was on his way out. He had a friend who lived in our complex. Anyway, he recognized me and offered me a ride to the bar."

When I turned, I found horror in Sean's eyes. "He was there?"

"Yeah."

My legs wobbled, and Sean caught me before I crumpled in a heap on the floor. "Jesus, Anna. I'm so . . ." He cursed, stifled his apology if that's what it was, and then he vowed, "We'll fight this. I promise."

My thumb grazed the emerald ring, Sean's last broken promise. When I went to move away, his hand slid into my hair, and he rested his forehead against mine. "You're coming home with me."

I shook my head. "I can't."

Sean's mouth crashed into mine, silencing my protest, and when he pulled away, he looked deeply into my eyes.

"I got you, Anna-baby. I swear it."

# CHAPTER TWENTY

**Sean**

*a* brick wall inlaid with stone butterflies in all shapes and colors surrounded the tranquility garden in the courtyard at the hospital. Since nothing about Brackenridge rose to the level of tranquil, I had my doubts.

But then I passed under an arbor and into the shade of a cluster of maple trees, and the façade of the stark white building faded behind the dense leaves.

It was like a world within a world. The peace in the eye of the storm.

I slid into a wrought iron chair at a table in the corner facing the center of the garden. On the other side of the courtyard, a little girl staked out a spot on the grass. What little sun peeked through the trees shined on her bald head as she arranged her toys in a semi-circle around the hospital-issued water pitcher and plastic cups. Her mother watched from a nearby bench, a weary smile playing on her lips.

"You want to tell me why you didn't let me kick that douchebag's ass?" Logan asked, dropping into the chair across from me.

Shifting my gaze from the little girl's makeshift tea party to my best friend, I stared at him blankly as he pulled a burger out of the greasy white bag. When he offered me one, I blanched, shaking my head.

Logan sat back in his chair, unwrapping his sandwich. "Something you want to get off your chest, Hudson?"

Reading Logan was nearly impossible for most. But we'd known each other since the second grade. Not well, though. Logan was the kid everybody feared. The fighter. It wasn't until I was ten that I got a glimpse behind the mask.

Banished to the cafeteria when my mother had forgotten to sign a permission slip for a class field trip, I'd sulked at the end of one of the long tables. I wasn't a crier, even then, but that day, my mother's cancer conspired with my disappointment, and tears welled.

Logan was stretched out flat on his back on a bench at an adjoining table, and he popped up when he heard me sniffle. "What are you crying for, Hudson?"

Embarrassed, I'd swiped the lone tear dribbling down my cheek. "I'm not."

He plopped down across from me. "Are too."

It wasn't a condemnation, just a fact.

Noting the bruise on Logan's cheek, I figured he'd gotten into a fight, and this was his punishment. "Why aren't you on the field trip?" I shot back, hoping to shut him up.

He caught me staring at the purple welt, but instead of hiding, he lifted his chin. "Why aren't you?"

"My mom didn't sign my slip." I shrugged. "No big deal."

"She kinda left you hanging, huh?" He snickered. "Sucks to be you."

Taking on the class brawler wasn't a smart move. But that didn't stop me from rearing out of my seat and leaning across the table. "She didn't leave me hanging," I spat. "She's got cancer."

It was the first time those words had ever left my lips. Before that, whenever anyone would ask, I always said my mom was "sick" or "not feeling well," but something about Logan's smug grin made me want to wipe it off his face.

He cocked his head, a ripple of emotion crossing his arctic blue eyes. "My mom's dead."

Sinking back onto the bench, a shot of fear ran down my spine. Because I knew someday that would be me, that Logan's life and mine were destined to intersect in that place where grief and loss collided. He just had a head start.

"What about your dad?" I asked weakly.

"He's a piece of shit." Another ripple passed over his ice blue orbs. "Yours?"

"Dead."

Logan looked around, absently touching the bruise on his cheek. "Lucky."

I didn't know what to make of that, so I ripped open the sack lunch my aunt Melissa had packed. And that's when I found the permission slip she'd forged.

Glancing out the window at the kids milling around by the buses, I spotted our teacher and rose automatically, the slip clutched in my hand.

Logan looked up at me. "Where are you going?"

My gaze darted to the window and then back to his face as yet another wave broke in his stormy blue eyes.

Plopping back onto the bench, I dumped out my lunch. "Nowhere." I pushed half of my bologna sandwich across the table along with one of my Little Debbie snack cakes. "Want some?"

After that we were inseparable. And when my mom died two years later, Logan was the only one who understood. Even when Christian and Cameron joined our little duo Logan and I were just a little closer.

Stirring from my memories, I locked our gazes, blue on blue. "Why didn't you tell me Anna came to the bar the night before we left?"

Logan stretched his legs, crossing them at the ankle. "You didn't seem too concerned with your past life." Lacing his fingers behind his head, I saw the ripple spread from the center of his blue eyes. "I made an executive decision."

"What makes you think—?"

"I didn't have to think." Logan snorted derisively. "My bunk was right across from yours. I knew. Everyone knew. You weren't thinking about Anna when you were banging your way through every groupie that spread their legs for you."

That's where Logan was wrong. I never thought of anything but Anna. But I couldn't admit it. Not then, and not now.

"You sure that's all there was to it?" I asked, cocking a brow. "From what I heard, you were quite the hero."

Logan laughed, dry and humorless. "I'm nobody's hero. But if that's how Anna wants to remember it, I won't argue."

My stomach twisted uncomfortably as my mind veered to a place it never went. To Anna and Logan. *Together.*

"What exactly happened between you two?"

"Didn't Anna tell you?"

Logan searched my face, but I had nothing to hide. All my secrets met the light of day long ago. All he was going to find was bleached bones.

"I want you to tell me."

Sighing, Logan took another bite of his burger. "What do you want to know?"

Not a damned thing. But that was the pussy way out, so I braced myself and said, "Everything."

Logan dropped his head to the back of the chair, and patches of sun peeked through the trees, casting his face in light and shadow. "I texted Anna when we got to the bar. Just to let her know you were safe." Working his jaw, Logan closed his eyes. "I never thought she'd show up."

Guilt isn't something you wear. It wears you. You can't escape it. And that's what I saw when Logan swung his gaze to mine. Guilt.

"It wasn't your fault."

Begrudgingly, I offered the small piece of solace.

Logan shook his head. "I ain't asking for your forgiveness. I just never thought . . ." He smiled a smile I'd never seen. "You surprised me, that's all. I thought you went out for a smoke. I didn't notice that Darcy was gone too." His gaze returned to the trees, and he continued, "I didn't realize what happened until I heard Anna screaming her guts out in the parking lot. She had Darcy by the hair, and she was wailing on her pretty good. I would've let her go." A shudder rolled off his shoulders, slight but noticeable. "But she was barefoot, and that fucking parking lot was a disaster. She didn't even feel the glass crunching under her feet." He pinned me with his gaze. "That skank wasn't worth the blood Anna was spillin', so I broke it up."

Schooling my features, I swallowed the bile crawling up my throat. "Is that all?"

Logan grunted. "Isn't that enough?" When I remained silent, he rolled his eyes. "Fine. I took her home and cleaned her up and then I tucked her into bed. And after she fell asleep I took a shower. When I got out, she was gone."

A dull pain spread through my limbs. "You didn't say goodbye?"

Logan smiled that smile again. "Nope, and neither did you. So I guess that makes us both pricks." Hauling to his feet, he shoved the chair against the table with enough force to shake me in my spot. "If you're done wallowing in the past, we need to talk about our trip to LA next week."

Numb, I picked at a crack in the black paint on the side of the table. "What trip?"

"Benny's PR department wants us to make a guest appearance at some party he's throwing." Logan fished his keys from his pocket. "You think you can get your personal shit straightened out by then?"

I looked past him to the bricks hidden behind the trees. "Yeah, I got it covered."

Logan leaned forward and looked me in the eyes. "This is everything we've ever wanted. Don't get yourself all twisted." He raised his closed fist for a bump, which I reluctantly returned. "Eyes on the prize, bro."

My eyes were on another prize at the moment, but there was nothing that said I couldn't have both.

The woman on the bench watched with mild curiosity as Logan sauntered out of the tranquility garden. Then she turned to me, recognition glinting in her eyes. I thought she might ask for an autograph or maybe a picture. But instead, she sank onto the grass next to her daughter and joined the imaginary tea party.

I sat back, casually thumbing through my messages. Over the top of my screen, the little girl caught my eye.

As I watched her crawl into her mother's lap, I scrolled through the unanswered texts from my Aunt Melissa dating back a week.

*Call me, sugar.*

*Call when you get a chance.*

*I haven't heard from you. Are you in town?*

*Sorry to bother. I need to talk to you.*

Bother?

Guilt nipped at my shoulders. Melissa had raised me. It was our sad little family tradition, dating back to when my mom took custody of Melissa when my grandmother died before I was born.

Melissa was there for all the important firsts in my life. First steps. First day of school. My mom's first treatment, and every one after that.

I blew out a breath as I waited for her to answer my long overdue call.

"Hey sugar," Melissa said in her lazy southern drawl. "Where you been?"

"Sorry. I've got a lot going on."

"I looked for you after the concert. But you boys were already gone."

*Shit.*

I pinched the bridge of my nose. "Yeah . . ."

A sigh forced its way from my lungs like a gale wind, and I heard Melissa's sharp intake of breath.

"What is it?" she demanded, her tone rising in alarm. "Sean Jacob, you tell me this instant."

That's all it took. The story came out in a rush. Anna. Willow. The hospital. All of it. When I paused to take a breath, a soft chuckle drifted over the line.

"You think this is funny?"

"Life is funny, sugar."

A nurse's aide entered the courtyard, and the young mother reluctantly pushed to her feet. Abandoning the pitcher and plastic cups, she picked up her sleepy daughter and then headed for the sliding glass door.

"Yeah, it's fucking hilarious," I muttered, dropping my gaze to the slate patio.

"Help me out," Melissa said. "Should I be happy or sad about this?"

I couldn't even begin to answer that question. There were too many caveats. I'd convinced Anna to stay at my house for a couple of days. Beyond that, I wasn't sure.

"It's . . ." I cleared my throat. "I've got some work to do. With Anna, I mean."

Another soft laugh. "I bet you do. Why don't you start by bringing her and that baby 'round. I need to talk to you anyway."

"What about?"

In my whole life, I only remembered a couple of times when Melissa didn't have a quick response. The day I asked if my mom was going to die. And the day the funeral director asked what color casket we wanted.

"What is it, Melissa?"

"Not now, sugar. Get Anna settled, and I'll have y'all over for supper."

The cheer returned to her tone, so I didn't push.

"Okay." I rubbed my tired eyes. "How's Chelsea?"

That drew a belly laugh from Melissa, which I was glad to hear. "She's seventeen. How do you think she is?"

"Please tell me she's not pregnant." I relaxed against the metal chair. "I've got enough on my plate. I don't need to take time out of my day to kick some little fucker's ass for knocking her up."

"That would be a little hypocritical don't you think?" Melissa chortled. "Speaking of, has Brian paid you a visit yet?"

Alecia was right about one thing. I'd known Willow all of one day, and I'd kill for her. Brian had twenty-six years to plot the perfect murder. My murder, as it turned out.

I smiled at the orderly gathering the child's toys from the grass as I strolled out of the garden. "I haven't seen him yet."

"Didn't think so. You sound like you still got all your teeth."

"Very funny. Can you be serious for a second? I need your help."

"Okay." Melissa sighed. "Shoot."

I pulled Anna's hand-written list from my pocket.

"What do you know about car seats?"

# CHAPTER TWENTY-ONE

**Anna**

*P*eyton stalked around the room with Willow in her arms. Despite the jiggling, my baby looked perfectly content being hauled around by a crazy woman. I guess she was used to it.

In between making funny faces at my little girl, Peyton ranted, "And just who the fu—" Our eyes met before the word tumbled out, and she slammed her mouth shut, "—the fudge does he think he is?"

Sadly, I wasn't sure which of the men in my life Peyton was referring to, so I stayed quiet.

Incredulous over my silence, her eyes bulged. "You don't seem too concerned that D-E-A-N is kicking you out of your own home."

Willow cocked her head, looking up at her godmother like she knew exactly whose name Peyton was spelling out.

"It's his house, Pey," I replied. "Not mine."

Slumping into the chair Sean had slept in, I curled my hands over the armrests, hoping a little of his unwavering belief lingered in the cheap wooden frame. He'd sounded so sure when he told me everything would be all right.

Peyton settled onto the bed and gave Willow her phone to play with.

A long moment of silence ensued, and then, as if she could see inside my head, Peyton said, "You don't have to go home with Sean, you know. I've got plenty of room."

Without meeting her gaze, I gave a little nod of acknowledgment. I couldn't look Peyton in the eye or she'd see, she'd know, that I wanted to go home with Sean.

Forever wasn't in the cards for us.

I'd taken the liberty of checking my work email, and Conner was serious about the tour.

Soon, Sean would be back on the road, and he'd forget about me. Not completely. I'd be there, at the edge of his thoughts. But he'd get on with his life. He'd done it before. I just wanted a few days, a week maybe, to live the life we should've had.

And then we'd move on.

Only this time we wouldn't be strangers. I'd seen the way Sean looked at our daughter, cataloging her every move, her smile. We'd always be a part of each other's lives. And that would have to be enough.

Plastering on a fake smile for my best friend, I said, "Sean is going to be leaving soon. He deserves a chance to get to know his daughter."

Peyton lifted a pale brow in challenge. "And he can't do that without you living in his house?"

I pushed out of the chair and faced her, hands on my hips and wry smile firmly in place. "You live in a loft. One big room. As much as you love Willow, you have no idea how hard it would be if we moved in."

Peyton's eyes skated to my daughter. She knew I was right.

But just to keep her off balance I added, "Maybe after Sean leaves for the tour, I'll stay with you for a while."

Peyton nodded without reservation, and for that, I gave her a genuine smile. If I were going anywhere, it would be to my parents.

But hopefully Dean would be reasonable with his demands, and I could afford a little apartment close to the bridge on highway 360.

My phone buzzed, and Avenged Sevenfold's "So Far Away" bled from the speaker before I could silence it. Pressing ignore on Sean's call, heat rose in my cheeks.

Damn it. I needed to change that ringtone before Sean heard it.

Peyton scooted to the edge of the bed, eyes on my phone. "Well, that's my cue. I need to leave before Prince Charming shows up," she hopped to her feet, "or I'm liable to throat punch him."

I had to laugh at the visual. Peyton would go to war for me. But I hoped that someday she'd quit hating Sean. For Willow's sake.

Peyton kissed me on the cheek before folding me into a hug. "I won't let Dean hurt you. Legally, at least."

I nodded into her hair. "Thanks."

Breaking our connection, she held me at arm's length, steel gray eyes clouded with worry. "You're on your own with Sean, though."

I gave her a weak smile. "I can handle it."

Peyton bit her lip. After witnessing the devastation following my split with Sean, I commended her for withholding her censure.

Another hug, and Peyton was out the door.

I waited until I was sure she was gone to check Sean's text message.

*Just picked up the car seat and a few other things. Be there soon.*

Butterflies took flight in my stomach. The boy made me stupidly happy.

Biting back a smile, I tapped out a response.

*Meet you downstairs. Waiting for the discharge papers.*

Right on cue, Jennifer the nurse strolled in pushing a wheelchair. Her cheery smile wilted the minute she looked around and noticed Sean wasn't here. She let out a sigh as she maneuvered the chair next to the bed.

"Looks like someone's getting sprung today." Willow's eyes rounded in response to Jennifer's roar.

People typically shouted when they found out that Willow was hearing impaired. The trick was to raise your voice a couple of octaves without adding any edge to your tone.

Jennifer held out her arms and my daughter promptly shrank against the bed railing.

I rushed to intercede. "I'll get her. She's a little shy."

Jennifer nodded, then did a slow circuit around the room. Snagging a soda can resting on the window ledge in front of the chair where Sean had been seated, she stowed it in the pocket of her scrubs when she thought I wasn't looking.

Seriously? Was she going to sell it on eBay, or what?

"Do you need help getting Willow downstairs?" Jennifer offered, a little overeager.

Picturing the petite nurse jumping into Sean's arms and attaching herself like a spider monkey, I shook my head. "No. I'm good. Thank you, though."

*Psycho.*

Another nod, followed by a bereft little sigh, and then Jennifer turned on her heel and walked out.

I settled Willow into the wheelchair, rolling my eyes when the door swished open. Expecting to find Jennifer, possibly with flowers and maybe candy, I blinked at the well-dressed woman standing in the doorway.

"Mrs. Kent?"

My gaze fell to the hospital ID pinned to the lapel of her blazer before shifting to the manila folder tucked under her arm.

"Yes." I cleared my throat. "I'm Anna Kent."

She walked toward me, hand outstretched. "Valerie Tustin." Sliding my palm into hers, I gave her a firm shake, and she continued, "I work in the hospital's accounting department. I've been assigned to your case."

*My case?*

Valerie dropped the file on top of the rolling table and then took a seat in the plastic chair. "Do you have time to discuss your bill?"

The question was obviously rhetorical since Valerie was already picking through the file.

"Sure."

Willow started to squirm, so I crouched to eye level, and said close to her ear, "One minute, okay, baby?"

Willow nodded and reached for my phone, which I gave up without question. Another text from Sean lit the screen.

*I'm downstairs.*

Shit.

I took a seat across from Valerie. "I have a payment plan in place. I should've hit my insurance maximum by now, so they should pick up everything from this point forward."

Valerie stopped sorting, a tight smile frozen in place. "The credit card on file has been declined, Mrs. Kent."

I cocked my head, a nervous laugh bubbling out. "That's impossible." She slid a printout in front of me, and there it was in black and white—*declined*. I picked up the paper and looked it over. "There's got to be a mistake."

Valerie shifted, and the chair creaked beneath her. "I took the liberty of contacting the issuer. The account was closed. Were you aware of that?"

I put down the paper, then met her gaze. "I don't understand . . . the account was closed?"

Valerie's eyes softened, but not her tone. "Perhaps you should speak to your husband? The bank said he closed the account."

*Dean.*

As mad as he was this morning, I never expected such swift retribution.

*How could he do this to me? To Willow?*

"I'll do that." My voice broke under the weight of my humiliation. "Can I write you a check?"

Did I even have my checkbook? Or money in my account?

While I was contemplating, Valerie sighed again. Clasping her hands on top of the pile of papers, she tipped forward slightly. "Mrs. Kent, this is your fourth visit to the hospital this year. Your second this week. Your bill." She shook her head. "It's quite substantial. I've looked over the charges. Many of the tests you insisted upon were not covered by your insurance."

"My daughter needed those tests." My voice rose, and I could feel the tears stinging the back of my eyes. "Willow's been diagnosed with Conductive Hearing Loss. The tests . . ."

As I struggled, unable to find the words, Valerie slid a box of tissues in front of me. The gesture was more perfunctory than genuine, like she did this a million times a day.

Anger overshadowed my embarrassment, and I went on, "As I said, I can write you a check for this month's payment. If you could just work with me on—" I jumped when the door swung open, the handle meeting the wall with a loud thump. Sean's gaze skipped from Valerie to me before coming to rest on Willow in the wheelchair.

"What's happening, baby?" Sean asked as he closed the distance between us.

"I . . ."

Sean stood behind me now, hands resting on the back of my chair and thumbs caressing the space between my shoulder blades.

When Valerie started to introduce herself, I jumped to my feet, nearly knocking over the rolling table. I held out my hand, defiant. "I'll be in touch, Valerie. Thank you for stopping by."

My eyes locked with hers as she took my hand. Somewhere in her file, I'm sure they listed Dean's profession. And while I was no lawyer, I was very familiar with the HIPPA laws. Unless Valerie was prepared to break confidentiality, she had no choice but to leave. But that didn't mean she was happy about it.

Frowning, she gathered her papers. "Very well, Mrs. Kent." She pushed back from the table. "But I need to hear from you within seventy-two hours."

"No problem."

When I turned to get Willow, I bumped into Sean's chest. He didn't move, his hand curving around my hip.

"Hold on a minute," he said, his narrowed gaze volleying between Valerie and me. "Can someone please tell me what's going on?"

I felt my cheeks ignite when Valerie gave a pointed look to Sean's hand, resting just below my waist.

Perfect.

Since wiggling free wasn't an option, I looked up at Sean and said through a clenched smile, "We'll talk about this later, okay?"

Sean took my hand, and then entwining our fingers he dropped into the chair I'd vacated. "Seeing as we're all here right now, there's no reason for that." He glanced at the paperwork. "How much is the outstanding bill?"

Valerie shifted her gaze to mine. "May I?"

As she waited for my answer, Sean's thumb made little circles over mine.

Defeated, I finally gave in. "Sure. That's fine."

Valerie handed Sean the invoice. "The balance is twenty-two thousand four hundred twenty-six dollars and change."

Cringing, I felt my cheeks flame, but Sean didn't miss a beat. "Do y'all accept American Express?"

Valerie sat up straighter, flashing a bright smile. "Absolutely. The payment is—"

"All of it." Sean pulled out his wallet and then placed the black card on the table. "Including the change."

# CHAPTER TWENTY-TWO

**Sean**

*I*t wasn't my style to creep around in hallways and listen to private conversations, but in this case, I'm glad I did.

When that bean said that Dean had closed the account, I could practically hear a piece of Anna's heart crack. And after what she'd told me this morning, she didn't have a lot to spare.

But now, as we rode down the elevator locked in silence, I was rethinking my decision.

Anna tensed when I laid my hand on hers, gripping the handle of Willow's wheelchair. "You mad about the bill?"

When she nodded, I took it in stride, but what did she expect, that I'd sit there and allow Dean to pay my kid's hospital bill?

We both spoke at the same time, and I clamped my mouth shut so Anna could say her piece first.

"That's a lot of money, Sean," she said, quiet concern creasing her brow. "I have a small amount coming from Gran. I don't know how much yet."

Anna worried her bottom lip, and I almost laughed.

The smile on my face was enough to make her scowl. "What?" she asked, irritated. And cute. So fucking cute.

I dipped my head and kissed her lips. "Do you think I can't afford it?"

The meek shrug she offered was all the answer I needed.

Discussing money with anyone, even my aunt, was a nonstarter. But this was Anna. We'd pooled our money when she was the one that earned more than I did working at a fucking coffee house.

Once we were in the lobby, I pulled her close. "Money is the last thing you need to worry about."

You'd think with my house and all the useless toys I had laying around, she'd know this.

Anna gave a little snort like the very idea was preposterous. And then she tried to wiggle free.

*Not going to happen.*

"Anna, listen to me." When her eyes found mine, I tucked a strand of hair behind her ear. "We made a lot of coin from the albums, but that's not why you don't need to worry. Chase is a wizard with money. He invested everything we made, doubled it after the first tour. That piece of property the house is sitting on? I own it outright, and two more parcels just like it. Got 'em dirt cheap." I shrugged. "Anyway, Chase worked his magic for the next two albums, and now, we've got more money than we can spend."

Anna processed the information, her worry fading to confusion or disbelief. "I thought that was the reason for the tour. I mean, that y'all needed money."

I laughed. "No baby. The reason for the tour is because we're a touring band. It's never been about the money."

While I thought the notion might comfort her, Anna seemed to grow more despondent. Hiding her dismay with a smile, she said, "Thank you. I'll look over my finances and reimburse you what I can."

That was never going to happen. But before I could tell Anna that, she was crouched in front of Willow's wheelchair, extracting our little girl from the clunky contraption.

Once on her feet, Willow stood perfectly still while Anna placed a braided twine around her neck with a metal cylinder attached.

"Kiss," Anna said, tapping her lips, and Willow gleefully complied, cupping her mother's cheeks. Trust and love and everything good swirled between them, and I just wanted to be a part of it. Since I couldn't yet, witnessing the little miracle would have to be enough.

When Anna stood, I motioned to the odd shaped pendant around Willow's neck. "What's that?"

"That's what'll ensure you don't spend twenty grand every time you take Willow to the park," Anna said, smiling at my confused expression. "It's her inhaler."

Suddenly the little cylinder took on mythical proportions. Whatever was in there stood between my daughter choking to death and breathing without distress.

"Should she, um, be wearing it? What if she loses it?"

An honest to goodness smile broke on Anna's lips. "Do you think that's the only one I have?" A laugh tumbled out when I didn't answer. "I have one in my purse, at least two in the car—front and backseat, and one in nearly every room of the house." She gazed down at Willow, who had a hold of her hand. "I'm a little OCD when it comes to the inhaler thing. I've also got a portable nebulizer in the car."

I roughed a hand through my hair. "I have no idea what that is."

I made a mental note to look it up, but I needn't have bothered.

"It's like the machine attached to her bed at home." Anna frowned, her good mood evaporating. "At Dean's house, I mean."

As we walked through the automatic doors and into the bright sunshine, I slipped my arm around Anna's waist. "I'll take care of you, baby."

She squinted up at me, shielding her eyes from the light, but I still saw the wall she was hiding behind. She didn't believe me.

I was about to tell Anna all the ways I'd accomplish this feat when she caught sight of the box strapped to the top of my SUV. Her eyes widened, and she stepped out of my grasp.

"You bought her a car?" Anna whirled on me, incredulous.

I rubbed the back of my neck, regretting not taking the store up on their delivery option. "Well, yeah, I had to. It matches the Dream House." Anna's brows shot to her hairline, and I added weakly, "It's a set."

It sounded better when the salesperson had said it.

Releasing Willow's hand, Anna slowly approached the car, then tipped forward to peer inside the tinted window. "Oh my God. Is there anything left at the store?" She stepped back, hands on her hips, looking over at me like I'd lost my mind. "Did you remember what I sent you for in the first place?"

I hit the button on my key fob, then proudly opened the back door, smiling. "Of course I did."

Anna ducked her head inside, then jumped back. "What the hell is that?"

Confused, I shifted my focus to the space-aged apparatus taking up a third of the bench seat. "That's the best car seat on the market. And it's appropriate for her age and weight."

Cutting my gaze to Willow, I hoped she wasn't oversized. Or undersized. Hell, I wouldn't know the difference.

A bubble of laughter tripped from Anna's pretty lips. "Read that off the box, did you?"

I scowled. "Better safe than sorry."

"Oh, she'll definitely be safe." Anna's snicker turned into a full belly laugh. "And well on her way to a career in NASCAR. Did that thing come with a helmet with one of those microphones attached?"

Folding my arms over my chest, I watched Anna dissolve into a hysterical fit of laughter. If I wasn't so happy to see the worry lines fade, I might have been offended.

Once she got herself under control, Anna slid her arm around my waist, the first touch that she'd initiated in, well, forever.

"She's not breakable," she said, smiling softly. "I promise."

Wiggling free of my hold when I bent to kiss her, she left me confounded.

"It's not you," Anna said in a faint whisper, swinging her gaze to Willow. "I don't want to confuse her. She doesn't know you."

Every nerve in my body twitched in protest. The more time we spent together, our fractured little family, the stronger my need to make us whole became. To seal the cracks.

"No worries." I shoved my hands in my pockets. "I get it."

Anna relaxed and then scooped Willow up. "Be a big girl while mommy tries to figure out your fancy new car seat."

After placing Willow in the front seat, she joined me in the back, and together we tried to assemble the state-of-the-art piece of equipment I'd bought to keep my daughter unharmed while we tooled around the treacherous streets of Austin in one of the safest SUVs on the planet.

After five minutes, tugging and pulling on the buckles, I realized I might have been over-cautious.

"Ma!"

Anna stopped what she was doing, then leaned into the front seat. Willow pointed at the center console as she peered hopefully at her mother.

Anna glanced over her shoulder at me. "Where are your CDs?"

I climbed out of the backseat and then slid behind the wheel to hook up my phone. "I've got a playlist. Let me plug it in."

"Do you have any Caged on there?"

"No," I replied automatically. "Do I look like an egomaniac or something?"

Anna cocked a brow.

God, the girl knew me.

I reached under the seat where I kept my stash.

"Here," I handed over the dusty, leather-bound case. "Happy now?"

Anna smirked. "Yep."

As soon as she flipped open the case, Willow's mouth dropped open, and she clutched the sleeve of Anna's blouse, trying to grab the CDs. "Ma! Ma!"

Anna gently outmaneuvered her eager hands. "No, no, this isn't yours."

After removing the debut Caged CD from the plastic pocket, Anna handed it to me. "Third track."

She patted me on the shoulder before disappearing into the backseat to continue her battle against the mighty car seat.

The sun shimmered off the CD as I turned the silver disc over in my hand. My greatest triumph and deepest sorrow, all pressed into four inches of plastic. It was everything, and nothing at all.

"The sooner you pop that puppy in, the easier the drive is going to be," Anna chimed in. "Trust me on that."

Willow's eyes never left my hand as I popped the shiny disc into the rarely used CD player.

Any single accomplishment related to my music paled in comparison to the look on my daughter's face when the drums began to pound through the speakers.

Bobbing her head, Willow closed her eyes, her little legs keeping perfect time with the beat.

"She's dancing." My voice cracked in two, along with my heart. "Anna-baby, she's dancing . . . to my music."

"Yes, she is." Anna jumped out of the backseat and then lifted Willow into her arms. Rocking her gently, Anna smiled at me. "Why are you so surprised? Her father's a musician."

Adjusting the bass on the equalizer, I watched Willow in the rearview mirror as Anna buckled her into the seat. My jaw went slack when Willow altered the intensity of her swaying. Most people wouldn't notice the slight variation. But I did. And my baby did. Willow had the same beat in her head that had accompanied me my whole life. She didn't need to read the music or hear the lyrics. She carried the rhythm with her.

Anna blew a strand of hair from her face as she sank into the passenger seat. "Finally."

Enthralled by the tiny figure in the backseat, my gaze shot to the rearview mirror every few seconds as I pulled out of the parking space. "What else does she like? I mean, besides music?"

Anna yawned, propping her foot on the dashboard. "The usual stuff. Those fluffy little puppies on YouTube, I forget what they're called. Sponge Bob. Finger painting." She wrinkled her nose. "McDonald's."

Taking Anna's hand, I pressed a kiss to her palm as I committed to memory all of my daughter's favorite things, making a quiet vow to get her every single one.

# CHAPTER TWENTY-THREE

**Anna**

*S*ean watched from the door of the guest room as I sorted through Willow's suitcase.

We'd stopped by my house—Dean's house—on the way here. And like a thief, I'd hastily packed a couple of bags, jumping at every noise.

And now, as I sat in front of Willow's small rollaway, I realized I didn't bring any of her nightclothes.

*Stupid.*

It's not like we needed much. Only enough for a few days. A week tops.

I'd heard Sean on the phone making arrangements to fly to Los Angeles. And as soon as he left, so would I.

As I closed the flap on the suitcase, Sean said, "You can use the drawers, you know."

The Victorian dresser, polished cherry wood with beautiful clawed feet and brass handles, sat like a monument against the wall. I was afraid to touch the damn thing, let alone store Willow's clothes in there.

Clutching one of my old T-shirts and Willow's little pink underwear to my chest, I gave Sean a nervous smile. "This is fine."

His jaw torqued as he stared at me. "Okay."

Willow sat on the bed, quiet as a mouse. I thought she might be a little dazed, but when I held out my arms, she jumped to her feet and started bouncing on the mattress.

Cringing, I turned to Sean to apologize, but he wasn't there.

I shook my head at Willow, and she stopped, then flung herself at me, dangling from my neck like a little monkey.

A half hour later, I pulled her slippery body from the bathtub.

"No! No! No!" she protested, arms and legs flailing as she tried to claw her way out of my arms.

Normally Willow hated bath time, but the garden tub in the adjoining bathroom was large enough to swim in.

The one in Sean's room was even bigger. Thank God she didn't see *that*.

"Willow," I said sternly as I tried to wrap her in a towel. "Stop squirming. You can take another bath tomorrow."

Without the benefit of her hearing aids, Willow couldn't hear me. But my tone should've been enough. It wasn't. The back of her head collided with my nose, and I saw stars. Reeling backward, I fell straight into Sean's arms.

He chuckled, his hands settling on my hips as I looked up at him with watery eyes.

"She really likes her bath, huh?"

I sniffed, sure my nose would start gushing any second. "Not usually."

Spinning toward the mirror, with Willow still attached, I checked for blood. But it was my daughter's blue eyes meeting Sean's in the reflection that had my full attention. I swear something passed between them.

In all the years of Willow's life, Dean had never looked at her that way. And I knew it had nothing to do with flesh and blood. After the trouble I had delivering Willow, Dean was all on board with adoption.

I guess that's when he started withdrawing from me, from Willow, when I nixed the idea of another child. Dean saw it as a betrayal. And a defeat. Proof that I'd never love him enough to commit to a life together. And in the end, I guess he was right.

Willow was quiet now, staring at her father, beguiled, like every other damn female on the planet. After securing the towel around her little body, I turned and impulsively held her out like a sack of potatoes.

*Real smooth, Anna.*

"Hold her for a sec, could you?"

Sean took a step back, even as he reached for her.

His eyes met mine, panic sparking in the silver threads. "Are you sure?"

Hell no, I wasn't sure. I only knew that Willow was curious and Sean looked almost desperate for contact. It was a perfect combination, because really, she was a toddler. And I didn't want their first touch to end in her screaming and him cringing.

Gingerly, Sean took Willow from my arms, holding her like she was made of glass.

Under the guise of wiping the mascara smudges off my cheeks, I grabbed a tissue and then turned back to the mirror, all the while vigilantly watching their exchange.

Willow reached up, tiny hands fisting Sean's hair. She gave the long strands a tug, thoroughly pleased with herself. Far from put out, Sean relaxed and made a face, like he intrinsically knew how to communicate with our daughter, to break the barrier created by her hearing loss.

My heart swelled, only to deflate when his phone rang. Logan's ringtone, "Come As You Are," the Nirvana anthem, echoed off the high ceilings. All these years and Sean hadn't changed it.

"Let me have her." Sean reflexively pulled Willow closer when I held out my arms. I smiled. "Your phone. Lo's calling."

The room went silent as the music stopped.

"I'll call him back." Sean gazed down at his daughter and then up at me. "What's next?"

His eyes wandered to my breasts before snapping back to my face.

I hadn't seen Sean blush since the first time he saw me naked when we were sixteen, but his cheeks were certainly red now. I guess staring at my boobs while holding our child was a little too confusing for him. Though, if things would've worked out the way they were supposed to, the way he'd promised, Sean would've known the two weren't connected in the least.

"Jammies," I said. "Then bed."

Bed.

Sleep.

My limbs were jelly, and all I wanted was crisp sheets and a soft pillow. That is until my arm brushed Sean's on the way out of the room. Every nerve in my body came to life at the contact, and cursing my erect nipples poking the hell out of my thin cotton T-shirt, I hauled ass before Sean noticed.

"Should we, I mean you, dry her hair?" Sean asked from his perch on the edge of the bed. His eyes found mine, and again, I was floored by all the questions swimming in the blue depths. An ocean of concerns. "I don't want her to get sick."

"That's an old wives' tale. People get sick from bacteria." Or in Willow's case—dust, pollen, smoke, and about a hundred other things. But I didn't want to freak Sean out. I held up a small hair-brush. "But I do have to get the knots out."

I lifted her from Sean's hold, and neither of them seemed happy about it. After slipping the T-shirt over Willow's head, I settled her on my lap and began to brush her wavy locks.

Sean hissed a breath when she whimpered. Willow noticed it too, not the sound but the painful grimace as his lips pulled back. She whimpered louder and got the same result.

"She's only doing that because you keep making those faces," I advised Sean in a tone too low for the little manipulator to hear. "I'm not hurting her."

"It doesn't sound like she's having a good time," Sean countered, folding his arms over his chest.

Resisting the urge to shoot him a look, which would only give Willow more reason to squirm, I said, "I need to settle her down. We'll talk in the morning."

Dead silence hung between us, and when I chanced a peek, Sean was staring at me. "You're not going to . . ." He frowned, then amended, "You're sleeping in here?"

Despite my aching nipples and the tightening in my belly, I nodded. "Yeah."

When I stood with Willow in my arms, Sean pulled the sheet back. He molded his palm to my hip as I tucked Willow between the covers, and I could feel the questions in his touch, the sexual tension that was always there. His hand fell away as I followed Willow under the blanket.

I met his confused gaze, which quickly morphed into something else. Resignation?

Brushing his lips against my forehead, he murmured. "Night, Anna-baby."

He touched Willow's hair but stopped short of a kiss.

And then he was gone, and the room was dark, and for the first time, falling asleep with my daughter in my arms wasn't enough.

An hour later, I slid out of bed to take a shower. That was the routine, get Willow to sleep and then tend to my own needs. I hadn't explained that to Sean. But after I dried off and applied some baby lotion, I tiptoed to his room. He'd stowed my suitcase in there, and at the time I didn't object, but now I needed my toothbrush.

At the door, I heard music playing softly. Chris Cornell's "Can't

Change Me" spilled into the dark hallway. My heart broke as I listened, the lyrics forming on my lips. Sean lived through music. And that song told me everything he couldn't. Sean wasn't changing.

I considered going back to bed, but then his voice rose over the music. "I don't care what you think." And then a pause. "I *am* taking care of Anna, believe that."

Hearing my name, I turned the doorknob and stumbled into the room.

Phone pressed to his ear, Sean's gaze crawled over me from tip to toe. Our eyes met, and a tempting smile curved his lips.

And that's how I found myself in his bathroom brushing my teeth. I didn't want to eavesdrop, or rather, I wouldn't allow myself to listen. But for some reason, I couldn't find the will to grab my bag and leave.

I flipped the switch on my way out, and to my confusion the bedroom was dark.

Muted light from a small, frosted bulb mounted on Sean's massive headboard outlined his body.

"Come here, Anna-baby," he said, voice rumbling above the music that still played.

I made my way to the side of the bed, and I could see him clearly now, my eyes adjusted to the dark. He was on his side, sheet low on his waist, all that luscious ink shading his sculpted chest.

His hand curled around my leg, just above my knee. "Is she asleep?"

"Yeah. Out like a light."

His palm skimmed over my thigh, under my baby doll nightgown, and came to rest on my ass. "I don't know where the line is, Anna." He gave me a gentle squeeze. "Help me out?"

I should be concerned about helping myself out. Out of this room, where the scent of him surrounded me, and the feel of his skin made me think stupid thoughts. But no, that would require more will power than I currently possessed.

Dropping a knee onto the mattress, I said, "You haven't crossed it yet."

In a heartbeat, I was on my back, Sean's hands in my hair and his lips on my throat. "You still use the same shampoo. I fucking love that shampoo."

I giggled, and he pulled away, his long hair tickling my heated skin. "What's funny?"

"Nothing."

*Everything.*

I didn't have time to ponder the meaning of life or how I got here, because Sean's lips were on me again, blazing a trail to the square of lace covering my breasts.

I groaned, arching into him as his mouth closed around my nipple, still trapped beneath the fabric. The extra friction sent a shock straight to my core.

He swept away the strap on the opposite shoulder, and when my sensitive skin met the rush of air from the ceiling fan, my nipple pebbled immediately. I felt him smile as he twisted the stiff peak, just enough.

"Fuck," I hissed.

A throaty laugh. "Yeah, that's what I had in mind too." His fingers dipped into my panties, and parting my folds, he grazed my needy bud. "But I want to taste you first."

Who was I to object? It's not like anyone had spent an inordinate amount of time between my thighs in the last four years. And that was my fault too.

Before I got lost in my head, in the guilt that contoured all the empty spaces where only Sean had ever dwelled, his breath was on my belly.

Sean yanked my panties down with a jerk, and the dainty seams ripped. He looked up, smiling. "Sorry."

He wasn't sorry. Not a bit.

"It's okay. I can buy some . . . oh God . . ."

I gripped his hair as his tongue explored. He was inside and outside and everywhere all at once. Two fingers slipped inside my channel, filling me.

"Eyes, Anna." The command held no weight until he pulled away.

And then my lids flew open, and I met his gaze. "Good girl."

Sean's eyes never left mine as his mouth closed over my clit. I could drift in those blue oceans forever. But we didn't have forever. We had now. Something about that notion pushed me to the edge, and I shattered, a silent surrender, gritting my teeth to keep from calling his name.

When he continued to work me, I shook my head. "I can't . . . I can't . . ."

And then Sean found that spot that assured he'd get his wish. This time, I couldn't hold it in. His name escaped in a rush as I came. And came.

Sean kissed my quivering belly and both breasts on his way up, and I shuddered involuntarily.

Fumbling around under the pillow, he waggled his brows when he showed me the condom.

I laughed, but it came out a snort because I hadn't caught my breath.

After Sean slid the latex in place, his fingers dove into my hair, and sealing his mouth over mine, he rolled onto his back with me on top.

With wobbly arms, I pushed myself up, straddling him. I knew what he wanted. I always knew.

"Ride me, baby," he roughed out. "Slow."

I dropped my gaze to his cock, moving a fraction until his tip nudged my entrance.

Sinking onto him with a groan, I squeezed my eyes shut, reveling in the feel of him, hard inside me.

Sean gripped my waist, his fingers digging into my flesh with just enough pressure to cause a little pain.

"Look at me, Anna."

My heart cracked at the request. Sean had never been so insistent on seeing my eyes in the past.

"Why?" I gritted out, wondering whose gaze he sought. "What are you looking for?"

He traced a finger over my jaw. "You. Always you."

# CHAPTER TWENTY-FOUR

**Sean**

*O*ur little family fell into a simple routine over the next few days. In the mornings Anna worked from the couch with Willow at her feet, playing with her toys or coloring, while I sat on the loveseat drinking coffee and watching. Always watching.

*How could you miss something you never knew existed?*

But I did. I was jealous as fuck of anyone who'd shared the last four years of Anna and Willow's lives.

The only time I left the house was to go to band practice.

And like today, I was pissy about it.

In forty-eight hours, I'd be on a plane headed for Los Angeles. Away from Anna and Willow.

The band had just finished running through our set list when I climbed down from my kit. "I'm out."

Pausing with the water bottle halfway to his lips, Logan narrowed his eyes. "What do you mean 'you're out'? This is our last practice before Benny's party."

Shoving my sticks into my back pocket, I faced my best friend, and though I could feel the icy wind blowing between us, zero fucks were given. "I've got a lunch date."

"Any girls included in your plans?" Logan asked.

Christian and Cameron dropped onto the couch to watch the fireworks. Wound tighter than usual, Logan was itching for a fight. But I didn't have time to give him one.

"Two," I replied, and with a laugh, I slung my backpack over my shoulder and headed for the door.

"Since your house is occupied," Logan called after me, "where are you planning on hosting this threesome?"

Anger flared as Logan's blade sunk deep into my back. After our conversation in the tranquility garden, I'd made my intentions clear to the guys. I told them I'd do anything to make things right with Anna. And this is how Logan wanted to play it?

Obliging, I spun around, and moving with purpose, I closed the gap between us in four quick strides. "What the fuck did you say?"

I wasn't waiting for an answer, my fists balled tight and ready to fly.

Just before I lunged, Christian and Cameron dove between us.

"Whoa, dude," Cameron said in that easy-going tone of his. "Calm down."

"Fuck that," I growled.

Christian was busy mumbling something to Logan along the lines of "not cool," and "what the fuck are you doing?" but my best friend wasn't paying attention.

I'd get him to pay attention.

"Sorry," by Buckcherry, echoed through the tension filled space.

I let Anna's call go straight to voicemail and said to Logan through gritted teeth, "Take it back."

It wasn't a request, but a demand, and after a few strained moments, Logan shook off Christian's hand and said, "Just making conversation." He grinned, his eyes cold and detached. "No need to get all worked up."

My gaze shifted to the clock on the wall. I had just enough time to pick up lunch and meet Anna and Willow. Or I could roll around on the floor with Logan and make him eat his fucking words.

"We're not done with this conversation," I said before turning on my heel.

Logan's laughter followed me as I stomped to the door. "We'll have plenty of time to talk on the plane, Hudson."

It sounded more like a threat than a promise.

Anna tossed me a smile when I jumped out of my car. "Hey." Refocusing her attention on the mountain bike sitting in the middle of my garage, she asked, "Did you bring lunch?"

My gaze darted to Willow, looking adorable in a pink helmet. And then I shifted my focus to the little plastic carrier on the back of Anna's bike.

Did she seriously take Willow on the road in that thing? It was made of plastic, for fuck's sake.

"Um . . . yeah, I brought McDonald's." I cleared my throat and took a couple of cautious steps. "What's all this?"

Anna's tongue darted out as she tried to turn the knob on the seat. "My dad brought over my bike." The proud smile gracing her lips slid away when our eyes met. "I hope you don't mind. I thought I'd take Willow for a ride later."

I shook the image of them lying in a heap on the side of the road out of my head.

"I don't mind at all." I walked over to examine the carrier. Gauging the weight of the straps, I asked, "Do you ride a lot?"

"Every day when the weather's nice."

Despite the irrational fear taking root in my chest, I smiled. "We could go now. There's a park about a half mile from here."

*Inside* the gates. Where it's safe.

Anna beamed right back at me. "That'd be great."

I set the food on the hood of my car before retrieving my bike from a hook on the wall. I'd never ridden the damn thing. It was just another way of connecting to my old life, to the times when Anna and I used to ride the trails at Volente Beach.

"That's pretty fancy," Anna said, her eyes roaming lovingly over the composite frame. "Is it heavy?"

I shook my head, a little embarrassed. "No. It's an ultra-light." An idea wove its way through my brain. "Why don't we trade?"

Anna shook her head, disappointed. "I can't. Willow's seat is already attached to this one."

Which was exactly the reason I'd offered. I didn't want Anna maneuvering her bulky bike down the driveway, let alone onto the street. Add Willow to the equation, and it took all my self-control not to insist.

"She can ride with me," I suggested.

The look Anna gave me was like an arrow to the chest. It was somewhere between "no" and "fuck no."

But then to my surprise, Anna knelt in front of Willow. "Sean wants to give you a ride to the park." Willow's eyes locked on mine over Anna's shoulder. "If you don't want to, you can ride with Mommy."

Tucking her thumb between her lips, Willow pondered for what seemed like an eternity. When she jerked a nod, my heart swelled to twice its size.

The trepidation in Anna's gaze sent me crashing back to earth. "You can't go fast. I mean it."

Was she serious right now? The mere thought of navigating the little hill at the end of my street with Willow on board had my palms sweating.

"Of course not."

With a sigh, Anna pushed to her feet, and I thought she'd waffle. Instead, she scooped Willow into her arms, regarding me over the top of the baby's soft ringlets.

"I guess we should get her strapped in."

Anna raced past me as soon as we exited the gate.

"Where's the fire!" I called as she crested the hill and slid out of sight. Glancing over my shoulder at Willow, I cemented on a smile. "Your mother's killing me."

Willow smiled right back like she could read my mind.

Gripping the handlebars on the downhill slope, I swallowed hard when I spotted Anna gliding along with her arms raised at her sides. She'd done it a million times, but seeing her now, all I could picture was a deer running into the road. Or a car making a turn from one of the driveways.

Mentally, I punched the little douchebag in my head whispering doomsday scenarios. But he just talked louder.

By the time we got to the park, my heart was pounding so hard I'm surprised I hadn't cracked a rib. I jumped off the bike and then met Willow's expectant gaze. She started squirming, kicking her legs.

Anna jogged over. "Take this." She held out the lightweight pack containing our lunch. "And go find us a table." Her brow hitched up. "It's going to take me a minute to get her out of this deathtrap."

My hand flew to the back of my neck. "I guess it's sturdier than it looks, huh?"

Anna suppressed a smile as she went to work on the straps. "Better be. It set my parents back two hundred bucks. You can ask my dad about the safety features since he has them memorized."

Anna looked up when I brushed a kiss to the top of her head. "What was that for?"

*For keeping our daughter safe. For letting me share your lunch. For the awesome sex you gave me before you snuck out of my bed this morning.*

But I said none of those things. Instead, I discreetly squeezed her ass. "For wearing these shorts."

Since that was true too, I gave her a wink and then hightailed it to the picnic area with a clear conscience. As I spread our meal on the table, a couple of women planted on a nearby bench looked my way. I gave them a curt smile, hoping they wouldn't disturb us.

No worries there.

After glancing over my tattoos, long hair, scruffy beard, and the red Happy Meal box in my hand, they promptly got up and left. And that's when I realized I had a kid's meal, but no kid.

Setting the box in front of me to lower the creep factor, I glanced around.

On the playground, a little tow-headed boy not much bigger than Willow caught my attention when he flopped onto his belly at the top of the slide.

My brows shot together and I wanted to warn the little guy, but his mother didn't seem to share my concern. She waited at the bottom with a big smile.

I turned away before the kid met his fate, but when I snuck a peek a second later, he was already climbing the steps to do it again.

I had to wonder if the park was a good idea with all the obvious perils.

There's no way Anna would let Willow on any of these contraptions. Would she?

From the look of longing on my daughter's face as she pointed at the equipment, she was familiar. And Anna didn't look the least bit concerned about the children tempting fate all around us.

"You can play in a minute," I heard Anna say as she tried to get Willow's eyes and feet moving in the same direction. "Look." She tipped her chin at me. "There's a Happy Meal over there with your name on it."

Interest piqued, Willow snapped her attention to her mother.

Anna smiled down at her and cajoled, "Do you want a Happy Meal, baby?"

Willow's copper curls bounced up and down as she nodded.

I thought we were home free until Willow stopped in her tracks a couple of feet from where I sat. Despite the fact that she saw me every day at the house, and she'd just rode here on the back of my bike, she regarded me with a furrowed brow.

Unconcerned, Anna slid onto the bench across from me, and said loud enough for Willow to hear, "I wonder if there's a toy inside the box?"

I blinked at her, unsure if the question was rhetorical. Anna laid her hand on my arm before I could rip open the box and do a thorough inspection.

"What? A strangled voice rang in my ears. Mine.

Anna's lips curved into a heart-stopping grin. "Easy, Sean. You look kind of scared. What is it?"

I shrugged, unnerved by Willow's demeanor. "She doesn't seem too thrilled having me here."

Anna rolled her eyes and laughed, reaching for her burger. "She thinks you might give in and let her play before we eat."

"And we're not doing that?" I glanced from Willow to Anna who was now looking at me like I'd grown a third head.

"No." Anna drew out the word as if I were a child. "We're the adults, remember?"

I didn't feel like an adult, but I gave Anna a confident smile nonetheless. "Got it."

Sure enough, once we started eating, or in my case picking, Willow inched her way to Anna's side. I watched in fascination as she threw her chubby leg onto the bench while her equally chubby hand curled around the lip of the table to pull herself up.

Once she settled on Anna's lap, Willow made a grab for the red box.

Anna thwarted her efforts, looking down into her frustrated azure gaze. "What do you say?"

Willow scowled, and it was almost as perfect as her smile.

"Peese," she huffed, turning those baby blues in my direction.

Mesmerized, I shoved the box in front of my little girl.

Again, Anna outmaneuvered her hands. But this time Willow didn't balk. She bounced up and down as Anna felt around inside the box. Willow's lips formed a tiny *o* when Anna pulled out a little purple toy.

Was like this all the time? And if so, how did people walk around without their hearts flying out of their chests?

I finally understood the goofy fucking look on parents' faces when their kid did something simple like drink water from a fountain or toss a ball. Because as Willow settled against Anna's chest, the purple fuzzy action figure in one hand and a chicken nugget in the other, I'd never been so enthralled.

"Eat," Anna said as she inhaled her food.

I'd no sooner unwrapped my Big Mac than Willow was on her feet, pointing at the sandbox.

Balling up her wrapper, Anna smiled at my untouched burger. "I never thought I'd say this, but you better learn to eat quicker or you'll starve."

I was already on my feet, chuckling as I cleaned up our mess. "Noted."

After emptying the trash, I took a seat on the bench next to Anna, and to my horror, Willow headed straight for the sandbox where a snot-nosed kid with a loaded diaper was playing.

Panic struck as I glanced over the germ-infested box. There was probably Ebola in there. "Don't you think it's kind of dirty?"

As I pulled out my phone to check for known contaminants in the Austin area, Anna caught my arm. "That's the whole point, babe. It's dirt."

Outside the bedroom, Anna hadn't used a term of endearment on me in four years. Basking in the glow, I didn't give the Google search another thought.

When Willow began arranging the soft powder into neat piles, I sat up straighter. "What's she doing?"

Responding through a yawn, Anna said, "Making a sandcastle, I guess."

I felt my chest constrict with pride and something more. *Love.* How was it possible to love someone so thoroughly in a week?

Taking Anna's hand, I looked down at our entwined digits. "If I didn't show up at your house, I wouldn't be sitting here right now, would I?"

Anna's frown said it all, but I waited for the words.

"If I stuck to the plan, neither of us would be here." She sighed, looking away. "I wasn't going to keep her."

After my conversation with Alecia at the hospital, Anna's declaration didn't come as a shock. But I had to wonder, how did this happen at all? Anna was meticulous about birth control. From the first day we picked up the pills at the free clinic, Anna had set an alarm to remind herself to take them.

Kids were a far off "someday, maybe" proposition.

After law school.

Marriage.

*Music* . . .

The question dancing on the edge of every thought found a voice. "How did it happen?"

"Rifampicin." The name rolled off Anna's tongue with familiar ease. Like she'd said it a million times. Before I could respond, she continued, "It's an antibiotic. Remember when I cut my leg at the gym?" She looked down at our joined hands, frowning. "No, I guess you wouldn't."

I brushed my lips to her temple. "On the leg press at 24 Hour Fitness? I remember."

Anna's looked up at me, and seeing the happiness in her eyes only made it worse.

Had I been that inattentive? Disinterested? Douchey? Apparently so.

"Um . . . anyway," Anna went on, "the doctor prescribed Rifampicin to wipe out the infection. It lowers the effectiveness of birth control pills by reducing the level of estrogen in the . . ." She exhaled a ragged breath. "It doesn't matter. That's how it happened."

Without a doubt, I knew Anna could recite every detail if I asked. All the statistics.

My stomach turned as I pictured her scouring the net for information and explanations. Alone.

I stroked my thumb over hers. "What happened next?"

"Before or after you left?"

I shook off the glancing blow. "After."

"Two trips to the clinic for an abortion—never made it past the front door. And then a meeting with a woman from an adoption agency. You know the rest."

I wasn't sure if Anna was letting herself off the hook or sparing me, but there was a big piece she'd yet to explain.

"Where does Dean fit in?"

Anna's leg bobbed and she looked away, squinting. "I told you he gave me a ride that night. We met for coffee after that. He wanted to see if I was all right. And then I threw up in the middle of the Java Hut." Her focus shifted to Willow and she smiled. "So I broke down and told him about her."

My head swam as I absorbed that little nugget. "What about Peyton? She didn't know?"

"At that point, I was planning on having an abortion. Peyton was sure you were going to come back. But I knew you weren't." Anna met my gaze, her eyes devoid of any sparkle. "Unless she told you I was pregnant. And she would've, you know? So I had Dean take me to the clinic. And then to the meeting with the adoption lady. He asked me to marry him on the way home that day."

Ever since our confrontation at the hospital, I'd imagined all the ways I'd put the hurt on Dean the next time I saw him. I pictured my fist colliding with his face. The satisfying crunch of his nose against my knuckles. The blood. Not once did I see him as anything but some guy who took advantage of my girl. Until now.

My introspection drew a heated glare from Anna. "I'm not apologizing for that, Sean. Not for having Willow. Or marrying Dean, or—"

Sliding my hand to Anna's nape, I pressed a kiss to her mouth. To wipe Dean's name from her lips or share the burden, I wasn't sure.

"I'm so fucking sorry."

If I had a dollar for every time I'd said it or thought it in the past four years, I could pay Willow's way through college. Still, I would keep saying it.

"Ma?" We turned in unison and found Willow standing a few feet away. "Swing now?"

Anna wobbled to her feet. "Of course, baby." Miraculously, she smiled at me and held out her hand. "You coming?"

I didn't deserve Anna's kindness. But I wasn't about to turn it down. I linked our fingers as we traipsed through the sand, following the trail of dust to where Willow waited beside the swing, her fingers coiled possessively around the chain.

Before I could test the links, Anna scooped Willow up and said, "A little help?"

"Sure."

Dropping onto my knees, I held the seat, and when Willow slid into place her face was a foot from mine. Instinctively my hand shot up to smooth a curl that had fallen over her eyes, but then I stopped, looking to Anna for permission. Guidance. Something.

Anna nodded, and I awkwardly tucked the strand behind Willow's hearing aid.

Hauling to my feet before I scared the kid with my shaking hand and overall ineptitude, I smiled. "All set."

Willow stared up at me with furrowed brows, kicking her legs,

Anna took a seat on the adjacent swing, chuckling. "You're going to have to give her a push."

I waited for her to provide detailed instructions on the proper way to push a toddler in a swing, because surely there had to be a handbook somewhere for all that shit. But all I got was a smile.

"I can do that," I said, and with a confidence I didn't possess, I sank into the sand behind our daughter.

Placing my palm on Willow's back, I studied my hand, which spanned the width of her tiny frame. Soft wisps of hair brushed my fingertips, and the breeze carried her baby scent straight to my heart, where it nestled beside the space I'd carved out for Anna long ago.

I leaned close to her ear. "Ready, Willow-baby?"

Her head bobbed, and I swear I felt her heartbeat like butterfly wings under my touch.

I gave her a gentle nudge, and she glided forward, giggling. But I made sure I was right there when she returned. Regret for all the time I'd missed threatened to cloud the moment, as did the voice in my head, reminding me that I'd be leaving in two days.

Determined to do whatever the hell it took so I'd never miss another milestone in Willow's life, I let my little girl's laughter chase the storm away.

# CHAPTER TWENTY-FIVE

**Anna**

*A*fter Willow fell asleep, I snuck out of bed, but instead of going to Sean's room as I had every other night, I headed downstairs to the home theater next to his studio. I wanted to transfer some pictures I'd taken this afternoon onto his hard drive.

My heart pinched at the thought of Sean leaving. But he wasn't mine to keep, and I knew that going in.

After plugging my phone into the little black box attached to his projection screen, I took a seat on one of the couches.

Picking up the remote, I tried to remember the steps to download. A menu came up labeled personal photos, and when I pressed the button, the screen populated with dozens of pictures. All of Sean in places I didn't recognize with different women on his arm. In his lap. At his side.

Tears lined my eyes, but I just sat there, unmoving, barely breathing, with the pieces of Sean's life laid out before me.

Footfalls on the stairs jolted me from my trance, and I fumbled with the buttons until the screen went dark.

The door creaked open, spilling light into the room. Not a lot. But enough to see the look of concern on Sean's face.

He glimpsed the blank screen as he walked toward me. "What are you doing?"

I held up my phone as if that explained everything, and then finding my voice, I choked out, "Pictures. Of Willow."

Sean looked down at the remote clutched in my other hand. I wanted to throw it at him, but before I could, he took it from me. "Let's see what you got."

He dropped onto the sofa, and when the screen illuminated, the photos splashed across his face. All of his conquests superimposed on his skin.

He blinked slowly and then pressed delete, jabbing the button until they were gone, and it was just us, sitting in the dark.

"You didn't have to do that," I said thickly.

"They didn't mean anything."

"I get it."

I hauled to my feet, trying to break his hold when his hands curled around my waist.

"What do you get?" Sean gripped me tighter and then pulled me closer, pressing a kiss to my chest, right above my heart. "Tell me."

*Tell me. Show me. Look at me.*

All his whispered demands, and always it came back to this. To the beginning of our end.

Anger flowed through me, unjustified given the circumstances. But that's the thing about anger, it doesn't need a reason.

Sean's fingers inched north, and I cursed my traitorous body, my tight nipples, and wet panties.

He looked up at me, thumbs sweeping the underside of my breasts. "Let's go upstairs."

The thought of Sean's bed turned my stomach, so I shook my head. If he wanted to fuck, we'd do it here, with the ghosts of all the other women a few feet away.

I eased the thin straps over my shoulders, and let my nightgown slip to my waist.

Sean's gaze flicked to my taut nipples, the stiff peaks a testament to my weakness.

"Upstairs," he repeated, more forcefully this time.

A taunting smile formed on my lips. "You want to fuck me, Sean? Then fuck me right here."

He caught my wrist when I reached for the drawstring on his board shorts. Pulling me on top of him with our joined hands trapped between us, he searched my face. "You want to tell me what we're playing at here?"

I smiled, because he hit the nail on the head. This was a game. And in two days it would end.

My gaze shot to the blank screen for a half a beat. "Sex is a sport, right?" I palmed him through the thin fabric of his shorts, and his cock pulsed in my hand. "So why it does it matter where we play?"

Annoyance shadowed his features. But then he flipped me onto my back on the smooth leather couch. As he looked down at me, impatient hands yanking at my gown, I swear I saw something in his eyes. But then he nudged my legs open with his knee.

"You're right, baby. It doesn't matter where." My breath stalled as he pushed my panties aside, and sliding a finger between my folds, he smiled. "You're so fucking wet."

It sounded more like an accusation than a compliment. So I pressed my lips together to show him how unaffected I was. When he slipped a second finger inside my slick channel, my hips bucked of their own accord.

Stupid body.

Pissed now, mostly at myself, I made another attempt to claw at Sean's shorts, but he stopped me. "I don't think so."

I glared at him as his thumb grazed my clit. But when he started circling the tiny nub, I couldn't hold back, and a slew of curses tumbled from my lips.

Another smile from Sean, soft, despite his relentless assault. "You like that?"

I said nothing, surrendering to the rhythm of his thrusts, and right when I was about to fly, he stopped.

His shorts slid to the ground, and then fisting his cock, he stroked himself in earnest. "Is this what you want?"

Sean kept asking questions, upping the stakes, like maybe I'd give in.

He could have my body, hell, he *owned* my body, but he couldn't have my words. Not tonight.

I spread my legs wider in silent invitation.

Sean's eyes stayed glued to my face as he ripped the foil package, and once he was fully sheathed, he gripped my thighs and pulled me forward. His hands slid to my ass, tilting me at just the right angle so that his blunt head was positioned at my entrance.

"You want me?" he asked softly. Too softly. Gripping my chin when I turned my head, Sean forced me to meet his gaze. "Do you?"

He didn't wait for an answer, pushing in to the hilt with one thrust. I gasped, and Sean took full advantage, his mouth sealing over mine. Something about the tenderness stabbed at my heart, so I sank my teeth into his bottom lip.

Sean didn't stop, or even pause, despite the coppery taste on our tongues.

When he finally broke the connection, panting, I turned my head.

"Open your eyes," he demanded.

Defiant, I shook my head.

He stopped moving. "Open your eyes, *please.*"

Reluctantly, I complied. And I wished I hadn't. Because when I looked at him, it was much harder to deny my feelings.

Sean eased out slowly and then slammed home with punishing force.

"Do you feel that?" He grunted. I bit the inside of my lip to keep from whimpering when he repeated the motion. "Do. You. Feel. It?"

Turning my face away, I bit out, "Yes. I feel it."

Sean pressed a kiss to my neck, my tense jaw, and finally my lips, and fuck, I couldn't stop myself from seeking his tongue.

Slowing his pace, he touched his forehead to mine. "This isn't me fucking you, Anna-baby. This is me loving you."

# CHAPTER TWENTY-SIX

**Sean**

$\mathcal{I}$ ducked out of the liquor store with a bottle of Melissa's favorite wine and a pint of peach Schnapps for Anna. Though the Schnapps was really for me since I planned on licking it off her body later tonight.

Maybe I'd take her back to the theater room. Our make-up sex was hot as fuck, even if I didn't know what we were fighting about.

*The pictures.*

They meant nothing to me, those images. But as soon as I returned from LA, I'd sweep the house for possible landmines.

As I turned onto the backroads, I hit the hands-free and placed a call to Anna.

Willow's screaming drowned out my hello.

"No, no, no!!!" she chanted.

"What's going on?" The speedometer crept up as I leaned on the gas pedal. "Anna, what's happening?"

"Willow!" Anna grunted, ignoring my question. "Stop wiggling! You will wear shoes!"

I blew out a relieved breath and then chuckled. "Are you really lecturing the kid about wearing shoes? That's funny since you don't wear them half the time yourself."

"My daughter is not showing up at your aunt's house with no shoes. I don't want her to think I'm not a good mother."

"Anna—"

"I can take care of my daughter. I can!"

Confused by Anna's sudden wave of insecurity, I blew right past the guy at the guard shack.

"Anna-baby, don't stress," I said. "You've known Lissa since you were fifteen. She loves you. And she's going to love Willow too, shoes or no shoes."

Silence, followed by a sniffle. "Did you tell her about Willow's hearing?"

Impatient, I punched in the gate code. "Of course I did. Why would you ask me that?"

"Because Willow doesn't speak well." Another sniff. "You don't know anything about kids, so you don't notice it, but Melissa will."

Wedging my phone between my ear and my shoulder so I wouldn't drop the call, I turned off the engine and then grabbed the liquor and the flowers from the passenger seat. "Do you really think Melissa is going to love Willow any less because she can't recite the fucking dictionary?" Anger propelled me up the front steps. "That's pretty shitty, Annabelle."

"It's not Willow's fault," she said quietly. "It's mine."

"You know that's not true. Willow was born with a hearing problem."

"I'm not talking about her hearing loss! I'm talking about the diagnosis! I told them . . . I told the doctors she wasn't slow . . . or autistic. But they wouldn't listen . . . I couldn't make them listen." Anna rambled on, despair coloring her tone. "I saw the way she looked at me, Sean. Trying to mimic me. Maybe if I could've got the doctors to listen sooner, she'd speak better."

From the bedroom door, I watched my girl come apart.

Silent now, with the phone clutched to her ear, Anna stared out the window, tears spilling down her cheeks. Willow sat on the floor, playing with her sandals, oblivious. On the nightstand, I spotted her hearing aids.

I crossed the room, and when I touched Anna's shoulder, the phone slipped out of her hand. She looked up at me with watery eyes, anguish creasing her brow.

There was nothing to say, so I cupped her cheek, wicking her tears away with the pad of my thumb. And then I kissed her, tasting all her fears. The burdens she carried.

When Anna broke our connection, she took a fortifying breath and then smiled, ready to resume her battle.

But it was my turn to carry the load.

I scooped up our little angel along with her pink sandals. "Relax, baby. Let me worry about the kid's shoes."

"I told you," I mouthed to Anna, smirking.

I was right about Melissa. Enthralled didn't begin to describe the way she looked at Willow.

Anna rolled her eyes, then went back to picking at her food. It wasn't like she could eat anything with my aunt running around snapping photos every few seconds.

I shook my head at Melissa when she reached for her camera. Again.

She ignored me. "Smile, Willow-baby."

Willow grinned, her mouth full of mashed potatoes.

"Like you've got room for any more pictures," I said as I looked around at the photos lining the shelves and crowding the tables. The dead and the living, side by side. Not that it pained me to see my mother. Not anymore. But in this house, it was like she was joining us for dinner.

"Never you mind, sugar," Melissa said, dropping into her chair to check out the screen on her camera. "I'll figure something out."

"Where's Chelsea?" I asked, motioning for Anna to eat while she had the chance. "I thought you said she'd be here."

Melissa sighed. "Shopping for her prom dress. She's been gone all day." Her eyes darted to mine. "You did lower the limit on her credit card, didn't you?"

"Nah." Capturing Anna's foot under the table, I winked at my girl. "You only have one prom night, right, baby?"

Anna's cheeks flamed and she shifted, giving me the evil eye. Yes, we'd gone to prom, junior prom at least. But we'd stayed less than an hour, and the only thing I remembered about Anna's dress was the way it looked on the floor of her parents' cabin.

With a little grin, Anna picked up her sweet tea. "Let's hope Chelsea has as good a time as we did."

And then it hit me. Some little asshole was going to be trying the same moves on my cousin that I'd used on Anna.

My stomach turned.

I was still obsessing when Melissa put a framed picture on the table in front of me. One of the last photos of my mother. "Notice anything?"

After glancing at the image for a couple of seconds, I refocused on my dinner. "Yeah, nice shot."

Melissa nudged me. "You are so thick sometimes, Sean Jacob."

Anna stifled a snort, either because she agreed or she knew I hated it when people used my full name.

"Look," Melissa urged, holding the camera next to my mother's picture. "Your baby has Gracie's eyes."

Humoring my aunt, I picked up the pewter frame, and as I glanced from the small screen on the camera to the memory in my hand, I saw it. It wasn't only the color—we all shared the same azure hue—but my mother's eyes burned a little brighter. By the time she died, the disease had all but stolen the radiance, but there it was, that forgotten sparkle, in my daughter's eyes.

Clearing my throat, I said, "Yeah, she does."

Since I couldn't get any more food down, I pushed my plate away. This time Anna's foot found mine. She smiled at me in that knowing way, and all I wanted to do was drag her upstairs and kiss her stupid.

Melissa reclaimed her seat and said to Anna, "I'd love to get some of Willow's baby pictures if you have any copies lying around."

I bit down a smile because my aunt was the only person I knew who ordered photos in triplicate.

Anna picked up her bag, and to my surprise, she pulled a 3x5 from her wallet. "This is Willow's hospital picture." She handed the snapshot to Melissa. "You can keep it. I have more."

Sneaking a peek over my aunt's shoulder, the lump in my throat doubled in size. Willow looked so tiny, like a little doll. Her red hair stuck up in every direction. And that scowl. She looked mad at the world, her fingers balled into tight fists under her chin.

Melissa turned the photo over, and a gasp escaped. She blinked at Anna. "You named her after Gracie."

Anna blushed and shifted her attention to Willow. "It's a beautiful name."

Sniffling, Melissa wobbled to her feet and then folded Anna into a hug. They broke apart when the front door slammed.

"Sean, are you here?" Chelsea called, and before I could answer she rushed into the room. "You *are* here!" She tossed a black garment bag over the back of an empty chair and then threw her arms around me. "I thought you were out of town."

I brushed a kiss to her temple. "I'm leaving tomorrow. What've you been up to?"

Flipping her long, sandy brown hair over her shoulder, Chelsea sank into the seat beside me. "Not much. Just getting ready for the prom. I found the cutest dress and . . ."

Chelsea stopped speaking mid-sentence. Lips parted and eyes narrow, she glared at Anna. "What is she doing here?" she demanded, all her fury aimed at me.

The room went silent, and before I could answer, Anna said, "Hey, baby girl. It's good to see you."

Chelsea shot to her feet. "Don't call me that! Why are you here?

Don't you have a husband somewhere? Shouldn't you be eating supper with *him*?"

My chair hit the floor with a thud, Chelsea's rapid-fire questions echoing in my head. I towered over my cousin, too afraid to open my mouth and release the venom crawling from the pit of my stomach.

Melissa muscled her way in between us. "Chelsea Nicole," she snapped, "you apologize right now."

"Why should I?" Chelsea countered, her fierce gaze locked on mine. "She disappears for four years, and now she wants to come back?" She shook her head. "No. She needs to go."

I managed to take hold of Chelsea's arm. "Upstairs," I barked. "Now."

Chelsea lifted her chin, defiant. "You're taking her side?"

When her focus shifted to Anna, it was like someone let the air out of Chelsea's face.

"She's got a kid?" Chelsea spluttered.

My gaze collided with Anna's, and even with the animosity swirling in the air, I managed a smile. "Willow. Her name is Willow."

Melissa grinned as if my declaration should mean something to Chelsea. It didn't. My cousin bolted from the room without another word.

Flustered, Melissa wiped her hands on her apron. "I-I don't know what's gotten into her."

"It's fine," Anna said softly as she pushed back from the table. "I'm going to wash up. Be right back."

Willow's little face peered over her mother's shoulder as Anna walked out of the room.

"Dammit," I muttered, grabbing my chair and righting it. As I sank into my seat, I glared at Melissa. It wasn't her fault, but she was the only one in the room. "Why would Chelsea do that? None of this," I motioned around helplessly, "is Anna's fault. It's on me."

Nodding, Melissa laid a hand on my shoulder. "I know that, sugar. And so does Chelsea. But she can't put the blame where it belongs." She smiled. "On you. You're her hero. She doesn't want to hear about you leaving your girlfriend to chase other women. Hits a little too close to home."

Melissa rubbed my shoulder to soften the blow, but it didn't help. Chelsea's father was a pitiful excuse for a man, running out on his family when Chelsea was still a baby. The fucker came back, sniffing around for a handout when the first Caged CD hit the airways. The only thing he got was my fist in his face when I lit him up outside the Parish.

Being compared to that piece of shit twisted my gut.

Melissa sighed as she dropped into the chair beside me. "She'll come around. But you can't let this come between you."

I nodded, lost in my thoughts, my eyes on the doorway waiting for Anna to return.

"Sean," Melissa took my hand, "before Anna gets back, I need to talk to you."

An ominous feeling spread through my limbs, emanating from our joined hands. "What's up?"

My dread made a hard right turn straight into panic when Melissa averted her gaze. "I went to the doctor a couple of weeks ago. I wasn't feeling like myself. They found a lump."

The world tilted, and I feared I might slide off into space.

*Breathe.*

When my brain refused to follow the simple command, I sat there, contemplating death by suffocation. Which beat cancer.

Melissa patted my hand, which was numb, along with the rest of me. "It runs in the family. Maybe it's fate."

And with that, she stood up and gathered a couple of plates before walking to the kitchen. I stumbled after her and caught her arm, my grip slackening when I felt bone.

The dull roar in my ears grew louder as I looked at her. Really looked at her. Shadows bruised her eyes, and her cheeks were hollow.

How did I miss it?

*Because you weren't looking.*

"Are you sure it's—" The word wouldn't come. It never did. Not without a fight. "Cancer?"

Melissa glided away, and then shoveled some mashed potatoes into the garbage disposal. "Yes. But they caught it early."

"How early?"

She lifted a frail shoulder. "Not sure. They'll know more after they do the mastectomy. I've always wanted a boob job anyway."

Her light chuckle did nothing to lighten the mood. Breast cancer took my mother and my grandmother. I found no humor in that.

Grabbing a plate from Melissa's hand, I absently shoved it into the dishwasher. "What can I do? Anything, Melissa. The best doctors. The best plastic surgeons."

*The best funeral.*

She peered up at me, smiling, but when her lips parted nothing came out. Her focus was on the archway.

I felt her then. Anna. And when I turned, she was there, eyes wide, holding tight to Willow's hand.

She rushed out of the room and then I heard glass shatter.

"Shit," I muttered, following the sound.

On her knees, Anna gathered shards of crystal off the hardwood. "Sorry . . . I'm sorry . . ." she babbled, and I wasn't sure if she was talking about the Waterford bowl or my aunt or what.

I pulled Anna to her feet, carefully extracting her from the mess. "Don't move. Let me get a broom."

My attention shifted to Willow, huddled against the wall with her thumb between her lips.

I nearly collided with Melissa when I spun around. She shoved a broom into my hand and then joined Anna, and together they shuffled to the family room.

Crouching to sweep up the mess, I made eye contact with my daughter. "Stay there, Willow-baby," I said, my tone firm but gentle.

Soft with a hard edge. I'd finally mastered the technique.

"Sugar, you can't worry about that," Melissa said to Anna. "If it happens we'll be prepared."

A thunderbolt crashed in my skull, and everything went white.

*It.*

My grandmother, my mother, my aunt.

*My daughter.*

The pieces slid into place forming an unimaginable picture.

Glass crunched under my knees as I scooted toward the little angel who looked so much like her mother. Except for the eyes. Those were mine. Because she had my genes.

Pulling Willow into my arms, I pressed my lips to her ear. "Let's get some dessert."

Anna's watery emerald gaze met mine and she smiled. But I could barely look at her, let alone reciprocate. All I wanted was to feed my daughter a big bowl of ice cream. And hide from the truth.

# CHAPTER TWENTY-SEVEN

## Anna

*I* rubbed my swollen eyes as I sat up in the dark room. Pitch dark, thanks to the blackout drapes. Which meant I was in Sean's bed. But when I looked around he wasn't there.

*He left without saying goodbye?*

Gasping for air, my hand flew to my throat. I'd been here before. Maybe the room was different, and yes, Sean would be back, but still, he left without a goodbye.

After last night, and all the crying at Melissa's, I didn't think I had any tears left. But then they were there, tiny droplets of despair, stinging my eyes and falling onto my cheeks. I tasted them on my lips.

The door flew open, spilling light into the room.

"Baby, what is it?" Sean's face swam into view as he knelt in front of me. "Did you have a nightmare?"

I threw my arms around his neck. "I thought you were gone."

I cursed my stupidity. Because, holy hell, it was true. I was in love with him. Maybe I'd never stopped loving him. But this was different.

This was that old kind of love. The one that bound us so tight it eventually snapped and drove Sean away.

*I'm done. With you and this town.*

He stroked my hair and smiled. "I fell asleep in the chair in Willow's room."

Spotting his duffel bag and backpack by the door, my survival skills kicked in.

I made a move to break our contact, but Sean had other ideas. His mouth crashed into mine. The kiss was hungry, bordering on desperate. He eased me onto my back, his hands skimming my thighs and caressing my stomach. He grunted, pushing my loose T-shirt up to my neck.

In between pressing hot kisses to my breasts, he murmured, "I don't want to go."

Floating back to earth, I blinked at the ceiling. "What?"

Sean pushed onto his elbows. "I don't want to go. I mean it."

Our eyes met and I cupped his cheek. "You have to go. It's your job."

It pained me to say it, but it was the truth.

He leaned into my touch. "Come with me."

The words tumbled out, impulsive. Hasty. And then his lips touched mine, lightly this time.

Sean kept us connected, our tongues twisting and tangling while he stripped off his shorts. He yanked my T-shirt over my head and then I buried my face in the crook of his neck while he fumbled around for a condom on the nightstand.

With those magic hands, Sean was sheathed and inside me in seconds.

"Fuck, baby." He panted. "Come with me."

I wasn't sure if he was talking about the sex or the trip or both, but I wrapped my legs around his waist, determined to hold on. A few deep thrusts from this angle and the pressure on my swollen nub sent me flying.

"I love you, Anna-baby," he grunted as I spiraled to the bottom.

My body tingling from his words and the last gasps of my orgasm.

Sealing my mouth over his, I swallowed the declaration. Even if it were true, it didn't mean as much as it should, because what had love done for us in the past? Not a damned thing.

Still, a little spark ignited somewhere deep inside.

Hope?

I wasn't sure, but as Sean continued to work my body, I surrendered and let it engulf me.

Draped over Sean's chest, with our limbs tangled, I drifted in and out as he stroked my back.

When the alarm went off on his phone, he silenced the ringer. I expected him to get up, but he didn't, settling back against the heap of pillows.

"When do you have to leave?" I asked, peering up at him.

"Not for a couple of hours. The limo's picking me up last." He ran his thumb over my bottom lip. "It's only for three days."

Turning my face into his chest, I effectively ended the conversation. It wouldn't change anything. Conner was going to offer Caged a spot on the tour, and then Sean would be gone for a year.

Though the prospect was still terrifying, for the first time, I felt something other than despair. I quickly shut down the Disney music playing in my head. This wasn't a fairy tale.

But then did all happily-ever-afters have to end with a white picket fence?

As I pondered, tracing the words inked over Sean's heart, a new curiosity took hold. He'd added quite a few tattoos since we'd split, but this one wasn't even in English.

"What language is this?"

The question seemed safe enough. But apparently not, since Sean went rail stiff. "French."

Covering the ink with my palm, I rested my chin on top of my hand. "Did you get it in France?"

He nodded, then looked away, and I got the message. Whatever it said, or whatever it was, the topic was off limits. The font on the tattoo was loopy, or I might have been able to commit the short phrase to memory and look it up later.

But from Sean's reaction, I probably shouldn't.

His arm banded around my waist when I scooted to the edge of the bed. "Where are you going?"

I smiled at him over my shoulder. "Bathroom."

When I returned, Sean was propped against the headboard, looking down at something in his hand.

He held out an envelope—old, stained with a coffee ring, and unsealed.

Climbing onto the bed, I sat onto my heels, my knees brushing his side. "What's this?"

He caught my hand as I peeled open the flap on the envelope. "There's a story that goes with that."

The seconds passed into a full minute. "Do you want to tell me?"

Sean laughed, low and humorless. "Not really. But I will." And after blowing out a breath, he began, "We were in France when I heard about your engagement. Since none of us read newspapers, but didn't want to appear like hicks, we requested the Austin Statesman be delivered whenever possible. It was in our rider. The list we gave the promoters—"

"I know what a rider is." I smiled. "Please tell me that Lo didn't have any weird requests like no brown M&M's."

Another laugh. "Doesn't matter. Whatever we requested, they made sure it was done."

"That's not always a good thing. Do you really want someone's hands all over your candy?" I raised a brow. "Those brown M&M's aren't going to magically jump out of the bag on their own."

Sean wrinkled his nose like he just got the visual, and for a second, he relaxed.

Until I tapped his arm with the corner of the worn envelope. "So you got a copy of the Statesman . . . ?"

*With my wedding announcement.*

I didn't say it, but I knew where he was going—straight to the picture of me in the white dress in front of Barton Springs Country Club. The photographer had to crop out my belly to get me to agree to the session, so I remembered it well.

Sean took my hand, toying with my emerald ring. "I read your wedding announcement, and then I cut it out and read it again. And again." The column of his throat constricted as he swallowed. "Then I got shit-faced drunk. Plastered."

He paused to look at me, so I pinned on a semblance of a smile, urging him to continue. Even if this story ended with something as drastic as Sean proposing to someone else, I'd handle it.

Another sigh and he continued, "So I found myself wandering down the Champs-Élysées, drunk, and I stumbled into this gift shop. Nobody understood English. Or maybe I wasn't making any sense." His grimaced. "See, I wanted to buy you a card, but they didn't have anything that said, 'I hope your new husband dies a grizzly death,' so the salesgirl gave me that." He tipped his chin to the envelope. "Honestly, I don't remember buying it. But when I woke up the next morning it was on the nightstand."

With unsteady hands, I peeled back the flap and then took out a card with a drawing of the Eiffel Tower on the front. Inside, in bold font, was the phrase inked on Sean's chest.

*Tu me manques.*

After I tried my hand at the pronunciation, Sean laughed and then let the phrase roll off his tongue. "Tu me manques."

I ran a finger over the letters. "What does it mean?"

He took the card back. "In English, it means 'I miss you.'" He stared at the drawing on the front. "But in French, there's no such phrase, so it more closely relates to 'you are missing from me.'" Sean's eyes met mine, and he smiled. "So, I guess I wasn't as drunk as I thought. Or maybe the salesgirl was psychic. Because that's how I felt, like I was missing something." Sean laid my palm flat against the ink on his chest. "Right here."

The steady thump of his heart was the only sound in the room. In the world. And after a long moment, I crawled into his lap.

*I love you.*

The words were there, ready to break free, but instead of giving them wings, I pressed my mouth to his, and showed him in the only way I could allow.

# CHAPTER TWENTY-EIGHT

**Sean**

*T*he scene on the red carpet in front of Benny Conner's Brentwood mansion resembled a post-Grammy party, not the intimate meet and greet his PR team had described.

Flashbulbs lit up the night sky as I made my way down the rope line.

*"Sean, turn to the left!"*

*"Sean, look over here!"*

*"Can you take off your glasses."*

I did as the reporters asked, but after foregoing sleep to spend more time with Anna, followed by a bumpy flight, then an accident on the 405, I was in no mood to deal with the press. So instead, I took my time with the crowd. This much fan presence wasn't the norm, but I'd come to realize Conner Management had a method to their madness.

Since Caged was still in the courtship phase of our negotiations, our "spontaneous" appearance was calculated to gauge public interest.

It was a risk for Conner and all upside for Caged.

A favorable response assured our place on the bill, but a *very* favorable response gave the band a huge bargaining chip when it came to hashing out terms. And that's all I cared about.

If I was going to tour for a year, I wanted assurances. Time off being chief among them. No adding shows to fill the gaps. And no jetting off for a movie premier just to up our visibility. Before I stepped on a plane, the calendar would have to be set in stone. Something tangible I could bring to Anna.

She didn't trust me yet. But she loved me. I could feel her love in every touch and every smile.

That thought had me grinning like a goofy bastard.

Until I spotted Logan sauntering toward me, Kimber Tyson at his side.

*Logan and Kimber?*

Oh, the irony.

My humor faded when he coaxed her toward me, passing her off like a football.

"What the hell?" My eyes bored into Logan's as Kimber curved her arm around my waist.

"Have fun, kids." Logan smiled as he backed away. "Don't do anything I wouldn't do."

And then he was gone, strolling toward the coveted position at the head of the line where a reporter from *Rolling Stone* waited.

Instinct kicked in, and I covered Kimber's hand, hell bent on breaking free of her hold. But then pandemonium ensued, every reporter in the vicinity jockeying to get a shot of us.

I was trapped.

Pinning on a smile, I leaned close to Kimber's ear. "You mind letting go of me, sugar? I'm working here."

Flashing a row of perfect veneers, she said, "So am I."

To prove the point, Kimber popped up to kiss me.

Molding a hand to her hip to thwart the effort, I held her in place. "Why the fuck do you keep showing up when you're not invited?"

Kimber looked up at me with an adoring smile, but the affection didn't touch her eyes. "Because we've both got big things to promote. And I *was* invited."

Despite my efforts, the mask slipped, and I felt a scowl tugging my lips. Rather than lose my shit in front of everyone, I took Kimber by the arm and ushered her to the end of the rope line.

Stopping just out of earshot of the reporters, I glared down at her. "Who invited you?"

Away from the cameras, her smile withered. "It doesn't matter. Besides, it's not like it's a hardship. We've always had a good time together."

Kimber adjusted the strap on her dress, preparing for her next photo op. And I realized I was nothing more than a prop. Like her designer clutch and her thousand dollar shoes.

I was about to leave, when something caught Kimber's attention. She turned on that megawatt grin and grabbed my hand.

Reflexively, I pulled away. "I thought I made it clear, sugar. I'm not interested."

The warmth drained from Kimber's eyes. I suspected it was reflected light, reserved for those who didn't know her.

"Do you really think it matters if you're interested?" she scoffed, her New Jersey accent bleeding through. "Stop being so naïve."

Anger boiled under my skin, but I held my tongue. And then I walked away. Kimber called after me in that sugary sweet voice, but I was over it. Over her. And over this fucking party.

Spotting Ethan Bartell from *Alternative Nation* in the rope line, holding up a finger, I cringed inside.

"Sean!" He looked right at me. "A few words?"

Just walk away.

But I couldn't. So I forced a smile and ambled over. "Sure, man. Fire away."

He flipped to a blank page in the small notebook in his hand. "What can you tell us about the tour?" Ethan chuckled when I raised a brow. "Can't blame me for trying, right?"

Caged was under strict orders to maintain radio silence. And of course, Ethan knew that.

I felt a hand on my back, and the reporter's eyes lit up, a dimple winking from beneath his five o'clock shadow. "Kimber Tyson," he drawled. "What brings you out tonight?"

She anchored herself to my side, gazing up at me with that fake-as-hell smile. "I'm here to support Sean."

Catching her wrist in what probably appeared like an adoring gesture, I squeezed hard enough to get Kimber's attention. "Why don't you go get us a drink and let me take care of business. I'll see you inside."

Triumph sparkled in her sable gaze, and she skated a finger over my jaw. "Don't be long, baby."

Batting her eyelashes at Ethan's cameraman, she paused long enough for him to get a shot of her good side before strutting away.

Ethan took in every last shake of her ass. "So, you and Kimber?" He grinned. "Together again, I see."

I shook my head. "Nope. Just friends."

Ethan's attention returned to the door Kimber had just sashayed through. "I'd like to have a friend like that."

I shrugged. "Be my guest. She didn't come with me."

"But I bet she's leaving with you. Tough gig."

Assessing me with cool, gray eyes, he gauged my reaction. And I realized this was what made Ethan one of the best in the business. His ability to cut through the bullshit.

So I gave him what he wanted. The truth. "Not my kind of gig, man. I'm just here to play a little music with my band. I got a girl."

Ethan nodded slowly. "Care to spill any of the details?"

Anna's face flashed in my mind. Her pretty smile. Those emerald green eyes. And then I thought of Willow and the hold Dean had over both of them. "I'd love to, but I can't. Soon, though."

With that promise in his pocket, Ethan pumped the breaks on his interrogation and turned his questions to our upcoming performance.

Slipping back into character, I did the song and dance, praising Benny and his management team while avoiding any mention of the tour.

Once the interview was wrapped, Ethen extended his hand. "Thanks, Sean." He came in for a bro hug, and said quietly, "Keep me in mind for the exclusive when you make the tour announcement. And I'd love to hear a little more about your mystery girl."

I clapped him on the back. "Sure thing."

After saying my goodbyes, I waved to the crowd and then marched straight to the staging area where the rest of the guys waited in front of the big Conner Productions sign.

Throwing an arm around Logan's shoulder, I snarled, "What the fuck was that all about?"

"Not now," he replied through a pearly white smile. "Later."

"Fuck your later." My tone rose along with my frustration. "I want to know what you're trying to prove."

"Dude, I don't have to prove anything." Logan's frosty eyes met mine, a caustic smile painting his lips. "Your arm around Kimber's waist said it all."

Applause and calls for an encore rang in the air as I pushed away from my kit. Ignoring the loudest request—from Benny's table—I made a beeline for center stage and Logan.

My fingers curled around his upper arm. "It's later."

He didn't move, but his bicep twitched in warning. "Unless you want me to break that fucking hand, you'll remove it."

The crew for the next band took the stage, unplugging amps and tearing down equipment. Since the drums weren't mine, I had nothing keeping me here except Logan and my fury.

An hour behind the drums should've burned off my anger, but if anything, I was more enraged.

Cameron forced his way between us, a fake laugh rumbling from his chest. "Whoa, what's going on here?"

Logan snorted, then ran a hand through his hair. "Ask Romeo. I've got some business to attend to."

He sauntered to Conner's table, and the two men hugged it out like they were old friends.

Cameron raised his eyebrow at me in a silent question, then looked down at my hand, balled into a fist at my side.

Yeah, no. This wasn't good. For any of us.

"I'm out," I said. "See you at the shoot in the morning."

Blind rage rolled through me as I elbowed my way through the crowd.

*Get a grip.*

Since the only thing I wanted to grip was Logan's throat, I put my head down. When I ran straight into a warm body, I lifted my gaze to apologize and came face-to-face with Kimber.

"You ready, baby?" she purred.

She'd parked herself near a crowd at the door. Several people hovered nearby, holding drinks and feigning interest in their conversations, but really, their eyes and ears were on us.

Benny wasn't the only fish in this pond. Representatives from our label, gossip columnists, bloggers—all the players were out tonight.

I let out a slow breath. "I'm going back to the hotel. See you later."

Kimber grabbed my arm. "You read my mind."

Lowering my voice, I tipped forward into her space. "Not going to happen, Kimber."

That triumphant smile I saw earlier curved her lips. She knew damn well I'd never mow her down with a camera crew mere feet away.

Pressing my lips together, I barreled out the door with Kimber in tow.

With my height advantage and her five-inch heels, I figured I'd lose her. But no, she matched me stride for stride.

At the edge of the long driveway, I came to an abrupt stop at the door to my limo.

Shaking Kimber's arm off, I said, "Fun and games are over. Go back to the party. And take your cameras with you."

She fisted my shirt, hanging on for dear life as I planted one foot inside the car.

"Fun and games." Kimber licked her lips. "I like where you're going with that."

When I didn't respond, she dropped her hand along with the seduction façade. The lights from the video cameras went dark, and the head of her crew sighed in annoyance.

"This is going nowhere," he said to Kimber. "I'm going back to get some interiors. See you in there?"

She nodded, her eyes frigid.

As soon as the crew was out of earshot, she propped a hand on her hip. "Is there some reason you're making this difficult?"

Resisting the urge to roll my eyes, I slid onto the leather seat. "There is no 'this,' sugar. Never will be."

Kimber grabbed the door. "What the fuck is your problem?"

"At the moment, you. Now step back."

She searched my face, her eyes boring into mine. "You are an asshole, you know that?"

"Yep."

I slammed the door on Kimber's next insult. The driver met my gaze in the mirror. He wore and indifferent smile like he'd seen it all before. "Where to, sir?"

I grabbed a bottle of Jack and an empty glass from the minibar. "Hotel."

Thirty minutes later, I exited the limo in front of the Chateau Marmont, the bottle of whiskey tucked under my arm.

Skirting the usual crowd of gawkers in the lobby, I stopped by the gift shop for a pack of smokes. And then I marched straight to my bungalow, through the cozy living room, and out the sliding glass door to the patio that connected Logan's room with mine.

Sinking into one of the retro chic chairs, I lit my cigarette. My eyes closed as I rolled the smoke around my mouth. It tasted fucking awful in the best possible way. Like my best friend and worst enemy. I took a slug of whiskey to mute the flavor of ash on my tongue. And I waited.

Three hours later a light flicked on inside Logan's bungalow.

A white cloud hung over my head from the dozen butts littering the ashtray.

Logan eyed me as he slid the heavy patio door across the track. And then without a word, he retreated, leaving the sheer curtain to flutter in the balmy California breeze.

I sucked down the last of the Jack, then jumped to my feet and stalked after him. "What the fuck is the matter with you?!"

Logan dropped his key on the table. "You want a beer?"

Lunging, I grabbed his collar. "Don't fucking walk away from me. I asked you a question."

Eyes on mine, Logan latched onto my wrist and twisted just enough to show me he wasn't playing. "I ain't walking away from nobody. I'm getting a beer. Do. You. Want. One?'

"Does it look like I'm here to socialize?"

Logan ambled to the fridge where he grabbed two bottles.

Sliding a Pale Ale in front of me, he said, "I saw you leave with Kimber. Why the hell are you here?"

His fingers coiled tightly around the beer as he took a swallow. Yeah, he was ready to go. And I was just mad enough or drunk enough to unleash that part of him that might land me in the hospital.

Not that I couldn't fight. Hell, I could brawl with the best of them. But Logan had trained at the feet of the master—his old man. Jake Cage was a mean son of a bitch with a foul temper. It took Logan seventeen years to best him, but I was there the night he did.

A memory of Logan's bloody face and vacant eyes stole some of my anger.

Ripping a hand through my hair, I dropped onto the barstool. "Kimber had a fucking camera crew with her. Did you realize that?"

Logan leaned a hip against the counter. "So, did they cockblock you or is there a sex tape in the offing?" He smirked. "I'm guessing the former based on your temperament. Shake it off; there's a lobby full of willing pussy downstairs."

My brows drew together. "I'm with Anna. You know that."

Logan snorted. "That didn't stop you from fucking Darcy, now did it?"

Years' worth of pent-up hostility and resentment shone in his eyes. Amazing that I'd never seen it before.

"That was a mistake."

Disgust curled Logan's lip as he took another swallow. "Yeah, whatever."

Crossing my arms over my chest, I narrowed my gaze. "For someone who claims to care so much, it seems like you don't give a shit if Anna gets hurt."

Logan's bottle met the bottom of the stainless-steel sink with a loud crash. "Don't you fucking lecture me about hurting Anna. You disappeared for four fucking years, leaving her to raise a kid by herself." He jabbed his finger into my chest. "You—not me."

I searched his eyes, unflinching. "Did you know about my kid?"

"No, dude, I didn't. But even if I had, I probably wouldn't have said anything. You dumped Anna and never looked back. I don't want to see the kid's face when you decide to do it again."

Pain radiated up my arm when I landed the blow to Logan's cheek. Surprisingly, the shot to his nose left only a slight tingling in my fingers. And the counter punch he landed on my mouth? I didn't feel it at all.

The blow stunned me, though, knocked me back, giving him enough time to charge.

We tumbled to the ground, taking out the coffee table on our way down.

Pinning me on the hardwood floor, Logan wedged his forearm against my windpipe.

Kicking hard to gain purchase, I clawed at his arm. "Get the fuck off me!" I choked out.

"Now, now, you started it." A maniacal smile spread across his lips as a thick scarlet stream dripped from his nostrils. "So why don't you answer me a question: how bad you want me to hurt you?"

"Fuck you," I spat, spewing droplets of blood onto his T-shirt. "I'll fucking kill you."

Barking out a laugh, Logan rolled off me. "That's cute. I think we both know that ain't about to happen."

Fighting to drag air into my burning lungs, I sat up.

On the other hand, Logan's breathing remained slow and even, and despite the blood streaming freely from his nose and the gash on his cheek, he reclined on his elbows and stretched out like he was getting ready for a nap.

"You know," he began, "if a bloody nose or a black eye is what it's gonna take to get you to listen, that's fine."

I wiped my lip on my shoulder, trying not to wince. "What makes you think I'd give two fucks about anything you've got to tell me?"

Logan sighed. "'Cause I'm your best friend. And I know you. It's not that I don't think you're going to step up and take care of the kid. That's the easy part. You throw a couple of bucks her way, visit when you can—you're golden. It's the rest of it you're gonna struggle with."

Pain shot from my throbbing hand to my elbow as I flexed my fingers. "You don't know that."

"I know what I saw. And honestly? I kinda fucking respected you for breaking it off clean. But now you're trying to play happy family, and we both know you were never good enough for Annabelle. Not then, and not now. No matter how many willow trees you plant in your yard or paint on your arm."

A ripple spread from his pupils, rolling over his pale blue irises. He believed it, this shit he was spouting.

Staggering to my feet, I loomed over him, fists clenched at my sides. "I was with Anna for years, and I never looked at another woman." Acknowledging his cocked brow, I heaved a sigh. "Fine, maybe I looked. But I never acted on it. Just that one fucking time."

Logan snorted again, and a fresh rivulet of blood joined the tributary leaking from his nose. "Once is all it takes."

The fury clouding my perception burned away like fog, and I saw Logan clearly for the first time in weeks. Maybe years.

"Is this about my mistake, or yours?" His grin faded to a blank stare. "Maybe you're just salty because there's nobody coming to give you a second chance." The voice in my head blasted a warning as I pushed us past the choppy waters and into the eye of the hurricane. "You heard from Laurel lately, bro?"

This time I didn't need to look for a ripple. At the mention of his sister, a twenty-foot wave crested in Logan's eyes.

It'd been ten years since child protective services took Laurel away. Logan spent weeks looking for her, asking about her, nosing around in every group home in the city. When he came up empty, he never spoke of her again. And from the look on his face, he wasn't going to start now.

"Is that your ace in the hole?" Logan mumbled, averting his gaze. "Because you're going to have to do better than that."

There was nothing better than that. I'd ripped his still-beating heart from his chest. Which was only fair since he'd done the same to me.

Glass crunched under my feet as I walked toward the back door, leaving my best friend to deal with the wreckage of his past.

Inside my bungalow, I flopped onto the bed with the phone in my hand.

A half hour later, I was still staring at the empty box next to Anna's name, trying to think of one good thing to tell her.

Finding nothing, I went in search of some ice for my swollen knuckles.

# CHAPTER TWENTY-NINE

**Sean**

*S*hifting in the canvas chair, I glanced at my reflection in the mirror. The harsh lights in the dressing room weren't doing me any favors.

The makeup artist winced as she applied balm to my swollen lip. "Sorry."

I shrugged, too tired to care. "No worries."

Her cheeks warmed to a rosy pink as her fingertips grazed the angry contusion on my neck. "This looks painful." She rushed to apply powder to the dark purple bruise. "I don't think I can cover it completely."

"It's fine, sug—" I caught myself before the endearment tripped fully from my lips. All part of the new leaf I was turning over. "Do the best you can."

Across the room, Logan sat with his back to me, another member of the team trying valiantly to cover his battle wounds.

When our gazes collided in the mirror, his lips tipped upward at the corners in his trademark smirk. Taking the olive branch, I gave him a small nod.

Neither of us was likely to proffer an apology. And that was fine for now.

A smartly dressed blonde swept through the door. "We're going to need the room," she barked without looking up from her iPad.

Relieved, I pushed out of my chair. In less than twenty-four hours my nicotine craving had returned with a vengeance.

I tipped my chin at Cameron. "I'm going to go grab a smoke."

Blondie caught my arm as I made for the door. "Not you." Her slate gray eyes shifted to Logan. "Or you."

The four makeup artists scurried away like mice with their caddies in tow. Christian and Cameron weren't so easily commanded. They joined Logan and me, standing awkwardly with our hands in our pockets.

"If you two would excuse us," Blondie said to Cam and Christian.

Cameron shrugged. "Depends on who you are."

She pursed her lips, obviously unaccustomed to being questioned. With a sharp exhale, she held out her hand for Cam to shake. "Olivia Block, Conner Public Relations Management Team, West Coast."

"That's a mouthful," Christian muttered as he scrolled through his phone. "Do you have a card or something?"

Olivia cocked her head. "Excuse me, Cameron, is it?"

That caught his attention.

"You're with the public relations team, and you can't even tell us apart?" Glancing at Logan, Christian said blandly, "That inspires confidence."

Any response was drowned out by the flurry of activity when Benny Conner strode in, jabbering into his Bluetooth.

Olivia straightened up like she was preparing for inspection.

Wrapping up the call, Benny tapped his earpiece. "How's everyone doing today?"

"Hi, Benny," Olivia interjected, an eager smile curving her lips. "I was about to go over the schedule."

"Liv, if you wouldn't mind showing Cameron and Christian to the dining room." Sinking onto the leather sofa, Benny addressed my bandmates. "Our chef makes a mean ahi tuna steak. To die for."

Benny looked down and brushed a hand over his tie. I got the feeling if Cameron and Christian declined, he had no problem telling them to wait in the bathroom.

Olivia blinked. "Benny . . . are you sure . . . ?"

He lifted his gaze without moving his head, and Olivia swallowed. "Of course. This way, gentleman."

Reluctantly, Cameron and Christian followed her out the door.

We were supposed to be on camera in thirty minutes with the host of Entertainment Tonight. Since Logan and I looked more prepared to shoot a promo for a *Fight Club* reboot, it was safe to assume that wasn't going to happen.

Benny stretched his arm over the back of the couch, amused. "I heard all the rumors about you boys before I ever took a look at your band." A thick New York accent etched his tone. "Lindsey Barger is a well-respected manager in this town, and she said you were trouble. But I don't give a fuck about rumors. What I care about is dissension in the ranks. You want to tell me what the hell happened last night?"

Adopting a casual posture, Logan dropped into the canvas chair. "What makes you think there's any dissension?"

Logan's blue eyes shifted to mine, and noting the silent plea behind the bravado, I ambled to his side.

The promoter tipped forward, elbows on his knees. "For one, you made kindling out of the antique table in Logan's bungalow. Add to that your beat-to-shit faces, and I put two and two together."

Logan didn't respond, setting his jaw and staring at his boots.

It was safer to pick up the slack than risk letting Benny ignite Logan's short fuse, so I said casually, "That wasn't a beef, Benny. That was Tuesday. I've known Logan all my life. Sometimes things get heated. Doesn't mean shit."

The tension ebbed from Benny's face but didn't recede entirely. "So, you're telling me that this was all just a squabble between friends?"

"Best friends," Logan said flatly, "Or else Sean over here wouldn't be standing. Know what I mean?"

I barked out a laugh. "Your confidence is astounding, asshat, considering that shiner you're sporting."

Logan shrugged. "Lucky shot."

Benny shoved to his feet, mollified. He didn't notice the strain in our exchange, but then, why would he?

"Typical Sixth Street band," the promoter said with a smile. "You guys are all the same. Work hard, play hard, fight hard. Conner Productions made Damaged a household name with their first tour. I've seen a couple of black eyes and trashed hotel rooms."

Logan and I sat up straighter, waiting for Benny to elaborate. He didn't.

Instead, he leveled a serious gaze and said, "I'm not likely to put up with that shit from you guys. Keep it off my tour. Are we clear?"

Logan accepted Benny's outstretched hand. "Crystal."

I nodded. "Absolutely."

Benny sighed, rubbing his fingers over his mouth. "Since you two look like you met the business end of a billy club, I'm sending you home. Put some ice on your faces. I'll see you back here in a week or so to discuss terms."

And then he was gone, barking into his Bluetooth before the door clicked shut behind him.

Logan gave me a sidelong glance. "I guess that means we're in."

My stomach tightened, but I wasn't sure it was from excitement. "Looks that way."

After gathering our things, we headed for the dining room to pick up the guys.

In the elevator, Logan asked, "Are we good, bro?"

I liberated my lucky drumsticks from my pocket, stroking my thumb over the *A* carved into the base.

We weren't good. Not even close.

"Yeah, man. We're fine."

Logan examined his reflection in the shiny doors. "Shit, I'm too pretty to be this banged up. I hope my face heals by next week."

He shoved his sunglasses on the bridge of his nose.

"Me too."

Staring at the floor, I hid my eyes. Or the lie behind them. The bruises were a reprieve. A stay of execution. And the longer the evidence stayed on my skin, the more time I'd have with Anna and Willow.

# CHAPTER THIRTY

Anna

*I* sighed into the phone, one eye on Willow as she sat on top of the large granite island in Sean's kitchen, scrupulously sorting vegetables for our salad.

"Are you even listening to me, Anna?" Peyton's voice boomed in my ear.

Honestly, I wasn't. My best friend had been droning on for fifteen minutes, peppering me with questions about my plans. And really, I didn't have any.

Something had shifted yesterday morning before Sean left. The way he'd looked at me, touched me as he moved inside me.

And that damned card.

*Tu me manques.*

You're missing from me.

The phrase rolled around in my brain.

"Anna?" Peyton prompted, growling her discontent.

"I'm listening," I lied, turning my attention to the pot of marinara simmering on the stove. "I just don't see why you're pushing this so hard. I mean, with everything going on with Dean, and now Melissa, I haven't had time to think about moving."

Peyton went silent for a long, uncomfortable moment. "Have you heard from Sean today?"

My skin prickled, because, no, I hadn't heard from Sean. Not since his plane landed.

"He had that party last night at Benny's and then a bunch of press engagements today." My tone held more bite than expected, and I mentally chastised myself. "He's busy."

More silence, and goose bumps rose on my arms.

I looked up at the air conditioning vent above the stove, but it wasn't that.

Closing my eyes, I asked, "What aren't you telling me, Pey?"

I could hear her shifting, grappling with whatever she needed to tell me.

"I have something to show you," she finally said. "Don't freak out."

Well, that didn't sound good.

I took a deep breath. "I won't."

When my phone beeped with an incoming text, I pulled the device from my ear and stared at Peyton's message. Enlarging the thumbnail, I swallowed hard when a photo of Sean and that reality star, Kimber Tyson, populated the screen.

They were smiling. Happy.

After scrutinizing the picture for much longer than necessary, my attention slid to Willow. The urge to grab my daughter, our belongings, and the last scrap of my dignity almost sent me running for the door.

But then I heard Peyton calling my name over and over.

I put her on speaker.

"He was at a party," I said listlessly. "It's his job."

The minute the excuse tumbled out, I shuddered. Because I knew I'd always make excuses.

*Don't you want more for your daughter?*

Dean's words trickled through my brain as Peyton sighed. They pitied me, both of them.

Dragging a wooden spoon through my spaghetti sauce, I said quietly, "I'll meet you tomorrow morning, and we'll go look at that apartment by the bridge." A sharp pain corkscrewed through my chest. "I've got to drain the noodles now. I'll call you later."

Without waiting for her reply, I disconnected the call. I wasn't mad at Peyton, just disappointed in myself. A week in Sean's house and the wall encasing my heart had started to crumble, leaving me vulnerable. Exposed.

I had to think about Willow.

If I allowed the man I loved to run around with other women, so would she one day.

With a sigh, I switched on the boom box. Music throbbed from the speaker, and Willow's foot began to rock.

*So much like her father.*

I returned to my cooking, and a moment later a strong arm banded around my waist. Frozen with fear, all I heard over the blood rushing to my head was a low rumble. "Fuck, baby—"

I howled, jabbing my elbow into the intruder's stomach. When I spun around, wielding the spoon like a Samurai sword, I met Sean's azure gaze. He clutched his ribs, feigning an injury. Willow giggled but I wasn't amused.

"What the hell, Sean?" I dropped the weapon, splashing marinara all over the floor. "What are you doing here?"

I pressed my lips into a firm line when I realized how that sounded. This was his house, not mine.

Sean chuckled. "Getting my ass kicked, apparently."

As he crouched to pick up the fallen utensil, he swiped a finger over a glob of sauce resting on the top of my foot. With a seductive glint in his eyes, he rose to his full height and made a show of licking the red goop from his thumb. Which naturally drew my attention to his split lip and the bruise on his cheek.

My hand flew to his face. "What happened to you?"

He seemed shocked by the question, but when my fingers skated over the tender flesh, he winced.

"Just a little accident." He shrugged. "It's nothing."

Sean held my gaze and then slowly, deliberately, shifted his focus to Willow who was taking in the scene with curious blue eyes.

Capturing my hand, Sean kissed my palm. "Later, okay?" His lips traveled to my wrist where he pressed another kiss over my pulse point.

The intensity in his stare and the tenderness in his touch wore me down. "Okay."

As soon as our contact was broken, my anger returned. I shut off the music, then lifted Willow from her spot.

"Dinner's ready," I mumbled. "I have to feed her."

Sean blocked my path. "You set the table, and we'll go wash up."

He held his arms out for our daughter, and though every instinct told me to deny him, I couldn't. Willow was his. And regardless of what he felt or didn't feel for me, she wasn't a pawn to be used as punishment.

Not that I could.

The little traitor was squirming in my arms, reaching for her daddy with a smile.

Reluctantly, I handed her over. "You do that."

Striding out of the room, he cooed to our little girl while I sorted through the silverware drawer, fighting the tears lining my eyes.

# CHAPTER THIRTY-ONE

**Sean**

*A*t the archway to the kitchen, I paused to glance at Anna. Shoulders curved inward and head bowed, she stood at the counter with her back to me. She didn't look up even though I could tell she knew I was there.

Clearly, she was pissed. And yeah, I should've called. Should've texted. Something.

I was about to double back, take Anna in my arms and explain the whole fucking mess when Willow laid her head on my shoulder. Once I brushed my nose over her coppery curls, inhaling her sweet baby scent, my problems melted into the background.

"How was your day, Willow-baby?"

She shimmied down my legs and landed in front of the pedestal sink, a little cough erupting from her chest. "Goo."

I crouched behind her to turn on the faucet. "Did you have fun at school?"

Nodding, she squirted soap into her hand as another cough rattled her tiny frame. And then another.

Spluttering, she whirled around, eyes wide. "M-ma."

My heart stalled, and I took her by the shoulders. "Willow, what is it?"

Wheezing, she fisted my T-shirt with a soapy hand. "M-ma."

Scooping her up, I hopped to my feet. The rattle in her chest was more pronounced, like thunder against my skin. "Hold on, baby."

I flung the door open, colliding with Anna.

"Something's wrong . . . She can't breathe. I don't know what happened."

Anna took Willow from my arms. "Calm down, Sean," she snapped, her eyes locked on mine as she sank onto the travertine floor. "Don't panic. *Never* panic."

Panic didn't begin to describe what I felt. Ripping a hand through my hair, I watched the scene unfold, helpless.

Anna dug around in her pocket while Willow flailed on the floor like a fish out of water. "It's okay, baby." Producing one of the magic silver cylinders, Anna yanked the cap off with her teeth, then held the inhaler to Willow's lips. "Big breath."

Willow squirmed, fighting her mother every step of the way.

I sank to my knees beside my girls. "Tell me what to do."

Anna outmaneuvered Willow's hands. "Nothing. She just needs her medicine." Pressing the inhaler to Willow's lips once again, she cupped her cherub cheek. "You gotta breathe for Mommy. Now. Big breath."

Willow stopped squirming, her blue eyes wild with fear.

Unable to take it anymore, I focused on Anna. The firm set of her jaw. The determination in her eyes. The reassuring smile on her lips.

*How in the fuck was she so calm?*

"That's it," Anna soothed. "Big breath. One . . . two . . . three . . ."

I counted along, my lungs expanding when the inhaler released its life-saving mist.

Anna dropped the cylinder, and it fell to the floor, rolling to a stop in front of me. I picked up the tube and stared at it, dazed.

When I looked up, Willow was in her mother's arms.

"It's all right," Anna cooed to our daughter, her palm flat on the baby's chest. "You're okay."

I blinked at Anna, because holy fuck, she'd done it. She'd saved Willow.

After a long moment, I helped her to her feet. "Should I call anyone?"

My voice was hollow, weak. And I fucking hated it. I'd give anything to protect them. And I couldn't.

Anna smiled at me, her eyes soft. "For what? It's over." She motioned to the stairs. "Come on."

Chilled by the sweat soaking my T-shirt, I trudged along behind them.

Anna laid Willow on the comforter while I just stood there and watched. A machine whirred to life, and I recognized the little blue penguin from that first night in Willow's room. The nebulizer.

Anna secured the mask over Willow's nose and mouth and then settled against the headboard with the baby resting in her arms.

"She's fine," Anna assured me. "Why don't you go get something to eat?"

*Was she serious?*

Dropping like a stone onto the side of the bed, I cleared my throat. "I'm not hungry."

Propping my elbows on my knees with my hands clasped in front of me, I waited. For what I wasn't sure.

The end of the world?

Anna nudged me with her foot.

Tearing my attention from Willow, I blinked at her. "What . . . what do you need?"

Another smile. "There's no way I can put her to bed with you in here. The minute I take this mask off she'll be all over you. Go get something to eat. Everything's fine. I promise."

A mild protest lodged in my throat. But looking into Willow's heavy-lidded blue eyes, I held it back when my baby smiled a sleepy smile.

"Are you sure I can't do anything?"

Anna shook her head, so I got up, knees knocking and stomach pitching. It felt like I was on a boat in the middle of the ocean.

"Night, Willow-baby," I whispered.

And then against every instinct, I left the room.

As I padded down the stairs to grab my suitcase, the smell of Anna's spaghetti wafted from the kitchen. My stomach growled, but the thought of food was unimaginable.

After checking the burners on the stove, I turned out the lights, grabbed my bag from the foyer, and then headed to my bedroom.

Sagging on the couch, I stared at the ceiling, making mental notes of everything we needed. An intercom in every room. A private nurse. No, a live-in nurse.

About an hour later Anna slipped through the door, and I bolted straight up. "Is she all right?"

Anna nodded and took a seat on the opposite end of the sofa, the baby monitor in her hand. "She's fine. Asleep."

Nothing felt fine. In fact, something was way the fuck off. Anna wouldn't even look at me.

"Are you sure?"

"Positive."

I closed the gap between us, but Anna sank farther into the corner of the couch and looked at me. "How was your party?"

I chuckled, probably from exhaustion, though I could feel the adrenaline coursing through my veins.

"It sucked." Dropping my head back, I closed my eyes. "There was this girl I used to . . ."

"Fuck" was accurate, but I wasn't going there.

I lost my train of thought, jerking to attention when the cushions dipped.

Anna gazed down at me with cold eyes. "I don't need to hear your confession, Sean. You don't owe me an explanation."

"Whoa." Grabbing her hips, I tugged until she relented and shuffled between my knees. "In order to confess, I'd need to have done something wrong." Anna's expression was dubious, so I continued,

"Kimber . . . that's the girl's name, was only there for a photo op. She didn't come with me if that's what you're thinking."

Folding her arms over her middle, Anna nodded. "Okay."

I pulled her a little closer. "You don't believe me?"

Her lips parted as if to answer, but then she cocked her head. "Were you smoking?" Her attention shifted to my plain white T-shirt, and before I could answer, she plucked the Marlboros from my pocket. "You *were* smoking."

She held the red and white box in her open palm, staring at it like she'd just discovered a murder weapon.

"Yeah, I picked up a pack after the show. I just had a couple." A couple of dozen, but that wasn't the point. "It's not a regular thing."

She threw the pack at my chest. "You can't smoke."

I'd never taken well to demands, even from Anna.

"Can't?" I blew out an annoyed breath. "I get it, smoking kills. I've read the warning label."

Anna grabbed the baby monitor and turned on her heel.

Bolting to my feet, I overtook her in seconds, caging her against the door. "If it's a problem for you. I'll stop."

"It's not my problem," Anna said quietly. "Cigarettes cause asthma attacks. Willow can't be around smoke."

My heart took residence in my throat. "What? Are you saying . . ."

Anna was out the door before I could finish the thought, confirming my suspicion. I caused this.

Picturing Willow on the floor, I braced a hand on the wall to keep from falling over.

I'd smoked thousands of cigarettes in my life, my first just one room away from my mother, dying of cancer at the time. Even my own collision course with the disease never gave me pause. But right now, the faint scent of ash on my shirt was enough to make me want to puke.

Fighting the bile rising in my throat, I dragged my suitcase to my closet and then dumped the contents into the hamper. I stripped off my clothes, tossing the offending garments on top of the pile. If smoke weren't an issue, I'd burn the heap.

Inside the bathroom, I gazed at my reflection in the mirror. Bruises, bloodshot eyes and a crease between my brows so deep you could park a car in it.

When I couldn't stand the sight of myself a minute longer, I stepped inside the shower. Steam rose and I struggled to catch my breath.

Turning the faucet to the left, the shock from the blast of cold water forced air into my lungs.

If only it were that easy for my daughter.

Some minutes later, Anna nudged me aside. "Why are you standing in the cold?"

Frigid water seemed like a small penance for nearly killing my kid.

Pinning on a smile, I wrapped Anna in my arms and reversed our positions to block the stream since she was already shivering. "Didn't know you'd be joining me, baby."

A frown tugged her lips. "I'm sorry, Sean. I was just . . ." She focused on the soap dish. "I was mad about the girl."

*The girl?*

And then I remembered the conversation I'd started before our talk about the cigarettes. "Kimber?"

Anna nodded.

I sighed and turned off the water.

Sliding my hands to Anna's hips, I walked us backward to the stone bench. I took a seat and then searched for her eyes. "Look at me, baby."

When she didn't comply, I continued, "I told you nothing happened with Kimber. She just showed up." Delicately side-stepping the issue of Logan's part in the debacle, I pulled her closer. She looked at me then, her gaze so wounded and mistrustful, I shuddered inside. "Anna-baby, I love you. Don't you know that?"

Her brows dove together. "Then why didn't you call me?"

*Why didn't I?*

"'Cause I'm a fucking moron sometimes," I admitted. "It was a bad night, and I didn't have anything good to say."

"So you didn't get the offer from Conner?"

I heaved a breath, my mind all over the place. Surprisingly, none of my thoughts concerned the band.

"Uh, yeah, I think Conner's going to make an offer. We'll know next week."

"Then how did your night turn out so bad?" Anna's eyes flicked to my busted lip and further down to the bruise on my neck. "You seemed to be having a good time in the pictures I saw."

Pictures? Of course there were pictures.

"I know what it must've looked like." I pressed a kiss to her chest, right below the hollow of her throat. "But nothing happened. Kimber just showed up on the red carpet."

Half-truths—were they as bad as a lie? Probably, the voice in my head warned.

"Maybe I overreacted," Anna conceded, and fuck, that made me feel worse.

Banding my arms around her waist, I looked into her eyes. "Don't. It was my fault. I didn't call." I blew out a breath. "And then I almost put our kid in the hospital."

Anna sloughed off my hands and then backed away. And who could blame her?

"It wasn't a serious attack, Sean, and you didn't put her in the hospital. But I have."

She dropped her gaze at my stunned expression.

"When?" I croaked.

"A couple years ago. Cold air can trigger an attack. I p-put her in the car seat, and I was late." She winced. "It wasn't that cold. I didn't think it was that cold. But she had an attack on I35." Tears flooded Anna's eyes, and she slid down the wall, landing with a splat. "She spent thirty hours in the hospital. I know, because I counted."

I joined her on the floor, the pebbled tiling digging into my knees as I crawled to her side. "Was that supposed to make me feel better or worse?"

The corner of Anna's lips ticked up. "I don't know. I just wanted you to understand that things happen. Even to me. And I was more pissed at myself about the smoking thing than you."

I laced our fingers. "Why?"

"Because I didn't notice the smell when you walked in. Maybe because you, I mean we, used to smoke. I would've picked it up on anyone else, but you just smelled like you."

I laughed. "So you smell like peaches, and what, I smell like an ashtray?"

Laying her head on my shoulder, she sighed. "No. You smell like a memory. Another life."

Anna's sweet nostalgia tore through me like a hollow point bullet, exploding in my chest. Because I didn't want to be a memory. I wanted a foothold in this life, the one she shared with Willow.

I settled her onto my lap, and she looked up at me and asked, "So, are we just going to sit in here all night?"

I kissed her shoulder, skimming my hand up her thigh. "No." My mouth moved to her ear as I reached between her legs, my fingers creeping toward her sweet pussy. "But I am going to fuck you in here. And when we're finished you're going to tell me all about Willow's asthma. So I'll know exactly what to do when this shit happens again."

# CHAPTER THIRTY-TWO

Anna

*L*ight poured through the window, a yellow haze settling on Willow's side of the bed. My heart slammed against my ribs when all I saw was rumpled sheets where my daughter should've been sleeping. But then I heard a giggle drift up from somewhere in the house, followed by Lola's voice.

Surmising that Sean must've taken Willow downstairs for breakfast, I wilted against the pillow to catch my breath. I was so used to doing everything on my own, I wasn't sure what to make of all this help.

Still, I was exhausted, so I wouldn't turn it down.

As promised, Sean'd fucked me into oblivion last night and then instead of letting me sleep off the euphoric bliss, he proceeded to ask me every question known to man about Willow's condition.

Rolling onto my side, I pulled the covers to my chin, intent on catching an hour of sleep.

My phone rattled violently against the nightstand, and I groaned, reaching for the device without opening my eyes. "Hello?"

"Anna . . . It's Trevor."

My heavy lids popped open. I hadn't seen Trevor in over a year. In fact, I'd avoided him whenever possible after I'd married Dean.

"Hey, Trev."

I pinched the bridge of my nose, chiding myself for the informality. Trevor was Sean's friend, not mine. I zipped my lip.

After a beat, Trevor sighed. "This is awkward, huh?"

Since I didn't know what "this" was, I mumbled something noncommittal and sat up.

"Sean asked me to call," Trevor said, sounding unsure of himself.

Suspicion churned in my gut, and I swung my legs over the side of the bed.

"Really? Why's that?"

Another long pause. "I'm just going to cut to the chase. I have a couple of names of attorneys that specialize in family law. You know how lawyers don't like to go head-to-head with each other. But these guys aren't afraid of Dean, and none of them have a conflict with the attorney Sean hired."

My suspicion moved north, and a lump formed in my throat. "Sean has an attorney?"

A string of muttered curses from Trevor followed by more silence from me. He finally blew out a breath. "Yes, Sean hired an attorney. I thought he'd tell you. But you don't need to worry."

Oh, but I *was* worried.

Trevor was using his lawyerly tone with me. The calm, courtroom demeanor that we were taught to adopt our first day of law school.

I could play that game too. But my weapon of choice was silence. People hated it, and it usually led to someone spilling their guts.

In less than thirty seconds, Trevor folded. "Christ, Anna, will you just check out the names? Find someone you feel comfortable with? Sean wants to make sure you've got proper representation."

My breath hitched. "Representation?"

Trevor quickly jumped to assuage my fears. "For your divorce. Sean wants you to have the best. He's paying for it, of course."

*Of course.*

Sean was paying for it, but he didn't *tell* me about it.

Closing my eyes, I loosened my grip on the phone. "Peyton's my lawyer."

"Are you sure that's wise? I mean, Peyton's great, but she practices corporate law."

Up until Dean showed up at the hospital, it never occurred to me that our divorce would be anything but civil. Now, I wasn't so sure.

"It's all good, Trev." I willed my voice to stay even. Calm, just like his. "Dean's not going to cause any problems." Trevor's silence told me he wasn't convinced, but before he could mount an offensive, I said, "I've got it covered."

Trevor let out a resigned sigh but didn't push.

We talked for a few more minutes, catching up, and then I ended the call. I tumbled into the chair facing the window, ready to send Peyton a text.

That's when I saw Sean sitting beside Willow on the deck, his long legs crisscrossed in what had to be an uncomfortable position. But the look on his face, the mixture of pride and unconditional love as he watched Willow, it melted my heart.

*He's got a lawyer.*

The thought hung over me like a dark, ominous cloud, crowding out everything else. Before I gave into the feelings of gloom, I pushed to my feet, resolute. I plucked a cheery sundress from my suitcase and then headed to the bathroom to shower so I could meet Peyton. And look at that apartment by the bridge she kept talking about.

# CHAPTER THIRTY-THREE

**Sean**

*I* kissed Willow on the top of her head, then left her to play with Barbie and her Dreamhouse at the edge of the deck.

Noting a missed call from Melissa, I dropped into the patio chair under the umbrella and hit redial.

"Hey sugar," Melissa said. "You called?"

"Yeah, I was just checking to see when the, um . . ." Words like mastectomy and chemo didn't belong in the English language, so my tongue refused to comply. "Thing is scheduled for."

Melissa snorted. "The 'thing' where they cut off my boobs and then pump me full of chemicals to kill off the cancer?"

Considering Melissa had never gone for any tests, never had her yearly exams, and not a fuck was given about our family history, her jokes fell on deaf ears. I might not be able to say the words, but I wasn't the only one avoiding.

"Yeah, that."

"Two weeks from next Thursday. The oncologist sent my PET scan for a second opinion."

My shoulders tensed, and I rolled my head from side to side to relieve the pressure. "PET scan? Sounds like something they give a dog."

Melissa laughed. "It's a full body scan. They're going to try and schedule my next surgery in a couple of months."

Spots danced at the corners of my eyes. "Next surgery? Why would you need another surgery?"

"Sean . . ."

Disappointment laced Melissa's tone. She'd sent me the information about her treatment, but I'd yet to open the email.

Since she had no room to lecture, I ignored her censure.

"So, two weeks from next Thursday, huh?" Roughing a hand down my face, I wondered where in the fuck I'd be two weeks from next Thursday. Here, I realized. "Okay, I'll be there."

Anna stepped onto the deck, smoothing the front of her white, eyelet sundress. Her auburn hair was back in a messy bun, and she was wearing makeup. My already queasy stomach somersaulted.

"Sugar, I don't want you to put yourself out," Melissa said as I watched Anna take a seat across from me.

"I really don't care what you want, Lissa." My tone held sincerity and warmth, but Anna cocked her head. I smiled and threw her a wink. "I'm going to be there."

Melissa sighed. "If that's what you want, I guess I can't stop you."

There was no mistaking the smile in her voice, the pride. Since I wanted to end things on a good note and find out why the hell my girl was up and dressed at 9:00 a.m., I quickly said goodbye and ended the call.

"Morning, baby," I said as I poured Anna a cup of coffee from the french press. "You're up early."

Out of the corner of my eye, I spotted a brochure peeking from her tote. Shiny images of the Colorado River and the 360 Bridge. *Lake View Townhomes.*

Anna squinted, looking out at the water. "Trevor called. He said you wanted him to give me some names of divorce lawyers."

Anna was easier to read when she was agitated. Like now.

Proceeding with caution, I surveyed her over the rim of my cup as I took a drink. "I did."

Her eyes blazed when she turned, the emerald hue dark with irritation. "What makes you think I need an attorney, Sean? What makes you think I need anything from you?"

"I wanted you to have options." Since this sounded suspiciously like what Alecia told Anna four years ago, I changed tactics. "My attorney said that this could get messy."

Anna's fingers balled into a fist on the table. "And what exactly do you need an attorney for?"

"For Willow." I took Anna's hand, and despite a meager protest, she let me. "I can't sit by and let another man claim my child, baby. That's not going to happen. Dean's a lawyer. And since Willow has his name, and y'all are married, he's holding a lot of cards."

"We're separated," she bit out. "And I can take care of my daughter."

"She's my daughter too."

My tone was as soft and gentle as my thumb stroking over hers, but the subject was not up for debate. I would put my family back together. And hiring the best damned attorney in Austin was a step in that direction.

As Anna stared at our little girl, silence yawned between us. The awkward kind.

"I only want Willow to know me," I finally said. "To know that I did everything to make that happen."

Focused on me now, Anna snapped, "Because I didn't, right?" Her gaze slid to her emerald ring, and her voice fell to a whisper. "You wouldn't even know about Willow if I hadn't come to the concert. You never even tried to contact me."

Would we ever get past this?

Without letting go of Anna's hand, I changed seats, so that I was sitting next to her. "I love you. I've always loved you." Threading my free hand into her hair, I looked into those green eyes that held all my tomorrows. "Whether you were there or not, I missed you. Every single day."

Anchoring my forehead to hers, I fought her silent resistance.

Anna's eyes drifted closed, and she asked in a small voice, "Do you know what I remember?"

I shook my head.

"Eight hours."

"What does that mean, baby?"

A shuddering breath wracked her body. "You sent me a text that day . . ."

She didn't have to finish the thought. It always came back to that day, the day that changed everything.

But I nodded, accepting her invitation into the past. "Go on."

Her lashes fluttered over wounded eyes, staring right into my soul. "You told me you loved me. You wrote it. And then eight hours later you walked out. For a long time, all I remember was the eight hours. That grace period when I didn't know everything was going to end."

There was nothing I could say. No words to magically heal us. So I sealed my lips over hers, pouring every bit of my regret into the kiss. "I was wrong. So fucking wrong. But I never intended to stay away. It just—"

"Ma!"

We broke apart as Willow powered toward us, her bare feet slapping on the deck.

"Ma!" Willow pointed excitedly to the lake. "Daw!"

I followed her finger to the Labrador retriever splashing around in the water next to its owner.

"Want daw," Willow said with an expectant look at her mother. "Ma?"

Smiling, Anna lifted Willow onto her lap and then spoke close to her ear. "We'll get one, baby. Mommy will find you a special dog."

Willow nodded glumly before sliding off Anna's lap. She reclaimed her spot on the edge of the deck, watching the dog until it paddled out of sight.

Something about Willow's wistful look made me want to go ask the dude on the shore to name his price for the mutt.

Shelving the wayward thought, I mused, "I guess she's never had a dog."

Anna gave me a patronizing smile as she picked up her cup of coffee. "I can't just go to the local pet store." Rolling her eyes when I offered a "why not" kind of stare, she sighed. "Shit-zu, Poodle, Bichon Frise—that's about it. And they have to be purebreds. Because of her asthma. They need to be hypoallergenic. And even then, it's not a guarantee. I wouldn't want to give her a dog and then have to take it away."

Taking her hand, I kissed her palm, grateful our little trip into the minefield didn't blow off one of our limbs. "I get it."

Anna finished her coffee, then glanced at her phone. "I'd better get going."

She quickly gathered her paperwork, including the folder for Lakeview Town Homes. And then she stood and smoothed out her dress once again.

I caught her arm before she could get away and then my palm skimmed over her elbow, past her shoulder, and landed on her nape. "Kiss?"

Not that I was asking.

Pulling her in, I explored her mouth, staking my claim. If Anna was going out into the world, she'd do it with my taste on her tongue.

Breaking our connection, she said breathlessly, "I'm going to be late."

Since locking her in the house wasn't an option, I bit my lip and acquiesced, staring vacantly at the lake as she prepared to leave. For how long, I didn't know. An hour. Half the day. Forever.

A protest from Willow caught me off-guard as she scrambled onto my lap.

"No!" She scowled at her mother. "No . . . stay!"

Anna slid her hands under Willow's arms and tried to peel the kid off me. "Mommy's got an appointment. Get your shoes."

Without thinking, I chimed in, "I'm not going anywhere. She can stay with me."

The "she" in question buried her face in my neck, nodding. I needed to work on my patience because this was about to get ugly.

Anna's lips parted, and she blinked at me, telegraphing the message loud and clear.

Not happening.

Burying my disappointment, I shifted, prepared to take Willow to Anna's car, kicking and screaming. But then Anna's fingers unfurled from our daughter's arm.

"Are you sure?" Eyes narrowed, she surveyed me for chinks in my armor.

I had a shit ton, but not when it came to the little girl on my lap.

"I'm sure. Lola's here."

Anna sighed and then pulled a notepad from her bag. "It doesn't inspire confidence if you're depending on the housekeeper to help you out."

She scribbled a long list and then laid the paper in front of me. "This is her doctor's number." She smirked when my face went blank. "You won't need it."

Line by line, Anna rattled off information while I nodded intently, all my focus on the list.

When she finished, Anna crouched and said to Willow, "Last chance. Mommy's leaving. Are you sure you want to stay?"

Willow cupped her mother's cheeks and nodded.

Anna stayed there for a long moment, then exhaled slowly. "Okay."

Anna wobbled to her feet, her face pale and a crease between her brows. I took her hand. "I got this." I kissed her clammy palm. "We'll stay in the house. Don't worry."

Anna jerked a nod, brushed a kiss to the top of Willow's head, and then rushed away. But I knew she wasn't gone. I could feel her, hovering by the edge of the deck.

Glancing over my shoulder, I mouthed, "Thank you."

Anna's face contorted with emotions she tried to hide. And I let her have that, her mask of strength.

Shifting my attention to the lake, I watched the sun skitter off the water with Willow in my arms.

Moments later, a car door slammed. I waited until the engine purred to life to lean close to my daughter's ear. "You want to learn how to play the drums, Willow-baby?"

Willow sat on the floor in my basement studio, her eyes glued to the twenty-seven-inch monitor in front of her.

"Hep, peese." She held out her hand.

Smiling, I adjusted her grip on the plastic drumstick. "How's that feel?"

She nodded, oh so serious. "Goo."

Stretching out behind my baby girl with my MacBook on my lap, I ran the program I'd created for her. In order to show Willow what music looked like, I'd rigged the portable percussion set to run a feed from my laptop to the screen in front of her.

It was kind of like the game "Simon," with blinking lights that she could follow.

The speakers in my studio were a higher quality than anything Willow had ever experienced, so it only took her a few tries to play the combinations flawlessly.

After mastering the latest riff, she looked up at me expectantly. I set the laptop aside, dropped a kiss on the top of her head, and then stood.

I held up my hands in the way I'd seen Anna do. "Wait."

Willow nodded, and her eyes followed me as I ran to the booth.

I smiled at her through the glass as I set up the recording.

When I reentered the studio, I took a seat behind my kit and then pointed at the pads. "Play, baby."

Willow looked so much like her mother when she worried her bottom lip, it nearly cracked me in two.

I smiled wide and hit the high hat, encouraging my daughter to do the same. "Play," I repeated.

Squaring her little shoulders, Willow tapped the pad tentatively before swinging her gaze to me for approval.

When I nodded, she began to play a simple eight beat riff of her own creation. Halfway through her second repetition, I added the snare and the kick drum—the two pieces that weren't a part of her portable set.

Somewhere between the here and the there, we created a song. It was a crude little thing, but I'd never been prouder of a piece of music. I only wished I'd had a video to show Anna.

Inspired, I launched into a solo, and before I knew it, Willow was on her feet, her palm resting against the kick drum.

Closing her eyes, she swayed in time with the rhythm.

My heart swelled with a love I'd never felt, along with a twinge of regret.

Was it too late for Willow to feel for me what I felt for her?

I let it go, squashing the remorse behind the pounding beat. Right now, I had Willow and music. Two of the three things I loved most in the world. The rest would come.

# CHAPTER THIRTY-FOUR

**Anna**

*I*t was dusk when I pulled up to Sean's house. Parking in the circular driveway, I sat for a long moment, just staring out at the lake.

My phone lit up in the cupholder. A text from Peyton.

*You did the right thing. But maybe for the wrong reasons.*

When I heard the leaves rustling in the meadow, drawing my gaze to the willow tree, I felt at peace with my choice.

Grabbing my phone, I headed for the front door. As I entered the foyer, my footsteps echoing off the high ceilings, a twinge of unease slithered through me. The house was silent. Still.

I peered into the kitchen and found it dark. The living room was quiet as well, everything in its place like nobody had been here all day.

Calling to Sean, my heart raced when he didn't answer. Up the stairs I went, my anxiety growing with every step. Standing in the guest room with Willow's toys neatly piled in the basket Lola had purchased, I pulled out my phone and sent Sean a text.

*Where are you?*

Biting my lip, I stared at the screen, willing him to answer. Thankfully, I didn't have to wait long.

*Basement. Are you home?*

Home . . .

Was I home?

Willow was here, and so was Sean, so, yes, I guess I was home.

Smiling, I descended the narrow staircase and headed for the basement. Expecting to find them in the theater room watching a movie, I was surprised to hear music coming from Sean's studio.

I peeked my head in the door.

Sean was banging away on his drums, his long hair flying in every direction, and for a moment my breath caught.

He looked . . . beautiful. And so young. Just like the image tucked in my memory.

And then I saw Willow in front of Sean's kit, palm pressed to the bass drum, smiling at her daddy.

Mesmerized, I took in the scene.

The music stopped as Sean's arms fell to his side. He pointed at me, smiling, and Willow's gaze followed his finger.

She squealed, and in a flash, she took off in my direction.

Sean nearly knocked over his drums in his haste to get to her, scooping her up with one arm to keep her from stumbling over the cords on the floor.

"Ma! Ma!"

Opening the door, I hovered at the threshold. They seemed so perfect at that moment, I hated to intrude.

Sean closed the gap in four strides. "Come in, baby." Wrapping me in a hug with Willow between us, he kissed my forehead and murmured, "Missed your face."

It was one of our old phrases, straight out of our past, and it warmed me in places where the sun hadn't shone in a long time.

Breathless, I looked up into Sean's azure eyes. "Hey."

The silver threads flickered to life, and he bent to kiss me.

"Ma!" Willow squirmed, demanding my attention by snaking an arm around my neck.

Settling her onto my hip, I ventured farther into the room. There was stuff everywhere. Abandoned instruments. A portable kit like the one Sean carried with him on the road. Sheet music. "What's going on in here?"

Sean was at my back, his chest so close that I could feel the heat through our two layers of clothing.

"Just messing around," he said a little sheepishly.

"I see that."

Willow shimmied down my body, and grabbing my hand, she led me to the portable percussion set and proudly announced, "Dums." She looked up at me, her little chin high. "My dums."

Sinking next to her on the floor, I said, "Your drums, huh?"

Sean took a seat behind us. We were like nesting dolls, the three of us.

Willow pressed a plastic drumstick into my hand. Indulging her, I hit one of the small pads, and to my amazement, a light flashed on the monitor in front of me.

"Did I do that?" When I repeated the motion with the same result, I twisted to look at Sean who was biting his lip and rubbing the hell out of the back of his neck.

"Yeah," he said and then cleared his throat. "I wanted to teach Willow how to play, so I, um, rigged up the pads to the computer." He took the stick from my hand and then tapped out a sequence, and the screen danced with blue, green, and red lights.

Tears welled out of nowhere, stinging the back of my eyes. "You showed her the music," I said to him quietly. "That's brilliant."

Sean laughed it off. "It wasn't hard." He handed the stick to Willow who began to pound out another sequence. "She's a natural, baby."

Relaxing against his chest, I watched our daughter. "How can you tell?"

"Intuition." Sean linked our fingers. "It's hard to explain. Remember how I used to tell you about hearing songs in the rain?"

I nodded.

"Well, it's like that. She hears it." He tapped his temple. "Up here." And then he nuzzled my neck, his voice a whisper only for me. "Everything has a rhythm, Anna-baby."

"Everything?"

"Yes." He pressed a kiss to my shoulder. "You have a rhythm."

I snorted. "I don't have any rhythm. You've seen me dance."

Lifting my hand, Sean turned my palm one way and then the other, like he was performing an inspection. "Not your rhythm—the rhythm of you. The way you sound when you move. When you breathe." As he brought our joined hands to my waist, his lips found the spot on my neck that drove me crazy. "The sound you make when you come."

So caught up in Sean's words, his breath fanning my skin, I didn't notice when the room went silent.

"We have an audience," he said with a chuckle, tipping his chin to Willow, who watched us with interest.

Fighting the blush heating my cheeks, I sat up. "Okay . . . well, you can show me more about that rhythm thing later."

Sean nipped my earlobe, and I felt him smile. "Oh, don't worry, Anna-baby. I plan on it."

# CHAPTER THIRTY-FIVE

**Sean**

*I* waited in the dark, my back pressed against the bark of the willow tree.

For a week, I'd planned this surprise, and since I was leaving for Los Angeles in the morning, this was my last chance.

The front door creaked open, and then Anna's bare feet pattered on the flagstone pavement. The moon cast just enough light to glimpse the sheen of her peach nightgown. I licked my lips. I fucking loved that nightgown. The feel of it, whisper soft against my skin when she slept spooned in my arms.

Anna slipped inside the gate. "Sean, are you out here?" She knew I was. I'd left her a note. But when I didn't answer, she hissed, "Great, I'm probably going to get eaten wandering around out here in the dark."

That was an invitation I couldn't pass up, so I moved toward her voice, my feet sinking into the dew-covered grass.

"You're going to get eaten, all right." I banded my arms around her waist. "That's a promise."

Anna yelped, but I captured her mouth, stifling the little cry as I
lifted her off her feet. She responded with her usual fervor, wrapping
her legs around my hips.

We were still working through our issues, but this we always had.
Her body spoke the words she wouldn't say out loud.

Sucking her bottom lip between my teeth, a hint of the wine we
had for dinner lingered on her soft flesh. "Fuck, you taste good."

Carrying her to the base of the tree, I dropped to my knees when I
felt the wool blanket under my feet.

As I laid Anna down on her back, her eyes widened. "Oh, God.
Look at the stars."

"Uh, huh."

At the moment, the stars were the last thing on my mind. Anna's
silk nightgown slid under my palms as I explored her body. Growling
when I reached the curve of her ass, I said, "You're not wearing
anything underneath this." Her nipples strained the sheer lace
bodice as I cupped her breast. "Damn. You're killing me."

I thought about taking her right here. Right now. Quick and dirty
the way she liked it sometimes. But I spent half the day keeping her
in the house to bring this plan to fruition.

"I have a surprise for you. And I really want to blindfold you so I
can reveal it." Kissing my way to her nipple, I flicked my tongue
against the sheer fabric. "But if I do that, chances are the surprise
would have to wait."

Anna arched, offering her perfect tits. "I can wait," she panted.
"I'm good with waiting."

Scoring my teeth across the taut peak, I bit down, and she
jerked.

"Patience." Rising to my knees, I pulled her upright. She pouted at
me, so I kissed her nose. "Close your eyes."

Anna's hand found its way under my shirt. "It's already dark," she
huffed when I caught her wrist.

"It won't be." I kissed her palm. "Trust me."

*Trust me. Please trust me.*

It was a mantra I practiced daily, hoping Anna would hear me.

Tonight, I got my wish. Her fingers locked with mine, and when I stood up, she followed suit.

"Don't move," I ordered as I reached behind us to locate the two flutes of champagne and the bucket with the bottle.

Anna snickered, and I had to laugh too. We were more of a Pale Ale couple. Maybe I should have brought a six-pack and called it good instead of the expensive as fuck Cristal.

Too late now.

Pressing the glass into her hand, I whispered, "Are you ready?"

"I guess." A nervous bubble of laughter tripped from her lips. "But—"

Anna's thought ended with a sharp inhalation of breath when I flicked the switch on the remote, illumining the two spotlights pointed at the tree.

I kissed her softly. "Open your eyes, baby."

Smiling against my lips, Anna slid her hand into my hair, seeking my tongue. I allowed her to explore my mouth for a moment before breaking away. The pout was back as I turned her toward her surprise.

Anna blinked several times, staring at the rustic swing. It wasn't much, I guess, just a few ropes hanging from a willow tree in a meadow. But the carpenter used teak wood for the seat, and even from our short distance, the words carved into the beveled edge were visible: Anna-baby.

The white ribbon twining the rope and the large bows on the sides of the seat wouldn't survive the first storm, but right now the scene looked like something out of a picture book. A fairy tale. Our fairy tale, the one I'd promised her.

Anna spilled champagne as she shuffled to the swing. The twin spotlights outlined every curve of her body as she ran her fingers down the coarse rope to the bows. She knelt in the worn grass, trampled from the five sets of work boots it took to hang the swing with little notice.

A quiet sob pierced the night air as Anna traced the inscription on the seat.

Sinking on the ground behind her, I wrapped her in a tight hug. "You don't like it?"

She nodded, sniffing. "I love it."

This would've been the perfect time to give Anna the two-karat solitaire in my safe that I'd purchased with my first royalty check. But I wanted to show her in a thousand ways how much I wanted her here, in this house. And later, when she got used to the idea, I'd give her the rock.

"I love you, Anna-baby."

We stayed like that for a long time, sipping champagne that I wished was beer, but, oh well.

Then she settled in the crook of my arm and looked up at me. I tensed when her finger ran the length of the fading bruise on my neck. "When were you going to tell me about your fight with Logan?"

Something akin to anger, or maybe jealousy rolled through me.

"How do you know about that?" I tilted Anna's chin to look into her eyes. "Your pen pal send you a little note?"

She shook her head, cupping my cheek. "Of course not. I talked to Lily. Everyone's wondering what happened, and you didn't even tell me about it."

"You talked to Lily?"

Shifting, she created a small distance. "Yes. Is that a problem? She dropped by when you were at practice to see Willow. I guess I forgot to tell you."

"It's not a problem." I blew out a breath, still unwilling to give her any details about Logan. "It was just a disagreement like I said. No big deal."

Anna's sigh told me she knew differently. "It seems like a big deal."

A gentle breeze brought the swing to life. "You can ask him yourself if you want. I'm flying out tomorrow, and you can come with me. I'll even let you sit next to him on the plane." Shadows crept across her face, and I sighed. "I've got to work, baby. But I want you and Willow with me."

Anna bit her lip. "What's going on with the tour? When do you leave?"

"*We,*" I corrected. "And I don't have any details yet."

Given our history, my ultimatum, I should've held back. But the thought of spending a year on the road without Anna and Willow caused a pit to form in my stomach. And it grew every day.

Anna's lips brushed the hollow of my neck. "I thought you wanted to show me your rhythm?"

She was distracting me. And worse, it was working.

Fisting her hair, I looked down into her hooded eyes. "It's not my rhythm . . . it's yours."

Lithe fingers traced the stubble on my jaw. "I told you. I don't have any rhythm."

I hauled to my feet, and then took Anna's hand to pull her up. "Come on. I'll teach you about your rhythm."

Easing onto the blanket, I motioned for her to join me. She did, stretching on her side to face me with a smug smile that I planned to kiss right off.

Propping my head on my palm, I looked into her eyes as I fingered the hem of her gown. Sliding my hand underneath the silky fabric, I skimmed her smooth skin as I moved north to cup her ass. She curled into me, her hips rocking slightly as I caressed the firm globe.

When I slipped my leg between hers, she increased the movement, craving the friction. Through the denim, I could feel her warmth beckoning me. Before I forgot all about the lesson, or anything but her sweet pussy, I thrummed my fingers against her thigh, matching her rhythm as she flexed against me.

Anna was all breathy moans and soft whispers. Needy, just the way I liked her.

Pressing a kiss to her mouth, I pulled her flush against me, so our rocking was in sync. "There's your beat."

"I don't hear anything," she breathed, adding depth to her tune.

Sliding my hand between her legs, I parted her slick folds, and this time I didn't stop. "Don't listen, baby. Feel."

# CHAPTER THIRTY-SIX

**Anna**

Sean pushed to his feet and then turned off the spotlights, plunging the meadow into darkness. I sat up, a shiver running down my spine.

Except for the house looming a few yards away, we might as well have been in the wilderness. It wasn't unusual to see deer every morning in the meadow, and who knows what other animals lurked in the trees.

As if he could read my thoughts, Sean let out a small chuckle. "What's the matter, Anna-baby?"

He was teasing me. And if I wasn't completely turned on and soaking wet I might be inclined to do a little teasing myself, and saunter straight into the house just to have him chase me.

But then a million twinkle lights flickered to life, spreading a warm glow across the meadow. There had to be a hundred or more strands intricately woven around the tree trunk and hanging from the branches.

"Oh, wow." Rising to my knees, I looked around in awe. "When did you do all this?"

Sean yanked his T-shirt over his head, grinning. "I didn't. I called Chase, and he sent one of his crews over this afternoon."

Which explained all the distractions. The bath Sean drew me after lunch. The movie marathon in the theater room with all my favorite Rom-Coms that he hated, but sat through without a peep. Dinner in the formal dining room.

Sean winked, a smug smile curving his mouth as he unbuttoned his jeans. I guess our dirty minds where on the same filthy track because he hadn't bothered to put on any boxers, and now he was right in front of me in all his glory, bathed in soft light.

I slid my gown off my shoulders, and when I crawled toward him, his lids fell to half-mast.

Fisting his hard length when I knelt in front of him, his free hand went to my hair. "What've you got in mind, Anna-baby?"

It wasn't so much a question as a taunt. He knew what I had in mind. The one thing I hadn't done since we'd been back together. Because I feared if I didn't hold something back, some small part of myself, we'd pass the point of no return.

But who was I kidding?

We'd blown by that mile marker a long time ago. Maybe the first night.

Peering up at him, I sealed my lips over his crown. He groaned, and I felt it all the way to my core.

"Fuck . . . Anna."

His fingers tightened in my hair, but he didn't move. Didn't push. I knew how he liked it. Hard. Fast. Punishing. So I took as much of him as I could, hollowing my cheeks and sucking hard.

Sean groaned again, but kept his resolve, barely rocking into me.

I took it as a challenge, and deeper I went until I felt him at the back of my throat. Gagging, I blinked up at him with watery eyes.

Sean smiled, not his normal smile, but the one that told me I was asking for trouble and he was going to give it to me.

"What do you want, baby?" His thumb skated over a tear that slid down my cheek. "You want me to fuck your mouth? Is that it?"

Relaxing my throat, I breathed through my nose, nodding.

Sean waited for a beat, so I pulled back, swirling my tongue over his tip. I barely had a chance to inhale a shallow breath before he jerked his hips, guiding my head to where my hand was curled at the base of his throbbing cock.

Sean set a punishing rhythm, both of his hands in my hair now, fisting the strands as he rocked into me.

Tasting him, salty on my tongue, I prepared for his release. Welcoming it.

And then he was gone.

I blinked at him through blurry eyes when he dropped to his knees.

"I want inside you." His hand cupped the back of my head a second before he pushed me onto my back. And then he froze. "Condom?"

My lips parted, yes, no, or maybe dancing on the tip of my tongue. I was on the pill, and I wanted to feel him so badly, the way I used to, with nothing between us.

In the few seconds it took me to grapple with my decision, Sean chose for me, stretching to grab a foil packet from the pocket of his jeans.

Maybe it was all the emotions slamming me at once. Or just the realization that I couldn't give this to him, this one last thing, but the tears I didn't know were there slid from the corners of my eyes.

Sean finished rolling on the condom before he noticed, and me, like an idiot, hadn't bothered to hide the traitorous little drops soaking into my hair.

He eased on top of me, alarmed, his thumbs working furiously to wick away the moisture. "Baby, what's the matter? What did I do?"

Throat burning and breath ragged, I shook my head. "Nothing. I'm sorry. I just . . . I can't do that yet."

Sean kissed my cheeks, my jaw, then buried his face in the crook of my neck. "Please don't fucking cry. It's my fault. All my fault."

He jerked when my legs wrapped around his waist, and I knew I was sending all kinds of mixed signals, but I wanted him. I always wanted him.

"Sean ... please ... I'm sorry," I choked out. "I love you." He stilled as the words tripped from my lips, and I pulled him close to look in his eyes. "I love you ... Please ..."

I didn't know what I was asking for. His body. His soul. His promise. But then he slid inside me, and all the chaotic thoughts ceased. It was just him and me. Us. Perfect and peaceful and primal.

"I love you," he roughed out as he thrust, deeper and harder. "I love you so fucking much."

Sean's words sent me tumbling into the sweetest oblivion. And then he called my name, and I felt him shudder as he chased me to the bottom.

For a brief moment, everything was exactly as it should be.

We were whole.

A warm breeze drifted across the meadow, and I shivered, my skin still a little damp with sweat and maybe some tears.

Sean shifted me in his arms and gazed down at me, concern creasing his brow. "Are you cold?"

Not trusting my voice, I shook my head, but he reached for my gown anyway. Once it was secured around my body, he pulled on his jeans and then took me in his arms again.

Drowsing as he stroked my hair, I mumbled, "I'm sorry about the crying. I don't know what got into me."

"I got into you." I chuckled, but then he blew out a breath, twining a strand of my hair around his finger. "Do you believe me, Anna?"

My eye snapped open. "About what?"

He shifted his focus to the lights, avoiding my gaze. "That I love you."

"Yes."

Sean relaxed, unaware I'd only given him half my response. Love was never the problem. He loved me the day he stumbled off to the bar, irrevocably tearing us apart a few hours later. And now, with Willow in the mix, I wasn't even sure if he knew what he felt.

Sean kissed me, smiling now. "You want to go inside?"

Gazing up at the stars, I wished for the millionth time things were less complicated. "In a minute. I should probably check on Willow."

Sean tightened his grip, and I wasn't sure he was aware that he was doing it. At the mention of her name, all his senses heightened. He was everything and more I could ask for when it came to our daughter.

Tracing a figure eight on his arm, I told him, "Willow's got an appointment in a few weeks at Cooks in Ft. Worth."

His back went board straight. "Cook's Children's Hospital? Why?"

I shrugged. "It's just a hearing test. But I figured I'd consult with the surgeon while I was there."

Sean practically knocked me over as he sat up. "Surgery?"

His brows drew together like he couldn't fathom it. And honestly, neither could I.

I hauled myself upright, and now we were facing each other. "I told you she'd probably need surgery."

Sean's eyes darkened, almost black in the dim light. "Is it dangerous? Because if it's dangerous, I don't think she should have it. She's fine."

Taking his hand, I turned his palm up so that I'd have something to concentrate on besides those steely blue orbs. "She's not having it tomorrow." I ran my nail along a particularly deep groove in his skin. "But if there's a chance her hearing will improve, we should take it. Surgery scares the hell out of me too, but I want Willow to have every opportunity—"

"She will," he blurted. "I'll make sure of it."

My focus shifted to the house where our daughter slept. Willow was the link on the broken road between Sean and me, and perfect in every way.

I kissed his palm before letting his hand drop. "Let's just see what happens."

Threading his fingers through my hair, Sean pulled me toward him, and just before our lips met a light flickered against the limestone veneer of the house. Someone was coming.

Sean squinted into the darkness. "What the hell?"

Grabbing his T-shirt, I yanked it over my head, since my flimsy nightgown didn't hide a damn thing.

"How did they get in the gate?" I asked, more put out than alarmed, at least until I caught sight of the police cruiser following one of the blue security trucks that patrolled the neighborhood.

Sean jumped to his feet. "Stay here."

*Screw that.*

I brushed the leaves and grass off my gown as I followed, staying on the pavement while he cut through the lavender bushes and trampled the spring flowers.

By the time I reached Sean's side, he was standing in front of a Travis County Sheriff.

"What's this all about, officer?" Sean asked, voice as gruff as his posture.

The cop looked Sean over, from his bare feet to the tattoos covering his arms and chest. "Are you Sean Jacob Hudson?"

Sean replied with a nod, and I linked our fingers when the cop turned his attention to me. "Are you Annabelle Dresden Kent?"

Before I could answer, Sean stepped in front of me. "I asked you once—what's this all about?"

But I knew.

Nudging Sean out of the way, I schooled my features. "I'm Annabelle Dresden Kent."

The officer withdrew two stacks of papers, and then handing one to each of us, he said, "Y'all have been served."

# CHAPTER THIRTY-SEVEN

**Sean**

*A*nna sat on the couch in our bedroom, staring out the window while I paced, my phone clutched to my ear. On the other end of the line, Trevor let out a weary breath. "Sean, you don't understand, this is way over my head. You need to call Scott in the morning."

"Scott." I snorted derisively. "I've spent all of five minutes with that dude. You told me he was the best family law attorney in Austin. He hasn't done shit."

"You don't know that," Trevor retorted. "Look, things have changed. From what you just read, Dean's gone on the offensive. He's filed a motion to prevent Anna from taking Willow outside of Williamson or Travis County, and he's joined you in the action. Scott will need to decipher the paperwork. Find out the scope. Let the man do his job."

I sank onto the couch next to Anna. "Scope? What does that even mean?"

"Ask your girl. She's got the documents." Trevor stifled a yawn. "She was a law student; she knows what they mean."

I cut my gaze to Anna, who'd yet to move. Or speak. She could barely lift her Dr. Pepper can without shaking, so delving into complex legal documents was probably out of the question.

I managed to force out a breath. "Okay, okay."

"This doesn't prevent you from doing anything you have to do," Trevor repeated for the fifth time. "It just means that until Anna and Dean come to terms, she can't do it with you."

Thoughts of the tour crept into my mind. Twelve months. *Impossible.*

I scrubbed a hand down my face. "Which lawyer did she pick? Is he good? He better be fucking good. Because I'm on a deadline."

Trevor cleared his throat. "Anna said Peyton is handling it."

*Peyton?*

Sitting up straight, my gut twisted in a knot. Peyton Hollis wouldn't piss on me if I were on fire. And for all I knew, she was squarely on Dean's side.

"I've got to go, Trev. Thanks for the help."

My phone landed with a thud on the table, rousting Anna from her haze. She rubbed her eyes with the heel of her palm. "What did he say?"

"He said you'd explain it to me." Bolting to my feet, I resumed my pacing, punishing the carpet with every step. "And while you're at it, why don't you tell me why you turned down his help?" Stopping behind her, I gripped the back of the sofa. "This is our daughter we're talking about, Annabelle. And you're letting Peyton handle it?"

When Anna slowly raised her head, I expected to see some acknowledgment of her mistake.

Instead, she rose mechanically, fists clenched at her side. "What the hell are you talking about?"

I snatched the summons from the table. "I'm talking about the fact that you let Dean get the upper hand. You should've hired one of the attorneys Trevor recommended and filed first."

Anna pushed me out of the way as she stomped to her suitcase.

For a minute I thought she might bolt. But from the look on her face, leaving was the last thing on her mind, at least not until she killed me and figured out where to bury my body.

"What you know about the law would fit in a thimble," she spat. "Do you want to know why Dean filed?" The papers she'd pulled from her bag crumpled in her balled fist. "Because I filed. And that," her angry gaze shifted to the summons in my hand, "is Dean's response. And just so you know, I don't need your help to figure shit out. Because in my experience, when you give me something, you know what that means?" She tossed the papers at my feet. "Absolutely nothing."

Anna stormed out of the room, with me on her heels.

"I didn't know," I said, my tone gruff with leftover anger. "Anna, listen to me." I grabbed her arm. "*I didn't know.*"

She turned to me, eyes moist but fierce. "Of course you didn't know. Because you didn't ask. You just assumed. I'm not hiding anything from you."

"*Anymore?*"

The word flew from my lips like a dagger, and fuck if I didn't want to turn the blade on myself.

"Is that how you see it?" She cocked her head, and when I said nothing, she nodded. "I'm sorry that my divorce is fucking up your plans. But you don't have to worry. You've got a good attorney." She broke free of my hold and then marched toward the guest room, calling over her shoulder, "Not that you will. I'm sure you'll have plenty to keep you occupied on your tour."

In the seconds it took for me to recover from Anna's blow, she was gone, behind the door of the guest bedroom. Gripping the knob, I pictured Willow, asleep in her bed on the other side.

*Fuck.*

Resuming my pacing, I burned off the anger and then rapped softly. "You're not playing fair, Anna-baby. Willow's in there. We need to talk."

She pulled the door open, just a crack. "I'm tired. We can talk later."

I leaned against the frame. "We can't. I'm leaving in the morning."

Only half of her beautiful face was visible through the small opening.

But that's all I needed.

Nudging the bottom of the door with my foot, I said, "You'll be missing from me."

A small smile ghosted her lips. "You're not French."

Breaching the space, I took her hand and then pulled her into the hallway. "You want me to be French?" I backed her against the wall, anchoring my forehead to hers. "I can be French."

Her eyes shone like polished emeralds. "What do you want, Sean?"

I kissed her lips. "*You*."

# CHAPTER THIRTY-EIGHT

## Sean

*E*xhaust fumes drifted through the vents as the taxi crept
along in the downtown Los Angeles traffic. I rubbed my
tired eyes as my phone pinged, the screen cluttered with another text
from my lawyer. After our conversation this morning, Scott gleefully
invoked the clause in his retainer allowing him to up his fee due to
the time-sensitive nature of the summons. For the bargain basement
price of a thousand bucks an hour, I now had his undivided attention.

I tapped out a perfunctory response.

*Stepping into a meeting. Do whatever you need to do. Just do it fast.*

Hoisting my backpack over my shoulder when the cab screeched
to a halt in front of the Conner Management Building, I gazed up at
the thirty-story glass and steel building that pierced the layer of over-
cast sky. June Gloom, they liked to call it here. It was fucking smog,
no matter what fancy name they slapped on it.

Pushing through the revolving doors, I spotted Cameron and
Christian at a table in the atrium.

Dropping my bag next to an empty chair, I flopped into the seat. "What are y'all doing out here?"

"Waiting for you," Cameron replied wearily. "We need to have a chat before we go in there."

My eyes narrowed when he shot Christian a look. "Why's that?"

Cameron slid a thick stack of papers in front of me. "Logan thinks we're being too demanding. He said if we let this deal slip through our hands . . ."

We all knew what could happen if we didn't get something set up soon. Our temporary gig at the Parish would become permanent. We'd be right back where we started. On Sixth Street, waiting to be discovered. Or re-discovered. And the chances of that were slim to none.

Noting all the red ink on the contract, the revisions we were requesting, I blew out a breath. "What do you think, Christian?"

The bassist looked thoughtfully into the paper cup he held. He was the most soft-spoken of our group, wearing his fame with the ease of an overcoat he could remove at will. If he weren't such a talented musician, he'd probably be teaching math at UT and banging co-eds.

Christian finally lifted his gaze, his blue eyes calm as ever, but deadly serious. "I don't have a problem with the tour. Unless we can't agree. Then it's a big fucking problem. I don't consider it a tragedy to play music in our hometown. Melody is there." He glanced at Cameron, then back to me. "She's not like Lily. She can't take her work on the road. So I'm giving up a lot. I'll do this thing, but only if we do it together."

I nodded, taking a brief look around. Memorabilia from some of the greatest bands in the world lined the walls. Tributes frozen in time.

Across the atrium, Logan stood stock still in front of a Lucite case.

"Let me see if I can straighten shit out with Mr. Personality before our meeting," I said as I pushed out of my chair.

"Try not to throw any punches." Tension laced Cameron's tone despite the wry smile. "We've already got a reputation."

"It's all good," I assured, smiling.

Logan didn't acknowledge me when I strolled up. Gaze fixed on the two Stratocaster guitars in the sterile case, he chewed the inside of his lip.

My stomach bottomed out as I read the inscription on the gold plaque.

*In memory of the fallen. Rocking it out in the great beyond.*
*Rhenn Grayson and Paige Dawson.*
*Damaged—Sixth Street Takeover Tour*
*Photo courtesy of Conner Productions ©*

Brief bios of Rhenn and Paige sat in steel frames along with several pictures from the band's last tour.

Glancing over the tribute, I stood silently, reverently. Their deaths paved the way for my career. Which in turn blew Anna and me apart. It was a circle with all roads starting and ending in Austin. For all of us. Even Rhenn and Paige.

"This is all I've ever wanted," Logan finally said, his voice thick with emotion.

I studied the mangled wreckage in the final picture. "You want to die in a fiery crash?" I chuckled. "Because if that's the case, I ain't boarding any tour buses with you in the near future."

Logan faced me with frigid blue eyes. "I want to be remembered. I want the music to mean something."

It's what I wanted too. And until now, there was nothing more important.

"Dude, it does mean something. This tour isn't going to change that one way or the other."

Logan looked down, kicking the polished stone with the toe of his boot. "Sounds like you're getting ready to bail. Is that what I'm hearing?"

Maybe. Possibly.

"I want to be remembered too." I tipped my chin to the photo of Damaged performing at Wembley Stadium. "And not by ninety thousand strangers on another continent. I want Willow to know me. I've already wasted too much time."

A cold wind swirled around us. "So that's all the last four years have been?" Logan cocked his head. "Wasted time?"

There was no explaining this to Logan. He'd never loved anything more than the music. Maybe Laurel, but that was a long time ago.

Still, I tried. "The music, what we do, it means more to me than almost anything." Looking him in the eyes, I smiled wistfully. "Almost."

An impeccably dressed blonde sauntered our way, her heels clicking against the stone floor. Benny must have a thing for blondes because they were crawling out of the woodwork in this place.

"I'm Amber, Benny Conner's personal assistant." The blonde waited for Cameron and Christian to join us and then continued, "If you're ready, Mr. Conner is waiting in the conference room."

She turned on her heel, and I followed while Logan took one last look at the Lucite box.

He fell into step beside me a few paces from the elevator. "I'm glad you decided to show up for this, Sean." Jaw set, his blue eyes stared straight ahead. "But don't think for a minute you're going to change my mind. We're doing this shit, bro. With or without you."

If you were planning something important in this town and you wanted people to know without actually admitting it, you marked the occasion with dinner at Mr. Chow. We'd yet to iron out all the details, but our meeting with Benny's team had gone well enough to warrant a little public display of our future alliance.

I'd just finished my plate of sea bass when three servers hustled to our table with buckets filled with champagne.

"We haven't even signed yet," Christian whispered out of the corner of his mouth. "What's up with the champagne?"

I polished off my first glass in one gulp.

"All part of the show," I mumbled, holding up my flute for a refill. The perky server scurried over, cheery smile in place as she filled my glass. "Thanks. You can leave the bottle."

Christian chuckled as the waitress retreated. "Anna-baby's got you whipped into shape, huh?"

Smiling at the thought of Anna, whip or no whip, I shifted my gaze to Christian. "What are you babbling about, dude?"

He pointed his fork at me, pecan pie dangling from the tines. "You barely made eye contact with that waitress, and I haven't heard you say 'sugar' all day."

Twisting the stem of the flute, I shrugged. "Whatever it takes, you know?"

The tinkling of crystal drew my attention to the front of the table where a member of Benny's publicity team pushed up from her seat.

The woman's overly plump lips curved into a smile as she addressed us.

"Sorry to interrupt. I'm Mandy, VP of public relations at Conner. I apologize for missing the meeting this afternoon, but I set up this little outing so we can get a jump start on your publicity."

Our strategic location in the center of the restaurant accentuated that fact. At the surrounding tables, people stopped eating, whispering behind their hands while they stole glances at us.

Mandy focused on Logan first.

"From what I've seen, you boys manage to keep yourself in the news on a regular basis." She lifted her glass, toasting my best friend. "Some of you more than others."

She let the chuckling die down and then continued, "What we want to do is keep your press manageable. Within reason, it doesn't matter what you do in your private life. It's your public persona that's of interest to Conner. Sometimes, when a particular story catches the public eye, we'll need to hone the copy for your benefit as well as ours. What we don't want are surprises."

She pivoted to Cameron, and the rest of her team followed. "Cameron, since your story has already grown legs, I only ask that should you change your status, you inform our office immediately."

Cam sat back, the easy smile never reaching his hazel eyes. "And what status would that be?"

"Your relationship status, of course," Mandy quipped, thumbing through her paperwork. "If you and Lillian decide to part ways, just let us know."

"Her name is Lily, and that's not going to happen." Cameron's semblance of a smile disappeared. "And even if it did, I'm not about to hold a press conference to discuss the details."

An awkward silence fell over the table, but to Mandy's credit, the dust barely settled before she moved on without acknowledging Cameron's decree.

As she flipped through her notebook, her fake smile landed on Christian. "I don't have any information here about a girlfriend or significant other, Chris. Does that mean you'd be open to a link with one of our hot properties from another division?"

The bitch was zero for two in the name department, but at least she wasn't referring to us as one of her "properties." Yet.

"It's Christian," my bandmate said dryly. "And just to clarify, are you running a dating service, or setting up our tour? There are enough bogus stories out there; I don't need you fueling the fire."

Mandy relaxed, clearly in her element now. "That's the point, *Christian*. It doesn't matter who you're seeing. It matters who you see in public."

Regarding her with no humor whatsoever, Christian replied flatly, "That would be my girlfriend, Melody."

Mandy's angular jaw ticked as she tried to keep her smile in place. "As you're probably aware, it's better for your image if you're single. So if you wouldn't be opposed to a couple of outings, that'd be super."

Christian maintained his composure. Outwardly. But I knew him. His bobbing leg told me his patience was wearing thin.

"Actually, I would," he said. "And more importantly, Melody would. So I'm going to have to decline your *super* offer."

Another round of silence ensued as Mandy glared at Christian.

"Don't worry, Mandy," Logan piped up, drawing her fierce gaze. "If you wanna give 'em something to talk about, I'm free after dinner."

Laughter broke out from the Conner contingent, snapping the tension like a twig.

Mandy smiled the first genuine smile of the evening. "Even if I wanted to take you up on that, Logan, Benny frowns on fraternization in the workplace."

Ignoring everyone, including Benny, Logan smiled slyly. "I'm not planning on taking you back to your office, darlin'. Unless that's your thing."

A pink flush dusted Mandy's hollow cheeks. "I'll keep that in mind for future reference. But right now . . ." She pulled a glossy rag from the stack in her hand. "I've got to congratulate Sean on his front-page story."

I blinked in confusion as she held up the *Star Magazine*.

"Your appearance on the red carpet provided the opportunity for some free publicity," Mandy said. "Good publicity. You even managed to get Conner mentioned in the piece. That makes my job a hell of a lot easier." Her second genuine smile of the evening was reserved for me. "Well done, Sean."

Blocking out the light smattering of applause, I gazed in horror at the photo of Kimber and me splashed across the cover.

Pleased with herself, Mandy opened the tabloid and began to read the story. "'*Sean Hudson, handsome drummer for the Grammy-nominated band Caged, made his first public appearance in months at an impromptu event at Benny Conner's mansion. On his arm was rumored love interest, Kimber Tyson, with whom the musician has a long romantic history. The two were seen leaving the party shortly after Caged performed. Sources at the Chateau Marmont confirm Ms. Tyson spent the night in Mr. Hudson's suite.*'"

Wrapping up her commentary, Mandy tossed the magazine on the table. "Now that's what we're looking for." She beamed. "Kimber is under contract with the Starline Network. And since Conner Productions has a large stake in Starline, orchestrating the appearance was mutually beneficial." Her smile turned self-satisfied. "Promos started running on the network this morning."

"P-promos?" That was all I could manage since my lungs felt like someone had sucked the air out with an industrial strength vacuum. "What promos?"

Mandy offered a patient, albeit annoyed, smile as she passed her iPad to her assistant. "Kimber has graciously agreed to weave your future encounters into her story line on *Beach Babes*."

Time slowed to a crawl as Mandy's girl Friday set the iPad on the table in front of me.

When she pressed play, a video of Kimber and me standing next to the limo filled the screen. Our faces were in shadow, but I could see Kimber's hand on my chest plain as day.

*"I'm going back to the hotel." My voice bled through the speaker.*

*"I like where you're going with that," Kimber replied. "Let's get out of here."*

My head snapped up as the announcer urged the viewers to "tune in next week."

"That's not . . . it didn't happen like that," I stammered.

"That's the beauty of editing. It makes the impossible possible," Mandy said, and then all business, she consulted her notes. "We've put Kimber up at the Chateau Marmont for the night. If you could make yourself available in the restaurant for breakfast at say, ten o'clock, I'll have a couple of photographers on hand."

Christian's fingers coiled around my forearm when my ass rose from the chair.

"I'm not with Kimber," I growled, glancing at Logan, who was staring into his glass of champagne. "Logan brought her to the event. I didn't—"

"A love triangle?" Mandy interrupted. Almost giddy at the prospect, she looked over at Benny and said, "That could work."

Shaking his head, Benny countered, "Too messy. We need the boys to present a united front. We don't want any rumors affecting ticket sales."

"Didn't you hear me?" I barked, slamming my hands on the table. Benny and Mandy abandoned their strategy session, jerking their heads in my direction. "I'm not with Kimber!"

Mandy gave me a patronizing smile, a technique she must've picked up from her boss since Benny wore an identical expression.

"That doesn't matter," she said, her tone icy and efficient. "The story will garner us a ton of free press as we launch the tour. If you're not happy with the way it plays out, we can easily arrange to unwind the romance aspect after Kimber makes a couple of appearances on the road."

As I glanced down at the iPad with my image frozen on the screen, my insides turned outside. "I want this out of the press now," I demanded. "Print a fucking retraction. Do what you gotta do. I have a..." My mouth went dry as I tried to conjure up a word to describe Anna. "I'm in a serious relationship with the mother of my child."

Mandy's brow furrowed as she stared at her notes. "I don't see anything in your bio about a girlfriend or a child." She heaved a sigh. "It doesn't matter; the story hit the newsstands this morning and traffic is up on the Caged website by three hundred percent. We're going to run with it."

Not even Christian's iron grip could hold me in place. The chair hit the ground as I shoved to my feet.

"Listen, lady, if you're interested in having me sign up for this tour, you'll get this shit out of the press and stay the hell out of my business."

The table erupted in chatter as I snatched my duffel from under the table. Shouldering my backpack, I avoided eye contact with the peanut gallery full of spectators as I stomped toward the exit.

When I pushed through the doors, a dozen reporters greeted me, hurling questions about Kimber's whereabouts.

"No comment," I bit out, fighting my way to the cab stand.

A firm hand gripped my shoulder as I yanked the door open to the taxi. Logan backed up a foot when I spun around, fists balled at my sides.

"Don't leave," he said calmly. "Let's go back inside and get this shit straightened out."

"The shit you started?" The question ripped from my chest in a roar. "I came out here to make things right and get on the same page. But I don't think that's possible." I slid onto the seat. "And I wouldn't be sending Annabelle any more emails. I doubt whether she'll answer."

Slamming the door with enough force to shake the chassis, I turned my stone-cold gaze to the driver.

"Where to?" he asked, setting the meter.

"LAX."

# CHAPTER THIRTY-NINE

**Anna**

*E*xhaustion weighed me down as I poured my first cup of
coffee. I was behind at work, so I'd stayed up half the night
to meet a deadline. Sean wanted me to quit, but that was out of the
question. For now, at least.

"If you're tired, Miss Anna, I'll watch the little bug for you," Lola
said with a smile. "It's no trouble."

Though I rarely trusted anyone with Willow, Sean's housekeeper
was the exception. Lola was kind in a no-nonsense way, and she
adored my child.

Smiling, I took a sip of the caffeinated glory. "I might doze on the
couch. If you wouldn't mind checking on Willow in a little while, I'd
appreciate it. I might be passed out."

"Do you know when Mr. Sean is getting back?"

I felt the heat rise in my cheeks, but I wasn't sure why.

Lola's chuckled. "I take it things are going well with you two?"

I bit back a smile. "We've known each other a long time. We were
high school sweethearts." I shrugged, sheepishly. "Anyway, Sean

should be back in a few days. But he'll probably be leaving for a long tour shortly after that."

Fighting the frown tugging my lips, I banished any notion that I'd made a mistake staying here, letting Sean back in.

*We're going to make it.*

It was the first time I'd felt it with such certainty. And even after our fight, I believed it to be true. Because Sean was fighting for us.

Lola patted my arm. "He loves you. I can see it." Her gaze followed mine to Willow. "And that little girl? She hangs the moon for him."

My heart swelled, and I nodded. "I better get some work done. Or try, at least."

I grabbed my laptop on the way to the couch and then, settling into my favorite corner, I pulled up a deposition, and soon I was lost in all the legal mumbo-jumbo.

"Sen!"

Expecting to find him standing in the doorway, I whipped my head around when Willow squealed Sean's name.

But no.

*No. No. No.*

Bile crawled from the depths of my stomach when I saw Sean's image on the television screen, Kimber Tyson's hand molded to his chest.

"Ma! Sen!" Willow jumped up and down, pointing at her daddy.

Stumbling to my feet to grab the remote, I plopped onto the coffee table to rewind the footage. My vision clouded, and I couldn't breathe as Sean's voice filled the room in surround sound.

I don't know how long I sat there, rewinding the scene over and over.

Willow finally settled down, taking a seat on the floor with her thumb in her mouth, like she could sense something was wrong.

Vaguely, I heard a knock at the front door, followed by footsteps on the travertine.

Too late, I wiped the tears dripping from my chin. Peyton was already in front of me, wrestling the remote from my hand, cursing under her breath.

Pity swam in her eyes when she looked down at me.

*She knew.*

Everyone knew.

"I've got to c-call Sean," I stammered, but Peyton's firm grip on my shoulder held me in place.

"Not yet."

Anger flared, and I knocked her arm away. "You don't understand."

*I* didn't understand. But Sean would explain. He had to explain.

Peyton shook her head, digging something out of her purse. "No, sweetie, *you* don't understand. Sean's attorney sent these over this morning."

Staring at the document she'd shoved into my hand, the words blurred and then came into focus, clear as a bell.

Everything was clear now.

*Sean Jacob Hudson vs. Annabelle Dresden Kent*

That's as far as I got before my whole world went dark.

# CHAPTER FORTY

**Sean**

Squinting, I shielded my bloodshot eyes from the ravages of the mid-morning sun as I climbed out of the cab.

The redeye out of LAX included a layover in Dallas, so by the time I trudged up the front steps of my house I was closing in on thirty hours with no sleep.

The whir of the vacuum cleaner added to the white noise as I stepped into the foyer.

"Anna!" I called, dropping my backpack. "Where are you, baby?"

Lola turned off the Dyson as I strolled into the great room.

"Morning, Lola." I gave her a weary smile, heading for the stairs. "Is Anna awake? She's not answering her phone."

"She's not here."

Lola gave me a go-to-hell look before returning to her chores.

*What the actual fuck?*

Surmising Lola didn't want me to mess up the clean floor, I dropped onto the first step to take off my boots.

"Lola?" I growled over the vacuum, trying to keep my temper in check.

She flipped off the switch but didn't face me. "Yes?"

"Is there something you need to tell me?"

The pint-sized dictator chewed me out good and proper last week for buying the wrong kind of milk, so it could be anything.

"Miss Anna's gone."

Stifling a yawn, I pushed to my feet. "Did she say where she was going?"

I was so damn tired, all I wanted to do was crawl into bed with Anna for a week. And then there was the matter of my career, which I'm pretty sure I'd blown to hell. Strangely, I didn't know how I felt about that.

Lola leveled stony brown eyes on me, clasping her hands in front of her. "She left this morning after her friend came. She took little Willow with her."

Confused, I cocked my head. "Which friend?" She pursed her lips when I closed the gap between us. "Lola, which friend?"

I stopped short of where she stood, aware of my height advantage. But Lola didn't seem to care. If anything, she looked more enraged by my proximity.

"Miss Peyton."

I tried not to roll my eyes. I'd need to buy that girl a bottle of Tito's, and then we'd get drunk off our asses and sort through our differences like we did in the old days.

"It's a good thing she was here," Lola quipped, her brows drawn together in an angry slash. "Miss Anna was a mess after she saw that commercial with you and that . . . woman. And then when Miss Peyton showed her those papers."

A sinking feeling hit my gut and kept right on going. "What are you talking about?"

Lola ignored me and turned on her heel, heading for the kitchen like the very sight of me was distasteful.

I followed, but kept my distance, pressing my palms flat on the granite island while she cleaned the countertops on the other side. "Will you please tell me what the hell is going on?" She shot me a look over her shoulder, and I heaved out a sigh. "Just tell me what you're talking about."

Lola gestured to the dining room table, not bothering to hide her disdain.

Before the other night, I'd never seen a summons up close. But now, even from a distance, the document was unmistakable. The bold print—the borders inside the pages—even the paper looked different. Stiff and formal.

"I'm going to kill that son-of-a-bitch." I ripped my sunglasses off the top of my head and smashed them on the counter. "What the hell is he serving her with now?"

Lola folded her arms over her chest. "Which son-of-a-bitch would that be?"

I pulled out my phone, firing off a text to Anna.

"Dean, Anna's ex." Sliding a hip onto the barstool, I stared at the screen and waited for a reply.

Lola picked up the crumpled pile of papers. "These came from you."

"Yeah, I don't think so."

The laugh scraping my throat threatened to strangle me when Lola shoved the documents under my nose.

*Order to Show Cause*

*Petitioner: Sean Jacob Hudson*

*Respondent: Annabelle Dresden Kent*

Frantic, I took the papers and began to skim the pages. "Peyton brought these?"

Lola nodded.

"Tell me exactly what happened." She pressed her lips together defiantly, and I shook the summons. "This is a misunderstanding. I didn't do this."

Glancing at the papers again, I noted my attorney's seal at the bottom.

I did do this.

Lola showed some mercy when I braced my hands on the edge of the island, trying to drag air into my lungs.

"Like I said," she began, her tone somewhat less harsh. "Miss Anna was very upset. She took her suitcases, and her and the little bug left with Miss Peyton. That's all I know."

I met Lola's eyes, pleading. "Did she say where she was going?"

She shook her head, gathering the debris from my sunglasses. "Miss Peyton seemed intent on taking them to her house, where ever that is."

I took Lola's hand, and she stilled. "If Anna calls you, will you tell me?" I swallowed over the dry lump in my throat. "Lola, promise me, please. I didn't mean for this to happen."

Hell, I didn't even know what had happened.

Through the fog, I tried to recall the texts that flew and back and forth between Scott and me, but my attorney never said anything about serving Anna.

*Because you didn't ask.*

My last message to Scott flashed in my head.

*Do whatever you need to do.*

"I'll let you know if she calls," Lola conceded. "But I won't tell you where she is if she asks me not to."

I squeezed Lola's hand, and to my surprise, she returned the gesture.

"Thank you." I offered a weak smile before sprinting to the garage.

My Bluetooth engaged as soon as I turned the key. Scott's secretary answered on the second ring, informing me he wasn't in the office yet.

"Tell him I'm on my way. I need to talk to him."

Slamming the car in reverse, I ended the call before she could respond.

# CHAPTER FORTY-ONE

**Sean**

*I* stared out the window in the waiting room of Scott Devaroux's downtown office. Not that I cared about anything going on below, but a few members of his staff had gathered around the receptionist's desk, eyeing me like they might want to strike up a conversation. And I was in no mood to talk.

Glancing at my phone for the hundredth time, I chewed the hell out of my lip. I'd sent Anna a dozen texts, but all of them remained unopened.

Desperate, I'd even swallowed my pride and called Peyton. Her secretary informed me in no uncertain terms that my attorney would need to facilitate any conversations, and then she slammed the phone down so hard my eardrum nearly burst.

The group in the reception area scattered like ants when Scott strode through the door, jabbering into his phone.

"See you in court, Counselor." He laughed, running a hand through his windblown hair. "Drinks sound great. You'll need something to numb the pain after I kick your ass in court tomorrow." His eyes lit up when he saw me. "Hey, I've got a meeting. I'll catch you later."

I tried to hide my disdain as Scott ambled toward me. Custom suit. Italian footwear. Keys to his overpriced convertible dangling from the Tiffany fob swinging on his index finger.

Everything about the dude screamed excess. But then, I'd hired him, paid his exorbitant fees. What did I expect?

Saccharine grin firmly in place, Scott extended his hand. "Hey, Sean. Got your text."

Shifting my focus from the diamond-studded cufflinks to his cosmetically engineered smile, I buried my contempt. For the moment, at least.

"I need to talk to you about my case."

Since I couldn't bring myself to shake the prick's hand, his arm fell to his side.

"Of course." A quizzical look painted his features. "Let's go to my office."

Scott took the two bottles of Perrier his secretary offered and then leaned forward and said in a hushed tone, "Pencil Mr. Hudson in for an appointment for our records department."

Records department, my ass. Mr. Pay-by-the-Hour was making sure to get every last billable second recorded for posterity. I was now in the unenviable position of paying this asshole a thousand bucks an hour to find out how badly I'd put the screws to Anna.

Scott took a seat behind the ornate mahogany desk while I paced in a tight circle.

"Sean, man, you seem upset. Have a seat. I've got you squared away."

The attorney shriveled in his chair when I glared at him. "Squared away? Is that what you call it?"

A look of genuine confusion passed over the prick's features. "Well, yes, I filed your motions with the court and—"

"You had my girlfriend served!" Incredulous, I yanked the summons from my back pocket and flung the papers on the desk. "At my house."

Brows furrowed, Scott looked down at the crumpled-up mess. "No . . . I served those papers to Peyton Hollis."

Flexing my fingers to keep from throttling him, I inhaled slowly. "What did I ever say that gave you the impression that I wanted Annabelle served with anything?"

The picture of self-confidence, Scott leaned back in his chair. Steepling his fingers he motioned to my file. "I've got copies of two dozen message you sent in there. Along with every electronic document that you signed."

Rage darkened my vision, but I couldn't tell if I was angrier at Scott or myself.

Laying my palms flat on the polished wood, I tipped forward. "I don't remember you explaining them, Scott."

"And I don't remember you asking."

*Fuck.*

Reining in my fury, I took a seat in the chair. "I'm asking now."

Scott eyed me as he pulled a blue folder from his drawer. As if contemplating, he tapped it against the side of the desk. "I've got a client consult in fifteen minutes. Maybe we should discuss this later. When you're calm."

Leaning back, I crossed my legs, foot to ankle. "I'm calm, man." I shifted my focus to the folder. "But if you don't explain exactly what's in that file, I might get a little riled."

Scott took me for my word and, blowing out a breath, he opened the folder. Our eyes met as he placed the first document in front of me. "Remember, I only did what you asked me to do."

If Scott was expecting a medal, he wasn't going to get one from me. Snatching the paper, I scanned the page. But the only thing that stood out was my signature on the bottom and the official court seal next to the red stamp that marked the item as filed.

I looked at my attorney. "What is this?"

Scott shifted in his seat, the leather squeaking under the fabric of his expensive trousers. "It's a motion to compel...for the DNA test."

My mouth dropped open, and Willow's azure eyes flashed in my head. My mother's eyes. Jesus.

"What?" I croaked.

Scott picked up his water. "Anna stipulated under penalty of perjury that the child is yours. But as your attorney, I filed this motion, on your behalf, compelling her to present the child for a mouth swab."

On my behalf.

"So this came from me?"

Scott clasped his hands on top of the folder. "Everything came from you. I just filed the paperwork."

The clusterfuck of events replayed in my head as I stared at the electronic signature. My signature. Anna thought I'd trapped her. No, she knew I'd trapped her.

My anger slowly turned to self-loathing.

"What else?" I asked meeting Scott's gaze. "What else did I request?"

Emboldened by my change of demeanor, Scott pushed out of his seat. Pulling another item from the folder as he rounded the desk, he handed me the paper and then slid a hip onto the mahogany as if his proximity was something I welcomed.

"That's the emergency request for visitation." Scott pointed at Anna's signature. "Anna signed it this morning. She'll present the child for your first official visit as soon as possible. I called Ms. Hollis when I got your text. Haven't heard back yet, but I told her secretary you were back in town."

I ripped a hand through my hair. "Peyton knows. I called her before I got here."

Scott clucked his tongue. "As your attorney, I'm advising you to cease contact with opposing counsel."

Glancing over Anna's shaky scrawl, I cringed inside. "I know Peyton. We went to school together." I reached for the glass bottle of imported water. "How did this happen so quickly?"

"That's why they call it an emergency request. If Anna hadn't signed, we'd have a court order in her hand mandating her to turn over the child within days. At least this way she gets a little say so." Scott snapped his fingers, then pulled out a note. "Which reminds me. Anna's only sticking point was that the visitations take place at her parents' or your aunt's. If you want me to hold her feet to the fire on that, I can—"

"No." I shook my head. "I'm fine seeing Willow at Anna's parents'. I don't . . . I don't want to scare her."

Scott shrugged, handing over the next document. "Let me know if you change your mind." He motioned to the paper. "We can fast track this now." My eyes bulged when I looked down.

*Request for Custody.*

Scott offered me an expensive looking pen. "Just sign at the bottom."

"I . . ." Words failed me as I read the first passage. Legalese about my rights to "the child."

"It's probably safer to wait for the results of the DNA test," Scott mused, folding his arms over his chest. "But since you seemed sure, I had the papers drawn up."

"It's not filed, though?" I roughed out.

He shook his head. "Nah. But I did share a copy with Ms. Hollis to show your intent. There will likely be heavy negotiations when it comes to actual custody. But, who knows, Anna might want a break from parenting. I've seen these cases turn on a dime so you should be prepared."

Scott's brows climbed to his hairline when I sat up straight, glaring. "Anna would never do that. She would never hurt Willow."

The papers spread out on the desk mocked me.

I hurt Willow. *Me.*

My silent introspection gave Scott his second wind. "As far as money," he said, shifting to stretch his legs. "Anna's waived all but nominal support—very nominal considering your means. She's requested all future monies beyond that amount be put in here."

Scott handed me a thick, leather folder. My shoulders sank as I ran a finger over the delicate gold leafing embossed on the portfolio.

*The Willow Grace Hudson Trust*

"As requested, I drew up the trust," Scott continued. "But Anna declined to serve as trustee. And Ms. Hollis returned the lump sum you offered as a settlement."

*A settlement . . .*

It was never that.

Stunned into silence, I took the check stub for the money I set aside for Anna. The vessel of my guilt.

"Put the money in the trust," I said thickly, placing the stub into Willow's folder. "Get Peyton to appoint Alecia Dresden as the trustee."

Scott gathered the papers, shoving them neatly into a file. "Sure, I can do that. You must've been born under a lucky star, considering the timing."

Every time Scott said the word "lucky," I felt like the unluckiest motherfucker on the planet. But I took the bait.

"How so?"

"Peyton, er, Ms. Hollis settled Anna's divorce. There's an interlocutory period, and the judge has to approve, but you don't have to worry about Dean Kent, considering he dropped his case."

"Why . . . ?" I cleared my throat. "Why would he do that."

Scott leaned across the desk and plucked another file from his inbasket. After perusing the contents, he smiled. "Guess Anna's not much for confrontation. She gave Dean everything he asked for, quitclaimed the deed to the joint residence and relinquished all the personal property. As far as I can tell there was only one stipulation."

I didn't want to know, but again, I had to ask. "And what was that?"

Scott frowned and I could see the wheels turning.

My pulse raced. Maybe there was a mistake. A loophole and all of this could be unwound.

"Anna's only stipulation was a full release from Dean vacating the order. Ahh . . . see it's right here. The judge released the hold on the kid's passport. It looks like Anna might be eager to do a little traveling."

My mind jumped to the only possible conclusion, landing with a thud. *The tour.* Anna gave Dean the golden ticket, the rights to everything she had in the world, in exchange for her freedom. And Willow's. I'd taken every piece of security Anna had glued together and smashed it in one fell swoop.

Mistaking my stunned demeanor for concern over this new wrinkle, Scott said, "I'll have my paralegal prepare a new order to replace Dean's. It will bind Anna under the same conditions."

*Bind her?* I'd already ruined her life, stolen her dreams, not once, but twice.

"No." I shook my head. "Don't file anything else. Are we clear?"

Scott pushed off the desk. "Whatever you say. I work for you."

The truth sank in, hard and cold and unmistakable. Scott *did* work for me.

I gulped down half the bottle of Perrier, but no amount of fancy water could wash the bitter taste from my mouth.

*Air.*

I needed to breathe something untainted by the stench of the paperwork and all it represented.

"Is there any way that I can talk to Anna?" I asked, shoving to my feet. "Can you get her a message for me?"

Scott sucked in a breath. "I've already worked miracles." He cocked a dark brow when I glared at him. "Whether you see it that way or not, nobody else could've moved this fast. You'll have the right to co-parent the child, but I can't make Anna talk to you."

"Willow."

"Pardon?"

"The child," I said thickly. "Her name is Willow."

"Of course . . ." Scott pulled one last document from the file. "Willow Grace Hudson." He laid the application to change my daughter's birth certificate on the desk. "I'll file this as soon as we get the results from the DNA test. Sign here."

Attached to the application was the only document that didn't cause me physical pain. Willow's birth certificate. I skimmed over my daughter's vital statistics—date of birth, weight, height—committing each to memory.

After scanning the rest of the application for ticking time bombs, I jotted my name in the box. "File it now."

"Will do." The clueless fucker clapped me on the back, and my skin crawled. "Congratulations, Daddy, it's a girl."

Scott's assistant tapped on the door. "I'm glad you're still here, Mr. Hudson." She walked in, holding out a note for Scott. "Peyton Hollis just called. Anna will present Willow at her parents' house as soon as tomorrow morning if you want to set up a visit."

Relief flooded me.

"Of course, "I replied. "What time does Anna want to meet?"

Her smile faded, dashing the flicker of hope blooming in my chest.

"Anna's not meeting you. She's dropping the child off for a custody exchange. She's requested that you don't show up at the property until after eight so the two of you don't bump into each other."

Holding the folder full of my betrayals, I waited until the assistant was gone to address Scott. "Is there any money left from my retainer?"

"Yeah, let me check and see what you've got."

Scott turned to his computer, but I stopped him.

"Consider it a bonus," I said as I strode to the door. "Send all my paperwork over to Trevor. You're fired."

# CHAPTER FORTY-TWO

**Sean**

The halo from my headlights spread from the garage door to the red brick exterior as I pulled into Melissa's driveway.

The in-dash clock jolted me out of my stupor: 10:22 p.m. I'd been driving for hours, ever since I left Scott's office.

Bone weary and emptier than I'd ever been, I slid my key into the lock on the front door.

"Hello?" I called, flipping the deadbolt behind me. "Anybody home?"

Melissa's raspy voice drifted from the family room. "In here, sugar."

Sinking onto the edge of the recliner, I buried my head in my hands. Melissa scooted to the end of the couch, and the scent of rose petals and vanilla enveloped me. By intention or by design, she smelled just like my mother.

"What is it?" Melissa wobbled to her feet when I didn't answer. "Sean, look at me."

I didn't have the strength. Or more likely I didn't want Melissa to see it all. The failure, the shame, the fucking mess I'd made of things. *Again.*

If the road to hell was paved with good intentions, many of the bricks had my name on them.

Tears pricked the back of my eyes as I stared down at my boots. When Melissa laid a hand on my shoulder, I gave up, wrapping my arms around her waist and letting her soothe me like I was a child.

Her thin, birdlike frame brought me back to the present—her present—and I clenched my teeth and straightened.

"I'm fine." I managed a weak smile, regretting my decision to come here in the first place. "There's just some shit going on."

Melissa's blue gaze clouded with concern. I didn't do this kind of emotion, and she damn well knew it. Yet, here I was, in a dimly lit room, looking up at one of only a handful of people who could read me like a book.

Before I could set her mind at ease, Melissa dropped a copy of *Us Weekly* face up in my lap. "Does it have something to do with this?"

*Reunion! Sean Hudson and Kimber Tyson rekindle their romance as the bad boy drummer prepares to announce plans for a European tour.*

As Mandy had predicted, the story had grown legs.

"I'm guessing that's all bullshit." Doubt flickered in Melissa's eyes. "Right, sugar?"

Tossing the rag on the floor, I pushed out a breath. "Of course it is. But it's not just that."

A humorless laugh rumbled from my chest. It seemed my fuck-ups had now reached the point where more than one could cause this kind of grief.

That took talent.

Melissa sank back onto the couch and drew in a labored breath.

"Are we playing twenty questions? Because I'm not up to it, Sean. Why don't you just tell me what happened."

Apparently, my selfishness knew no bounds. Because instead of leaving and dealing with my mess on my own, I looked down at my clasped hands and let it all pour out. When I finished, my guts lay in a puddle on the floor at Melissa's feet.

My aunt shifted, her rigid posture warring with the sympathy etching her brow. "I can see why Anna would think you set her up. What is she saying about it?"

"She won't talk to me."

"So you haven't spoken to her, and now you're in a legal battle?"

*I wish.* I'd face Anna's wrath over her silent exile any day.

"Nope. No legal battle." I dropped my head to the back of the chair. "She agreed to everything. Visitation. DNA testing—"

"You asked for a DNA test?" Melissa's feet hit the floor with a thud. "Sean, how could you do that?"

For the hundredth time, Willow's blue eyes flashed behind my lids. But it wouldn't have mattered if they were green, or brown, or yellow with polka dots. She was mine.

"It's standard procedure. I was following my attorney's orders."

Melissa saw right through my bullshit. "Since when do you follow anyone's orders?"

"What do you want me to say?" I growled, shoving to my feet. "I didn't mean for it to go down like this!"

Melissa jabbed her finger against my chest, then roared, "Dammit, Sean! Stop making excuses."

Disappointment curved her shoulders, and she grabbed my arms, for support or to shake me, I couldn't tell.

Shame washed over me, and I eased her onto the couch.

"I shouldn't have come. I'll deal with it, Lissa, I swear."

"Horse shit. We'll figure it out together." Her hand flew to her throat as a coughing fit ensued. "Get me a Dr. Pepper," she wheezed. "So I can think."

When I returned with the soda, Melissa was sitting at the far corner of the couch, glancing over the pictures on the side table. I recognized the 8x10 of Anna and me in our graduation garb. Three brightly colored chords hung from her neck, a testament to all her achievements. Her unlimited promise. At the time, I had nothing but a dream and the love of a girl who was way out of my league.

"You know, technology is pretty useful sometimes," Melissa said softly as I handed her the can. "Chelsea showed me how to send those snapshots I took straight to Walgreens. Do you know they had them ready in an hour?"

Two smaller pictures I'd never seen sat in silver frames. One of Willow on Anna's lap, her little face tilted to her mother in adoration, and the other, a candid shot of the three of us.

The pain in my chest threatened to break me in half.

*My family.*

"Are you going to hide out here for a couple of days?" Melissa asked. "It's your house too. You know you're always welcome."

Flopping onto the sofa, I draped my arm over her shoulder. "I've got visitation with Willow tomorrow morning at Alecia and Brian's."

She cackled. "That'll teach you. Brian's going to tune you up but good."

I sighed. "I could have had Willow's visits here if I wanted. Anna gave me the choice."

She'd always given me choices. I'd been the one who'd refused to negotiate.

Reading my mind, Melissa huffed, "That girl's amazing. Still making it easy on you. You need to do whatever it takes to get her to talk to you."

The weight of Melissa's expectations added to the exhaustion spreading through my limbs. "There's not much I can do if she won't answer me."

She hummed, lacing our fingers. "Do you remember when that guy hit your pickup truck when you were in high school?" I nodded, and she laughed. "When you found out he didn't have insurance, you followed him around for a month to make sure he paid for that dent. Not that anyone would notice one dent in that old rust bucket."

Dropping my head back, I closed my eyes. "Is there a point coming anytime soon?"

"My point is," Melissa jabbed me in the ribs, "you've got a lot of tenacity when it suits you. But when it doesn't, you let things fall through the cracks. "

I gave her a sidelong glance. "Are you comparing Anna to an '85 Chevy?"

"No. I just want you to get your priorities straight. And it's not just about Anna. Willow's not your girlfriend. She's not your aunt or your cousin. She's your daughter."

I sat up, my fatigue all but erased by the indignation stiffening my spine. "Are you saying I don't take care of my family?"

Melissa's gaze followed mine as I glanced over the expensive furniture and top of the line electronics I'd purchased.

"You're a generous man," she conceded. "But Willow doesn't need any grand gestures. She needs you. Remember that."

Signaling an end to the discussion, Melissa laid her head on my shoulder and flipped to a re-run of *Buffy the Vampire Slayer*. We used to watch the series religiously when I was a kid. Or rather, Melissa watched while I fantasized about Sarah Michelle Gellar, the only good thing about the show, in my opinion.

Still, I'd sat through every episode more than once because Melissa enjoyed it.

Thinking back over the last four years, I tried to remember the last time I did anything to suit anyone but myself.

*My needs. My time. My terms.*

Sadly, my actions proved I was still that guy, looking out for myself and rolling over anyone who got in my way.

Including Anna.

*My Anna.*

I chased her away. And now I had to face reality—my daughter didn't make me a better man.

I had to do that for myself.

# CHAPTER FORTY-THREE

**Sean**

*W*aiting in my car a block away from the Dresden house, I checked the clock, and seeing as I had a few minutes, I fired off another text to Anna.

*Talk to me, baby. I'm right outside.*

While I waited for a reply that would probably never come, I scrolled through the last batch of messages I'd sent.

*I didn't know what the lawyer was going to do.*

*Let me explain.*

*All I wanted to do was protect you.*

I didn't even mention Kimber. The lawsuit and threat to wrangle custody of our daughter was enough.

When the clock on the dash read 8:00 a.m., I pulled alongside the house, then got out of the car and made the trek up the rose-lined path.

After climbing the steps, I stood at the front door and looked around. The same porch swing hung in the corner, and I could practically feel the wooden slats against my back from all the hours Anna and I had spent in that very spot.

*What the hell are you doing here?*

As if by magic, the door swung open and my question was answered.

"Sen!"

Willow reached for me, but she was firmly entrenched in her grandfather's arms, and Brian looked pissed as hell, so I made no move to grab her.

"Hey, Willow-baby." I shifted my attention to Anna's father and smiled grimly. "Brian."

He set Willow on her feet, and she coiled her fingers around mine, but Brian seemed intent on blocking my path.

In a menacing tone, too low for Willow to hear, he growled, "You don't seem too sure of yourself, son. If you changed your mind, I'd be happy to show you to your car."

The nineteen-year age gap separating Anna's father and me seemed more pronounced when I was young. Brian was always imposing with his broad shoulders and thickly muscled arms, but back then, I thought he was old, and I laughed off his thinly veiled threats.

*Don't ever hurt my daughter or there won't be enough of your body left to identify, we clear, son?*

Brian's comments usually earned him a light slap on the arm from Alecia and an eye roll from Anna.

But now, glimpsing the ink peeking from the sleeve of his T-shirt, I didn't notice the gray hair dusting his temples or the faint lines around his eyes. All I saw was a man of similar height and build, ready to show me the business end of his rather large fists.

Weighing the options—a knockdown, drag-out fight on the porch of his home while my daughter watched, or taking Willow to Melissa's, I prepared to exercise the out-clause Anna had given me.

"Listen, Brian," I began. "I think it would be better—"

Alecia shoved her husband out of the way. "Quit glaring at the boy, Brian." She faced me with a forced smile. "Please come in, Sean."

There was pleading in her eyes that I couldn't ignore.

"Thanks," I said, letting Willow pull me into the house.

After I took a seat on the couch, Willow flopped on the floor a few feet away, leaving me to deal with her grandparents.

"Go get us some sweet tea," Alecia said to Brian, shooing him away. "And grab Willow some of that organic pear juice."

Once he was gone, Alecia turned her emerald gaze on me. "I want you to tell me right now if this is some kind of game."

Propping my elbows on my knees, I clasped my hands and looked down at the carpet. "No game."

Alecia heaved out a breath. "Why couldn't you just be honest with Anna? Tricking her, telling her you loved her, that was cruel, Sean."

I felt Anna's presence, and I knew she was probably hovering on the staircase. So I sat up and spoke only for her.

"I didn't lie about loving Anna. I've never loved another woman."

*And I never will.* I left that part out because some truths were too painful to admit.

Alecia folded her arms over her chest and sat back, silently urging me to continue.

"I didn't know Scott was preparing that summons. Or the DNA test. None of it." Cursing the weary sigh that tripped from my lips, I shook my head. "I'm not going to fight Anna for custody. I just wanted to know my daughter. Give her my name." I glanced at Alecia. "Is that too much to ask?"

Her lips parted like she was about to let loose, and I prepared for her wrath. But then Anna's picture lit up the screen on the phone in Alecia's hand.

I heard the patter of footsteps on the stairs, and then Brian took off like a shot, following his little girl. The same way I'd follow mine.

Alecia shoved to her feet and left the room to take the call. Anna was saving me again, and fuck, I didn't deserve it.

Willow gave me the side-eye, and accepting her invitation, I slid onto the floor and crawled to her side.

"What are you doing, Willow-baby?"

"Payin wiff bocks."

I eased onto my stomach. "Need some help?"

She didn't answer, but after a moment she tapped my arm. Dropping a block into my hand, she waited while I chose a spot. After several more exchanges, she leaned against me, surveying our handiwork with a most serious expression.

"It's goo." Her little brow knit and she amended, "It's gooda."

She peered over at me for confirmation, and I smiled. "That's right, baby, it's good."

Grabbing her coloring book, she slid onto her belly right next to me. "Cowor now."

She smoothed the page before examining the box of Crayolas. Handing me a blue crayon, she smiled. "Buue."

Shoulder to shoulder, we worked in silence, and when the portrait was complete, I picked up a discarded brown crayon.

Willow's lips formed a little o as I sketched a tree in the corner right below where I wrote her name. She watched intently as I sorted through the crayons for just the right color.

"Green." Swallowing over the lump in my throat, I lovingly filled in the leaves on every branch. "Like mommy's eyes."

# CHAPTER FORTY-FOUR

**Anna**

*I* knocked on the door of my old house, and getting no answer, I slid my key into the deadbolt, hoping Dean hadn't called a locksmith.

The tumblers clicked, and I breathed a sigh of relief as I stepped into the foyer. A stack of mail sat on the small table below the art niche, and I grabbed the pile before heading to the kitchen.

I yelped, the letters slipping from my hands, when I rounded the corner and saw Dean sitting at the table.

"I-I'm sorry. I knocked. I didn't know you were here."

After studying me for a moment, he shoved to his feet and took out his earbuds. "I didn't hear you."

I backed up as Dean closed the gap between us, my cheeks flaming when he stooped to pick up the mail. "You don't have to be afraid of me, Anna."

Annoyance laced his tone, rightfully so, and I crouched to help him.

"I know that." Our eyes met when he handed me the stack, and I smiled. "How are you?"

Dean walked to the coffee pot and, taking a mug from the hook under the cabinet, he said, "Better than you, I guess."

He poured coffee into the cup, added sugar, and then set the steaming brew on the counter in front of me.

"Sorry, I don't have any cream." He motioned to the table. "Do you have time to talk?"

I had nothing but time. In fact, I'd seriously considered what I was going to do for the few hours Sean was with Willow. After the first visit when I'd lurked on the stairs, I decided it would be better if I wasn't around for any others.

I took a seat. "You're not going to the office today?"

He shrugged. "I've got court this afternoon. Just getting some notes together."

Glancing over the papers strewn over the table, I realized the intrusion and picked up my cup.

Dean sat back, scrutinizing me, and after a moment of yawning silence, he asked, "Where's Willow?"

The hot liquid burned my tongue when I took a larger gulp than I meant to. "Um . . . she's having a visitation with Sean at my parents' house."

Dean cursed under his breath and looked down. He'd always told me that nothing good would come of anything concerning Sean, but he was wrong.

"He's good with Willow," I said quietly. "And that's all that matters."

"And I wasn't."

Shocked, I jerked my gaze to his. "No, you were fine with her. It's just . . ."

*Not the same.* I left that part out. Dean didn't deserve it. He was a good man in a bad situation. And now he was free to get on with his life.

"Look, Anna," he began slowly. "I have my apartment downtown. Why don't you and the baby move back in here?"

For a brief second, I considered it. But then I shook my head. "That's really nice of you, but I've got some other things I'm looking into."

Dean sat back, brown eyes searching my face. "What kind of things?"

My mouth went dry, and I felt a strange sense of guilt discussing this with him since I hadn't told anyone else. But then, it wouldn't be the first secret we'd shared.

"I'm thinking about going back to school."

Dean leaned forward, smiling. "Law school?"

I nodded, suddenly shy about the whole thing. I'd always intended to go back, but then Willow's hearing problem came to light, and I'd spent every waking moment making sure that I was there for her.

"I think that's great," he said, covering my hand with his. I didn't flinch or try to move away. There was no spark, and we both knew it. "Have you talked to the admissions department?"

I gave him a tight smile because of course, he was assuming I was talking about UT Law. But that ship had sailed.

"Yes." It was an honest answer, at least that's what I told myself. I *had* spoken to the registrar's office at Baylor. "They're reviewing my transcripts."

We spent the next two hours talking about first-year courses and what classes I should take if I got in.

And then Dean shoved to his feet. "I've got to get ready for court." He smiled. "You can come with me if you'd like. I can dazzle you with my mad skills."

I laughed as I pushed out of my chair. "I don't think that would be a good idea."

Dean's eyes lost a little of their sparkle. "Because of Sean? Are you still holding on to that dream, Anna?"

"No," I said softly. "I've learned my lesson. It's time to dream a new dream."

A little piece of me felt bad about lying to Dean because a part of that dream would never die. But I'd bury it, just like I had for the past four years.

Dean's lips parted, and I could tell he wanted to say something else. But he didn't. Instead, he wrapped his arms around me and kissed the top of my head.

"You're the smartest girl I've ever met. If there's anything I can do..."

The invitation hung between us, but unlike before, I wouldn't be accepting his offer.

This time, I had to do things on my own.

For me and for Willow.

# CHAPTER FORTY-FIVE

**Sean**

*"I*'m out of here," Chelsea mumbled, jumping out of the Range Rover as we coasted to a stop. Tapping her foot, she waited for Melissa's garage door to open, then flounced into the house.

I met Melissa's unfocused gaze in the rearview mirror. "What the hell is her problem?"

Drugged up from the medication they gave her before we left the hospital, my aunt offered a drowsy smile. "She's scared, sugar. Give her time."

I understood all about the fear. The past two nights while Melissa recovered in her hospital room, I thought I'd choke from the weight of it. Even though the doctors had assured us that the surgery was a success, I hadn't slept more than a few hours, keeping vigil next to Melissa's bed.

Turning my attention to Willow, sitting quietly in her car seat, my anxiety abated at the sight of her little face.

"We're all scared, Melissa," I said as I pulled the car into the garage. "But Chelsea needs to step it up. If she's going to disappear into her room, I'm going to hire a nurse to make sure you're not alone."

Melissa tried not to chuckle. "Not much chance of that happening. Every time I turn around, you're underfoot."

She was right. But I didn't have a choice in the matter. I wouldn't violate Anna's rules about visitation. But Brian couldn't stand the sight of me, and I didn't feel comfortable spending my mornings in his living room.

Melissa touched my hand as I loosened the buckles on Willow's car seat. "Aren't you supposed to be somewhere in Europe or Asia or somewhere?"

Ignoring the question, I set Willow on her feet and then slid my arms under Melissa's legs.

Halting my forward progress with a firm hand to my chest, she frowned. "You haven't mentioned the tour. When do you leave?"

For someone hopped up on pain meds, she had a surprisingly strong will.

It was either answer the question or wrestle Melissa to the ground. "There is no tour."

Not technically correct. But not a lie either.

Melissa's eyes widened. "Sugar, what did you do?"

Motioning for Willow to follow, I carried my aunt through the house.

"You didn't answer my question," Melissa said weakly as I settled her onto the couch. "What did you do?"

"It's complicated. Now stop with the third degree and tell me what you want to drink."

A smile ghosted her lips. "Whiskey sour."

"Water it is. Be right back."

As I headed out of the room, Willow climbed onto the couch. I slowed to make sure she wouldn't disturb Melissa, but I should've known better. My aunt welcomed my baby with open arms and tucked Willow to her side.

When I returned a few moments later, Melissa was absently

sifting through Willow's auburn curls. "Let's hope Willow's hair color isn't the only thing she inherited from Annabelle."

Setting the glass on the end table, I dropped into the chair and then scrubbed a hand down my face. "I hope she picked up a few traits from our side of the family. They're not *all* bad."

Melissa's azure gaze darkened with fear. "It's not her personality that concerns me."

Chelsea started stomping around upstairs, and glaring up at the ceiling, I muttered, "I'm going to take that kid's car away if she doesn't adjust her damn attitude."

Melissa sighed, wincing from the effort. "Cut her some slack, sugar. She's got a lot to contend with."

Anger flashed hot through my veins. "Nobody's contending with you. Don't ever think that."

Melissa's pressed a kiss to Willow's head. "Not me. The disease. What it could mean for her." Her small smile returned. "I'm damn lucky; you know that, right?"

One glimpse of the bandages peeking from the top of my aunt's top proved how unlucky she was. "How so?"

Melissa managed a half shrug. "I watched Mama and Gracie die. And still, I didn't think it would happen to me."

With the medication loosening her tongue, Melissa's honesty had slipped into brutal territory.

Glassy blue eyes peered up at me. "I should've died, Sean. Stage two at my age? That's a miracle. And lightning doesn't strike twice."

Focusing all my attention on straightening her blanket, I avoided her gaze. "Time for a nap."

Melissa's fingers curled around my arm. "You don't understand. They want to run the tests on Chelsea."

The tests. *One test.* To determine your whole life.

The ever-present fear slithered through me, and I dropped onto the chair with a thud, holding Melissa's hand. "When?"

"Soon. But the thing is, she's about to turn eighteen, and I can't make her take the test."

With false bravado, I muttered, "I can."

Something akin to relief shadowed Melissa's features. "So you'll talk to her?"

Her blue eyes locked on mine, the silver threads beseeching, and I realized Melissa meant now. My façade of strength cracked, and I slumped. "Yeah, sure."

*Fuck.*

Blowing out a breath, I pushed to my feet.

Melissa smiled, curling her arm around Willow, fast asleep at her side. "Thank you."

Reluctantly, I climbed the stairs, following the music spilling into the hallway. Classical, of course.

"Come in," Chelsea grumbled in response to my knock.

Sprawled out on her stomach on the bed, she didn't look up when I walked in.

"Whatcha doing, kid?"

Chelsea shot me an evil glare.

Shoving my hands in my pockets, I took a look around.

Pausing at her desk to thumb through some sheet music, I asked, "Whose are these?"

When Chelsea didn't answer, I gathered the pages and then sank onto the edge of her bed.

She rose to sitting, eyeing me warily. "What are you doing?"

"What's it look like?"

Chelsea snorted. "Trying to read music."

"You think I can't read music?" I cocked a brow. "I play the drums, guitar, piano, and the bass. I think I can muddle through this."

She wrinkled her nose and then scooted to the head of the bed, drawing her knees to her chest. "Why did you choose the drums of all things?"

Ignoring her jab, I dropped to my elbow. "Because the beat in my head drowns out most of the other instruments."

A small smile curved Chelsea's lips. "I hear strings. Individual strings. You know, like when I'm walking around."

"How does that work?"

I knew how it worked, but the kid hadn't talked to me in two weeks without scowling, so I was running with the conversation.

Humoring me, Chelsea twisted up her mouth in contemplation. "Birds, they have a specific string. Crickets too. And people."

I fingered the sheets, nodding. "So you change the scores to fit the sound in your head?"

Indignant, her brows dove together. "Those are mine, Sean. My stuff. There is no score to change."

Pride filled me from some unknown place as I glanced over the intricate work. I'd purchased all Chelsea's instruments, including the six-thousand-dollar violin. But I had no idea she was this good.

I sighed. "I'm sorry you didn't get into Juilliard, Chels."

It was the first time I'd mentioned it. Because, apparently, I was a fucking dick.

Chelsea smirked. "I did get into Juilliard." She raised a brow when my lips parted in surprise. "I didn't want to leave Mama." She frowned and looked down at her hands. "Guess I made the right choice."

Sheets of paper fluttered to the floor when I sat up. "You can't give up your dreams, Chels. Your mama wouldn't want that."

"I'm not giving up shit. I don't want it." She glanced around the room at the pictures of me performing. "That's your dream, not mine."

Contentment sparked in her eyes, and I knew she was telling the truth.

"Fair enough." I managed a smile. "I'm going to take care of things. I don't want you to worry when you go to Dallas."

"I'm not going to Dallas either," she said flatly. "I only told Mama I would go to get her off my back. She believed me when I told her I didn't get into Juilliard. She wouldn't believe I didn't get into SMU."

I ran a frustrated hand through my hair. "So you're just going to hang around here and play the martyr? Good plan."

"I'm not playing the martyr, asshole," she hissed. "If I wanted to go, I would. But I'm not you. I don't suffer through family dinners and holidays. I like it here."

Direct hit, straight to the solar plexus. I had to look away, and when I did, a picture on Chelsea's mirror caught my eye. Christmas two years ago. Chelsea sat between Logan and me in front of the fireplace, and to my shock, he seemed happier to be there than I did. My focus wasn't even on the camera, but somewhere in the distance.

With the photo mocking me, I asked, "What are your plans then, after you graduate?"

"Music theory at UT." A smile played on Chelsea's lips. "I want to teach someday."

Like the other women in my life, Chelsea had a knack for making me feel unworthy. She didn't have to try since I suspected it was true.

Her scowl returned, and she crossed her arms over her chest. "So, when are you leaving anyway?"

Running through my list of errands, I rubbed the back of my neck. "I've got to make dinner and then I'll head to the pharmacy to pick up your mama's pain meds. But I'm going to sleep here tonight."

Rolling her eyes, an exasperated sigh tripped from her lips. "No, I mean for the tour."

"Oh, that." I picked at the fringe of her Hello Kitty throw pillow. "I'm sitting this one out." Saying it out loud, admitting it, lifted a weight, and I smiled. "I've got a few things to take care of here."

"Yeah." She snorted. "I figured that. Since your 'thing' decided to join us at the hospital."

A flame ignited in my chest. "That's my daughter you're talking about. And your cousin."

Turning that stone cold glare my way, Chelsea huffed, "Excuse me if I don't get all emotional, considering I might not see her again for years. Anna never came around after you dumped her. And you never bothered to tell us about your kid."

Chelsea couldn't have landed a more solid blow if she'd used a bat.

Deflating from the blunt force trauma, I sank back onto my elbow. "I would've. But I didn't know about her."

"You didn't?" Chelsea's tone thawed slightly. "Anna didn't tell you?"

I shook my head, the lump in my throat too massive to speak.

"Oh . . ." She shrugged. "I just thought you were too busy to bring her around."

And the hits keep coming . . .

"Nope. Just didn't know. But she's here now, and so am I." A few beats of silence while I tried to think of the right words, the right thoughts to keep Chelsea from shutting me out.

"I know you're scared," I finally said, "I'm scared too. But you don't have to handle this by yourself."

Guilt washed over me as Chelsea rested her chin on her knees. She looked grown, except for the eyes. I could still see the child in those blue orbs.

And when did that happen?

For years I'd put the people I loved in a box, taking them out on holidays, or when it suited me.

Chelsea outgrew her box long ago. And I'd missed it.

I tugged Chelsea's hand, and though she held out for a second, she finally relented and let me lace our fingers. Once, I was her hero. But I'd lost the title long ago if her hidden resentment was any indication.

"Listen to me," I said, seriously. "If you need me, I'll be here. I still have to work. I haven't figured everything out yet. But I'm just a phone call away, and I'll never be gone long."

Chelsea nodded, her gaze on our joined hands.

Brushing her calloused fingertips with my thumb, I dipped my head to find her eyes. "Your mom and I were talking about the . . . cancer. You have to promise me you'll do everything the doctors ask and that you won't avoid any of the tests." I tilted her chin with my finger. "I may need you to help me explain things when Willow gets older. So promise me, yeah?"

Chelsea blinked, tears gathering in her eyes. "B-but . . . Willow's just a baby."

She crumbled then, and I pulled her into my arms, my lips grazing her sandy brown hair. "So are you, sugar."

Fisting my shirt, Chelsea let go of all the emotion she'd been holding in. Sobs wracked her body as her fear and sorrow poured out in buckets. Rocking her gently, I waited for her breath to even out and then I took her face between my hands and bumped my forehead to hers like I did when she was little.

"I've got to go check on Willow. Can you come downstairs and watch your mom when I take her back to Alecia and Brian's?"

Chelsea pulled away, swiping her soggy cheeks. "Where's Anna? Isn't she coming over?"

Pushing off the bed, I gave her a soft smile. "It's complicated."

She caught my hand, squeezing my fingers. "Uncomplicate it. I'm sorry for what I said at dinner. I miss her."

*You're missing from me.*

The skin over my heart flamed as if the tattoo had a life of its own. And maybe it did.

"She knows that, sugar." Tilting her chin with my finger, I grinned. "Are we good?"

Smiling at me, she nodded, and I tossed her a wink before I left.

In the hallway, I leaned against the wall to catch my breath.

Life was easier when I could write a fucking check and be done with it.

But those days were long gone.

# CHAPTER FORTY-SIX

**Sean**

*T*he pounding beat from the Bose system rattled the windows in the empty bedroom. Leaning on the handle of the roller, I spread pale pink paint on the wall with even strokes. Sweat trickled down my back, due in large part to the humid air seeping from the open window. It was almost May now, and May in Austin meant air conditioning, but I had to release the fumes or I'd pass the fuck out.

My phone vibrated on the table, so I dropped the roller into the pan. Wiping my hands on a towel, I leaned over and glimpsed the screen. A text from Logan.

*Let me in. It's hotter than shit out here.*

Logan had a key to my front door, which was likely unlocked anyway, but since we hadn't spoken in a month, I could see why he was a little wary of barging in.

He didn't need to be.

Regardless of the role he'd played in my meltdown with Anna, he wasn't to blame. He was my best friend, and I didn't want him going on the road for a year with this hanging over our heads. Jogging down the stairs, I pulled the rubber band out of my hair and then opened the door.

Propped against a pillar in the archway with his arms folded over his chest, Logan stared at me with wary blue eyes.

Cocking a brow, I stepped back to allow him entry. "Do you want to come in, or are you planning on glowering at me from the porch all day?"

Logan flashed a grin as he pushed off the stone column. "Glowering?" He knocked me in the shoulder on his way inside. "Someone got a word of the day calendar for their birthday."

I followed Logan to the kitchen where he flopped onto a barstool at the breakfast nook.

Despite the smile, he looked like he might need alcohol to get through the conversation, so I dug a couple of beers out of the fridge.

"My birthday's not until next month, asshat," I told him, handing over a bottle of Shiner Bock.

He shrugged. "I know. I figured it took you eleven months to get to G." Twisting off the cap, he flicked the disc between his thumb and middle finger, aiming for the sink. The metal circle bounced off the faucet, landing on the counter. "Ohhh," he hissed a breath through his teeth, "so close."

Opening my bottle, I smiled and then took my shot. With one snap, the disc sailed into the nearby trashcan. I chuckled. "But yet so far."

Logan rolled his eyes. "Lucky shot."

My focus shifted to the spot on his cheek where I'd landed my punch a month ago. There was no bruise, no outward signs of our scuffle. Only the awkward silence we'd maintained. "Yeah, I guess it was."

After a few moments of avoiding each other's gazes, I hoisted myself onto the island, letting my feet dangle. "So, what brings you by?"

Setting his beer on the granite, Logan turned the bottle around and around slowly. "I need a reason to visit my best friend?"

"Nope."

He gave me the side-eye. "You still pissed at me?"

"Yep."

When I didn't elaborate, he sighed and ripped a hand through his long hair. "I didn't know Benny's team was going to pull that shit with Kimber."

The declaration lay between us like a dead fish, but ironically, I believed him. Logan's agenda was his own. But I still wasn't sure what that was. It was more than the music, no matter what he'd said.

Logan had fired our manager for fucking with Cameron and Lily's relationship, and he didn't even know the girl at the time. It was about Cameron. Logan loved with all his heart, he just extended that emotion to very few.

Leaning back, I pressed my palms against the stone. "What did you think was going to happen if you put the two of us together, Kimber and me?"

Hitching an arm over the back of his chair, Logan blew out a breath. "I thought you were going to fuck her."

Logan didn't move a muscle when I slid off the island, chewing up the small space between us in three strides. The height of his barstool didn't give me much of a vertical advantage, though he did have to look up to meet my eyes. Unusual for him.

"What would you have done then? Send Anna an email?"

He sipped his beer and then replied casually, "Better me than someone else."

Clenching my fists, I fought to keep my tone steady. "You got a thing for my girl, dude?"

It was an outlandish question, more for shock value than anything else, but to my surprise, Logan looked me dead in the eyes and said, "Yeah, I do."

My hand shot up with no real target. But Logan was too quick. Covering my fist with his large palm, he forced my arm to my side.

"Cool your fucking jets." He chuckled, which was usually a precursor to his own fist meeting someone's face. "It's not about that. I didn't want to see Anna get hurt again, that's all." His eyes darkened, and all traces of humor faded. "She's like a sister to me."

His words trickled through my rage.

Like a sister. Like Laurel.

I'd hit the nail on the head the night of our scuffle, but I still didn't know where Anna fit. Why he chose to elevate her to a coveted status.

Rarefied air.

To my knowledge, only two women had ever achieved that position in Logan's eyes. His mother and his sister.

Confused, I sank onto the stool next to him. "If you were so against me hooking up with Anna, then why didn't you say anything when you saw her in my room at the Four Seasons."

"I thought it was a revenge fuck." He took another drink. "Hers, not yours, and I figured you deserved that. Then I found out about the ki . . . about Willow. And all of a sudden they're living with you."

"So you thought, what, you'd set me up and see if I'd bite?"

Logan looked away, confirming my suspicion.

"Well, I didn't." I hopped off my stool. "I wouldn't, and I don't give a fuck if you believe me or not."

"I believe you," he said, glancing down at his hands.

Since this was as close to an apology as I'd ever get, I decided to get over it. I was learning to get over a lot of things. And I needed Logan in my life.

"Come on." I nudged his shoulder. "I need your help with something."

Grabbing the rest of the six-pack, I headed up the stairs. Before I reached the landing, Logan's heavy footfalls echoed on the marble behind me, and I let out a sigh of relief.

He had my back, like always. And the rest? It didn't matter.

Setting the beer on the tarp, I surveyed the empty room while Logan dropped on his ass to tug off his combat boots. "What are we painting?"

"Willow's room."

He nodded, so I synced my phone with the boom box, and then a thundering beat surged from the powerful speakers, drowning out the possibility of any conversation. We didn't need to speak anyway.

I took a roll of painter's tape and started on the far wall, covering the top of the baseboards while Logan worked on the other side of the room. An hour later we met in the middle.

Plopping onto the floor to unwrap a paintbrush, I snapped my head up when Logan cut the music off.

Easing onto the floor, he stretched his long legs. "Did you know the only reason I graduated was because of Anna?"

I shook my head, surprised. "No, man, I had no clue."

To my knowledge, the two of them never studied together. Hell, Logan never studied at all.

Staring into his bottle, Logan's long, blond hair fell over his eyes. "I think my old man hit me in the head one too many times. I have a hard time reading and shit."

Cocking my head, I waited for him to look up. He didn't.

"Reading what?"

He shrugged. "Everything. The letters get all jumbled. Math was okay. I could, you know, copy the numbers onto the calculator. I memorized the formulas."

My stomach twisted. In school, Logan always conned one of us into giving him the highlights of any assignment we were asked to read. He'd say he forgot his book, or he didn't have time.

"What's Anna got to do with this?"

Logan met my questioning gaze, smiling. "I asked her for some help one day. And by help, I mean, I wanted to copy her paper. But she wouldn't give it to me." He snorted. "The chick had morals, go figure, since she was with you." He looked away for a second, squinting like he was reliving the memory. "Anyway, we got to studying this chapter on the Civil War. I started following along in the book and talking about General Eel." He smirked at my raised brow. "Yeah, that's the same look Anna got. Apparently, the dude's name was Lee. Robert. E. Lee. But that's not what I saw."

I hid my shock around my next sip of beer as he continued, "So, I got pissed and stormed off. But that night Anna called me and read me the story and the next day she gave me some notes. She told me to pick out the letters on the test and go with the ones I could remember. We, um, developed this system that was pretty easy. I'd just count how many letters in a name if I got into a jam, and then look for anything familiar."

"And that worked?"

Logan lifted a shoulder. "Well enough to pass. But Anna only gave me the notes after she'd read me the whole damn chapter so I knew the answers even if I couldn't get them on the paper."

From experience, I knew that Logan's memory was flawless. He could spit anything back verbatim. I assumed it was a weird little quirk, not a coping mechanism.

"How come you never told me?"

He laughed and then took a pull from his beer. "I spent an hour on the phone with your girl almost every night. I wasn't sure you'd be cool with that."

Of course, that's where his mind went, but I was talking more about why he never mentioned his problem. To me. His best friend.

After a long moment, Logan blew out a breath, and then as if he could read my mind, he said, "I figured you'd get the hint after we all moved in together. You didn't think it was kinda weird that Anna read out loud all the time?"

Since I loved the sound of Anna's voice, I always figured she was reading to me. For my benefit. But now that I thought about it, Logan was always there, sprawled out on the couch, thumbing through a magazine.

A magazine he couldn't read.

*Fuck.*

Shaking my head, I tried to make sense of what he'd just told me.

"Dude, what about contracts and . . ." Inhaling slowly, I gathered my thoughts. "Okay, so we need to get you some help for this shit, right?"

A storm swirled in his blue eyes as he lifted the bottle to his lips. "Fuck no," he growled like a dog backed into a corner. "I didn't tell you so you could fix my problem. I told you so you'd understand. I'd never hook up with Anna, even if she was down for it, which clearly, she never was. I'm the one who's been emailing her for over a year, but it was your sorry ass she came running back to."

A familiar ache settled over me.

Logan was wrong about the running part, but Anna had come back. Whether she wanted to admit it or not, she had faith that I'd fix this thing I broke. And I let her down.

Hanging my head, I picked at the label on my beer. "There's some shit you don't know."

Logan laughed. "Are you talking about your brilliant legal maneuver?" My silence wiped the smile from his face. "Yeah, I heard about that."

"I guess that confirms your suspicions." I saluted him with my bottle. "Congratulations. I'm an unworthy douchebag."

Logan pushed to his feet and then filled a pan with paint from the five-gallon bucket. Glancing over his shoulder, he rolled his eyes. "No, you're just a fucking idiot that's all."

Again, I lifted the bottle in a mock toast because I couldn't argue with that either.

Rolling a swath of pink paint onto the white wall, Logan wrinkled his nose. "All this shit you're doing, painting the room, visiting the kid every day, rearranging your plans? Maybe I was wrong."

I jumped to my feet. "I fucking sued her, dude. Had her served. You weren't wrong, I did hurt her."

Scrubbing a hand down my face, I tried to erase the image of Anna's wounded eyes from my memory. It didn't help. The picture was etched inside my lids, all the times she'd looked at me with mistrust.

Logan let out a sigh. "I've only been wrong about a couple of things in the last decade, and this ain't one of 'em. Once Anna sees this God-awful paint, she'll probably fall right into your arms. Nobody would put this shit on their walls unless they were seriously whipped."

I laughed. He was right about that. And he hadn't even seen the furniture I'd ordered.

Logan gave me a sidelong glance. "What are you waiting for? We need to get this shit done. Chop chop."

Grabbing the roller, I went to work. With every swipe my optimism grew, balancing out the sadness. A clean slate, that's what I'd give Willow. Something fresh, untainted by all the missteps. Because she was the one thing we got right, Anna and me. The best of what we were.

Wrapped up in my own thoughts, I didn't notice Logan's uncharacteristic silence until he said, "Laurel's in Tennessee."

Shocked, I turned to find him staring out at the lake, a slight breeze rustling his hair.

Dropping the roller, I joined him at the open window. "Where?"

"Nashville."

"You talked to her?"

He shook his head and then picked up a finishing brush. Dropping to his knees, he meticulously covered the small seam above the baseboards.

"Dude, you've got to give me more than that," I said, taking a seat on the five-gallon bucket. "What's she doing in Nashville? Is she trying to break into the business?"

He cocked his head, seemingly transfixed by the painting. "I suppose she could be doing a little singing in between lap dances. You never know." He smiled at his handiwork before hopping to his feet. "I'm going to wash up."

Logan strode from the room, and when he returned, wiping his hand on his jeans, his brows drew together.

"What?" he asked, reaching for his beer.

I shoved to my feet. "What are you going to do?"

He drained the last half of his beer in two gulps. "About?"

*About your sister, the stripper.*

Logan's misdirection didn't work on me, so I crossed my arms over my chest and waited.

His mouth twisted into a frown. "What do want me to say? If Laurel wants to take her clothes off for money, ain't my deal."

"So it doesn't bother you?"

The doorbell rang, interrupting our stare-off. When Logan broke ranks first, it was more telling than an admission.

Pausing at the door, he held onto the frame but didn't turn around. "I hired a private investigator. As soon as he gets me an address, I'm heading out there. Satisfied?"

"Then what?"

His shoulders curved inward. "Then I bring her home." The bell rang again. "Sounds like the gang's all here."

I followed him into the hallway. "Huh?"

"Didn't I tell you?" Thundering down the stairs, he called over his shoulder, "We're having a band meeting."

I dropped onto the couch as Christian and Cameron shuffled into the room, beers in hand. They sank onto the love seat wearing identical looks of annoyance.

Guilt gnawed at me for fucking with their plans. Our plans.

Logan propped up the wall next to the entertainment center, arms folded over his chest, staring down at the floor. Now that he wasn't angry anymore, I suspected he was having a hard time coming to terms with my decision to beg off the tour.

Nestling into the corner of the sofa, I waited for the penalty phase of the trial to commence. No need for closing arguments, I'd made my position clear: I wasn't going.

Pissed off, Cameron looked me over with mild contempt. "How's Melissa? Do you know anything yet?" I blinked at him, stunned, and he added in a softer tone, "About the cancer?"

My focus shifted to Logan. Lips pressed together in a grim line, concern etched the corners of his pale blue eyes, overshadowing any other emotion.

Guilt consumed me, and when I couldn't look at him anymore, or

find the words to apologize for not telling him, I turned my attention
back to Cameron and Christian.

Clearing the thick lump of tar from my throat, I said, "Um, she's
okay. Really good, actually." Nodding more for my benefit than theirs,
I shifted uncomfortably. "They caught it early. Stage two. She had a
mastectomy. How did y'all . . . um . . . ?"

"Find out?" Cameron cocked a brow, barely able to contain
himself. "From my girlfriend, who found out from your girlfriend.
That's all kinds of fucked up, dude."

Logan's gaze shifted to the window, and he no longer resembled
the self-assured rock star who showed up at my door a few hours ago.
He looked like the little boy Melissa comforted whenever he showed
up with a bloody nose or a black eye.

Christian slammed his beer on the table, his easygoing manner
disintegrating into a cloud of anger. "How could you not tell us?"
Ripping a hand through his thick mane of hair, he muttered,
"Melody's a research scientist, for fuck sake. You ever think that might
be helpful?"

"We'll sort that out later," Cameron cut in. "Right now, I'd like to
discuss what kind of douche-nozzle sends an email, a fucking email,
to inform us that he's quitting the band."

*Quitting the band?*

Pinching the bridge of my nose, I squeezed my eyes shut. "That's
not what—"

"He didn't say he was quitting," Logan interjected calmly. "The
asshat only said he couldn't do the tour."

"In an email!" Cameron roared, shaking the offending piece of
correspondence in his fist. "I wasn't keen on saddling up for a year,
and you didn't see me offering to find a replacement." He pinned me
with a brutally disdainful glare. "You don't replace family."

Despite their posturing, a definite air of disappointment
hung in the room. And I had to laugh. I'd only offered them a
few names because I thought it was the right thing to do—find
a fill-in drummer for the tour, nothing more. Not a
replacement.

Three sets of eyes swung my way as the inappropriate chuckle spilled from my lips.

"This isn't funny," Christian muttered.

"Yeah, I know," I conceded. "But I was trying to do the right thing. I'm not quitting; I just need some time to sort out my shit with Anna."

"Did you send her an email too?" Cameron crumpled the paper into a tight ball. "Knowing you, you probably did. Which is why you're here, looking like Tim the Tool Man with paint all over your hair, and your girl's over at my place having dinner with Lily."

I perked up. "Anna's at your place?"

"Yes, Anna's at my place," Cameron mocked in a nasally tone. "With Willow. Lily was going to come with me and act as Anna's stand-in just in case you wanted to serve her with another summons."

They were pulling out every stop on the hit parade. Not that I didn't deserve the ribbing, but much more and they'd break a bone.

Grimacing, I rubbed the back of my neck. "I didn't think that one through. It wasn't supposed to go down like that."

"Maybe you should've sent her a damned email after all, since you obviously have a problem with oral communication," Christian said dryly. "At least she would've had some notice."

Cameron tossed the crumpled paper at my head, and the messy wad landed in my lap like a grenade.

Though I'd vowed to maintain my silence, I couldn't resist asking, "So who did y'all decide on for the tour?"

I'd provided a list of studio musicians. Good, but not great. I wasn't stupid. I fully intended to take my place behind the kit as soon as I could swing it.

Christian and Cameron shifted their attention to Logan who was stretching like a cat.

"We turned down Benny's offer," he said offhandedly. "I talked to him as soon as I got your email."

My lips parted, but nothing came out, so I bowed my head, grateful and indebted in equal measure.

And guilty.

What if we didn't get another shot?

Before I could voice my reservations, Christian said, "You're not replaceable. If you got shit to handle here, we'll sit our asses at home and wait until the right gig comes along."

Praying my words wouldn't fail me, I cleared my throat. "That means a lot, y'all, but . . ."

Cameron groaned dramatically. "Why does there have to be a 'but'?"

I looked at each of them, hoping to convey my gratitude. The love I felt. And the responsibility. "Because of Willow. I've got to be here for her. No matter what."

"Do you see anyone preventing you from doing that?" Christian grumbled, annoyed. "You're the one that keeps stepping on your dick."

Logan barked out a laugh and dropped on the couch next to me.

"Impossible," he scoffed. "Sean couldn't step on his dick if he tried. I'm the only one that could pull off that particular feat. But enough about me. I've got some news."

Smiling into his sip of beer, Logan relished the silence as we waited for him to speak. Sadistic prick.

"Looks like we might be able to get an audition with Tori Grayson after all," he finally said. "Twin Souls is planning a memorial concert at Zilker Park on the five-year anniversary of the accident, using only talent from their roster. It's all on the down low, but Taryn Ayers is putting out feelers. She's signed a dozen new acts."

If anyone could pull off that kind of show, it was Tori's management group. Or rather, Taryn Ayers. She'd single-handedly wrestled control of the three biggest bands in the country from Metro Music's iron fist. The "Big Three." Leveraged, Revenged Theory, and Drafthouse, respectively. The heirs to the throne Damaged vacated. All Sixth Street originals.

The atmosphere turned decidedly upbeat, and everyone spoke at once. Gesturing wildly, we made plans that might never come to fruition. But that's how this all started to begin with. We dreamed big.

In the midst of the chaos, Logan stood up and wandered to the fridge.

Grabbing a twelve pack of beer, he said solemnly, "I hate to pump the brakes on the celebration, but this could take a few months. Leveraged is still in LA working on their never-ending album. Anyway, we got bigger fish to fry at the moment."

"What kind of fish fry are we talking about?" I asked.

Logan thumped the back of my head on his way to the stairs.

Scowling, I rubbed the sting out of the tender spot while Cameron and Christian laughed. I tossed a pillow in their direction and they promptly lobbed two back at me.

Logan whistled through his teeth from his position at the top of the stairs. "Am I the only one with any priorities?" he asked. "Willow's room ain't gonna paint itself."

Cameron and Christian plodded up the steps, assuring me that they'd only stick around for as long as the beer held out.

But I knew better.

They'd be here until all the walls were painted. No matter how many coats it took.

# CHAPTER FORTY-SEVEN

## Anna

*S*eated in front of my laptop at my childhood desk, I gazed out the window at the swaying leaves on the oak tree. Willow slept a few feet away, clutching a bear that Sean had given her.

Butterflies fluttered in my stomach as I brought up my email.

No, Sean and I weren't talking. Not in the strictest sense. But every night he sent me a message. Mostly about Willow, what they'd done that day and what they had planned for the next visit. He usually included pictures, and at the bottom, there was always a small poem or a lyric. Something for me alone.

It was driven by guilt, more than likely. For the Kimber debacle. And though I refused to take any blame in that, I knew what I was getting into when I moved into Sean's house. I wasn't enough for him, and that was nobody's fault.

From the first day, I'd suspected that his feelings for me were more of a reflection of his undying love for Willow. And the legal action proved it. Sean wanted his daughter, and I was an afterthought. One he could forget as soon as he stepped foot out of our little bubble.

Sighing from the weight of it all, I opened Sean's latest message, and a picture of Willow populated the screen. Parked behind her custom drum kit, she wore specially made pink earphones and a big smile.

Scanning through Sean's notes about the bed he'd commissioned for Willow's room at his house, my heart swelled with pride and then broke into a thousand pieces. Willow was about to begin her overnight visits, and Sean was pulling out all the stops to make her comfortable. Still, she'd be gone.

*Missing from me . . .*

When I got to the bottom of the page, there it was, Sean's latest musing.

*I never knew love*
*Until you showed me how to love you*
*I never knew pain*
*Until you took it all away*
*I never knew want*
*Until I looked into your eyes*
*I love you. I'm sorry.*
*Sean*

A sharp pain lanced through me, because I wasn't sure if Sean was sorry for loving me or sorry for not loving me enough.

And he did love me.

*Because you're Willow's mother.*

Even with that knowledge, I couldn't help but bring up his private Facebook page. The one he kept under another name.

Biting the bullet, I fired off a friend request. I was about to turn off my computer when a message popped up, alerting me that Sean had accepted.

Opening his page, I smiled at the dozens of pictures of our daughter on his feed. And one of me that I didn't recognize, with the simple caption *"Anna-baby."*

Nostalgia won over, and I opened my Messenger. My fingers

hovered over the keyboard as I tried to think of something safe to say. Since there was nothing, I gave up and typed: *What are you doing?*

The dots jumped around in the little box, then stopped, before starting again.

Considering how long it took Sean to compose his response, I figured he was recounting whatever he'd done tonight.

But only two words popped into the box.

*Missing you.*

# CHAPTER FORTY-EIGHT

**Sean**

*L*ola raised a worried brow as she dunked the battered slice of beef into the skillet of bubbling grease. "Are you sure you want to serve Miss Anna chicken fried steak?"

I hovered behind my housekeeper, supervising.

After two weeks of chatting on Facebook, Anna had finally agreed to come for dinner. She'd actually suggested it. And now I was nervous as fuck.

"I'm sure," I replied, scooping up a handful of cornhusks and potato peels from the counter. "It's her favorite meal."

Flipping the steak, she splattered grease onto the stainless steel, and I thought I heard her curse. "You're plum wacko if you think Miss Anna's going to let that baby eat this oily mess."

I set the pot of fresh corn on the back burner. "Willow's not coming." I winked at her surprised expression. "Just Anna."

If the smile crinkling the corners of Lola's eyes were any indication, she approved wholeheartedly of my plan. Not that I had an actual plan. But Anna was coming, and that's all that mattered.

Lola's grin fell away as she glanced me over from tip to toe. "You're a wreck. Get upstairs and take a shower while I finish up. I'll be out of here in fifteen minutes."

"Yes, ma'am." I squeezed Lola's shoulder, tempted to kiss her cheek. "Thanks for your help with dinner."

Lola nodded, her signature half annoyed, half amused smile firmly in place.

I narrowly missed another snap from her dishtowel of doom as I snagged a cherry tomato from the salad bowl on my way out.

Entering my room, I passed the unmade bed, and exhaustion slowed my steps.

Usually, I slept like the dead, but not lately. I spent most of my nights staring at the ceiling, adding items to my to-do list. Remodeling Willow's room, childproofing the house, grocery shopping for Melissa. Those things were easy. Tending to the emotional needs of those I loved—infinitely more difficult.

And Anna . . . always in the background. Close, but not close enough.

I showered quickly, eager to head downstairs and finish setting the scene for our dinner.

As I stepped into the hallway, one of Willow's original compositions, a sixteen-beat riff with me accompanying her on guitar, drifted from her room. Following the music, I paused just inside the door when I spotted Anna through the white netting cocooning Willow's handcrafted princess bed.

She looked gorgeous, auburn hair tied up in a loose bun on top of her head, accentuating her delicate features.

It seemed like longer than a month since we'd seen each other, and I wanted nothing more than to drag her to my bed and show her how much I missed her. How much I loved her.

Instead, I played it cool, venturing to the castle that Logan and I had constructed.

"What do you think?" Startled, Anna jerked her emerald gaze in my direction. Running a hand over the steeple with the flag bearing

Willow's initial, I laughed. "I bet this thing is bigger than our old bathroom."

She smiled softly. "It's beautiful, Sean."

And then she looked away. Something about the gesture felt off, but then she hadn't been in the house since everything had gone down with Scott. I'd explained everything to Anna in my emails, and reiterated it in chat, but she never responded with more than one-word acknowledgments.

Closing the gap between us, I parted the white mesh so I could see her face.

"You look beautiful," I blurted when our eyes met. "I'm glad you're here."

She nodded and then looked down, fiddling with her emerald ring. I took it as a good sign that she was still wearing it.

"The bed isn't just for show," I said. "The netting will keep the dust away." Flipping open the cubby on the headboard, I grinned. "And then there's this."

Glimpsing the nebulizer and small cylinder of oxygen tucked inside the compartment, Anna frowned up at me. "You thought of everything."

Gingerly, I swept a fallen curl behind her ear. "That's a good thing, right?"

She blinked at me, lips parted, a tiny crease between her brows. I saw the affection in her eyes, and just as quickly, it disappeared. "Yeah, it's good." She pushed to her feet, clutching the strap on her purse like a ripcord on a parachute. "Can we talk now?"

Icicles formed under my skin, freezing the blood flowing to my vital organs. "Sure."

Instead of heading for the stairs, Anna veered right at the door to my bedroom and then walked straight to the wet bar. Pulling the bottle of Jack from the shelf, she poured three fingers of whiskey, and I watched with detachment as she gulped it down.

She glanced at me. "Do you want one?"

My legs suddenly felt like lead. "Yeah."

Taking the lead crystal tumbler she offered, I sank onto the couch while she took a seat in the overstuffed chair.

"What's going on, Anna?"

She stared into her glass, brows drawn together. "I got accepted to the law program at Baylor."

Blood rushed to my head and my fingers closed around the arm of the sofa.

"It won't affect your visitation," she was quick to add, and then studying my blank expression, her shoulders sagged. "Please don't make this hard for me, Sean. It's only ninety miles away. You can have two overnight visits in a row during the week, and I'll be responsible for transportation."

Anna's voice trembled as she laid out the concessions. Compromises I probably didn't deserve but had no intention of turning down.

As she spoke, I drained my glass, surveying her over the rim. Grabbing the bottle, I emptied the last of the whiskey into my tumbler. "When did you decide all this?"

Crossing her legs, Anna clasped her hands over her knee, and her foot began to bob. "What do you mean?"

I polished off the second drink, and calculating the amount of liquor I'd need to get through this conversation, I headed for the bar.

"I mean, why are you doing this now?" I took a shot straight from a new bottle and then retraced my steps. Standing over her, I splashed whiskey onto the table as I filled her glass. "Are you going to answer me?" I growled.

Anna lifted her gaze, and the light seeped from her eyes. I'd seen the look before, but only once. A million years ago in our little apartment. The night I broke us apart.

Dropping onto the couch, I pushed out a breath. "I'm sorry."

Two words, pitifully overused, but accurate.

I *was* sorry. Sorry that I'd made it impossible for Anna to trust me. And sorrier still that she didn't know how much I loved her.

Despite the pain shredding my insides, I draped my arm over the back of the couch. And I smiled. "Tell me about your plans, Anna-baby."

The tension lines bracketing her mouth faded as she spoke about Baylor, the second chance she never thought she'd receive after foregoing her scholarship to the only school she'd ever dreamed of attending.

I was zero for a hundred in the concession department, so I buried any objections, and like the adults we were supposed to be, we discussed daycare and the two overnight visits a week she'd proposed.

Some two hours later, Anna pushed to her feet. "I need to ask you a favor."

I sat forward. "Sure."

Shifting her weight from one foot to the other, she fiddled with the hem of her blouse. "If you're going to have any overnight guests during your visits with Willow could you, I mean, would you please take her to my parents' house?"

A tingling spread from my chest as I fought the urge to lash out. But since that had never worked before, I downed the last of my drink to calm my frayed nerves.

"I'm not going to be having any overnight guests unless you're planning on coming by on the weekends." Taking her hand, I pried open her fist and then pressed a kiss to her palm. "Anna, things got fucked up. I was just trying to do the right thing by Willow."

"So am I. That's why I can't do this." She looked around with sad eyes. "Whatever *this* is. It'll always end up the same."

I could argue. Plead my case. Throw myself on her mercy. But the one thing I couldn't do? Make her choose. Not again.

Slipping my arm around her waist, I took her down with me as I eased onto the cushion. She didn't fight me, just braced a hand on the back of the couch to keep from crashing into my chest.

"One night?" My palm slid to her hip, molding to the spot I loved.

Anna searched my face, her fingers skimming my brow, my cheek, and finally my lips. "I can't stay all night."

I didn't trust my voice or the words that might spill out, so I nodded, and then took her hand.

Anna led me to the bed where we undressed, and it was so quiet, just the sound of our breathing and the rustle of the fabric. She stretched out on the mattress and smiled, but there was no joy in her upturned lips. Only resignation. Sadness. And goodbye.

But if my choice was having Anna one last time or never having her again, I'd take a few minutes in heaven with her and deal with the hell of it all later.

Skimming my hands up her calves, I stopped at her knee and then bent to kiss the little scar, the tiny piece of our past marring her perfect skin. Someday, Anna might regard me that way. A blemish on her otherwise unsoiled life.

*No*, I thought as I kissed my way to the scar above her mound. Willow was my redemption. No matter how this ended, it would never truly end.

Settling between Anna's legs in my favorite place on earth, I slipped two fingers inside her warm channel. Her back bowed as my tongue slid over her swollen nub.

"I love the way you taste, baby."

As if she knew what I wanted, Anna gazed down at me over the swell of her breasts. With every twist of my tongue and thrust of my fingers, she fought her heavy lids. But she didn't let go, those green eyes holding tight to mine. And when her orgasm hit, and she clenched tight around me, calling my name, I memorized it all. The sound and the taste and the feel of Anna coming undone. For me.

I waited until the last shudder left her body, then kissed my way to her breasts. As I toyed with her nipples, she reached between us, wrapping her fingers around my length. I bit back a groan as she brushed her thumb over the head of my cock, spreading the pre-cum over the crown.

"Lie back," she whispered, tightening her grip.

I pressed my lips to hers in a lame refusal, but she wasn't having it. She stroked me hard, and her shoulder pushed against my chest in an effort to reverse our positions.

Cupping the back of her head, I crushed my mouth to hers in a searing kiss as I rolled onto my back. Anna's teeth scraped my skin as she moved south.

Hissing a breath when she took me in her mouth, I twined my fingers into her hair. Anna sucked hard, taking as much of me as she could while she slid her hand along my base.

My stomach coiled to the point of pain as I guided her head, coaxing her into my favorite rhythm. Or hers. Probably hers. There was no rhythm without her. Everything started and ended with her.

"No more," I grunted.

I knew she wouldn't stop. And normally that was fine. But not tonight.

Gritting my teeth, I met her soft eyes as I teetered on the edge. "Please, baby, no more."

Anna rolled over, lying still as I took a condom from the cubby in the headboard.

And then she was under me. I looked into her eyes as I slid inside her, and for a brief moment, I was on the other side of the wall she'd built.

She kissed me hungrily, her sweet lips chasing away the bitterness threatening to overtake me.

Gripping her thigh, I brought her leg to my hip as I thrust, the beat in my head pushing aside any rational thought. I don't know how long I was there, moving with her, loving her. I felt her shatter, once, twice.

Our sweat mingled as I rested my forehead against hers.

If I could just hold on . . .

Anna's fingertips brushed my cheek. "Let go, Sean."

She pressed a kiss to my mouth, sealing her request as she toppled over the edge again, and God help me, I followed her, like I feared I always would.

Chasing her to the bottom, I spilled my release as the last notes to the unfinished symphony I started the day we met faded to nothing.

When I finally rolled off of her, there was no sound. It was odd, the silence in my head.

I disposed of the condom and then wrapped Anna in my arms and whispered, "Just for a minute."

Begging wasn't my style, but I'd beg. Anything so I wouldn't be left alone with this awful quiet.

An hour later, Anna slipped from my hold, and feigning sleep, I latched onto the pillow. Her bare feet slapped the marble stairs, the sound growing fainter until there was nothing left. Nothing of us. Maybe nothing of me.

I would love Anna until my last breath. But I couldn't force her to love me, to trust me. Even though every instinct told me to run after her, to beg and plead and offer her anything she ever wanted or needed, that would only make things worse.

For Willow's sake, I had to try to let Anna go.

# CHAPTER FORTY-NINE

**Sean**

*G*lass orbs hung from the ceiling in the secluded dining area at Uchiko, bathing the long, rustic dining table in a faint orange glow. And I wondered for the millionth time, what the fuck I was doing here.

I spent nearly every evening holed up in my house, but tonight, I'd agreed to go out to dinner with the guys. Drea, Trevor's assistant, came along for the ride, eagerly accepting the invitation to join us after she'd shown up at band rehearsal with some contracts for us to examine concerning a mini-tour Caged was doing in Tennessee.

Yeah, I knew it was a setup. Trevor had admitted as much when I sent him an angry text. But, I was here now. Trying to make the best of it. Unfortunately, I was distracted.

Anna had sent me a message after she picked Willow up from her parents' this afternoon. Apparently, she'd had a minor asthma attack, and though Anna assured me that it was the result of a cold, I remained unconvinced.

Sneaking my phone from my pocket, I texted Anna as a line of servers filed into the room carrying trays of sushi and Sapporo beer.

*How's Willow's cough? Is she running a fever?*

When I got no response, I set my phone down and met Drea's soft brown eyes. Trevor was right; the girl was pretty. A real fucking knockout. Dark, glossy hair. Creamy sun-kissed skin. Pouty, natural lips.

All wasted on me since my dick didn't even twitch.

"Sorry about that," I said, discreetly shifting my leg to dislodge Drea's hand from my thigh.

"Don't apologize. I know how it is." She smiled, revealing a hint of her straight, white teeth. "I dated Danny Amado when I was in college. He was always busy too. Interviews, fans." She waved a dismissive hand. "All that stuff."

"Amado?" Cameron piped up, lifting out of his chair to peek over Lily's head. "The football player?"

Grinning, Drea glanced over the array of sushi, transferring two lonely pieces onto her plate. "The one and only."

Cameron's eye narrowed to slits. "Didn't Amado desert the Cowboys for the Patriots?"

"Hell yeah, he did." She snorted. "He's not going to get a Super Bowl ring in Dallas."

Gaping, Cameron stared a hole in the side of Drea's head as she nibbled on her cucumber roll.

"Ditch her," he mouthed before sinking back into his seat.

I rolled my eyes, and a moment later my phone lit up. I dove for it.

"Shit," I muttered, dismissing the text from Cameron repeating his request.

I didn't respond because I had no intention of taking things further with Drea. At least, I thought I didn't. But at some point, I'd have to try the dating thing. And the sex thing. Though, the prospect of doing either with anyone but Anna turned my stomach.

"Problem?" Drea asked, knocking me from my thoughts.

Forcing my lips to bend as her wandering hand found my leg again, I said, "Not really. My daughter has a cold, and she's on her way . . ." *Home.* I couldn't bring myself to say it. Two months after Anna's move, and I still wasn't comfortable with the label, so I amended, "She's out of town with her mother."

Drea paused, a piece of sushi halfway to her lips. "You have a child?"

"Yep. Willow. She's almost four."

Setting down her chopsticks, Drea wiped her mouth and then picked up her glass of wine. "I didn't know you had a child. Your bio says you've never been married."

*She checked my bio?* I was going to kill Trevor.

Chewing slowly, I worked the tension out of my jaw. "Nope. Never been married."

Drea pondered this for a moment, then shrugged and took another sip of wine. "Well, accidents happen, I guess."

Lily dropped her fork, snapping her focus to my date. A hush fell over the table as Cameron, Christian, and Melody followed suit. Even Logan tore his attention from the brunette perched on his lap to scowl at Drea.

It took me a second to react, a long second where I thought about some woman, some *nice* girl, dropping that little bomb on Willow. Because, honestly, wasn't that what this was all about? Finding someone worthy of meeting my kid someday?

Shoving to my feet, I tossed my napkin on my plate.

Drea's eyes widened when I bent within an inch of her pretty face. "Willow wasn't an accident." I smiled in sharp contrast to the venom lacing my tone. "She's a gift."

Drea's voice rose up from behind me, calling my name, apologizing as I slipped through the glass partition and into the main dining area. Busting out of the front door, I looked around for my Range Rover, and laughing to myself, I walked over to my old pickup truck. Yeah, I wasn't ready to move on. There was something sick about driving the '85 Chevy to a date, even if Drea came in her own car.

I slid behind the wheel, shaking my head. The fucking heap of junk even smelled like Anna, like peaches and hot summer days.

Yanking the column shifter into reverse, I glanced over my shoulder to check for traffic. Noting the amber glow pouring from the window in the back of the restaurant, guilt collided with my urge to drive off. My southern manners took over, and I grabbed my phone from the ashtray to contact Drea and smooth things over.

As I swiped my finger over the screen, a text from Anna appeared. *She's good. No fever.*

A picture of Willow asleep in her car seat accompanied the message.

Relaxing into the cracked vinyl upholstery, I replied: *Don't text and drive.*

A photo of a half-eaten burger popped up ahead of Anna's response: *I'm not. Stopped to pick up dinner.*

My fingers itched, and I longed to tell her how I'd like to share that burger and then eat her for dessert, but instead, I tapped out: *Be careful. I love you.*

Wincing, I pressed the back button, and my stomach knotted as the endearment disappeared one letter at a time, leaving only the safe, appropriate reply.

I squinted as the dome light flickered above my head.

Logan hopped onto the seat. "If you're trying to get some pussy," he hitched a thumb over his shoulder, "you might want to take the girl next time."

"That pussy comes with too many strings." Sighing, I pushed the door open. "But I'll go back in an and apologize."

Logan snickered. "Don't bother. You'll ruin Lily's fun. She wants to show that girl the door. And probably the pavement."

A loud voice drew my attention, and when I turned, I spotted Drea hustling across the parking lot with Lily close on her heels.

"Go back to trolling the benches for a basketball player!" Lily shouted as she veered right and stomped toward my truck. Heads bowed, Cameron, Christian, and Melody skulked along behind.

"Stupid bitch," Lily muttered as she ground to a halt at my open door.

Cameron slipped an arm around his girl. "It's football, darlin'," he corrected, and when Lily glared up at him, he kissed the tip of her nose. "Drea dates football players."

"She probably eats them for breakfast too," Melody piped up, glaring at Drea's BMW as she whizzed past us. "What the hell were you thinking, Sean?"

"He wasn't thinking with his head," Christian interjected. "Not the big head, anyway."

Two sets of narrowed eyes, one green and one blue, both female, swung in my direction. Lily looked fiercer at the moment, but Mel was kind of scary in general, so I didn't discount her solidarity with the petite blonde in Cameron's arms.

"Climb on up here, Veronica," Logan said, patting his legs when the brunette ambled up. "This is going to be good. Lily's about to rip Sean's balls off. Melody's going to supervise. She's a doctor."

We all watched in stunned silence as the girl negotiated the step on the side of my truck. Sliding into Logan's lap, she gave us a ditzy smile, then peered up at her knight in shining armor and asked, "Who's Veronica?"

A laugh ripped from Cameron's chest, snapping the tension. And even Lily, in all her righteous indignation, couldn't hold back a snort.

Logan's lip twitched as he ran his palm from the crown of the brunette's wavy hair to the sun-lightened ends. "You are." He pressed a quick kiss to her lips. "You don't have a problem with that, do you?"

Anyone else would have gotten a slap. Or at the very least a vicious retort.

But Veronica merely smiled, tucking closer to Logan's chest. "Nope."

Logan shifted his amused gaze to Lily. "Carry on, Lil."

Stifling another bubble of laughter, Lily shook her head. "I just . . . I can't. You ruined it."

Christian shifted his weight, propping his chin on Melody's shoulder. "We left four hundred dollars' worth of dead fish in there," he said. "I'm fucking starving. Where are we going to eat?"

Staring out the window at the Frost Building jutting into the night sky, its glass façade reflecting all the lights of the city, my chest squeezed painfully. Our once tiny hometown swelled its borders, but out of a million people, I felt the loss of only two.

"Let's get burgers." I smiled through the ache. "I'm buying."

Two hours later I was stretched out in the booth at the What-A-Burger on Guadeloupe, watching through the smudged window as Lily, Christian, and Melody climbed in Cameron's SUV.

"Do me a favor, sweetheart," Logan said to Veronica as he handed her his keys. "Go warm up the car. I gotta talk to Sean for a minute."

Brows scrunched, Veronica looked down and ran her thumb over the Mustang logo on the fob. "It's ninety degrees." Batting her puppy dog eyes at Logan, she smiled hesitantly. "You want me to put on the heater?"

I bit my lip so hard I tasted blood while my best friend sighed patiently. "It's just a figure of speech." Logan smiled. "Just, you know, wait in the car."

Veronica grabbed her milkshake, which Logan promptly took from her hand. "Not in the Mustang, darlin'."

She shrugged, then wiggled her fingers at me and slid out of the booth.

"Dude." I snickered, watching her flounce to the door. "I think Veronica is a little slow."

Slumping in the corner of the booth, Logan tucked his arm behind his head. "No man, she's a little fast." He waggled his brows. "Which is why she's going home with me. What's your excuse?"

Collecting garbage from the table, I tossed the mess onto the tray. "Excuse for what?"

"Dina, the ice queen in the Beamer."

"Drea," I corrected. "It was Trevor's idea. He figured I might want to give a regular girl a chance."

Snorting, Logan slurped his chocolate shake. "That wasn't a regular girl."

"Yeah, well, she's not a groupie."

A smirk lifted Logan's lips. "You're right. She's a star-fucker with an agenda. Which is worse than a groupie. At least Kristin is upfront about what she wants."

"Who the hell is Kristin?"

Logan tipped his chin to the brunette waiting patiently in his '69 Mustang.

Following his gaze to Kristin/Veronica, I said, "Maybe I want a little more than a quick fuck. Ever think of that?"

Pushing upright, Logan clasped his hands in front of him on the marred Formica table. "But not with Anna?"

In the past two months, I'd endured Lily's disapproving gazes, Cameron's gentle prodding, Christian's transparent analogies, and now this. I wasn't up for it.

"Anna's gone. We're not together. She's Willow's mom, that's it. Get the fuck over it."

Logan cocked a brow. "I will if you will."

The schizophrenic bastard was standing on my last nerve. Logan had thrown the match on the gasoline that burned the house to the ground, and now he wanted to sift through the charred remains for survivors.

Yeah, no.

"I have." I smiled through clenched teeth. "Hence the almost date with Drea."

A dry laugh spilled from Logan's lips. "If you were over it, you'd be begging Veronica to call a buddy. You ain't over it."

"You don't know what you're talking about."

Challenge lit his pale blue gaze. "All right then, let's go find you a real date. The kind you don't have to buy dinner or worry about seeing in the morning."

I rolled my eyes. "I don't pay for sex, asshat."

"Yeah, you do. Right here." With lightning speed, Logan's arm shot out, and he tapped his fist against my chest, right over my heart.

"You paid for that last go around with Anna-baby in bones and flesh. And you still let her walk away."

"I didn't let her. She just did it."

"You're right." Annoyance bled into Logan's tone as he pushed to his feet. "You couldn't stop her from leaving. But you're a fucking coward for not chasing her down."

Glaring, I crunched an orange wrapper in my fist. "You can't catch someone if they don't want to get caught."

Logan took in my silent fury with a furrowed brow, which quickly faded to indifference. "I get it. You'd rather play daddy on your terms than put in the fucking work."

Incredulous, my jaw dropped open. There was nothing easy about my situation. "You don't know what you're talking about."

Grabbing the tray of garbage, I hopped to my feet, but Logan blocked my path.

"I know you're still hedging your bets. Anna gave you the perfect opportunity to step up."

"I did step up." My voice rose, drawing the attention of a handful of patrons. "If you'll notice we're not in Europe. I didn't sign on for the fucking tour so I could be here for Willow."

I stepped around him, but he followed, like a shark circling the water.

"That's right," he growled as I dumped the leftover french fries in the trash. "You're here for Willow. You get to take her to your mansion two nights a week while Anna does the heavy lifting in Waco." Laying a firm hand on my shoulder, he continued, "And when you get tired of daddy duty you can jet off to one of those mini-tours we're negotiating with a clear conscience. Sweet gig. Where do I sign up?"

Knocking Logan out of the way, I headed for the door. "Go play with your little friend. I'm driving to Waco tomorrow to check on Willow."

I stomped to my truck with Logan close behind.

"Make sure you don't wear out that hand!" he called as I slid behind the wheel. "We got a show this weekend!"

Flipping him off, I threw the truck into gear and peeled out of the parking lot.

As I sped toward the freeway entrance, the Caged disc pounding from the speakers, I skipped to the last track, the one I never played. The opening riff for "Crimson Pain" echoed in the cab.

*You wrap me in strands of crimson pain. All my screams cried in vain. I'll never escape, I'll never be free. Your crimson pain, always coming for me.*

The melancholy lyrics filled the God-awful silence in my head where my beat used to reside. Years of practice, and I could play anything by heart, but I couldn't compose anything new. Not since my last night with Anna.

Bypassing the turnoff for my house, I continued down the winding road. As the last notes of Anna's anthem faded to nothing, I pulled into the parking lot of the Oasis.

Sliding past a group of patrons lingering inside the doors, I headed for the bar, and I dropped onto a stool facing the large wall of glass.

A few minutes later, sipping my Jack and Coke, I stared at the twinkling lights from the houses on the other side of the shore. Anna's monument stood in the center, a burnt-out bulb in the otherwise pristine strand.

"You look like shit," came a familiar voice. With a smile in her tone, Darcy plopped onto the barstool beside me. "Want some company?"

Meeting her gaze in the large mirror behind the bar, I lifted my glass to my lips. "Are you working tonight?"

Motioning to the bartender, Darcy held up two fingers. "Just got off."

She swiveled in her seat, legs brushing mine as she handed me the shot. My attention slid from her face to a scrap of lace peeking from the plunging neckline of her blouse. And then I shifted my focus to the glass in my fist, examining the red stained liquor.

"Fireball whiskey," Darcy said.

I smiled. "Crimson pain."

A laugh tripped from Darcy's painted lips. "I guess you could say that."

I threw back the shot. "I just did, sugar."

Darcy tilted her head, searching my face. "You want seconds, Sean?"

I knew she was talking about more than a drink, and with the whiskey warming my insides, whispering promises of oblivion, I shrugged.

"Sure. Why not?"

# CHAPTER FIFTY

**Sean**

$\mathcal{W}$illow careened around the corner and into my bedroom.

Hopping onto my lap, she pressed a pink hairbrush into my hand, then looked up at me with expectant blue eyes. I ran my thumb over the soft bristles, unsure of how to proceed. Usually, Lola was entrusted with taming Willow's auburn locks. But today it was my turn.

Blowing out a breath, I began the arduous task of dragging the brush through Willow's wild curls, wincing every time I hit a snag. Unfazed by the torturous procedure, she didn't move a muscle.

When I finished securing the rubber band, Willow peered up at me. "Dums today, peese." She pursed her lips and amended, "Puhlease."

The speech coach Anna hired was working wonders. Which was a good thing, since I didn't have the heart to correct my baby girl. Everything Willow said sounded perfect to my ears.

I tugged at her off-center ponytail, smiling. "Sure, baby."

Sliding her arms around my neck, Willow hugged me tightly. "Luva you, da."

*Da.*

The day my daughter stopped calling me Sean my heart had doubled in size.

*One word.*

How could it mean so much?

Smiling into her hair, I splayed my hand across her tiny back. "Love you more. Lola's making you a special breakfast. I'll be down in a minute."

Willow slid off my lap and then took off like a shot. My blood pressure spiked as her little feet pounded against the marble steps.

"Careful!" I called, vowing for the millionth time to carpet the stairs.

But Anna had vetoed the idea when I brought it up during one of our Facebook chats. She said the fibers might aggravate Willow's asthma, but all the hard edges in this house weren't good for my nerves. Leveling the place to the ground and building a one story was an option. Or selling the house outright.

Hot air blasted my face as I stepped onto the patio. Sipping my coffee, I took in the view while contemplating the idea of living somewhere else. Closer to Melissa, maybe.

The notion drifted away on a breeze as I watched prisms of morning light dance off the water spilling over Mansfield Dam.

No, I'd never sell.

As I followed the length of shoreline to the Oasis, an uncomfortable twinge tightened my chest. Not quite guilt. Certainly not shame. But unease.

Having drinks with Darcy wasn't the best decision. If I wanted to prove that Anna didn't own my ass, returning to the scene of the crime wasn't the way to do it.

But nothing had happened with Darcy. I'd rather burn that bridge than cross it. After that second shot, I'd made my excuses and come home alone.

Sighing, I secured the umbrella on the patio set and then covered the chairs. I took one last look around before pulling out my phone and adding another item to the list for the property manager.

*Clean the gutters on the master bedroom deck once a month.*

After securing the deadbolt and the latches on the top and bottom of the door, I turned my attention to the pile of clothes on my bed. Answering Logan's call, I wedged the phone between my shoulder and my ear as I continued to pack.

"Hey, I'm kind of busy," I said as I continued to pick through the messy heap.

"You're just packing, not performing brain surgery."

"Funny." A faint peach scent wafted to my nose when I came across a T-shirt that Anna used to wear to bed. Instead of tossing it back into the drawer with the other items I never wore, I folded the worn scrap of cotton and tucked it into the corner of the suitcase. "Willow's downstairs. I got to go."

"Whatever." Logan yawned. "I just got home. I need sleep. Pick me up as late as you can."

A smidgeon of jealousy crept in. I couldn't remember the last time I was getting in at eight in the morning instead of getting up. As I counted back the months, Willow's laughter drifted up the stairs, and I abandoned the pursuit. The hours I spent with my daughter were priceless.

"You can sleep on the plane," I said. "I'll pick you up at four."

Disconnecting the call, I cut off Logan's unintelligible goodbye.

The mouthwatering smell of Lola's pancakes proved too much to resist, so I headed downstairs. Brushing a kiss to the top of Willow's head, I dropped onto the barstool beside her.

"Morning, Lola." I smiled as I took the plate she offered. "Anna's going to have a fit if she finds out you made the kid weekend food on a Wednesday. You're spoiling her rotten."

"Hush," Lola said, smoothing a soft curl behind Willow's ear. "I'm not going to be seeing her for a while. I can spoil her a bit."

I picked at the crispy end of the hot cake. "It's just for a few months."

Hopefully. I wasn't sure.

Lola said nothing, folding her arms over her chest.

"I know what I'm doing," I mumbled, annoyed at my need for approval from the woman I paid to clean my house.

But Lola was much more than a housekeeper. She was part of the village it took to help me raise my child, and I trusted her.

To my surprise, Lola gave my hand a quick squeeze. "I know that. I'm just gonna miss the little bug."

Jerking a nod, I picked up my coffee, and my attention shifted to the clock on the microwave. My stomach pitched, threatening a full-on revolt.

*Was I doing the right thing?*

While I pondered, Willow slid off her chair. Quiet as a mouse, she dragged the step stool to the rack of keys hanging on the wall.

Popping out of my seat, I closed the gap in two strides, sliding my arm around her waist before she reached the second step. "What do you think you're doing, Willow-baby?"

Feet dangling, she peered up at me through auburn lashes, gracing me with her most innocent smile. "Dums, da."

Setting her on her feet, I gave her a stern look. *Boundaries.* It was a recurrent theme in Anna's messages.

But the little manipulator had other plans, and she propped a hand on her hip. "You poomised."

It was the pout that did me in. Or maybe the resemblance to her mother. Either way, I was toast, so I dropped the single key into Willow's waiting palm.

Lola chuckled as I picked up my plate.

"What happened to 'no food in the studio'?" she asked, using her best baritone to mock me.

"It's my studio," I grumbled, not sure if it was true anymore. "I can eat in there if I want."

Lola's rumbling laughter followed me all the way down the narrow staircase. Shaking my head, I slid into the chair in front of the control panel.

Seated behind her miniature drum kit with her custom pink earphones in place, Willow frowned at me through the glass. "Da...?"

I turned on the microphone. "You play, sunshine. I'm going to stay in here. "

Willow's eyes darted to my kit and back to me, and I nodded reassuringly. She didn't need me or anyone else, the beat in her head was enough.

Relaxing in the soft leather chair, I smiled as Willow hit the kick drum, and soon she was lost in the rhythm, pounding away. The kid amazed me with her stamina as well as her versatility. I'd outfitted the studio with miniature versions of a number of instruments, and Willow had familiarized herself with each one. She was more gifted than I was by a mile.

Detecting a change in the riff, I flipped on the recorder, overlaying her new composition with tracks I'd recorded during previous sessions.

A couple of hours later, Willow wandered into the booth, her hair falling out of her ponytail. Pushing my arm aside, she climbed into my lap and then cocked her head, watching in fascination as I affixed the custom label with her name and the Caged logo to the CD.

Placing the disc in the clear plastic case, I smiled at her.

"This is you, Willow-baby." Her eyes widened as I laid the box in her hands. "Play it for Mommy so she can see how talented you are."

# CHAPTER FIFTY-ONE

Anna

The waitress at Kettle dropped my plate of pancakes on the table.

"Ya know," she drawled. "We reserve the right to refuse service to anyone. We don't. But we can. You better rethink your attire next time you come in here, missy. If you know what I mean."

I didn't.

I blinked up at her, cheeks burning, and then I surveyed the crowd. Denim, faded T-shirts, flip-flops.

"I . . . um . . ."

The waitress slowly shifted her gaze to the Baylor Bears poster on the wall, then back to me. Specifically, to my UT baseball cap, and then lower to the matching Longhorn tank top.

The flush spread to my chest. "Um, yeah . . . thanks for the advice, ma'am. I'll remember, for next time."

Hand on hip, she pursed her lips. "Make sure that you do."

She sauntered away, and I sank lower in the booth, acutely aware of my wardrobe as I sipped my coffee. All around me there was a sea

of green. Green shirts. Green hats. All with that damned bear embla-
zoned on them. I frowned because I'd never truly fit in here. Baylor
was a means to an end. A concession. I'd get my law degree, and more
importantly, I could focus on my studies without obsessing
over Sean.

Much.

He was back on the road, a mini-tour of Nashville and a couple of
dates in the surrounding states. Still, he'd managed to send an email
every night and FaceTimed with Willow at least twice throughout
the day.

Banishing Sean from my thoughts, I finished my breakfast and
then tucked into the corner of the booth with my textbook. The
restaurant was full, so when an audible gasp rippled through the
crowd, it caught my attention.

My mouth dropped open when I lifted my gaze and saw Sean
following the hostess to a table in the front. A smartly dressed
woman, mid-to-late twenties, slid into the booth across from him. My
stomach turned when I noticed the way her eyes glinted. She was
facing me, while all I could see of Sean was the back of his head, his
long hair pulled into a loose bun, and his left arm with the willow
tree tattoo on his bicep.

*What was he doing here?*

Anger rooted me to my seat while every cell in my body screamed
to march over to his table. Several people were whispering now, and I
heard Sean's name. The woman he was with must've noticed, because
she sat higher, looking around like she was the queen of England.
And then she touched him. Just a pat on his arm, but I felt it like a
burn on my skin.

My next class was starting in a half hour, but there was no way for
me to leave without Sean seeing me. So I waited, my pulse climbing
to dangerous levels. And just when I thought I couldn't take it
anymore, they got up and left. Walked right out the front door.

With a shaky hand, I pulled my phone from my backpack and
fired off a text.

*What time are you getting in so I'll know when to have Willow ready?*

It took Sean a long time to answer. I was already in my car, driving aimlessly when his message came through.

*I can meet you after your last class.*

I pulled over and studied the text.

He hadn't answered my question, but then, why would I expect him to?

Tears pricked the back of my eyes as I fumbled with the keyboard.

*No class today. I'll pick Willow up from daycare now and meet you in the park at one.*

No message came back. And I shuddered to think of what Sean was doing. But I couldn't confront him. I'd lost that right the day I'd walked away.

Rubbing my chest, I eased into traffic, wondering when the ache would finally go way.

# CHAPTER FIFTY-TWO

**Sean**

$\mathcal{J}$ sat under the tree in the park where Anna and I usually met for custody exchanges. I hated that fucking phrase —*custody exchange*. It sounded so formal. And hopefully, after today, Anna and I would be on more intimate terms.

Skimming the lease that Vanessa, the realtor, had drawn up for the three-bedroom house on the quiet street not far from the Baylor campus, I wondered again if I should bite the bullet and buy the place. It's not like I wanted to pay someone else's mortgage for three years.

*Fuck it.*

I signed on the dotted line and then dug my journal out of my backpack. The leather-bound notebook contained every thought, poem, and lyric I'd written about Anna over the last year.

Turning to a blank page, I mused over some broken phrase about new beginnings.

"Da!"

Willow's voice carried from the parking lot, and when I looked up, she was racing across the grass. Flinging herself into my arms, she smothered me with kisses that I gratefully returned.

Five fucking days. I'd missed five days, and it felt like five hundred.

Anna paused a fair distance away, surveying our reunion with a frown.

The box containing her diamond jabbed into my thigh, a constant reminder of what I'd lost and what I had to gain.

"Hey Anna-baby," I smiled at her. "What are you standing way over there for?"

Reluctantly, she shuffled over, and without addressing me, she bent down and spoke to Willow. "Why don't you go play while I talk to Daddy, okay?"

Willow looked at me, and my stomach flipped, but I nodded. As I watched her walk away, I searched my memory for anything that could've upset Anna. There were constant stories about the band in the press, but I made sure I was never photographed alone with a woman. It was comical, really, the way I hid whenever the band did meet-and-greets.

As soon as Willow was out of earshot, Anna sank onto the grass in front of me, three feet of space between us. "I thought you weren't getting in until tonight?"

Something about the way she was looking at me felt off.

"I flew in last night after our show."

Her eyes narrowed in that way they did when she was sussing out a problem. Or jumping to a conclusion. "And you drove in this morning?"

"No, I came straight here from the airport."

"You were here last night?" She cocked her head, her brow furrowed. "Where did you stay?"

I leaned forward, my boot brushing against her knee. "Home-wood Suites, why?"

"A hotel . . ." Her shoulders slumped. "I didn't see you online."

"Yeah, sorry we didn't get to catch up the last few nights. With the shows," I blew out a breath, "it's been crazy. And then my plane didn't get in until after ten, and by the time I got here, it was after midnight."

Our Facebook chats were the highlight of my day. But I had little latitude when it came to shows. Getting a promoter to agree to a matinee performance for our hard-rocking band was out of the question. That kind of shit didn't happen unless you were Justin Beiber and your fan base had a 10:00 p.m. curfew.

Twisting her fingers in her lap, Anna searched my face. "Why would you spend the night here, Sean?"

I picked absently at the dry grass. "I'm moving here, baby. To Waco."

The column of Anna's throat constricted as she swallowed. "You're what?"

Scooting closer, I caught a whiff of her hair and the speech I'd planned escaped my memory. "Listen . . . I want to be close—"

"No!" Anna hauled to her feet. "You can't . . .You can't do this to me."

As I looked her over, from the fury in her eyes to the flush coloring he chest to her fingers balled into tight fists at her side, a million thoughts collided, but only one found its way to my lips. "Are you seeing someone, Anna-baby?"

She swayed as if I'd slapped her, and when she found her voice incredulity trembled her tone. "You're asking *me* if I'm seeing someone?" Pointing her finger at me, she roared, "You're the one who showed up at Kettle with another woman."

In the silence that swelled between us, the aftermath of Anna's accusation, I swung my attention to Willow, perched on the carousel.

"The other woman was my realtor," I replied. "But you still haven't answered my question."

Processing the information, Anna rubbed her forehead with the heel of her hand. "Of course I'm not seeing anyone," she finally said.

I let out the breath I didn't know I was holding.

But when Anna finally met my gaze, nothing had changed. "What do you want from me, Sean? I signed over joint custody of my . . ."

She closed her eyes and then sighed. "Of *our* daughter. Without a fight. I've tried everything to make this work."

She tracked my movement as I stood. "I want to make it work too. You're here, so I'm here. It's as simple as that. I came for you."

Before I'd even finished, Anna was shaking her head. "You're not here for me. You're here for Willow."

"No—"

"Stop! Just stop!" She backed up a foot when I stepped forward. "I want you to leave. This isn't Austin. It's a small town, and there's no place for me to hide here."

"Why would you hide from me?"

After a long moment, her shoulders sagged. "Because I love you," she said quietly and a tear spilled onto her cheek. "And not because you're Willow's father. She's the result, not the reason. I won't be some obligation you were content to leave in the past until you found out you knocked me up. You wanted a different life. I wasn't enough for you."

My lips parted to mount a protest, but she shook her head.

"Don't say it. I'm not blaming you or myself. But you can't just come here and think you're going to mold me into something you want."

The last brick of the wall between us crashed to the floor, revealing something deeper than hurt and mistrust over my long-ago betrayal.

"What do you think I want?"

She sucked in a breath. "It's not about you. I'm raising a daughter, Sean. I want her to believe in the fairy tale. The one that you left behind. I want her to have that. And I don't want her to see her mother pining away for a dream that someone else forgot."

I moved blindly, but Anna shook her head.

"If you've ever cared for me at all, Sean, you'll leave. I hope you find what you're looking for, Sean. But I'm not it."

With one last look into my eyes, Anna spun on her heel and ran to our daughter.

Confused as fuck, I dropped on my ass and watched as she knelt in front of Willow and gave her a quick kiss. And then she marched to her car without sparing me another glance.

I pulled into Melissa's driveway sometime after dusk. Why I always ended up here, I couldn't say. Taking my phone from the charger, I glanced at the screen. Nothing from Anna, but a shit ton from Vanessa, the realtor. I got the distinct impression she wanted to do more than rent me a house.

I knew the deal. It wasn't me that she wanted, but Sean Hudson, drummer for Caged. The rockstar.

Was I even that guy anymore? There was no beat in my head. No music in the rain.

Cursing the damn silence, I got out of the car and then freed a sleeping Willow from her car seat. Burrowing against me, she pressed her face to my neck as I entered the house.

Holding a finger to my lips when I walked through the living room, I warned Melissa to stay quiet. She glanced at Willow and nodded, quiet concern painting her features.

On the way up the stairs, I passed Chelsea and she ran a hand over Willow's back and then kissed my cheek.

That's why I was here. *Comfort.*

After tucking Willow into bed, I trudged downstairs where Melissa and Chelsea waited, looking appropriately confused.

Melissa folded me into a hug, and I no longer felt all of her ribs protruding, so I didn't worry about breaking her when I returned the embrace.

"What are you doing here?" she asked. "I thought you were in Nashville."

I dropped into the chair, exhausted. "I was. I got in last night and then went to Waco."

Chelsea sat forward, a grin breaking like dawn on her face. "So you spent the night with Anna?"

Rather than answer their questions one at a time, I laid it out there. Told them about my surprise. The house. All of it.

And when I was finished, I waited for the consoling to begin because, damn, I needed it.

My gaze flicked between my aunt and my niece when they said nothing.

Melissa was the first to react, pinching the bridge of her nose like she was fighting a headache. "You didn't tell Anna you were coming?"

She ventured a peek, sighing when I shook my head.

"How could you do that?" Chelsea chimed in, scowling.

*What the actual fuck?*

"Excuse the hell out of me for trying to put my family back together." I hauled to my feet in search of alcohol.

When I reclaimed my seat, bottle in hand and no glass in sight, Melissa glared at me.

"Don't you think before you decided to put your family back together you might've wanted to include Anna in the plans?" my aunt asked, and Chelsea nodded her agreement.

I eyed the crazy women as I gulped from the bottle.

Chelsea let out a little snort as she stood up. "Lucky you have your looks," she brushed another kiss across my cheek, "'cause you're thick as a brick."

I grunted, taking another drink as she strode out of the room and up the stairs.

"Go ahead," I said to Melissa, sinking further into my seat. "Lay it on me. Obviously, I don't know what the fuck I'm doing."

Or, as I feared, it was too late, and Anna was done with me. Recalling her declaration of love in the park, I cringed inside. It was more of an indictment, something she was forced to endure, like a wound that wouldn't heal.

"I want you to look at something," Melissa said as she handed me a brightly colored box. "Anna brought this by before she left town."

Curious, I lifted the lid, and at least a hundred pictures in various sizes stared back at me.

My insides turned outside when I picked up the first photo.

Clad in a pink sundress, Anna stood beside a cake with a toy bassinet on top, forcing a smile for the camera. The momentary joy I felt at seeing the baby bump was eclipsed by the vacant look in her eyes. She wore the identical expression in the next picture. And the next. I shuffled through the stack for one image not tainted by her sorrow.

And then I found it.

Swathed in her hospital-issued pink blanket and beanie, Willow peered up at her mother, and despite the tubes attached to each arm and her ghostly, pale skin, Anna looked happy.

Resting the box on my knee, I traced the corner of each photo that marked every event I'd missed.

When I finally stepped out of the past, I met Melissa's soft blue eyes.

"That's what she remembers, sugar. What's etched into her soul."

I hung my head, the weight of all my mistakes weighing me down. "Don't you think I know that, Lissa? That I regret it every day? That I wish it were different?"

Melissa grabbed my hand. "Tell me what you'd change."

I laughed, because there was only one answer. "Everything. I love her. I've always loved her."

*Only her.*

Sighing, Melissa shook her head and then eased back against the cushions. "You still don't get it. Your problem has never been love. You just . . . you do what you want. You don't think. That little snafu with your lawyer didn't teach you a damn thing. And it wasn't always like that. You and Anna, you used to talk. I'd hear you from my room, making plans. Now you seem to think you can build her a big house and she should live in it. Or that she should forget about the things you promised her."

"No." I shook my head. "No. That's not it. I—"

"You what? Hired a realtor and got her another house?" She snorted. "Same shit. The only thing you changed was geography."

Suddenly it was so clear to me, like a blinding light shining from the heavens. I glanced around the room at the photos of Anna and me from a different time. A different place. When I included her. When her opinion mattered.

And that's when I realized, to give Anna a future, first I'd have to give her back our past.

# CHAPTER FIFTY-THREE

**Anna**

*P*eering over the top of my textbook, I frowned at my laptop on the desk. A message from Sean flashed in the corner of the screen.

After our dustup at the park last month, he didn't contact me for two weeks. My mom facilitated his visitation exchanges, and he stopped sending me emails about the time he spent with Willow.

So I threw myself into my studies, my volunteer work at legal aid, Mommy and Me classes with Willow—anything so I wouldn't have to think of him. It was our new normal.

And then last week, he'd sent me three words.

*Lemon or lime?*

Back in high school, we used to play this game. Sean would throw out two choices and I'd have to pick one. Sean knew I was a lemon girl, but I'd indulged him.

And that's how we made the leap from lovers to friends. Sean didn't tell me he loved me or beg me to talk to him about our future. Because there was no future beyond co-parenting our child.

For Sean, it seemed effortless. He was happy.

Me? I was trying. But the fact that I looked forward to his stupid messages more than I'd liked to admit proved that my heart still belonged to him. And his belonged to Willow. Our daughter got the best of Sean, and for that, I was supremely grateful.

With a sigh, I set my book aside, then doing my best impression of a contortionist, I slid out of bed. Willow never even stirred.

Grabbing my laptop, I headed to the kitchen for some wine. After filling a teacup with some cheap Moscato, I settled on the couch to read Sean's message.

*Cookies or Brownies?*

Biting my lip, I typed: *What kind of cookies?*

Dots jumped around in the box as I sipped my wine.

Laughing when he replied: *You're breaking the rules*, I responded with an angel emoji.

When nothing came back for a long moment, my heart sank just a little. It was still early. Maybe Sean was getting ready to go on a date.

Sipping my wine, I pulled up my browser to find a movie to watch. When Sean's picture appeared on the screen, I startled, spilling Moscato all over myself.

Incoming FaceTime call.

Butterflies swarmed in my stomach as I accepted.

And then Sean was there, his handsome face taking up the entire screen.

His brows turned inward. "Why can't I see you?"

"Oh . . . Hold on." I ran my fingers through my hair, straightened my soggy T-shirt, and then tore off the piece of electrical tape covering the webcam. "Better?"

Sean smiled as he relaxed against the headboard. "Yeah."

We stared each other for a minute and then both spoke at once. My cheeks heated and I wondered if Sean could detect the blush in the dim light.

"Sorry, go ahead," I prompted with a laugh.

"I was just asking about your day."

I took my last sip of wine to cool myself down. Sean was making it all kinds of difficult to concentrate. He was shirtless with his arm resting casually behind his head. And damned if I didn't want to lick the screen.

"Let see," I began. "I made homemade macaroni and cheese for dinner. And then Willow—"

"I'm asking about you." He smiled into a sip of beer. "What did *you* do today?"

Thrown off by the heat in his azure gaze, I pondered for a moment. Think. "Um . . . the usual. I went to class and—"

"Which class?" His tongue darted out to sweep some liquid off his bottom lip, and I forgot my own name. "Well?"

I rattled off a few classes that I wasn't even sure were on my schedule while Sean continued to look at me like he wanted to eat me for a midnight snack.

"Sounds like fun," he said when I finished babbling.

Fun would be if he lowered his camera so I could see where that happy trail led, but I wasn't about to tell him that.

"Is everything all right?" he asked, adjusting his computer so only his concerned face lit the screen.

I finally managed to push out a breath. "Yeah . . . of course."

He looked down and sighed. "Anna . . ."

Nothing good ever started when Sean said my name that way. Infusing steel in my spine, I braced myself for whatever was coming.

Raking a hand through his hair, he met my gaze and smiled. "I want to see you."

Blood rushed to my ears. *Why would he want to see me?* It had to be something big.

"You are seeing me."

"In person. Can we do that?"

Excuses filled my head. But I couldn't form any words, so I nodded.

Sean visibly relaxed. "Cool. Day after tomorrow?"

Resisting the urge to rub the ache in my chest, I nodded again. "Sure."

My voice was thin and reedy—but Sean didn't seem to notice. He was too busy grinning. The pain spread to my limbs, and I couldn't feel the cup in my hand.

"It's getting late." I forced my lips to bend. "I'm going to go, okay?"

A crease formed between his brows. "Yeah, sure." Before I could sign off, he blurted, "Wait! Blue or Green?"

I looked deep into the azure pools of his eyes, momentarily silenced by the silver threads that sparkled when he smiled again.

"Blue."

# CHAPTER FIFTY-FOUR

**Sean**

Sitting on the open liftgate of my old truck, I scrolled through the list on my phone. Most of the items had a little red check beside them but a few details I'd left to others. I shot a group text to Logan, Christian, and Cameron.

*All set?*

Christian replied almost instantly, enumerating every detail.

Cameron answered a moment later: *Yeah. Stop worrying.*

It took a good five minutes for Logan's response, an emoji of a middle finger. Not an answer but the best I was going to get from him.

Pocketing the phone, I reclined on my palms and looked up at the bowl of stars. I didn't pray. Not the way most folks did. But as I gazed at the night sky, I whispered a few words, likely to my mother. If there was a heaven, she was there.

The hum of an engine pulled me from my thoughts, and I sat up straight when Anna swung her car into the parking space next to mine.

She hopped out, smiling.

God, she was fucking gorgeous. Like a summer day. Her hair hung in loose waves around her face and she wore a black Damaged T-shirt, the letters faded and the fabric threadbare from too many trips through the spin cycle.

How I ever went four years without seeing her was a mystery, because right now, one day shy of a month from our last face-to-face, and all I wanted to do was grab her. Kiss her. Fuck the truth into her.

I hid my true intentions behind an innocuous grin as I climbed off the tailgate of my truck. "Hey."

Anna tucked a strand of hair behind her ear. "Hey, yourself."

She looked from the dim façade of the building, then further to the grass that made up the football field. The lights were on, illuminating the Westlake High "Chaps Nation" scoreboard.

"What are we doing here?" she finally asked, her voice thick with nostalgia.

Rocking back on my heels, with my hands buried in my pockets, I tipped my chin to the sign on the light post. "Do you remember this spot?"

Anna followed my gaze, and a flush rose on her pale skin. "You used to park here and wait for me."

When her eyes found mine, she bit her lip to keep her smile in check.

"Yep." I motioned to the field. "Let's go."

She blinked down at my hand, extended for her to take. It could all end here. This was our journey, but I wouldn't drag her kicking and screaming.

Hesitantly, she slid her palm against mine, and I locked our fingers.

Anna fell into step beside me as we crossed the blacktop. I let her go when we got to the gate on the chain link fence. She stared intently at the padlock, beaming when I gave it a tug and the bolts disengaged.

"I can't believe they haven't fixed that," she said, ducking under my arm as I held the gate open for her.

Joining her at the edge of the field, I reclaimed her hand. "I guess they're more worried about kids breaking out than breaking in."

Anna looked at me out of the corner of her eyes as we strolled along. "But we're not kids," she whispered.

Reality warred with the fantasy I'd constructed, and Anna hesitated. But I wasn't going to stop now. Not when we were this close. So I urged her along.

As we neared the gym, she squeezed my hand. "We're not going to break in . . . are we?"

A sly smile curved my lips, deceptive enough to distract her until we reached the double doors. "No, we don't have to break in."

I knocked lightly, and when Coach Riley appeared, Anna yelped.

She slipped behind me, fisting my shirt, and I could practically feel her trembling.

Pushing aside my nerves, I said, "Hi, Coach."

Amazingly, the guy hadn't aged in ten years. Riley's Westlake Nation T-shirt stretched across his muscled bicep as he pushed the door open, granting us entry.

"Hudson, good to see you're still breathing free air. I thought you might be in prison by now."

"No, sir." I chuckled. "Thanks for the favor."

"You can thank Christian." Coach clapped my shoulder, tipping forward. "You got fifteen minutes, and there are cameras everywhere. So no funny business." Shifting his no-nonsense gaze to Anna, he smiled. "Annabelle, keep him in line."

Anna swallowed hard. "Yes, sir . . . Coach Riley, I mean."

Snapping her mouth shut, Anna trapped any further squeaks behind tight lips. Because she was squeaking. Like a little mouse.

It might have had something to do with the fact that Coach Riley caught us behind the equipment locker our senior year. I had Anna caged against the wall with my hand up her shirt, and as I remembered, we were so into the kiss Riley had to blow his whistle to get our attention.

From the look on Anna's face and the color flaming her cheeks, she was reliving the same memory.

"Fifteen minutes," Riley repeated and then turned on his heel and strolled toward the gym.

"Let's go before he changes his mind," I said, and Anna nodded, her head bobbing long after we'd turned the first corner and disappeared into the maze of hallways.

It was eerily quiet, with only a few lights illuminating our path, but I knew exactly where we were going.

Anna stared down at the rose on the tiled floor when we reached our first destination. "Third row, second seat," I said as I crouched to pick up the flower.

Anna took the rose and ran her fingertips over the petals. "I don't understand."

Molding my hands to her hips, I maneuvered her to the glass window in the classroom door.

"You were sitting right there." I pointed at the metal desk. "Looking out the window."

"When?"

My lips grazed the shell of her ear as I told her what she already knew but assumed I'd forgotten.

"The first day I saw you. You had on a green shirt. That was before you started boycotting green because it's Baylor's color."

Ironic, since she was now attending the university. But I didn't comment on that. Because right now, it was ten years ago, and the only thing in Anna's future was UT Law. And me.

She tilted her face to mine, but my eyes never left the desk. "Your hair was pulled back," I continued with a smile, conjuring all the sights and smells and sounds from that long-ago day. "And I knew I had to meet you, so I waited for the bell. But I couldn't speak. I just stood there like an idiot when you passed, breathing in your peach scent and looking at your ass. You had on Abercrombie low-rise jeans."

When I finally chanced a peek at Anna's face, she was frowning.

"Abercrombie? Did you have to remember those?"

I swept a loose curl behind her ear. "I remember everything." I brushed my thumb over her jaw from ear to tip before taking her hand. "Come on; we're running out of time."

Anna didn't ask where we were going, and I felt no reluctance as her fingers laced with mine. When we reached the row of lockers a few corridors away, she snagged her lip between her teeth.

Extracting the rose from the vent in the metal cabinet, I said, "This was the first place—"

"You ever kissed me."

I'd vowed not to push her. Not to use the physical spark we shared to influence her decision, but then Anna looked up at me, and it was like the first time. So I slipped my hand into her hair and brushed a chaste kiss to her lips.

It took all my resolve to pull away.

Anna's lids fluttered open, and she smiled. Shy, like she used to.

"You ready to go?" I asked, and she nodded.

We made our way to the parking lot without saying a word. Afraid to break the spell, I coaxed her to the passenger side of my truck.

She blinked up at me when I pulled the door open. "What about Willow?"

I wanted to tell Anna that there was no Willow tonight, but that would freak her out, so I slid my hand to her backside and gave her a nudge. "Willow's fine."

Anna pondered for only a second before hoisting herself onto the seat.

"Where's your Range Rover?" Anna asked as she ran her fingertips along the cracked Chevrolet emblem on the glove compartment, a smile ghosting her lips.

"At the house."

Once I'd hopped in the cab, I took the wicker basket from the floorboard and placed it on the seat between us.

Anna peeked inside the hamper as I pulled out of the parking spot. "What's this for?"

"Your roses." I smiled. "Let's hope they're all going to fit."

# CHAPTER FIFTY-FIVE

**Sean**

$\mathcal{F}$ingering the wilted petals on all her roses, Anna gazed at the serene water as I turned the truck onto the gravel road leading to her parents' cabin.

I'm sure she figured our journey through the past would end here, where we began, in the spot where I learned how to love her.

Anna hadn't said a word since we'd left the lookout at Mansfield Dam, listening intently as I explained the meaning behind the lyrics to the songs serenading us in the background—"Crimson Pain," "Rue the Day," and "Sunshine Smile," my three contributions to the Caged catalog. All for her.

Cutting the engine, I took in the grandeur of the willow tree. Moonbeams filtered through the snarl of branches, lighting tips of the drooping leaves here and there.

Earlier today, Willow accompanied me to the cabin so I could set the scene. Since it was easier to cut across the lake, we took my boat, and as we'd floated down the inlet, I'd pointed out the special tree, telling my daughter as much as I could about its storied history.

When I finished, Willow looked from the tree to the ink on my bicep. "Like Ma's."

"Just like Ma's. Daddy drew it."

"Why?"

"For you, Willow-baby."

It was true. I'd sketched the tree when Willow was nothing more than a hope, some distant future that only existed in a dream.

Tracing the gnarled limbs with her tiny fingertip, Willow had nodded, as though she'd just put it together, the pieces of our story, Anna's, hers, and mine.

When we reached the shore, Willow scrambled from the boat, racing toward the tree she was named after. And then as she watched, I added her initials to the heart I'd carved in the trunk for Anna and me all those years ago.

No matter what happened tonight, the circle was complete.

Anna's soft whisper knocked me from my haze. "This is the end of the road, huh?"

I took her hand and brought it to my lips for a kiss. "The road so far."

She blinked at me, doubt or fear shining in her eyes. Then she slipped out of my grasp and opened the door, jumping to her feet without a reply.

*It's not going to work . . .*

Until that moment, I never entertained the possibility.

Glued to the seat, I watched as she plucked a stray rose from the gravel. Then another. She had a handful by the time I got out of the truck.

"Careful," I warned. "Don't step on any thorns."

She shifted her gaze to the sea of roses, laid out like a red carpet from the edge of the cobblestone path to the door of the cabin.

"Oh, God . . ."

Since Anna wasn't wearing shoes, I had an excuse to scoop her up and carry her the rest of the way.

Sliding her arm around my neck, she asked, "How many roses did you buy?"

I chuckled. "All of them."

I'm not sure Anna believed me until I shouldered my way through the door. Dozens more roses sat in vases and Mason jars on every table, their vibrant peach petals muted by the soft glow of the candles strategically placed throughout the room. The dainty little buds arrived this morning on a truck from Tyler, Texas, where roses of all colors and sizes were grown year-round.

"I know the red ones are your favorite," I said, easing her onto the couch. "But I like the peach."

"Why?"

She knew the answer. It was always the same.

"Because they remind me of you."

Taking a seat beside her, I placed a worn composition book in her lap.

Anna looked up at me, confused. "What . . ."

"Humor me. Open it up."

She did as I asked and when she turned to the first page, her eyes widened. "This is eight years old."

"I must've given you the wrong one then." As I tapped the stack beneath the coffee table with the toe of my boot, the little tower crumpled and landed in a heap at her feet. "I'm sure there's an older one in there."

I can't say I was sorry to see the tears drop onto the dog-eared pages as Anna read. With every bit of ink that ran, my optimism grew.

Anna thumbed through the book, scanning some items and stopping to read others over and over.

Hours later, after she'd gone through every spiral pad, bound notebook, and binder, her eyes found mine.

"You told me you wanted to be the reason, and you are," I said, glancing over all my confessions. "You're the reason for everything. I wrote all of this stuff before I ever knew Willow existed. Most of it after I left. And if you ask me 'why,' the answer will always be the same. Because I love you."

Anna refocused on the book resting in her lap. "But that wasn't enough before. I wasn't—"

"You were enough, baby. It was me that was lacking." I took her hand, looking down at the emerald ring. "Do you remember when I gave you this?" She responded with a little hum, and I laughed, the sound brittle to my ears. "I was so fucking pissed at you that day."

Looking up, I met the shocked expression I knew I'd find.

Before Anna found the words to ask why, I continued, "I thought if you agreed to marry me right then and there it meant that you'd never leave."

She tilted her head, confused. "Leave? I was seventeen. Where was I going to go? I told you I'd marry you after—"

"After you got out of school." I hissed out a breath. "I know. I remember."

I remembered everything, but now I saw it clearly. Tipping forward, I rested my elbows on my knees, still holding her hand.

"It took my mom almost two years to die." Anna went still at my abrupt change in topic. Or maybe it was because this was something I'd never shared. "When she went into the hospital the last time, she packed everything up, stacked all her clothes with instructions for which charities they should go to. She sat me down and told me," closing my eyes, I swallowed hard, "she told me it was going to happen, that she was going to die."

Anna tightened her grip, and I bit the inside of my cheek, a habit I picked up way back then so I wouldn't cry.

"Anyway," I went on after clearing my throat, "she may have thought it was time, but nothing happened right away. She just kept getting weaker. Sleeping more. Then one afternoon she didn't wake up. Melissa cried, but I couldn't understand why. Because she was going to wake up. She told me before she went to sleep we'd play cards . . . after."

I met Anna's gaze with a sad smile. "But there was no after. She died the next day. And even with everything I knew, everything she'd said, I was shocked." I shrugged. "I guess that's when it started, this feeling I've always had."

Anna rubbed small circles on my back. "What feeling?"

"That everything could end in the blink of an eye. It's a restless kind of thing. I felt that way with you sometimes." All the time. I kept that to myself because there was only so much I could admit about this particular weakness. "So I figured, you know, if I held on tight enough you wouldn't disappear."

"But I didn't," Anna said, confusion suffusing her tone. "You did."

Laughing softly, I shook my head. "This is going to sound like an excuse. It *is* an excuse. But that doesn't mean it's not the fucking truth. Fact is, I couldn't deal with the separation. I had to stay or go—no in between. So I decided to go. But not before I burned everything to the ground. I thought . . . I thought I'd forget about you eventually. Like..."

Too much. I'd said too much. And now I could feel Anna waiting for the end of the sentence I couldn't push past my lips.

After a long moment, she slid forward, and we were side-by-side. "Like what?"

"Like my mom." It took a second for me to swallow the shame and continue. "I never forgot her, I just put her memory away. But one day when I tried to retrieve it, I couldn't see her face. It wasn't like that with you though. I saw you everywhere. So I tried harder."

I didn't give Anna the details of all the methods I'd used. She could probably guess. The fact that it was always her face I saw when I was with another woman wouldn't provide any comfort.

"Did it work?"

I laughed. "Never."

"It didn't work for me either."

I welded my back teeth together, the thought of her with someone else causing me pain in places I didn't know had feeling. When the silence turned heavy, I gathered enough air to force out the last of my truth.

"I love you, Annabelle. I can live without you. I've done it before. But please don't make me."

Spent, I fell back against the cushions and waited. I was always waiting for this girl, and whatever her answer, I feared I always would. But if Anna couldn't find a place for me in her heart, I'd stop pushing.

"I love you, Sean," Anna finally said, so low I had to strain to hear her. "I've always loved you. But I can live without you too." The weight of her last statement hit me like a ton of bricks. I was still reeling when she eased back and sighed. "I just don't want to."

The words rolled off her tongue, tentatively, and it took all my restraint not to grab her and worry about the rest later. But I didn't want to blow up the bridge we'd just built. It was a rickety little structure, propped up by memories, some good, some bad.

Twisting a lock of her hair around my fingertip, I ventured, "Does that mean we can negotiate the terms for my surrender?"

She tensed. "I don't . . ."

Cupping her cheek, I tilted her face to mine. "*My* surrender. Not yours."

Doubt lingered in her eyes, thick clouds, seeded with every misstep on our broken road. I had more work to do if I didn't want our bridge to crumble. Love wasn't enough. Not then and not now. But it was a start.

"Okay, here it is," I began after a big breath. "First, I'd like permission to rent a house in Waco. But don't expect me to wear green." I wrinkled my nose. "We can negotiate on the kid's attire if it makes you feel better, but I'm sticking with orange." Ignoring Anna's dumbfounded expression, I eased her onto her back. "Second, will you consider living with me at some point?" Her brows drew together, so I amended, "Part-time. I'll do part time if that's what you want." Emboldened by her nod of ascent, I slipped my hand under her shirt. "Third, can I take you away for spring break? Alone. We don't have to go far. San Antonio or Padre Island. Maybe—"

Her mouth collided with mine, and I twined my fingers into her hair. Our tongues battled, and I ceded to her wishes, letting her take the control she'd always had. She explored me hungrily, possessively, and I tasted everything in her kiss. The good and the bad. The sweet and the bitter.

I pulled away when my head began to spin. "I wasn't finished."

Anna smiled, and it touched every part of her beautiful face. "I'll agree to all your terms if you agree to a couple of mine."

"Done."

Her smile grew. "You don't even know what I'm going to ask."

I didn't need to hear it. But in order to maintain some dignity, I pretended to mull it over.

"You're right. Let's have it."

"Don't ever shut me out," she said, her brows scrunched up as if she were asking for the moon. "Whatever it is, just talk to me. We'll work it out or we won't, but nothing you could ever tell me is worse than you leaving without a word."

Nodding, I pressed my lips together.

I'd vowed not to bring Willow into our discussion, lest Anna think that anything I'd professed was because of our daughter. Even if Willow didn't exist, I'd like to believe we'd have found our way back to each other. But because she did, I'd never disappear again. Not for four years or four days or four hours.

"What else, baby?"

I expected some monumental demand, so I was surprised when she said, "Just . . . love me."

Love her . . .

I pushed off the couch with a sigh. "You need to learn a thing or two about negotiating."

"Is that so?"

I toed off my boots, then pulled her against me. "Yep."

Somewhere between the kisses and the groping we made it to the bedroom, leaving a trail of clothing on the dusty floor. Limbs tangled, we dropped onto the old mattress.

Braced on my forearms with Anna beneath me, I looked into her eyes. "Asking me to love you is like asking me to breathe. I don't have a choice, baby."

Anna rubbed her foot against my calf, and I went stone still when a soft beat echoed in my head, distant and unrecognizable.

"Do that again."

She smiled a funny smile and repeated the motion. "This?"

The beat got louder, more distinct.

Reversing our positions, I settled her on top of me, so she straddled my waist. As I ran my hands from her knees to her hips, a chorus of strings accompanied my movement. Anna didn't put the music in my head, but without her, I couldn't hear it. She was the muse.

As I plucked the little scar on her knee, a bass drum thundered in the background. I don't know how long I spent lost in the beat, brushing my fingertips over the same swath of skin, but apparently, it was long enough for Anna to get worried.

"What is it?" she finally asked.

Startled out of my euphoric haze, I shook my head. "You. Just you."

Cupping her nape, I guided her mouth to mine for a kiss. Before our lips met, Anna slid off me with a laugh and then fished my wallet from the pocket of my jeans. Retrieving the condom from the folds, she lifted a brow.

I shrugged. "Wishful thinking."

Anna climbed on top of me, and as she ripped the foil packet, I pressed my hand to her taut belly. Maybe someday she'd give me another baby. When she was ready. Right now, I had everything I needed. Anna and Willow and music. Not the kind I played in front of thousands of people. The kind that was all for her.

The steady hum between my ears grew louder as she sank on top of me, taking every inch until there was no her and no me. Just us. Dropping her head back, she moaned, adding lyrics to her sweet song.

"That's it, baby." Slipping my hand into Anna's hair, I rocked against her. "Play for me."

# EPILOGUE

## Ten Months Later

**Sean**

Cameron wrinkled his nose, as I hoisted my suitcase into the bed of the truck.

"Where's the Range Rover?" he asked, peering through the window without moving from his spot.

"Anna's got it." I shook my head, impatient. "Dude, you asked me for a ride. Carry your ass back to the tour bus and call a cab. I'm leaving."

Cameron mulled it over while I scowled. And, yeah, I might have apologized. To the truck.

Reluctantly he threw his bag into the bed next to mine.

"What about your Porsche?" he asked as he slid onto the worn bench seat. "You're telling me you'd rather drive this than a Turbo Carrera?" Looking around skeptically like he might pick up a flesh-eating virus, Cameron clasped his hands in his lap.

I *did* prefer the Porsche for some things. I could make the drive from Austin to Waco in about an hour.

But Willow loved the old pickup. Maybe it was the bumpy ride or her mother's heel prints on the dash or the smell of peaches, but the kid considered it a personal affront if I drove anything else.

"Dude, you've got no room to talk." I snickered. "That piece of shit you used to drive was much worse than this."

Grunting, Cameron pointed the air vents at his face. "Used to is right."

Once the air conditioning cranked up and we were on the freeway, Cameron's mood improved.

"So, you're here for the summer?" he asked. "No more trips to Waco?"

I nodded, smiling.

Three months of boat rides, picnics by the shore and skinny-dipping with Anna at Hippy Hollow. Or as I liked to think of it—heaven. Not that I minded Waco. I'd even gotten used to the sickening green splashed over every square inch of the little town. But it wasn't Austin.

A small smile lifted Cameron's lips. "Who knows? Maybe you can convince Anna to stay."

I shook my head. My convincing days were over. I was lucky if I got to choose the pizza toppings at my house.

"Nah, she's gotta finish school."

*At Baylor.*

A little of the old guilt crept in, but I pushed it away before it took hold.

Lily was digging groceries out of the back of her SUV when we pulled into the gate at Cameron's place.

"See you, dude," he said, his foot out the door before I'd rolled to a stop.

Grabbing his suitcase, he headed straight for Lily, and she was off the ground before I put the truck in reverse. She managed to wave at me as he carried her toward the house.

I pulled out my phone and then tapped a text to Anna.

*Be there in fifteen. You naked?*

Anna replied about the time I was crossing the red bridge spanning the Colorado River.

*Hardly. We're in the meadow. See you soon. Love you.*

She loved me. Still. *Always.* It never got old though, hearing it. Reading it.

I kneaded the muscles in my thigh, determined not to let the ache keep me from showing Anna how mutual the feeling was. The mini-tours Caged was doing once a month took a toll on my body. Six back-to-back performances in seven days with little rest between shows. But I wasn't complaining.

Anna's eyes met mine as I coasted to a stop in the driveway. A smile curved her mouth when the chaos ensued.

"Daaadddy!" Willow shrieked, her fiery curls bouncing like little springs as she tore across the grass.

Betty, the little Bichon puppy that Logan had given Willow for her birthday, beat her to the fence, yapping like a maniac and scratching at the wood posts.

I stepped inside the gate and into the fray.

"Pick me up, Da!" Willow demanded, arms outstretched.

Though I FaceTimed with her every single night when I was away, the small changes in Willow's appearance from week-to-week floored me. Scared me, really. I wanted to slow the clock. Keep her small enough to scoop into my arms.

Willow squealed when I did just that. "Daaaddy!"

"Have you grown?" Tossing her over my shoulder, I jiggled her around. "You *have* grown."

I sauntered toward the sexy redhead on the swing, prisms of light dancing from the stone around her neck. Anna had refused to wear anything but the emerald to mark our engagement so the two-karat diamond was now a pendant. Willow slid off my back as I crouched to kiss her mother.

"You taste good," I said, rising to my feet before my sore knees locked. "How was the drive?"

"Good." Anna smiled. "Long."

"Look, Da!"

My attention snapped to Willow as she gripped the rope on the smaller, identical swing on the other side of the tree.

Anna grabbed my arm. "Let her go, babe. She just wants to show you."

I waited until Willow righted herself on the seat before following Anna to the blanket. Dropping onto my ass, I kept one eye on my daughter. "Not too high, Willow-baby."

Anna squeezed my hand, shifting her focus to the pit of soft sand beneath Willow's swing. "She's fine. You brought the whole shore up here. There's enough dirt to cushion the fall."

Willow's halo of auburn curls whipped her face as she climbed to dizzying heights. Dizzying for me, at least.

"If she has to fall," I said, squinting at my little girl through the dwindling sunlight. "I want her to have a soft place to land."

Anna straddled my lap, blocking my view. "You didn't put any dirt under my swing." She wiggled her hips. "Does that mean I don't need a soft place to land?"

Molding my hand to the curve of her waist, I held her in place. "I'd rather give you a hard place to land."

"Promises, promises." Anna rolled off me and reclined on her elbows, her face tilted toward the sun. "Did Logan have any luck?"

Picking a few blades from the lush carpet of St. Augustine grass, I blew out a breath. "Nope."

Her eyes bored into the side of my head. "How's he taking it?"

I shrugged. "You know Logan, he says it's all good. But he got drunk as fuck last night and had a threesome in his hotel room if that tells you anything."

Six months ago, I would've left that detail out. But I'd slowly come to realize that once we were back on solid ground, Anna didn't worry about other women.

"I don't know if that has anything to do with Laurel," she said. "That sounds like a typical Saturday in Logan Land."

The women, yes. But not the booze. Whenever the private investigator unearthed a new lead about his sister, Logan set up a gig in a nearby city so he could check it out. Every dead end left him worse for wear.

Shaking off the morose mood, I tucked Anna to my side. "Anything on your finals?"

"I haven't checked."

I looked down my nose at her. The girl was a fanatic about checking her grades. She used to do it religiously when . . .

When it mattered. *When she was at UT.*

Anna fingered the pink bracelet on my left wrist, a smile curving her lips.

"Don't be making fun of my bracelet, woman," I warned. "I get enough grief from the guys."

Any father worth his salt would tell you—your baby girl makes you a pastel bracelet, you wear the fucking thing with pride. Even if you got teased about it. Relentlessly.

As the sun dipped below the tree line, Anna hiked her skirt up to soak up the final rays. "I wasn't smiling about that. I got some news today."

Tearing my gaze from her bronze thighs when Willow plopped into my lap, I asked, "What news?"

My daughter snatched the official-looking envelope Anna offered. "Give me that, squirt."

My smile faded as I glanced at the UT Law seal on the front.

I met Anna's gaze, and she nodded, eager. "Read it."

As I unfolded the thick parchment, my heart leapt into my throat.

*Dear Ms. Dresden:*

*We are pleased to inform you that your application for admittance to the University of Texas School of Law has been approved.*

I blinked, rereading the letter. Twice. "How . . . ?"

Anna's cheeks flamed as she sucked her lip between her teeth. "Chase talked to some big wigs on the alumni board and got them to review my transcripts and LSAT scores." She frowned. "But I met all the requirements, so I didn't take anybody's spot or anything."

Cameron's brother never ceased to amaze me. He was the largest land developer in Austin, owned two music venues, but still found time to look out for us. All of us.

The heavy weight of guilt I'd been carrying over Anna's education diminished somewhat as I fingered the envelope. "You deserve this, Anna-baby. You've worked so hard. It's what you've always wanted."

She snuggled against me, her eyes drifting to Willow and Betty running circles around the tree.

"This is what I've always wanted. You and me in a little house by the lake." Cutting her gaze to the McMansion, she smirked. "I guess you can't have everything, right?"

She was wrong. So wrong. Because I did.

I eased her onto the grass, and the branches of the willow tree reflected in her eyes along with the first star in the evening sky. A world painted in emerald green.

"You want everything? I'll give it to you. Anything."

Fingers coiling into my hair, Anna smiled. "I already have everything."

Grunting when Willow jumped on my back, I propped up on my elbows to keep from crushing Anna entirely. "I love you," I said, sweeping a tendril of hair from her brow.

Another smile. "I love you more."

That wasn't possible, but I didn't tell her. Because we had love to spare. And music. A never-ending symphony.

## THE END

# ACKNOWLEDGMENTS

**Jeff**—Love of my life. All of my life. Words and music, baby.

**Matthew and Victoria**— My true north. I love you both.

**Mary**—Can I be just like you when I grow up?
Love you.

**Dad**—You'll never read this. *Hopefully.* But I'll send you this page
anyway.

**Bonnie Marie**—Always in my thoughts. I love you. Forever.

**And finally—to all my readers—***thank you.*

# ABOUT THE AUTHOR

Jayne Frost, author of the Sixth Street Bands Romance Series, grew up in California with a dream of moving to Seattle to become a rock star. When the grunge thing didn't work out (she never even made it to the Washington border) Jayne set her sights on Austin, Texas. After quickly becoming immersed in the Sixth Street Music scene...and discovering she couldn't actually sing, Jayne decided to do the next best thing—write kick ass romances about hot rockstars and the women that steal their hearts.

Want to join the tour and become a Jayne Frost VIP?
Sign up for the **Sixth Street Heat Newsletter**
http://bit.ly/2fS3xiQ
to receive exclusive members only content, swag, giveaway
opportunities, and all the latest news.

*STALK ME!!*

www.jaynefrost.com/

jayne@jaynefrost.com

# ALSO BY JAYNE FROST

GONE FOR YOU

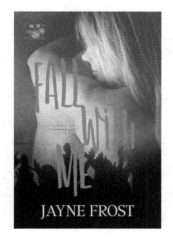

FALL WITH ME

CPSIA information can be obtained
at www.ICGtesting.com
Printed in the USA
BVHW040907050519
547383BV00016B/579/P